THE ROSE SOCIETY

Also by Marie Lu

THE YOUNG ELITES

LEGEND

PRODIGY

CHAMPION

THE ROSE SOCIETY

A YOUNG ELITES NOVEL

MARIE LU

G. P. Putnam's Sons

G. P. Putnam's Sons
an imprint of Penguin Random House LLC
375 Hudson Street
New York, NY 10014

Library of Congress Cataloging-in-Publication Data is available upon request.

Printed in the United States of America.
ISBN 978-0-399-16784-3
1 3 5 7 9 10 8 6 4 2

Design by Marikka Tamura.
Text set in Palatino Linotype.

For Cassie, sisters always, no matter what

THE
W
E
S
DUMOR
THE
The
Sun
Sea
Kenettra
Merroutas
The
Sacchi
Sea
TAMOURA
DOMACCA
THE

SKYLANDS
BELDAIN
Hadenbury
KENETTRA
The Sun Sea
Anjou
Campagnia
Serrata
Estenzia
Golden Valley
Triese di Mare
Udara
Dalia
Falls of Laetes
Petra
The Sacchi Sea
SEALANDS
The Ember Isles
SUNLANDS

Adelina Amouteru

When I was a little girl, my mother would spend long afternoons telling me old folktales. I remember one story particularly well.

Once upon a time, a greedy prince fell in love with a wicked girl.

The prince had far more than he needed, but it was never enough. When he grew ill, he visited the Kingdom of the Great Ocean, where the Underworld meets the living world, to bargain with Moritas, the goddess of Death, for more life. When she refused, he stole her immortal gold and fled to the surface.

In revenge, Moritas sent her daughter Caldora, the angel of Fury, to retrieve him. Caldora materialized out of the sea foam on a warm, stormy night, clad in nothing but silver silk, an achingly beautiful phantom in the mist. The prince ran to the shore to greet her. She smiled at him and touched his cheek.

"What will you give me in return for my affection?" she asked. "Are you willing to part with your kingdom, your army, and your jewels?"

The prince, blinded by her beauty and eager to boast, nodded. "Anything you want," he replied. "I am the greatest man in the world. Even the gods are no match for me."

So he gave her his kingdom, his army, and his jewels. She accepted his offerings with a smile, only to reveal her true angel form—skeletal, finned, monstrous. Then she burned his kingdom to the ground and pulled him below the sea into the Underworld, where her mother, Moritas, was patiently waiting. The prince tried once again to bargain with the goddess, but it was too late. In exchange for the gold he'd stolen, Moritas devoured his soul.

I think of this story now, as I stand with my sister on the deck of a trading ship, looking toward the shore where the city-state of Merroutas rises out of the morning mist.

Someday, when I am nothing but dust and wind, what tale will they tell about me?

Once upon a time, a girl had a father, a prince, a society of friends. Then they betrayed her, and she destroyed them all.

City-State of Merroutas

The Sealands

They were the flash of light in a stormy sky,
the fleeting darkness before dawn. Never have they
existed before, nor shall they ever exist again.

–Unknown source on the Young Elites

Adelina Amouteru

"I think he might be here."

I'm startled from my thoughts by my sister Violetta's voice. "Hmm?" I murmur, looping my arm through hers as we wind our way through a crowded street.

Violetta purses her lips in a familiar expression of concern. She can tell I'm distracted, but I'm grateful she decides to let it go. "I said, I think he might be here. In the main square."

It is early evening on the longest day of the year. We are lost in the thick of a celebration in the city-state of Merroutas, the wealthy, bustling crossroads between Kenettra and the Tamouran Empire. The sun has nearly dipped below the horizon, and the three moons hang low and plump, ripe golden orbs suspended over the water. Merroutas is alight with festivities for the Midsummer Feast of Creation, the start of a month of fasting. Violetta and I wander through the throngs of revelers, lost amid the celebration's rainbow of colors. Both of us are dressed in Tamouran silks tonight, our hair wrapped up and our fingers adorned with bronze rings. People draped in jasmine garlands are everywhere, packed into the narrow alleys and spilling out into the squares, dancing in long lines around domed palaces and bathing temples. We walk past waterways swollen with cargo-laden boats and buildings carved in gold and silver with thousands of repeating circles and squares. Ornate tapestries hang from balconies in the smoky air. Soldiers pass us by in small clusters, wearing billowing silks instead of heavy armor, a moon-and-crown emblem stitched onto their sleeves. They're not the Inquisition Axis, but no doubt they've heard news of Teren's orders from across the sea to find us. We steer clear of the soldiers.

I feel as if I were in a haze, the celebrations floating around me. It's strange, really, to look out at all of this joy. What do I do with it? It doesn't feed my energy. Instead, I stay silent, letting Violetta guide us through the busy streets, as I return to my dark thoughts.

Since leaving Kenettra three weeks ago, I have woken to whispers at my bedside that fade away seconds later. Other times, the hushed voices talk to me when no one else is around. They are not always there, and I cannot always understand them even when they are speaking to me. But I can always feel their presence lingering in the corners of my mind. There is a blade there, a rotation of sound and silence, a lamp that burns black. A grim, growing fire. This is what they say:

Adelina, why do you blame yourself for Enzo's death?

I should have had better control over my illusions, I respond quietly to the whispers. I could have saved Enzo's life. I should have trusted the Daggers sooner.

None of it was your fault, the whispers in my head argue. *You didn't kill him, after all—it was not your weapon that ended his life. So why are you the one cast out? You didn't have to return to the Daggers—you didn't need to help them rescue Raffaele. And still they turned on you. Why does everyone forget your good intentions, Adelina?*

Why feel guilty for something that isn't your fault?

Because I loved him. And now he is gone.

It's better this way, the whispers say. *Haven't you always waited at the top of the stairs, imagining yourself a queen?*

"Adelina," Violetta says. She tugs on my arm and the whispers scatter.

I shake my head and force myself to concentrate. "Are you sure he's here?" I ask.

"If not him, then another Elite."

We've come to Merroutas to flee the Inquisition's prying eyes in Kenettra. It is the nearest place outside of Kenettran control, but eventually we'll make our way south to the Sunlands, far from their reach.

But we also came here for another reason.

If you had heard stories about only one Young Elite, they would have been about a boy named Magiano. Raffaele, the beautiful young consort who was once my friend, mentioned Magiano during my afternoon training sessions with him. Since then, I've heard his name on the lips of countless travelers.

Some say he was raised by wolves in the dense forests of the Ember Isles, a tiny chain of islands far east of Kenettra. Others say he was born in the hot Sunland deserts of Domacca, a bastard brought up by wandering nomads. He's rumored to be a wild boy, almost feral, dressed from head to toe in leaves, with a mind and hands as quicksilver as a midnight fox. He appeared quite suddenly several years ago, and has since avoided arrest by the Inquisition Axis dozens of times, for everything from illegal gambling to stealing the Kenettran queen's crown jewels. As the stories go, he can lure you straight off a cliff and into the sea with music from his lute. And when he smiles, his teeth shine wickedly bright.

Though we know he is a Young Elite, no one can say for certain what his power is. We can only be sure that he was recently seen here, in Merroutas.

If I were still the same girl from a year ago, before I knew I had powers, I'm not sure I would have the courage to search for such a notorious Elite. But then I killed my father. I joined the Dagger Society. I betrayed them, and they betrayed me. Or perhaps it was the other way around. I can never be sure.

What I *do* know is that the Daggers are my enemies now. When you're all alone in a world that hates and fears you, you want to find others like yourself. New friends.

Elite friends. Friends who can help you build your own society.

Friends like Magiano.

"*Salaam,* lovely Tamouran girls!"

We enter another large square near the bay. All along the sides are food stalls with steaming pots and street operators in long-nosed masks, performing table tricks. One of the food vendors smiles when we look at him. His hair is hidden behind a Tamouran wrap, and his beard is dark and well-trimmed. He bows to us. I touch my own head instinctively. My silver hair is still short and scraggly from my attempt to cut it off, and it stays hidden tonight behind two long strips of gold silk, adorned with a headdress of gold tassels dangling above my brows. I have woven an illusion over the scarred side of my face. To this man, my pale lashes are black and my eyes are flawless.

I glance at what he's selling. Steaming pans of stuffed grape leaves, lamb skewers, and warm flatbread. My mouth waters.

"Pretty girls from the homeland," he coos at us. I don't understand the rest of what he says, other than "please, come!" and "break your fast." I smile back at him and nod. I've never been in a city so heavily Tamouran. It almost feels like coming home.

You could rule a place like this, say the whispers in my head, and my heart fills with glee.

Once we approach his stall, Violetta digs out a couple of bronze talents and hands them over to the man. I stay back. I watch as she makes him laugh, then he leans over to murmur something and she blushes demurely. Violetta responds with a smile that could devastate the sun. At the end of this exchange, she turns away with two skewers of meat. As she leaves his stand, the vendor stares at her back before turning his attention to new customers. He switches the language of his greeting again. "*Avei, avei!* Forget the gambling and come have some fresh flatbread!"

Violetta hands a bronze talent to me. "A discount," she says. "Because he liked us."

"Sweet Violetta." I arch an eyebrow at her as I take one of the skewers. We've kept our purses full so far because I can use my powers to steal coins from noblemen. That is my contribution. But Violetta's skill is entirely different. "At this rate, they'll be *paying* us to eat their food."

"That's what I'm working toward." Violetta looks at me with an innocent smile that's not innocent at all. Her eyes wander the square, pausing where an enormous bonfire burns in front of a temple. "We're getting closer," she says as she takes a delicate bite. "His energy isn't very strong. It shifts as we go."

After we eat, I follow Violetta as she practices her power, guiding us in a long, jagged pattern through the mass of people. Every night since we fled Estenzia, we've sat across from each other and I've let her experiment on me, like how she used to braid my hair when we were little. She pulls and tugs. Then I blindfold her and walk silently around the room, testing whether or not she can sense my location. She reaches out to touch the threads of my energy, studying their structure. I can tell she's getting stronger.

It frightens me. But Violetta and I made a promise after we left the Daggers: We will *never* use our powers against each other. If Violetta wants protection with my illusions, I will always give it. In return, Violetta will always leave my abilities untouched. That is all.

I have to trust *someone.*

We wander for almost an hour before Violetta stops in the middle of the square. She frowns. I wait beside her, studying her face. "Did you lose him?"

"Maybe," Violetta replies. I can barely hear her over the music. We wait a moment longer before she finally turns to her left, nodding for me to follow.

Violetta pauses again. She turns in a circle, and then folds her arms with a sigh. "I lost him again," she says. "Perhaps we should go back the way we came."

The words have only just left her mouth when another street vendor stops us in our tracks. He is dressed like all the other operators, his face entirely obscured by a long-nosed *dottore* mask, his body shrouded in colorful, mismatched robes. At second glance, I notice that those robes are made of luxurious silk, finely woven and dyed with rich inks. He takes Violetta's hand, holds it up to his mask as if to kiss it, and puts a hand over his heart. He gestures for both of us to join the small circle around his stand.

I recognize the scheme right away—a Kenettran gambling game where the operator places twelve colorful stones before you and asks you to choose three. He'll then mix the stones underneath cups. You often play as a group, and if you are the only one to guess where all three are hidden, then you not only win back your own money, but everyone else's bet along with the operator's entire purse. One look at the operator's heavy purse tells me he has not lost a round in a while.

The operator bows at us without a word and motions for us to choose three stones. He does the same to the others gathered beside us. I look on as two other revelers pick their stones enthusiastically. On our other side is a young *malfetto* boy. He is marked by the blood fever with an unseemly black rash across his ear and cheek. Behind his thoughtful façade is an undercurrent of fear.

Mmm. My energy turns toward him like a wolf drawn to the scent of blood.

Violetta leans in close to me. "Let's try a round," she says, her eyes also pinned to the *malfetto* boy. "I think I sense something."

I nod at the street operator, then drop two gold talents into his outstretched hand. He bows at me with a flourish. "For my sister and me," I say, pointing at the three stones we want to bet on.

The operator nods back at us silently. Then he starts to mix the stones.

Violetta and I keep our attention on the *malfetto* boy. He watches the cups spin with a look of concentration. As we wait for the operator, the other players look in his direction and laugh. A few *malfetto* jeers are thrown out. The boy just ignores them.

Finally, the operator stops spinning the cups. He lines up all twelve in a row, then folds his arms back into his robes and signals at all the players to guess which cups their stones are in.

"Four, seven, and eight," the first player calls out, slapping the operator's table.

"Two, five, nine," another player replies.

Two more shout out their guesses.

The operator turns to us. I lift my head. "One, two, and three," I say. The others laugh a little at my bet, but I ignore them.

The *malfetto* boy casts his bet too. "Six, seven, and twelve," he calls out.

The operator lifts the first cup, then the second and third. I've already lost. I pretend to look disappointed, but my attention stays focused on the *malfetto* boy. *Six, seven, and twelve.* When the operator gets to the sixth cup, he flips it over to reveal that the boy had chosen correctly.

The operator points to the boy. He whoops. The other players cast him an ugly look.

The operator lifts the seventh cup. The boy has guessed correctly again. The other players start to look at one another nervously. If the boy gets the last one wrong, we all lose to the operator. But if the boy has guessed the third one correctly, then he gets all of our money.

The operator overturns the final cup. The boy is correct. He wins.

The operator glances up sharply. The *malfetto* boy lets out a surprised shout of joy, while the other players glare angrily at him. Hate appears in their chests as sparks, flashes of energy that merge into black spots.

"What do you think?" I ask Violetta. "Do you sense anything about his energy?"

Violetta's gaze stays fixed on the celebrating boy. "Follow him."

The operator reluctantly hands over his purse, along with the money that the rest of us bet. As the boy collects the coins, I observe the other players muttering among themselves. When the boy leaves the operator's stand, the others trail behind him, their faces tight and shoulders tense.

They are going to attack him. "Let's go," I whisper to Violetta. She follows without a word.

For a while, the boy seems too happy with his winnings to recognize the danger he has put himself in. It isn't until he reaches the edge of the square that he notices the other players. He keeps going, but now at a nervous pace. I sense his inkling of fear grow to a steady trickle, and the sweet taste of it entices me.

The boy darts out of the square and onto a narrow side street where the lights are dim and the people are scarce. Violetta and I settle into the shadows, and I paint a subtle illusion over us to keep us hidden. I frown at the boy. A person as notorious as Magiano surely wouldn't be this tactless.

Finally, one of the other gamblers catches up with him. Before the boy can lift up his hands, the gambler trips him.

A second gambler pretends to stumble over his body, but kicks him in the stomach as he goes. The boy yelps and his fear changes to terror—now I can see the threads of it hovering over him in a dark, shimmering web.

In the blink of an eye, the other gamblers have surrounded him. One grabs him by his shirt and shoves him up against the wall. His head hits it hard, and in an instant, his eyes roll back. He collapses to the ground and curls up into a ball.

"Why did you run away?" one of them says to the *malfetto*. "You seemed to be enjoying yourself, cheating us out of all our money."

The others chime in.

"What does a *malfetto* need all that money for, anyway?"

"Going to hire a *dottore* to fix your markings?"

"Hiring a whore so you can find out what it's like?"

I just watch. When I first joined the Daggers and witnessed *malfettos* being abused, I would go back to my chamber and cry. I've seen it enough times now to stay composed, to let the fear of such a scene feed me without feeling guilty about it. So as the attackers continue to torture the boy, I stand by and feel nothing but anticipation.

The *malfetto* boy scrambles to his feet before the others can strike him again—he dashes down the street. They pursue him.

"He's not an Elite," Violetta murmurs as they go. She shakes her head, her expression genuinely puzzled. "I'm sorry. I must have sensed someone else."

I don't know why I feel a desire to keep following the group. If he's not Magiano, then I have no reason to help him. Perhaps it's pent-up frustration or the allure of dark feelings. Or the memory of the Daggers' refusal to ever risk saving *malfettos* unless they were Elites. Perhaps it's the memory of myself pushed against an iron stake, pelted with stones, waiting to burn before an entire city.

For a fleeting moment, I imagine that if I were queen, I could make the act of hurting *malfettos* a crime. I could execute this boy's pursuers with a single command.

I start hurrying after them. "Come on," I urge Violetta.

"Don't," she starts to tell me, even though she knows it's pointless.

"I'll be nice." I smile.

She raises an eyebrow at me. "Your idea of *nice* is different from others'."

We hurry along in the darkness, invisible behind an illusion I've woven. Shouts come from up ahead as the boy turns a corner in an attempt to throw off his pursuers. No use. As we draw near, I hear the others catch up to him and his cry of pain ring out. When we turn the corner too, the attackers have completely surrounded him. One of them knocks the boy to the ground with a blow to the face.

I act before I can stop myself. In one move, I reach out and push aside the threads hiding us from view. Then I walk straight into their circle. Violetta stays where she is, looking on quietly.

It takes a moment for the attackers to notice me there—not until I walk right over to the quivering *malfetto* boy and stand in front of him do they finally see me. They hesitate.

"What's this?" the ringleader mutters, confused for a moment. His eyes dart across the illusion still covering my scarred face. What he sees is a whole, beautiful girl. His grin returns. "Is this your whore, filthy *malfetto*?" he taunts the boy. "How did you get so lucky?"

A woman beside him gives me a suspicious look. "She was the other gambler in our circle," she says to the others. "She probably helped the boy win."

"Ah, you're right," the ringleader replies. He turns on me. "Do you have other winnings on you, then? Your share, perhaps?"

A couple of the other attackers don't seem so sure. One of them notices the smile on my face and gives me a nervous stare, then looks back at where Violetta waits. "Let's just finish this," he protests, holding up a pouch. "We got the money back already."

The ringleader clicks his tongue. "We are not making a habit of letting people go," he replies. "Nobody likes a cheat."

I shouldn't be using my powers so carelessly. But this is a secluded alley, and I can't resist the temptation anymore. Outside their ring, Violetta tugs faintly against my energy in protest, sensing my next move. I ignore her and stand my ground, slowly unraveling the illusion over my face. My features quiver, transforming gradually so that a long scar begins to emerge over my left eye, then the disfigured skin where my eye used to be, the rough, abused flesh from an old wound. My dark lashes turn pale silver. I've been working on the precision of my illusions, how fast and slow I can weave them. I can wield my threads of energy more accurately now. Bit by bit, I reveal my true self to the ring of people.

They stare, frozen in place, at the scarred side of my face. I'm surprised that I enjoy their reaction. They don't even seem to notice the *malfetto* boy scrambling out of the circle to press himself against the closest wall.

The ringleader scowls at me before pulling out a knife. "A demon," he says, with a subtle note of uncertainty.

"Perhaps," I reply. My voice comes out cold. It's a voice I am still getting used to.

The man is about to attack when something on the ground distracts him. He looks down at the cobblestones—and there, he sees a tiny ribbon of bright red snaking its way along the grooves. It looks like a little lost creature, wandering back and forth. The man's brows furrow. He leans down toward the tiny illusion.

Then the red line bursts into a dozen more lines, all darting away in different directions, leaving trails of blood in their wake. Everyone jerks backward.

"What in the gods—?" he starts.

I weave the lines furiously across the ground and then up along the walls, dozens turning into hundreds into thousands, until the entire street is covered in a harsh field of them. I blot out the light filtering down from the lanterns and create an illusion of scarlet storm clouds overhead.

The man's composure cracks, revealing alarm. His companions take hurried steps away from me as the bloody lines cover the street. Fear clouds their chests, and the feeling sends a surge of strength and hunger through me. My illusions make them afraid and, in turn, their fear makes me stronger.

Stop. I can feel Violetta pulling on my energy again. Maybe I should. These attackers have already lost their thirst for more money, after all. But instead, I shrug her off and keep going. This game is fun. I used to be more ashamed of such a feeling, but now I think—why shouldn't I hate? Why shouldn't it bring me joy?

The man suddenly lifts his knife again. I keep weaving. *You can't see the knife,* the whispers in my head taunt him. *Where is it? You just had it a moment ago, but you must have left it somewhere.* Even though I can see the weapon, he looks down at his hand with rage and bewilderment. To him, the knife has vanished completely.

The attackers finally give in to their fear—several flee, while others huddle against the wall, frozen. The ringleader turns and tries to run away. I bare my teeth. Then I snap the thousands of bloody lines across him, pulling them as tight as I can, making him feel the slice and burn of razor-thin threads ripping across his flesh. The ringleader's eyes bulge for a moment before he falls, shrieking, to the ground. I tighten the sharp threads around him like a spider trapping prey in her silken web. *It feels like the strings are sawing through your skin, doesn't it?*

"Adelina," my sister calls out urgently. "The others."

I take in her warning just in time to see two others gather enough courage to rush toward me—the woman from earlier and another man. I lash out, washing the illusion over them too. They fall. They think their skin is being ripped from their flesh, and the agony bends them over double.

I am concentrating so hard that my hands are shaking. The man struggles toward the end of the street, and I let him crawl. What must it be like, seeing the world right now from his point of view? I continue pouring the illusion over him, imagining what he must be seeing and feeling. He begins to sob, using all of his strength for every movement.

It is nice, being powerful. Seeing others bend to your will. I imagine this must be how kings and queens feel—that with just a few words, they can ignite a war or enslave an entire population. This must be what I fantasized about as a little girl, crouching on the stairs of my old home, pretending to wear a heavy crown on my head and look out at a sea of kneeling figures.

"Adelina, no," Violetta whispers. She's standing beside me now, but I am so focused on what I'm doing that I hardly sense her there. "You've taught them enough of a lesson. Let them go."

I tighten my fists and keep going. "You could stop me," I reply with a tight smile, "if you really wanted to."

Violetta doesn't argue my point. Perhaps, deep down, she even wants me to do it. She wants to see me defend myself. So instead of forcing me to stop, she puts a hand on my arm, reminding me of our promise to each other.

"The *malfetto* boy escaped," she says. Her voice is very soft. "Save your fury for something greater."

Something in her voice cuts through my anger. Suddenly, I feel the exhaustion of using so much energy all at once. I release the man from my illusion's hold. He collapses onto the cobblestones, clutching at his chest as if he could still feel the threads cutting through his flesh. His face is a mess of tears and spit. I take a step back, feeling weak.

"You're right," I mutter at Violetta.

She only sighs in relief and steadies me.

I lean down toward the trembling ringleader so that he can have a good look at my scarred face. He can't even bring himself to look up at me. "I'll be watching you," I say. It doesn't matter if my words are true or not. In his state, I know he won't dare test it. Instead, he just nods in a rapid, jerky movement. Then he staggers to his feet and runs away.

The others do the same. Their footsteps echo down the street until they turn the corner, where the sound blends into the noise of the festivities. In their absence, I release my breath, my courage spent, and turn to Violetta. She looks deathly pale. Her hand has clasped mine so tightly that our fingers have turned white. We stand together on the now-silent street. I shake my head.

The *malfetto* boy we saved couldn't have been Magiano. He isn't an Elite. And even if he were, he's already run away. I sigh, then kneel down and steady myself against the ground. The entire incident has only left me bitter. *Why didn't you kill him?* the whispers in the back of my head say to me, upset.

I don't know how long we stay here before a faint, muffled voice overhead startles us.

"So much for being nice, eh?" it says.

The voice is oddly familiar. I glance around at the higher floors around us, but in the darkness, it's hard to make out anything. I take a step back into the middle of the street. Off in the distance, the sounds of celebrations continue.

Violetta tugs my hand. Her eyes are fixed on a balcony across from us. "Him," she whispers. When I look, I finally see a masked figure leaning against the balcony's marble ledge, watching us in silence—it's the operator who ran our gambling game.

My sister leans close to me. "He's an Elite. *He's* the one I sensed."

The irony of life is that those who wear masks
often tell us more truths than those with open faces.
–Masquerade, *by Salvatore Laccona*

Adelina Amouteru

He doesn't react when he sees us looking back.

Instead, he stays slouched against the wall and unstraps a lute from his back. He plucks a few strings thoughtfully, as if tuning the instrument, and then flings off his *dottore* mask with a grunt of impatience. Dozens of long, dark braids tumble down around his shoulders. His robes are loose and unbuttoned halfway down his chest, and rows of thick gold bangles adorn both of his arms, bright against his bronze skin. I can't make out his features well, but even from here, I can tell that his eyes are a bold honey color and they seem to glow in the night.

"I've been watching you two make your way through the crowds," he continues with a sly smile. His gaze shifts to Violetta. "It's impossible not to notice someone like you. The trail of broken hearts left in your wake must be long and fraught with peril. And yet, I'm sure suitors continue to throw themselves at your feet, desperate for a chance to win your affection."

Violetta frowns. "I beg your pardon?"

"You're beautiful."

Violetta flushes bright red. I step closer to the balcony. "And who are you?" I call up to him.

His notes turn into a melody as he starts to play in earnest. The tune distracts me—despite his flippant attitude, he plays with skill. *Hypnotizing* skill. There was a place behind my old home where Violetta and I used to hide inside the hollows of the trees. Whenever the wind rustled through the leaves, it sounded like laughter in the air, and we would imagine it was the laughter of the gods as they enjoyed a cool spring afternoon. This mysterious person's music reminds me of that sound. His fingers run along the length of the lute's strings in fluid strokes, the song as natural as a sunset.

Violetta glances at me, and I realize he is making up the tune on the spot.

He can lure you straight off a cliff and into the sea with music from his lute.

"As for *you,*" the boy says in between notes, shifting his attention from Violetta to me. "How'd you do it?"

I blink at him, still distracted. "Do what?" I reply.

He pauses long enough to shoot an irritated glance at me. "Oh, for the gods' sakes, stop being so coy." His voice stays nonchalant as he plays. "You're obviously an Elite. So. How'd you do it, with the blood lines and the knife?"

Violetta gives me a quiet nod before I go on. "My sister and I have been searching for someone for months," I say.

"Is that so? Didn't know my little gambling stand was so popular."

"We're looking for a Young Elite named Magiano."

He stops talking and plays through a fast series of notes. His fingers fly along the lute's strings in a blur of motion, but the notes each come out crisp and clear, absolute perfection. He plays for what seems like a long time. There is a story in his notes as he makes up the melody, something cheery and wistful, maybe even humorous, some secret joke. I want him to answer us, but at the same time, I don't want him to stop playing.

Finally, he pauses to look at me. "Who's Magiano?"

Violetta makes a muffled sound, while I can't help but cross my arms and sniff in disbelief. "Surely you've heard of Magiano," my sister says.

He turns his head to the side, then gives Violetta a winsome smile. "If you came here to ask me my opinions about imaginary people, my love, then you're wasting your time. The only Magiano I've ever heard of is a threat mothers use to make their children tell the truth." He waves one hand in the air. "You know. *If you don't stop lying, Magiano will steal your tongue. If you don't pay proper tribute to the gods on Sapienday, Magiano will devour your pets.*"

I open my mouth to say something, but he continues as if talking to himself. "That's enough proof, I think," he replies with a shrug. "Eating pets is disgusting, and stealing tongues is rude. Who would do such a thing?"

A little ribbon of doubt creeps into my chest. What if he's telling us the truth? He certainly doesn't look like the boy from all the stories. "How do you operate your gambling game and win so frequently?"

"Ah, *that*." The boy continues playing his song for a while. Then he stops abruptly, leans down toward us, and holds both hands up. He smiles again, flashing his teeth. "*Magic*."

I smile back. "Magiano's tricks, you mean."

"Is that where the word comes from?" he asks lightheartedly before slouching backward again. "I didn't know." His fingers find the lute's strings and continue playing. I can tell we're losing his interest. "Nothing more than sleights of hand, my love, tricks of the light and a perceptive use of distraction. And, you know, the help of an assistant. He's probably still hiding somewhere, stupid boy, scared out of his wits. I warned him not to run." He pauses. "That's why I'm here talking to you, you know. I wanted to tell you both that I'm grateful you saved my helper, and now I'm going to leave you to enjoy your night. Best of luck to you in finding your Young Elite."

The other malfetto *was working with him all along.* I take a deep breath. Something about the way he says *Young Elite* triggers an old memory. He *does* sound familiar. I know I've heard his voice before. But where? I frown, trying to place the memory. *Where, where . . .*

And then I realize it.

My prison mate. When the Inquisition first arrested me and threw me in their dungeons, I had a half-crazed companion in the cell next to my own. A laughing, giggling, singsong voice, one belonging to someone who I'd thought had gone mad from his long imprisonment.

Girl. They say you're a Young Elite. Well, are you?

He sees the recognition in my eyes, because he pauses again in his playing. "You're making a very odd face," he says. "Did you eat a bad lamb skewer? That happened to me once."

"We were in prison together."

He stops at my words. Freezes. "I'm sorry?"

"We were in the same prison. In the city of Dalia, some months ago. You must remember—I know your voice." I take a deep breath, revisiting the memory. "I was sentenced to burn that day."

When I squint at him in the darkness, I notice that he has stopped smiling. He turns his full stare on me.

"You're Adelina Amouteru," he murmurs to himself, his gaze wandering across my face with renewed interest. "Yes, of course, of *course* you are. I should have sensed it."

I nod. For a moment, I wonder if perhaps I've told him too much. Does he know that the Inquisition wants us? What if he decides to turn us in to the Merroutas soldiers?

He considers me for what seems like hours. "You saved my life that day," he adds.

I frown in confusion. "How?"

He smiles again, but it's different from the sweet grin he gave Violetta. No, I've never seen a smile quite like this—cat-like, one that slants the corners of his eyes and gives him, for a moment, a fierce and savage look. The tips of his canines gleam. His expression has transformed his entire face, turning him into someone both intimidating and charismatic, and every thread of his attention is now trained on me, as if nothing else in the world existed. He seems to have forgotten about Violetta entirely. I don't know what to make of this, but I can feel my cheeks starting to flush.

He stares at me without blinking, humming with the music as he plays. Then he looks away and speaks again. "If you are searching for Magiano, you will have better luck finding him in the abandoned bath halls of southern Merroutas, a building once called the Little Baths of Bethesda. Go there tomorrow morning at first light. I've heard he prefers negotiating in private places." He holds a finger up. "But be warned—he doesn't take orders from anyone. If you want to talk to him, you'll have to give him a good reason."

And before Violetta or I can say anything in return, he pushes away from the balcony, turns his back, and disappears inside the building.

Raffaele Laurent Bessette

Fog. Early morning.

A memory of a young boy crouching barefoot outside the door of his family's squalid home, playing with sticks in the mud. He looked up to see an old man making his way along the village's dirt path, his bony nag pulling a wagon behind her. The child stopped playing. He shouted for his mother, then stood up as the wagon came closer.

The man stopped before him. They stared at each other. There was something about the child's eyes set in his thin face—one as warm as honey, the other as bright green as an emerald. But there was something more than that—as the man continued to stare, he must have wondered how someone so young could wear such a wise expression.

He went inside the little home to speak to the mother. It took some convincing—she did not want to let him in until he said that he had an opportunity for her to make some money.

"You won't find many customers in this region to buy trinkets and potions," his mother said to the man, wringing her hands in the tiny, dark room that she shared with her six children. He sat down in the chair she offered him. Her eyes darted constantly from thing to thing, never quite able to settle. "The blood fever has ravaged us. It took my husband and my eldest son last year. It marked two of my other children, as you can see." She gestured at the young boy, who looked on quietly with his jewel-toned eyes, and to his brother. "This has always been a poor village, sir, but now it is on the verge of collapse."

The child noticed the man's eyes darting to him again and again. "And how are you faring, without your husband?" the man asked.

The mother shook her head. "I struggle working in our fields. I have sold some of our possessions. Our bread flour will last another few weeks, but it is full of worms."

The man listened without a word. He showed no interest in the boy's marked brother. When the mother finished, he sat back and nodded. "I make deliveries between the port cities of Estenzia and Campagnia. I want to ask about your littlest boy, the one with the two-toned eyes."

"What do you want to know?"

"I will pay you five gold talents for him. He is a comely boy—he will fetch a high price in a large port city."

At the mother's stunned silence, the man continued, "There are courts in Estenzia that have more jewels and riches than you've ever dreamed possible. They are worlds of glitter and pleasure, and they are constantly in need of new blood." At that, he nodded at the child.

"You mean you'll take him to a brothel."

The man looked down at the child again. "No. He is too fine featured for a brothel." He leaned closer to the woman and lowered his voice. "Your marked children will have a hard time here. I have heard stories about other villages that have cast their little ones out into the forests, in fear that they will bring sickness and misfortune to all. I have seen them burn children, *infants*, alive in the streets. It will happen here too."

"It will not," the woman replied fiercely. "Our neighbors are poor, but they are good people."

"Desperation brings out the darkness in everyone," the man said with a shrug.

The two argued until evening fell. The mother continued to refuse.

The child listened in silence, thinking.

When night finally came, he rose and quietly took his mother's hand. He told her that he would go with the man. The mother slapped him, told him he would do no such thing, but he did not budge.

"Everyone will starve," he said softly.

"You are too young to understand what you're sacrificing," his mother scolded.

He glanced at his other siblings. "It will be all right, Mama."

The mother looked at her beautiful boy, admired his eyes, and ran a hand through his black hair. Her fingers played with his few strands of brilliant sapphire. She pulled him close to her and cried. She hung on to him for a long time. He hugged her back, proud of himself for helping his mother, not knowing what it meant.

"Twelve talents," she told the man.

"Eight," he countered.

"Ten. I'll not give up my son for less than that."

The man was silent for a while. "Ten," he agreed.

The mother exchanged a few quiet words with the man, and then released her son's hand.

"What is your name, little boy?" the man asked as he helped him into his rickety wagon.

"Raffaele Laurent Bessette." The child's voice was solemn, his eyes still fixed on his home. Already he was starting to feel afraid. Could his mother ever visit him? Did this mean he would never see his family again?

"Well, Raffaele," the man replied, tapping his mare's hindquarters with his whip. He distracted the boy by giving him a hunk of bread and cheese. "Have you ever been to the capital of Kenettra?"

Two weeks later, the man sold the child to the Fortunata Court of Estenzia for three thousand gold talents.

Raffaele's eyes flutter, then open to the faint light of dawn streaming in through the window. A flurry of snow is falling outside.

He stirs. Even the flickering fireplace and the furs piled high on his bed are not enough to keep away the bite of icy air. Raffaele's skin prickles from the chill. He pulls up the furs to his chin again and tries to fall back asleep. But two weeks on a ship sailing through stormy waters from Kenettra north to Beldain have taken their toll, and Raffaele's body aches from exhaustion. The Beldish queen's summer castle is a cold and dank place, unlike Estenzia's glittering marble halls and warm, sun-drenched gardens. He cannot get used to such a chilly summer. The other Daggers must be having trouble resting too.

After a while, he sighs, pushes away the furs, and rises from bed. The light outlines his taut stomach, lean muscles, and slender neck. He walks on silent feet to where his robe is draped over the foot of the bed. He'd worn this robe before, as it had been a present from a Kenettran noblewoman, the Duchess of Campagnia, several years ago. She'd become so infatuated with Raffaele, in fact, that she threw much of her fortune behind supporting the Daggers. The more powerful his clients, the more they tried to buy his love.

He wonders whether the duchess is well. After the Daggers fled Kenettra, they sent doves out to contact their patrons. The duchess was one of the patrons who had never responded.

Raffaele slides on the long robe, covering his body from head to toe. The fabric is heavy and luxurious, pooling at his feet, and shimmers in the light. He runs his fingers through the weight of his long black hair, then pulls it up into an elegant knot on the top of his head. In the cold morning sun, tiny traces of sapphire glimmer in his hair. His hands trace the cool surface of his sleeves.

He thinks back to the night when Enzo visited his chambers, when he had first warned the prince about Adelina. His fingers pause for a moment, suspended in grief.

No use dwelling on the past. Raffaele casts a glance back at the fireplace, then exits the chamber on silent feet. His robes pull behind him in a sheet of heavy velvet.

The corridors smell stale—centuries of old, damp stone and the ash of ancient torches. Gradually, they lighten until they open up to the summer castle's gardens. The flowers are dusted with a thin layer of snow that would melt by the time afternoon came. From here, Raffaele can see the castle's lower grounds and, beyond that, the rocky shores of Beldain. A cool gust numbs his cheeks and whips strands of hair across his face.

His gaze shifts to the main courtyard within the castle's front gates.

Normally, the space would be quiet at this hour. But today, *malfettos* fleeing Estenzia litter the grounds, huddled around small fires and under old blankets. Another shipload of *malfettos* must have just arrived in the night. Raffaele watches the clusters of people move and shift, then turns back inside the castle to head down.

Several *malfettos* recognize Raffaele as he makes his way out into the main courtyard. Their faces light up. "It's the Daggers' leader!" one exclaims.

Other *malfettos* rush forward, all eager to touch Raffaele's hands and arms, hoping for a moment of his ability to soothe. It is a daily ritual. Raffaele stands still in the midst of them. So many people, begging for comfort.

His eyes settle on a bald boy quite a bit taller than himself, his hair taken long ago by the fever. Raffaele had seen him waiting yesterday too. He gestures at the boy to step forward. His eyes widen in surprise, and then he rushes to Raffaele's side.

"Good morning," he says.

Raffaele looks at him carefully. "Good morning," he replies.

The boy lowers his voice. He seems nervous now that he has managed to get Raffaele's attention before anyone else. "Can you come see my sister?" he asks.

"Yes," Raffaele replies without hesitation.

The bald boy brightens at his answer. Like everyone else, he seems unable to tear his eyes away from Raffaele's face. He touches the young consort's arm. "This way," he says.

Raffaele follows him through the groups of *malfettos*. A rough, dark mark sprawled all across a forearm. A scarred ear and dark hair peppered with silver. Mismatched eye colors. Raffaele silently memorizes the markings he sees. Whispers erupt wherever he glides past.

They reach his sister. She is huddled in a corner of the courtyard, hiding her face behind a shawl. When she sees Raffaele approach, she makes herself even smaller and lowers her eyes.

The boy leans down to Raffaele as they reach her. "An Inquisitor seized her on the night they broke shop windows in Estenzia," he murmurs. He bends closer and whispers something in Raffaele's ear. As Raffaele listens, he studies the girl, noticing a scratch here, a bruise there, black and blue marring the skin of her legs.

When the boy finishes talking, Raffaele nods in understanding. He tucks his robe under his legs and kneels beside her. A wave of her energy washes over him. He winces. Such overwhelming sadness and fear. *If Adelina were here, she would use this.* He's very careful not to touch the girl. A few clients had done the same to him in his bedchamber, left him bruised and trembling—the last thing he ever wanted afterward was a hand on his skin.

For a long time, Raffaele sits and says nothing. The girl watches him in silence, transfixed by his face. The tension in her shoulders doesn't go away. At first, Raffaele senses a wave of resentment and hostility from her at his presence. But he doesn't look away.

The girl speaks at last. "The Lead Inquisitor is going to enslave us all. That's what we've heard."

"Yes."

"They say the Inquisition has set up slave camps around Estenzia."

"It's true."

She seems surprised at his refusal to soften the blow. "They say after they're done with us, they're going to kill us all."

Raffaele is silent. He knows he doesn't need to say anything in order to give her an answer.

"Are the Daggers going to stop him?"

"The Daggers are going to destroy him," Raffaele responds. The words sound strange in his gentle voice, like metal slicing through silk. "I will see to it personally."

The girl's eyes wander across his face again, taking in his delicate beauty. Raffaele holds a hand out to her and waits patiently. After a while, she extends her own hand. She touches his tentatively, then gasps. Through their contact, Raffaele tugs gently on her heartstrings, sharing in her heartache, soothing and caressing as much as he can, replacing her sadness with comfort. *I know.* Tears prickle the girl's eyes. She keeps her hand there for a long time, until at last she pulls away, huddling back into her crouch with her face turned down.

"Thank you," her brother whispers. Others cluster behind Raffaele, watching in awe. "It's the first time she's spoken since we left Estenzia."

"Raffaele!"

Lucent's voice cuts through the scene. Raffaele turns to see the Windwalker cutting her way through the crowd, her copper curls bouncing in the air. She looks every inch a typical Beldish girl here in her homeland, with furs thick around her neck and wrists, and a trail of beads clinking in her hair. She pauses in front of him.

"I hate to interrupt your daily healing session," she says, motioning for him to follow her, "but she arrived late last night. She's asked to see us."

Raffaele nods a farewell to the *malfettos* in the courtyard before matching Lucent's pace. She looks agitated, possibly at having to track him down, and she rubs her arms incessantly. "Kenettran summers have turned me soft," she complains as they go. "This cold is making my bones ache." When Raffaele doesn't respond, she turns her irritation on him. "Do you really have so much free time?" she says. "Making sad eyes at *malfetto* refugees every day isn't going to help us strike back at the Inquisition."

Raffaele doesn't bother looking at her. "The bald boy is an Elite," he replies.

Lucent makes an incredulous sound. "Really?"

"I noticed it yesterday," he continues. "A very subtle energy, but it's there. I'll send for him later."

Lucent glares at him. He can see the disbelief in her eyes, then annoyance that he has surprised her. Finally, she shrugs. "Ah, you always have a good reason for your kindnesses, don't you?" she mutters. "Well, Michel says they're out on the hills." Her footsteps speed up.

Raffaele doesn't add that his heart is still heavy, as it always is after he meets the *malfettos*. That he wishes he could have stayed longer, that he could do more to help them. There is no point in mentioning it. "Your queen will forgive me," he says.

Lucent huffs at that and crosses her arms. But underneath her nonchalant show, Raffaele can feel the threads of her energy twist painfully, a knot of passion and longing that has tightened and tightened for years, anxious to be reunited with the Beldish princess. How long has it been since Lucent was first banished from Beldain—how long has she been separated from Maeve? Raffaele softens toward her in empathy. He touches her arm once—the strings of energy around her shimmer, and he reaches for them, pulling on her powers, to soothe her. She glances at him with a raised eyebrow.

"You will see her," Raffaele says. "I promise. I'm sorry I kept you waiting."

Lucent relaxes a little at his touch. "I know."

They reach a high stone entrance that opens out onto the vast grasslands behind the castle. A smattering of soldiers are training out in the yard. Lucent has to lead Raffaele in a wide arc around the dueling pairs until they leave the castle behind and enter the tall grass. They crest a small hill. Raffaele shivers in the wind, blinking through the snow flurries, and pulls his cloak tighter around his shoulders.

The other two Daggers finally come into view as they reach the top of the hill. Michel, the Architect, has traded in his Kenettran attire for thick Beldish furs that hide his neck from view. He talks in a low voice to the girl beside him—Gemma, the Star Thief, still dressed stubbornly in her favorite Kenettran dress. Even she has a Beldish cloak draped over herself, though, and trembles in the cold. They both look up from their conversation to greet Lucent and Raffaele.

Gemma's gaze lingers the longest. Raffaele knows that she is still hoping to hear word about her father, that maybe Raffaele will bring news. But Raffaele just shakes his head at her. Baron Salvatore is another former Dagger patron who has not answered their doves. Gemma's face falls as she looks away.

Raffaele shifts his attention to the others in the clearing. Inside a circle of soldiers lining the edges are a handful of noblemen—princes, judging from their dark blue sleeves—and an enormous white tiger with stripes of gold. Its tail swishes lazily through the grass, and its eyes are narrowed into sleepy slits. Everyone's attention is fixed on two dueling opponents in the center of the clearing. One is a prince with light blond hair and a frown on his face. He stabs forward with his sword.

His opponent is a young woman—a girl, even—with furs lining her cloak. A fierce smear of gold decorates one of her cheeks, and her hair, half black and half gold, is tied up into an elaborate series of braids that resemble the hackles running down an angry wolf's back. She easily dodges the stab, flashes a grin at the prince, and swings her own sword to clash with his. The blade glints in the light.

Michel steps closer to Raffaele. "She is queen now," he murmurs. "Her mother died several weeks ago. I accidentally addressed her as Her Royal Highness—don't do the same."

Raffaele nods. "Thank you for the reminder." *Her Majesty Queen Maeve of Beldain.* He frowns as she duels. There is an energy around her, the unusual threads that must belong to an Elite. No one had ever mentioned this about the Beldish princess—but the signs are all there, glittering in a sheet of moving strings around her. *Does she even know?* Why would she keep such a thing secret?

Raffaele's attention then shifts to one of the princes watching. The youngest one. His frown deepens. There is an energy about this one too. But it is not like an Elite's energy, threads of vigor, of the world that is *alive*. He blinks, confused. When he reaches out to touch this strange force, his own strength immediately recoils, as if burned by something cold as ice.

The clash of swords brings him back to watching the duel. Maeve swings again and again at her older brother. She pushes him to the edge of their circle, where the soldiers stand guard—and then, all of a sudden, her brother starts striking back viciously, forcing her into the center again. Raffaele watches them closely. Even though the prince is taller than Maeve by a good foot, she doesn't seem intimidated. Instead, she calls out a taunt as she pushes against his blade, laughs again, and spins. She tries to catch her brother off guard, but he sees her move first. He suddenly crouches down, aiming for her legs. She catches her mistake too late—and falls.

The prince stands over her, his sword pointing at her chest. He shakes his head. "Better," he says. "But you still strike too eagerly before you can tell exactly where my attack will go." He gestures to his arm, then makes a slow, swinging motion. "See this? This is what you didn't catch. Look for the angle before you choose to strike."

"She caught it, Augustine," one of the other princes chimes in. He winks at Maeve. "She just didn't react fast enough."

"I would've reacted fast enough to dodge *your* attacks," Maeve calls backward, pointing her sword at her second brother. Several of the other princes chuckle at her answer. "And you'd be limping home by nightfall." She sheathes her sword, walks over to rub the tiger behind his ears, and nods at Augustine. "I'll do better, I promise. Let's practice again in the afternoon."

Raffaele looks on as the prince gives his little sister a smile and a bow. "As you wish," he replies.

Then, at her brothers' gesturing, she turns her attention to the Daggers. Michel and Gemma kneel immediately. Her eyes fall first on Lucent—a flash of recognition darts across her face—and her lighthearted mood instantly transforms into something serious. She says nothing. Instead, she waits while Lucent kneels and bows her head, her curls tumbling forward. Maeve watches her for a moment longer. Then her piercing stare darts to Raffaele, and he lowers his lashes. He follows Lucent's lead.

"Your Majesty," he says.

She leans one hand on her sword's hilt. Her cheeks are still flushed with excitement. "Look at me," she commands. When he does, she continues, "Are you Raffaele Laurent Bessette? The Messenger?"

"I am, Your Majesty."

Maeve regards him for a moment. She seems to study the summer green of his left eye, then the honey gold of his right. Her teeth flash at him in a wild smile. "You're as beautiful as they say. A lovely name, for a lovely face."

Raffaele lets himself blush, tilting his head in the familiar, subtle way he always did to his clients. "You honor me, Your Majesty. I'm flattered that my reputation has traveled as far as Beldain."

Maeve watches him thoughtfully. "You were Prince Enzo's most trusted adviser. He spoke very fondly of you. And now I see you have taken his place as the leader of the Daggers. Congratulations."

Raffaele's heartbeat quickens as he tries to ignore the familiar pang that Enzo's name brings. "It is not something I celebrate," he replies.

Maeve's eyes soften for a moment, perhaps in remembrance of her own mother's death. There seems to be something else about Enzo's death that intrigues her, a fleeting emotion that Raffaele senses in her heart, but she decides against mentioning it, leaving him to wonder. "Of course not," she says in the end.

Augustine whispers something in her ear. The young queen leans toward him—and although she focuses her attention on Raffaele, he can tell by the shift of her energy that she really *wants* to pay attention to Lucent. "Prince Enzo's death is not in my favor, as I'd hoped he would open trade between Kenettra and Beldain. Nor is it in your favor,

Messenger, because he has left you leaderless. But the king, too, has died. Giulietta rules in his place now, you say, and new *malfetto* refugees arrive in my country every day."

"You are kind for taking us in, Your Majesty."

"Nonsense." Maeve waves a hand impatiently, motioning for all of them to rise. When they do, she whistles for her horses. Her white tiger rises from his resting spot and saunters over to her side. "The gods created the blood fever, Raffaele," she says as they all pull themselves into saddles, "and so they also created the marked and the Elite. It is blasphemy to kill the children of the gods." She taps her horse's hindquarters with her heels, then starts leading them up a higher hill. "I didn't take you in out of kindness, though. Your Daggers are weakened now. Your leader is dead, and I hear rumors that one of your own turned her back on you, that she was working with the Inquisition. Your patrons have either given up and fled or have been captured and killed."

"Except you," Raffaele says. "Your Majesty."

"Except me," she agrees. "And I am still interested in Kenettra."

Raffaele rides in silence as the young queen guides them along the side of a sharp cliff, waves crashing against the rocks far below. "What have you sent us here for?" he asks.

"Let me show you something." Maeve leads them along the edge for a while, until they reach an area where the land curves in on itself, forming a shelter from the wild winds. Here, they ride up so close that Raffaele can see the entire bay.

The sight below is astonishing. Behind him, Lucent sucks in her breath.

Hundreds of Beldish warships dot the beaches of the bay. Sailors bustle up and down gangplanks to the decks, loading crates on board. The ships stretch far down and out along where the cliffs trail off into the distance.

Raffaele turns to Maeve. "You're planning to invade Kenettra?"

"If I can't have your *malfetto* crown prince sitting on the throne, then I will do it myself." Maeve pauses, studying Raffaele's face for his reaction. "But I'd like your help."

Raffaele just sits quietly. The last time Beldain went to war with Kenettra was over a hundred years ago. If Enzo could see all this, what would he think? Handing over his crown to a foreign queen? *It doesn't matter,* he reminds himself harshly. *Because Enzo is dead.*

"What help do you need?" Raffaele says after a moment.

"I hear that Master Teren Santoro was behind the king's death," Maeve replies. "Is this true?"

"Yes."

"Why did he want the king dead?"

"Because he is in love with Queen Giulietta. She keeps Teren at her side precisely for his help, among other reasons."

"Ah. A lover," Maeve says. At that, Lucent's eyes flick briefly to the queen, then dart away again. "She's young, new, and vulnerable. I need the Inquisition and her army weakened. What can you do to help me in this?"

Raffaele's expression is one of concentration. "Giulietta

is powerful with Teren at her side," he says. He exchanges looks with each of his Daggers as he goes on. "But Teren answers to something even more powerful than his queen—his belief that he has been ordained by the gods to destroy *malfettos*. If we can break their trust and separate them, then this invasion will have a better chance at success. And in order to break their trust, we'll have to make Teren disobey his queen."

"He'll never do such a thing," Lucent chimes in. "Have you seen Teren around Giulietta? Have you heard him talk about her?"

"Yes," Michel agrees. "Teren obeys the queen like a dog. He'd sooner die than insult her."

Even Gemma, who has been quiet until now, speaks up. "If you want to turn them against each other, we'll have to get into the city," she says. "Right now, it's nearly impossible to enter Estenzia. All *malfettos* have been forced outside the city walls. The Inquisition guards every street. We can't get over the walls or through the gates, even with Lucent's powers. There are too many soldiers."

Maeve's furs brush against her cheeks. "Kenettra has a new ruler," she says. "According to tradition, I must sail for Estenzia and see her in person, offer her gifts and a welcome. A promise of goodwill." At that, she raises an eyebrow and smiles. Behind her, Augustine laughs a little. Her eyes turn back to Raffaele. "I will get you into the city, my Messenger, if you can place a wedge between the queen and her Inquisitor."

"I am a consort," Raffaele replies. "I'll find a way."

Maeve stares in silence for a moment at her preparing fleet. "There is something else," she says, without looking at him.

"Yes, Your Majesty?"

"Tell me, Raffaele," she goes on, turning her head slightly in his direction, "that you can sense my power." She says it loudly enough for the other Daggers to hear. Michel, the closest, stiffens at her words. Gemma inhales sharply. But Raffaele notices Lucent's reaction the most—the sudden, sickly paleness of her face, the surprise in her eyes. She glances at Raffaele.

"Her power?" she asks, forgetting for the first time to refer to Maeve by her title.

Raffaele hesitates, then bows his head to the young queen. "I do," he replies. "I'd thought it rude to ask until you decided to share it."

Maeve smiles a little. "Then it will be no surprise to you when I tell you that I, too, am an Elite." She doesn't seem to react to Lucent's shock—although her eyes do dart briefly to her.

Raffaele shakes his head. "Not a surprise to me, Your Majesty. You may have had a different effect on my Daggers, though."

"And can you guess what I do?"

Raffaele reaches out once again to study the energy that surrounds her. It is a familiar feeling, one that leaves him with a chill. Something about her aligns with darkness, with the angels of Fear and Fury, the goddess of Death. The same alignments he felt in Adelina. The mere memory of her makes Raffaele clench his horse's reins. "I cannot guess, Your Majesty," he replies.

Maeve looks over her shoulder at the youngest prince, with his dueling mask still on, and nods. "Tristan," she says. "Let us see your face."

Her other brothers grow quiet at her command. Raffaele senses Lucent's heart lurch forward, and when he glances at her, he notices that her eyes have turned wide. The youngest prince nods, reaches up, and pulls the mask off his face.

He resembles Maeve, as well as his brothers. But while the others seem natural and whole, this prince is not—the eerie energy about him remains, haunting Raffaele.

"My youngest brother, Prince Tristan," Maeve says.

It is Lucent who finally breaks the silence. "You said in your letters that he had managed to pull through," she chokes out. "You told me he never died."

"He did." Maeve's expression turns harder. "But I brought him back."

Lucent goes pale. "That's impossible. You said—he almost drowned—and your mother—the Queen Mother—banished me for the near death of her son. This is *impossible*. You—" She turns to Maeve. "You never told me. I heard nothing about this in your letters."

"I couldn't tell you," Maeve answers sharply. Then she continues, in a quieter voice, "My mother screened every letter that left the palace, particularly those I meant for you. I could not risk her finding out about my power. She, like you, like *everyone,* assumed that Tristan never died, because I brought him back on the same night she banished you."

Raffaele only stares, hardly able to believe what he is witnessing. Threads of energy that do not belong in the land of the living. He understands it now, the unsettling, unnatural bond. He also understands immediately why Maeve is telling them this.

"Enzo," he whispers. "You want—"

"I want to bring back your prince," Maeve finishes for him. "Tristan, as you can see, is able to enjoy life again. Even more than that, though, he has brought some part of the Underworld with him. He has gained the strength of a dozen men."

The thought of Enzo alive again leaves Raffaele short of breath. The world spins for a moment. *No. Wait.* There is something else about Prince Tristan that the queen isn't telling him. "And what of Elites who are revived?" he asks.

Maeve smiles again. "Bringing an Elite back from the dead must amplify his powers too. And someone as powerful as Enzo was may prove nearly invincible once revived. I want his power at our side when we attack Kenettra. It will be a test, my creation of an *Elite* among *Elites.*" She leans toward Raffaele. "Think of the possibilities—of the other deceased Elites I could revive, of the unbridled power on our side."

Raffaele shakes his head. He should be overjoyed at the thought of seeing the prince again. But he senses the stain of the Underworld hovering over Tristan's energy.

"You doubt that it works," Maeve says after a moment. "Those I bring back must always be tied to someone from the living world. They need living threads to hold them away from the Underworld's constant pull. Tristan is tied to me, giving me a certain level of control—protection—over him. Enzo will need to be tethered to someone too."

Tethered to me. Raffaele's eyes narrow as he looks at her. *That is what she means to do.* "I cannot be a part of this," he finally says. His voice is firm, even in its hoarseness. "This violates the order of the gods."

Maeve's voice hardens now. "I am a *child* of the gods," she snaps. "I was gifted with this power. The gods bless it—it violates no order."

Raffaele bows his head. His hands are shaking. "I *cannot* agree to this, Your Majesty," he says again. "Enzo's soul has gone to rest in the Underworld. Pulling him back, away from the side of Holy Moritas, and into the real world again . . . he does not belong here anymore. Let him rest."

"I am not asking your permission, consort," Maeve replies firmly. When Raffaele looks up at her again, she lifts her chin. "Remember, Raffaele, that Enzo was the Crown Prince of Kenettra. A *malfetto,* an Elite, your former leader. He did not deserve to die. He deserves to *return,* to see his country's *malfettos* safe. I will rule Kenettra, but I will reinstate him in my absence." Her eyes are hard as stone. "Is this not what you and your Daggers have long fought for?"

Raffaele is silent. He is seventeen again, standing before a sea of nobility at the Fortunata Court, sensing Enzo's energy in the crowd for the first time. He is in the underground training cavern of the Daggers' former home, watching the prince duel with others. Raffaele looks at Michel, then Gemma, then Lucent. They look back, grave and silent. This should be what they all want.

But Enzo died. They grieved, and made their peace with it. And now . . .

"I *will* bring him back," Maeve continues, "and I *will* tether him to anyone I please." Then, her voice turns gentler. "But I'd rather tie him to those who care the most for him. The bond with the living is strongest that way."

Still, Raffaele doesn't reply. He closes his eyes, willing himself to silence his mind. To force away the churning sensation of wrongness in this idea. Finally, he opens his eyes and meets the queen's gaze. "Will he be the same?"

"We won't know," Maeve says slowly, "until I try."

SCENE VII

(Exeunt all but Boy.)

BOY. Are you an ogre?

(Enter Ogre.)

OGRE. Are you a knight?

BOY. I am not a knight! Nor am I a king, scout, or priest. Therefore, you can be sure I am not here to steal the jewel.

–Original translation of The Temptation of the Jewel,

by Tristan Chirsley

Adelina Amouteru

The Little Baths of Bethesda turn out to be a set of ruins at the edge of Merroutas.

Early the next morning, as the sun crests the horizon and fishing boats set out into the bay, Violetta and I make our way down the dirt path leading out of the city-state's main gates and to a smaller cluster of abandoned domed houses, all situated beneath the stone arches of a former aqueduct.

It looks like a place that once bustled with activity. But the bathhouse itself—or what's left of it—was built on soft ground, which must have sealed its fate. As people abandoned the bathhouse, so must they have abandoned the small settlement of homes around it. Or perhaps the aqueduct delivering its water crumbled first. The once-glorious pillars at its entrance have now collapsed, and the stone foundation has sunk into the marshy soil. Vines crawl up the stone, their flowers vibrant green and yellow. I feel a strong attraction to this place's ruined beauty.

"He's here," Violetta whispers beside me, her brow furrowed in concentration.

"Good." I adjust my mask across my own ruined face and approach the entrance.

The bathhouse is cool and dark inside, its arched stone ceiling covered with mosses and ivy. Narrow shafts of light cut through the ceiling's openings, illuminating the pools of water below. We step carefully through the halls of ancient marble colonnades. The air smells wet and musky, the scent of something green and alive. The sound of dripping water echoes all around us.

Finally I stop where the bath pool begins. "Where is he?" I whisper.

Violetta lifts her eyes to the ceiling. She spins in a half circle, then focuses on a dark corner. "There."

I strain to see into the shadows. "Magiano," I call out. My voice startles me—it bounces off the walls, over and over, until it finally fades away. I clear my throat, a little embarrassed, and continue in a quieter tone. "We were told we could find you here."

There is a long silence, so long that I start to wonder whether Violetta might be mistaken.

Then, someone laughs. As the sound echoes from surface to surface, a flurry of leaves rain down from the bathhouse's mossy banisters. A trail of dark braids flashes in and out of the light. I instinctively extend one of my arms in front of Violetta, as if that might protect her.

"Adelina," a voice calls playfully. "How nice to see you."

I try to pinpoint where the voice comes from.

"Are you Magiano, then?" I reply. "Or are you just taunting us?"

"Do you remember a comedy called *The Temptation of the Jewel*?" he continues after a pause. "The play opened in Kenettra a couple of years ago, to great fanfare, right before the Inquisition banned it."

I do remember it. *The Temptation of the Jewel* was about a dull, arrogant knight who continually bragged that he could steal a jewel from an ogre's lair—only to be bested by a cheeky young boy, who snatched the prize first. It was penned by Tristan Chirsley, the same famous scribe who'd written the *Stories of the Star Thief* collection, and its final performance had happened in Dalia, in a theater overflowing with people.

The Star Thief. I shake my head, trying not to think of Gemma and the others. "Yes, of course I do," I respond. "How is this relevant? Are you a Chirsley admirer?"

Another laugh sounds through the vast space. Another shuffle of feet and flurry of leaves high above us. This time, we look up and see a dark silhouette crouched on a rotting wooden beam right over our heads. I step aside to look more properly at him. In the shadows, all I can make out are a pair of bright gold eyes, fixed curiously on me.

"It's relevant," he replies, "because I was the inspiration for it."

A laugh escapes my mouth before I can stop it. "You inspired Chirsley's play?"

He dangles his feet over the beam. I notice that he's not wearing shoes today. "The Inquisition banned the play because it was about the theft of the queen's crown jewels."

I catch Violetta's skeptical glance. The rumors we'd heard along the way, about how Magiano had stolen Queen Giulietta's crown, come back to me now. "Did you inspire the clever boy, then, or the arrogant knight?" I tease.

Now I can see his bright white teeth in the darkness. That carefree smile. "You wound me, my love," he says. He reaches for something in his pockets and tosses it at us. The object falls in a clean line, gleaming as it goes. It splashes into the shallowest part of the pool.

"You forgot your ring last night," he says.

My ring? I hurry over to the pool, kneel, and peer into the water. The silver ring sparkles in a ray of light, winking at me. It is the ring I'd worn on my fourth finger. I roll up my sleeve, reach for it, and clench it in my fist.

He couldn't have taken it from me last night. Impossible. He didn't even touch my hands. He didn't even come down from the balcony!

The boy laughs before tossing something else down, this time in Violetta's direction. "Let's see, what else . . ." As it floats down, I see that it's a ribbon of cloth. "A sash from your dress, my lady," he says to Violetta with a mock bow of his head. "Right as you walked into this bathhouse."

He throws down more of our things, including a gold pin from my head wrap, and three jewels from Violetta's sleeves. The hairs on my arms rise. "You two are very forgetful," he chides as he goes.

Violetta bends down to retrieve her belongings. She shoots a glare at Magiano as she carefully clips the jewels back onto her sleeves. "I see we've found an upstanding citizen, Adelina," she mutters to me.

"Is this supposed to impress us?" I call up to him. "A demonstration of cheap street tricks?"

"Silly girl. I know what you're really asking." He hops into the light. "You're asking how I managed to do it. You have no idea, do you?" He's the same boy we met yesterday. Thick ropes of braids hang over his shoulders, and he's wearing a colorful tunic that has everything from patches of silk to enormous brown leaves sewn into it. When I look more closely, I realize that the leaves are actually made out of metal. Of *gold*.

His smile is the one I remember—feral, sharp in a way that tells me he is observing everything about us. Studying our possessions. Something about his eyes sends a chill through me. A pleasant chill.

The famed Magiano.

"I admit I don't know how you took our possessions," I say, with a stiff jerk of my head. "Please. Enlighten us."

He pulls his lute from behind his back and plucks a few notes. "So, you're impressed, after all."

My gaze shifts to the lute. It's different from the lute he had yesterday. The instrument he has now is an opulent one, encrusted with glittering diamonds and emeralds, the strings painted gold, the knobs on the lute's neck made out of jewels. The entire thing looks like a gaudy mess.

Magiano holds out the lute for us to admire. It twinkles madly in the light. "Isn't she amazing? It's the best lute that a night of gambling can buy."

So this is how a famous thief spends his winnings. "Where do you even *go* to buy a monstrosity like that?" I say, before I can stop myself.

Magiano blinks at me in surprise, then gives me a hurt frown. He hugs the lute to his chest. "I think it's pretty," he says defensively.

Violetta and I share a look. "What is your power?" I ask him. "All the rumors say that you're a Young Elite. Is it true, or are you simply a boy with a talent for theft?"

"And what if I'm not an Elite?" he says with a grin. "Would you be disappointed?"

"Yes."

Magiano leans back on the beam, hugs his lute, and regards me in the way that an animal might. He says, "All right. I'll enlighten you." He picks at his teeth. "You are a worker of illusions. Yes?"

I nod.

He gestures at me. "Create something. Anything. Go ahead. Make this broken place beautiful."

He's challenging me. I look at Violetta, and she shrugs, as if giving me permission. So I take a deep breath, reach for the threads buried inside me, pull them out into the air, and begin to weave.

All around us, the interior of the bathhouse transforms into a vision of green hills underneath a stormy sky. Steep waterfalls line one side of the landscape, and baliras lift ships from the ocean to the top of the falls, setting them safely on the shallow, elevated seas. Dalia, my birth city. I keep weaving. A warm wind blows past us, and the air fills with the scent of oncoming rain.

Magiano watches the shifting illusion with wide eyes. In this moment, his mischief and bravado vanish—he blinks, as if unable to believe what he's seeing. When he finally looks back at me, his smile is full of wonder. He takes a deep breath. "Again," he whispers. "Make something else."

His admiration of my powers makes me stand a little straighter. I wave away the illusion of Dalia, then plunge us into the twilit depths of a nighttime ocean. We float in the dark water, illuminated only by shafts of dim blue light. The ocean transforms into midnight on a hill overlooking Estenzia, with the three moons hanging huge over the horizon.

Finally, I take the illusions away, bringing back the ruins that surround us. Magiano shakes his head at me, but doesn't say a word.

"Your turn," I say, crossing my arms. My body hums with the ache of using energy. "Show us your power."

Magiano bows his head once. "Fair enough," he replies.

Violetta takes my hand. At the same time, something invisible shoves against my hold on my dark energy—and the world around us vanishes.

I throw my hands up to shield my eye from the brilliant light. It is searing bright—is this his power? *No, that can't be right.* As the light gradually fades, I chance a look around. The bathhouse is still here, still all around us . . . but, to my shock, it has transformed into its former self. No ivy or moss hangs from broken pillars, no holes in its crumbling dome roof let light paint patterns on the floor. Instead, the rows of pillars are new and polished, and the water in the pool—its surface adorned with floating petals—gives off clouds of steam. Statues of the gods line the pool's edge. I frown at the sight, then try to blink it away. Beside me, Violetta's mouth hangs open. She tries to speak.

"It's not real," she finally whispers.

It's not real. Of course it's not—with those words, I realize that I recognize the energy this place is giving off, the millions of threads holding everything together. The renewed bathhouse is an *illusion.* Just like something I would have created. In fact, the threads of energy that created this image of the perfect bathhouse feel exactly like my own threads.

Another illusion worker?

I don't understand. How could he have created something with a power that should belong to me?

The illusion breaks without warning. The brightly lit temple, the steaming water and statues—all disappear in an instant, leaving us back in the dark recesses of the broken bathhouse and its overgrown shell. Spots of light still float across my vision. I have to adjust to the darkness, almost as if I'd been blinded by something real.

Magiano swings his legs idly. "The things I could've done," he muses, "had I known you earlier."

I clear my throat and try not to look too stunned. "You . . . you have the same power as I do?"

He laughs at the hesitation in my voice. With a grandiose half bow, he jumps onto his feet and spins once on the beam, like he is dancing. It looks effortless. "Don't be stupid," he replies. "No two Elites have the *exact* same power."

"Then . . ."

"I imitate," he continues. "Whenever I encounter another Elite, and she uses her power, I can briefly glimpse the weave of her energy in the air. Then I copy what I see—if only for a moment." He pauses to give me a grin so large that it appears to split his face in two. "This is how you saved my life, and you didn't even know it. When you were in the dungeon cell next to mine, I mimicked you. I tricked my way out of my cell by making the soldiers think my cell was empty. They came over to investigate, and I stepped right out when they opened the door."

Gradually, the realization hits me. "You can mimic any Elite?"

He shrugs. "When I was lost and penniless in the Sunlands, I mimicked an Elite named the Alchemist, and transformed an entire wagon's worth of silks into gold. When I ran from the Inquisition in Kenettra, I mimicked the Lead Inquisitor's healing abilities in order to protect myself against the arrows his men launched at me." He spreads his hands, nearly drops his lute, and grabs it again. "I am the brightly colored fish that pretends to be poisonous. You see?"

A mimic. I look down at my hand and move my fingers, watching my ring glint in the light. I eye the sash Violetta has tied back onto her dress. "When you stole our things," I say slowly, "you used my power against us."

Magiano tunes one of the lute's strings. "Why yes. I replaced your ring with an illusion of it, slipped it off while convincing you that I was just idling on the balcony."

Of course. It's something I would have done—something I *have* done before—when stealing money from noblemen's purses. I swallow, trying to grasp the sheer extent of his power. My heart beats faster.

Violetta's mistrust of him has turned to fascination. "That means—around the right people—you can do anything."

Magiano pretends to have the same realization she does, and his jaw drops, mocking her. "Well, now. I do believe you're right." He swings the lute over his back again, skips along the ceiling beam until he reaches a pillar, then hops down to a lower beam so that he now crouches close to us, close enough for me to see the wide array of colorful necklaces hanging around his neck. More jewels. And now I can see what bothered me about his eyes. His pupils look strangely oval—slitted, like a cat's.

"Now, then," he says. "We have been introduced to each other and gotten all our pleasantries out of the way. Tell me. What do you want?"

I take a deep breath. "My sister and I are running from the Inquisition," I say. "We are heading south now, out of their reach, until we can gather enough allies to return to Kenettra and strike back."

"Ah. You want revenge against the Inquisition."

"Yes."

"You and the rest of us." Magiano snorts. "Why? Because they imprisoned you? Because they're horrible? If that's the case, then you're better off leaving them alone. Trust me. You're free now. Why go back?"

"Have you heard the latest news from Estenzia?" I ask. "About Queen Giulietta? And her brother's—" I choke on the mention of Enzo's death. Even now, I cannot bring myself to say it.

Magiano nods. "Yes. That news spread rather quickly."

"Have you also heard that Master Teren Santoro is planning to annihilate all *malfettos* in Kenettra? He is the queen's pet—she will give him the power to do it."

Magiano leans against the beam. If this news disturbs him, he doesn't show it. Instead, he gathers his braids and pulls them over one shoulder. "So, what you're trying to say is that you want to stop Teren's ruthless little campaign. And you are trying to gather a team of Young Elites to help you do this."

"Yes." My hopes rise a little. "And you are the Elite we hear about the most."

Magiano stands taller, and his eyes glint with pleasure. "You flatter me, my love." He gives me a rueful smile. "But flattery won't be enough, I'm afraid. I work alone. I'm quite happy right where I am, and I have no interest in joining a noble cause. You've wasted your time on me."

My rising hopes vanish as quickly as they came. I can't help letting my shoulders fall. With a reputation like his, of course he must have been approached in the past by other Elites. What made me think he would agree to side with us? "Why do you work alone?" I ask.

"Because I don't like to share my spoils."

I lift my head and give him a small frown. *He has to join us,* the whispers in my head urge. The Daggers would have killed for an Elite with his powers on their side. What would Enzo or Raffaele have said to entice him to join the Dagger Society? I think back to the way Enzo had recruited me, what he whispered in my ear. *Do you want to punish those who have wronged you?*

Beside me, Violetta squeezes my hand in the darkness. She glances at me from the corners of her eyes. "Find his weakness," she murmurs to me. "What he wants."

I try a different tactic. "If you are the most notorious thief in the world," I say to him, "and you are so good at what you do, then how did you get captured by the Inquisition?"

Magiano props an elbow up on one knee and swings his legs. He gives me a curious grin . . . but behind it, I see what I'd hoped for. A spark of irritation. "They got lucky," he replies, his nonchalant voice a little bit sharper than before.

"Or maybe you were careless?" I press. "Or are you exaggerating your talents?"

Magiano's grin wavers for an instant. He sighs and rolls his eyes. "If you *must* know," he mutters, "I was in Dalia to steal a chest of rare sapphires that had arrived from Dumor as a present for the duke. And the only reason the Inquisition caught me is that I went back for one more sapphire than I should have." He holds up both hands. "In my defense, it was a very heavy sapphire."

He can't help himself, I realize. This is why one of the world's most notorious Elites still runs petty street games for money, why he just spent an entire night's pouch of gold talents on a useless, jewel-encrusted lute, why he has gold leaves sewn into his clothes. There are never enough gold talents in his pockets or jewels on his fingers—not when he knows there are more to gain. I glance at his fine silks again. Money pours into his hands and flows right out between his fingers.

Violetta's tightened hold tells me she has come to the exact same conclusion. This is our opening.

"Kenettra's royal treasury holds a thousand times the

sapphires you tried to steal in Dalia. You and I both know this. You managed to steal the crown jewels once before—now imagine all the gold behind that crown."

As expected, Magiano's eyes take on a gleam so intense that I have to take a step back. He tilts his head suspiciously at me. "You tell me this as if I've never considered stealing the entire Kenettran royal treasury," he says.

"Then why haven't you done it yet?"

"You are so naïve." He shakes his head, disappointed in my answer. "Do you have any idea how many guards watch over that gold? How many locations it's scattered across? What a fool attempt it would be for anyone to think he could take it all?" He sniffs. "And here I thought for a moment that you had some magical idea to take it too."

"I do," I reply.

Magiano lets out a short laugh, but I can tell he's studying me seriously now. "Then please, Adelina, share it. You really think the entire Kenettran royal treasury can be yours?"

"*Ours,*" I correct him. "If you join us, you would never need to scramble for gold again."

He laughs again. "Now I know you're lying to me." He leans forward. "What—are you planning to cloak yourself in illusions and sneak into the treasury to take one armful of gold at a time? Do you know how many lifetimes that would take you, even if you made dozens of trips a night? And even if you *could* steal all that gold, how does one even begin to transport it out of the country? Out of Estenzia, even?" He stands up on the beam, hops lightly to a spot where he can reach a higher beam, and starts to turn away.

"I never said anything about *stealing* it," I call out.

He pauses, then turns to face me. "Then how do you plan to take it all, my love?"

I smile. A memory burns through my mind: the cold, rainy night; my father talking to the stranger downstairs; I'm sitting along the stairs, pretending from my perch that I am a queen on a balcony. I blink. The power of that desire rushes through me like a wild wind. "Simple. We take away the throne from Queen Giulietta and the Inquisition Axis. Then the Kenettran royal treasury becomes ours by right."

Magiano blinks. Then he starts to laugh. The laughter grows louder, until his eyes shine with tears, until he finally stops to let himself catch a breath. When he composes himself, his eyes slit, glowing in the darkness. In the silence that follows, I press on. "If you join us, and we take the Queen of Kenettra's throne, then *malfettos* will have a ruler like themselves. We can stop Teren's thirst for our blood. You can have more gold than you ever dreamed of. You can have a thousand diamond-encrusted lutes. You would be able to buy your own island and castle. You'd be remembered as a king."

"I don't want to be a king," Magiano replies. "Too many responsibilities." But his answer is halfhearted, and he doesn't move. *He's considering my plan.*

"You don't need to be responsible for anything," I say. "Help me win the crown and save the country, and you can have everything you've ever desired."

Another long silence drags on. His gaze wanders to my mask. "Take it off," he mutters.

I hadn't expected an answer like that. He's buying himself some time to think, distracting me in the process. I shake my head. After all this time, the thought of showing a new stranger my greatest weakness still sends fear through me.

Magiano's expression flickers, if only slightly, and some of the wildness seeps out of his eyes. Like he knows me. "Take off your mask," he whispers. "I do not judge a *malfetto*'s markings, Adelina, nor do I work with someone who hides her face from me."

When Violetta nods, I reach up and fiddle with the knot behind my head. The mask loosens, then swings completely off to dangle in my hand. The cold air hits my scar. I force myself to stare steadily back at Magiano, bracing myself for his reaction. If I'm going to have my own Elites, they will need to trust me.

He steps closer and takes a long look. I can see the slashes of honey gold in his eyes. A slow, lazy smile starts to creep onto his face. He doesn't ask about my marking. Instead, he lifts the lower corner of his silk shirt and bares part of his side.

I inhale sharply. A hideous scar snakes its way across his skin, then disappears up under his shirt. Our eyes meet, and a moment of understanding passes between us.

"Please," I say, lowering my voice. "I don't know what happened to you in your past, or what your full marking looks like. But if the promise of gold doesn't entice you enough, then think of the millions of other *malfettos* in Kenettra, all of whom will die in the next few months if no one saves them. You are a thief, so perhaps you have your own code of honor. Is there a place in your heart where you would mourn for the deaths of all who are like us?"

Something about my words strikes Magiano, and his eyes take on a faraway look. He pauses and clears his throat.

"It's just a rumor, you know," he says after a moment. "The story about the queen's crown jewels."

"The crown jewels?"

"Yes." He looks at me. "The Kenettran queen's crown jewels. I never stole them. I *tried* to—but couldn't manage it."

I watch him carefully. There is something shifting in the balance of our conversation. "Yet you still want them," I reply.

"What can I say? It's a weakness."

"So, what will you do? Will you join us?"

He holds up a slender finger covered with gold rings. "How do I know that you'll keep your promise, if I do help you get what you want?"

I shrug. "Are you going to spend the rest of your life stealing a handful of jewels at a time and running gambling stands in Merroutas?" I reply. "You said yourself, you wonder what you could have done if you'd known me earlier. Well, here's your chance."

Magiano smiles at me with something akin to pity. "The girl who would be queen," he murmurs thoughtfully. "The gods play interesting games."

"This is no game," I say.

At last, he lifts his head and raises his voice. "I do owe you a life debt. And that's something I never play games with."

I stare silently at him, thinking back to the night before, when he'd originally met us to pass along his thanks for saving his *malfetto* companion.

Magiano holds out a hand in my direction. "If you want to take on the Inquisition, you will need a whole host of people at your back. And if you want people at your back, you need to build a reputation. I don't follow anyone until I'm convinced that they're worth following."

"What can we do to convince you?"

Magiano smiles. "Beat me in a race."

"A race?"

"A little game between us," he says. "I'll even give you a head start." His smile takes on a wicked tilt. "A man called the Night King rules this city. He has many soldiers, as well as a secret army of ten thousand mercenaries scattered throughout the island. You may have seen his men patrolling the streets, with moon-and-crown emblems on their sleeves."

I fold my arms. "I have."

"He is the most feared man in Merroutas. They say that every time he uncovers a traitor in his ranks, he skins that man alive and has the skin sewn into his cloak."

As I imagine the scene, my skin prickles . . . not just from horror, but from fascination. *A kindred soul,* the whispers say. "What does that have to do with us?" I ask, raising my voice to drown out the whispers.

"Tomorrow morning, I am going to gain access to his estate to rob him of the prized diamond pin he always wears on his collar. If *you* can steal it before I can . . . then I will join you." He gives me a mock bow that makes me blush. "I only work with the worthy. And I just want to make sure you understand the risks of this mission."

Neither Violetta nor I am an expert thief. I can disguise us or make us invisible, but my powers are still imperfect. What if we are caught? I imagine us lashed to a pole, our skin stripped from our limbs.

It's not worth it.

Magiano smiles at my expression. "You're too afraid," he says.

The whispers in my head stir, urging me on. *The Night King controls ten thousand mercenaries. What wouldn't you give for ten thousand mercenaries at your service?* I shake my head—the whispers fade away, leaving me to ponder Magiano's offer. This is one of his games. His famous tricks. Maybe even just a challenge for himself. I watch him carefully, searching for what the right answer should be. Can I actually get to the prize before Magiano runs away with it? I don't know. Power and speed are two different things.

"I'm only giving you this chance, by the way," Magiano says in a lighthearted tone, "because you helped me escape the Inquisition Tower."

"How generous," I quip.

Magiano just laughs again, a bright, tinkling sound, and extends a decorated hand. "A deal, then?"

I need him. I need my little army. Even Violetta touches my hand and nudges it toward him. So I only hesitate for one more second.

"A deal," I reply, taking his hand.

"Good." He nods. "Then you have my word."

Teren Santoro

The outskirts of Estenzia, and a cool early morning. Along the wall that surrounds the city are dozens of dilapidated shelters of wood and stone, covered with mud from the evening rains. *Malfettos* wander between them.

Clusters of dirty white tents are scattered among the shelters. Inquisition guard points.

Teren Santoro lounges inside his personal tent on a long divan, looking on as Queen Giulietta dresses. His eyes wander up her back. She is exquisite today, as she is every day, wearing a brilliant blue riding dress with her dark locks piled high on her head. He watches as she carefully pins her curls back into place. Just moments ago, they had been loose, tumbling over her shoulders, brushing against his cheeks, soft as silk through his fingers.

"Are you running a full inspection of the *malfetto* camps

this morning?" she asks. They are the first words she has said to him since she came to his tent.

Teren nods. "Yes, Your Majesty."

"How are they doing?"

"Very well. Ever since we moved them outside the city, my men have put them to work in the fields and busied them with weaving. They've been very efficient—"

Giulietta turns so that he can see a profile of her face. She smiles at him. "No," she interrupts. "I meant, how are they *doing*?"

Teren hesitates. "What do you mean?"

"When I rode through the tents this morning, I saw the *malfettos'* faces. They're gaunt and hollow-eyed. Have your men been feeding them as much as they've been working them?"

He frowns, then pushes himself to a seated position. The morning light shows the pale maze of scars on his chest. "They're fed enough to keep them working," he replies. "And no more than that. I'd rather not waste food on *malfettos* if I don't have to."

Giulietta leans toward him. One of her hands rests on his stomach, then runs up his chest to the hollow of his neck, leaving a trail of heat across his skin. Teren's heart beats faster, and for a moment, he forgets what they were talking about. She brushes her lips past his. He leans into the kiss eagerly, bringing a hand up to the back of her slender neck, drawing her toward him.

Giulietta pulls away from him. Teren finds himself staring

into her deep, dark eyes. "Starving slaves don't make good slaves, Master Santoro," she whispers, stroking his hair. "You aren't feeding them enough."

Teren blinks. Of everything she should be concerned about, she is asking about the welfare of her slaves? "But," he starts, "they're expendable, Giulietta."

"Are they, now?"

Teren takes a deep breath. Ever since Prince Enzo's death in the arena, since Giulietta officially took the throne, she has been pushing back against his original plans. It is as if she had lost interest in what he thought was her hatred for *malfettos*.

But he does not want to argue with his queen today. "We are cleansing the city of them. For every *malfetto* that dies, we'll simply replace him with another, brought over from a different city. My men are already rounding up *malfettos* in other—"

"We are not cleansing the city of them," Giulietta replies. "We are *punishing* them for their abomination, for bringing misfortune down on us. These *malfettos* still have families within the walls. And some of them are unhappy about what's happening." She nods in disdain at the tent flap. "The water in their troughs is filthy. It is only a matter of time before everyone in these camps falls ill. I want them to work themselves into submission, Teren. But I don't want a *rebellion*."

"But—"

Giulietta's eyes harden. "Feed and water them, Master Santoro," she commands.

Teren shakes his head, ashamed to be arguing with the Queen of Kenettra—someone so much purer than he. He lowers his eyes and bows his head. "Of course, Your Majesty. You're absolutely right."

Giulietta smooths the folds at her wrists. "Good."

"Will you see me tonight?" he murmurs as she rises from the divan.

Giulietta casts him a casual glance. "If I want to see you tonight, I'll send someone to fetch you." She turns away and leaves the tent. The flap slaps closed behind her.

Teren keeps his head bowed and lets her go. Of course he lets her go. She is the queen. But a sinking feeling weighs down his heart.

What if I upset her, and she finds someone new?

The thought sends pain through his chest. Teren pushes the image out of his head and rises to grab his shirt. He can't stay here—he has to move, to go somewhere and think. He dresses in his layers of armor. Then he steps out of the tent and nods to the guard stationed outside. The guard nods back, pretending not to know what happened between Teren and his queen.

"Round up my captains," Teren says. "I'll be at the temple. Have them meet me outside, so we can discuss today's inspections."

The guard bows immediately. Teren can tell he's too

afraid to stare into his pale blue irises for long. "Right away, sir."

Temples to the gods are built against the wall at every mile, their entrances marked by looming stone pillars with wings carved against the ceiling. Teren heads for the nearest one on foot, ignoring the horse tied outside his tent. Mud splashes his white boots. When he reaches the temple, he makes his way up the steps and into the building's cool recesses. The space is empty this early in the morning.

Inside, the twelve statues of the gods and angels line both sides of a straight marble path. Plates of jasmine-scented water sit at the path's start. Teren removes his boots, dips his feet in the water, and walks along the path. He kneels in the center, surrounded by the gods' eyes. The only sounds in the temple are the occasional clinking of chimes hung outside the temple's doors.

"I'm sorry," Teren finally says. His eyes stay turned to the floor, their pale, pulsing color subdued. His words echo between the statues and pillars until they fade away, incomprehensible.

He hesitates, unsure how to continue.

"I shouldn't have questioned my queen," he adds after a moment. "It is an insult to the gods."

No one answers.

Teren frowns as he talks. "But you have to help me," he continues. "I know I am no better than the *malfetto* wretches out there in the camps, and I know I should obey Her Majesty. But my mission is to rid this country of *malfettos*.

The queen . . . she has so much love in her heart. Her brother was a *malfetto,* after all. She doesn't know how urgently she needs to destroy them. *Us.*" He sighs.

The statues stay silent. Behind him come the tiny footsteps of the priests' apprentices as they replace the plates of water and jasmine. Teren doesn't move. His thoughts wander from Giulietta and the *malfettos* to the morning in Estenzia's arena, when he'd run his sword through Prince Enzo's chest. He rarely dwelled on those he killed, but Enzo . . . he can still remember the feeling of the blade pushing through flesh, of the prince's terrible gasp. He remembers how Enzo had collapsed at his feet, how flecks of bright red blood dotted his boots.

Teren shakes his head, unsure of why he keeps thinking about Enzo's death.

A childhood memory comes to him, of golden days before the fever . . . Teren and Enzo, still little boys, racing out of the kitchens to climb to the top of a tree outside the palace walls. Enzo was first, being older and taller. He reached down to offer Teren a helping hand, pulled him up, and pointed toward the ocean, laughing. *You can see the baliras from here,* the little prince said. They unwrapped leftover cuts of meat from the kitchens and skewered them onto the branches. Then they sat back and watched in awe as a pair of falcons swooped down to grab the food.

That evening, when Teren's father struck him for being late to his Inquisition training, Prince Enzo stood between Teren and the towering Lead Inquisitor.

Let me discipline my son, Your Highness, his father said. *A soldier cannot be taught laziness.*

He followed my orders, sir, Enzo replied, lifting his chin. *It was my fault, not his.*

Teren's father spared him that night.

The memory fades away. Teren continues to kneel for a long time, until the metal of his armor cuts his knees, making him bleed even as the wounds heal immediately. He looks up at the statues of the gods, trying to understand the mess of emotions crowding his mind.

Was it right for me, he asks silently, *to kill your crown prince?*

A boy and girl—the priests' apprentices—come into view in their temple robes, placing fresh flowers at the statues' feet. Teren watches them with a smile. When the little girl notices his Lead Inquisitor uniform, she blushes and curtsies. "I'm sorry for interrupting your prayer, sir," she says.

Teren waves off her apology. "Come here," he beckons, and she does. He takes one of the flowers from her basket, admires it, and tucks it behind her ear. She's a perfect child—flawless, free of markings, with a head of red-gold hair and wide, innocent eyes. "You serve the gods well," he says.

The girl beams at him. "Thank you, sir." Teren places a gentle hand on her head and dismisses her. He watches her scamper away to join the boy.

This is the world he is fighting to protect, from monsters like himself. He looks up at the statues again, certain that the little girl and boy are the gods' way of telling him what he needs to do. *It was right of me. I* have *to be right.* He just has to convince Giulietta that he's doing this for the sake of her throne. Because he loves her.

Finally, Teren rises. He straightens his cloak and his armor, and heads toward the temple entrance. He throws open the doors. Sunlight washes over him, bathing his white robes and armor in gold. Before him is a sea of tents and dilapidated shelters. He looks on with disinterest as two Inquisitors drag a dead, whipped *malfetto* through the dirt, then toss the body onto a burning pile of wood.

Several of his captains are already waiting for him at the bottom of the steps. They straighten at the sight of him.

"Halve the rations for the *malfettos,*" Teren says, adjusting his gloves. His irises shine clear in the light. "I want this cleansing sped up. Do not inform the queen."

This Documente of Assurance, executed 11 Toberie of 1315, witnesses that Sir Marzio of Dalia may enter into monitored trade with His Eminence the Night King of Merroutas, with knowledge that failure to provide His Eminence with eighty percent of acquired monies will result in arrest and execution.

–Document of Assurance between Sir Marzio of Dalia and the Night King of Merroutas

Adelina Amouteru

Like everything else about Magiano, his little challenge to me is probably a trick.

"He said he'd make his move tomorrow morning," Violetta says to me that evening, as we sit together on the floor of a small tavern room on the edge of Merroutas. We are practicing our powers, just as we do every night.

"He'll make his move sooner than that." I weave a tiny ribbon of darkness on the ground and let it dance in a pattern. "Tricksters don't tell the truth."

"Then what should we do? We don't have much time if we want to beat him."

I shake my head, concentrating on weaving the ribbon into a miniature, dancing faerie. I mold as much detail as I can into its face. "Remember," I say, "our goal isn't to steal the diamond pin before Magiano can. Our goal is to convince him that we are worth following."

Violetta watches as I shift my illusion of the dancing faerie, hunching its back, replacing its beautiful hair with hideous spikes. I grow it into a hulking monster. "You're thinking about what he said, aren't you?" she asks after a moment. "How the Night King has ten thousand mercenaries and an army at his back. You'd love to have that kind of support at your disposal."

"How did you know?"

Violetta gives me a timid smile before putting her chin in her hands and admiring my illusion. "I've known you my whole life, mi Adelinetta. And I think Magiano told you about those mercenaries for a reason."

"And what reason is that?"

"Perhaps he wants you to win them over to your side."

We fall into a comfortable silence as I play with the illusion. The monster gradually changes into a sleek, golden doe, Violetta's favorite animal. My sister's smile expands at the sight, encouraging me to make it even prettier for her. "Magiano is arrogant," I say. "If we really want to win him over, we can't just steal a diamond pin." I look at her again. "We need to surprise him with what we can do."

Violetta looks away from the doe illusion and arches an eyebrow at me. "How do we plan on doing that? You heard Magiano. And you saw the soldiers during the Midsummer Festival too. They are all intimidated by the Night King. He rules with fear."

At that, the doe's golden hide turns black, and the

creature's eyes glow scarlet. Violetta instinctively shrinks away from it.

"So do I," I say.

Violetta realizes what I want to do. She laughs a little, both uneasy and admiring, then shakes her head. "You were always good at playing games," she replies. "I could never beat you."

I'm not that good, I think, even as her words warm me to her. *I tried to play Teren's game against him, and I lost everything.*

"Adelina," she whispers, seriously this time. "I don't want to kill anyone."

"You won't," I reply, taking her hand. "We are just going to show off what we can do. Mercenaries can be persuaded to turn against their employer. If we can show how much more powerful we are than the Night King—if we can make him *fear* us, and make sure his men see—some of them may switch their allegiance. They could follow *us*."

Violetta looks up at me and searches my gaze. There is guilt there, for how she had once left me to fend for myself. "Okay," she says.

It is her way of telling me that she'll never betray me again. I squeeze her hand, then lean back. "Go ahead," I say to Violetta. "Take my power away."

She reaches out and tugs at my threads of energy. My illusion wavers wildly. When Violetta uses her power, it feels as if an invisible hand were reaching down my throat and pulling the energy out of my body. She holds on to it tightly—my illusion dissolves. I try to access my power, but I can't anymore. A feeling of panic bubbles up like bile, the sudden and familiar fear that I will never, ever be able to defend myself again, that I am now exposed for all to see.

Don't panic. I remind myself of our promise and force myself to relax. "Hold on," I murmur to Violetta through gritted teeth. I have to let her do this. She needs to practice her stamina.

The seconds crawl by as I continue to push back my panic, trying to get used to the feeling. There is a certain solace in it, yes. The absence of darkness. The lack of twisted whispers in the night. But without it, I feel helpless, and I spiral into the version of myself that used to cower before my father. Again and again, I try to reach out for my energy. Again and again, I find nothing but air, emptiness where there had once been a churning pool of darkness. More minutes.

When I feel like I can't stand it any longer, I finally choke out, "Give it back."

Violetta exhales.

My power rushes back to me, and I crumple in relief as strength floods me again, filling every nook and crevice of my chest with its sickness. Both of us lean back in exhaustion. I give Violetta a small smile.

"How long was that?" Violetta asks after she manages to catch her breath again. She looks pale and fragile, as she always does after she uses her power, and her cheeks are unnaturally flushed.

"Longer than yesterday," I reply. "That was good."

To be honest, I want her to learn faster, so that we can

confront Teren again sooner. But I have to be careful when I practice with her, lest she fall ill. I go slowly, gently, encouraging her along. Maybe I also do this because I am afraid of her, because her power is the one that I can never defeat. She is, after all, partly responsible for all my childhood abuse, for holding me back without ever telling me. If she wasn't my sister, if I didn't love her, if she had a harder heart . . .

"Well, what do we do?" Violetta asks. I turn in the direction of the Night King's court. My eye narrows at the glow of the setting sun. The whispers in my mind awaken as they sense what I'm thinking, and then they start to twitch and chitter in excitement, pushing and shoving against my thoughts until they crowd every dark corner. This time, I listen to them. This is my chance to send a signal to the Inquisition that I am coming for them, that they have not crushed me.

"We make the Night King cower at our feet," I say.

It is a hot and humid evening, and the city shimmers under the light of a setting sun. Violetta and I make our way through the smoke-filled streets until we end up on a hill, overlooking a lush garden estate in the center of the city. Here, blue-and-silver flags depicting the symbol of a crown and moon hang from every balcony. The Night King's main quarters.

I can see why Magiano chose a night like this to steal the pin. Because it's so hot, everyone is eating and lounging outdoors, and a bustling outdoor space must be easier for a thief to work with. Sure enough, the garden inside the Night King's estate now buzzes with servants, all setting up for the evening meal.

Violetta and I hide in the shadows under a row of trees. We stare at the guards posted along the estate's walls. Farther down the hill, soldiers patrol near the main entrance.

"We can't go over the walls," I whisper. "Not without causing a scene." If the Windwalker were with us, she could have effortlessly lifted us onto the walls—but now that we are no longer with the Daggers, I can rely only on my own powers.

"Look," Violetta says softly, touching my arm. She points to the main entrance below. There, a cluster of young dancers gathers by the doors, waiting to be let in. They laugh and talk with the guards.

"Let's find a different way," I mutter. I don't like the sight of them. Somehow, their ornate hair and colorful silks remind me too much of the Fortunata Court—of sensual consorts I once knew, who could hypnotize their audience with a sweep of their lashes.

"Do you want to waste all your energy on keeping us invisible for hours?" Violetta says. "It will be the easiest way to get in. You said Raffaele trained you while you stayed in the—"

"I know," I interrupt, perhaps more harshly than I intended. Then I shake my head and soften my voice. She's right. If we want to get in, we should go as dancers, and we need to play nicely with the guards. "But I never could charm clients like Raffaele did," I admit. "I only played a novice who never needed to speak."

"It's not so hard, really."

I give her a withering stare. "Maybe not for an unmarked *malfetto* like you."

Violetta just lifts her chin and gives me a teasing look. It is the same look she used to give our father whenever she wanted something. "You are powerful, mi Adelinetta," she says, "but you have all the charisma of a burnt potato pudding."

"I *like* burnt potato pudding. It's smoky."

Violetta rolls her eyes. "My point is that it doesn't matter what *you* like, it matters what *others* like. All you have to do is listen and look for what makes the other person happy, and feed it."

I sigh. Violetta may not be able to lie about important things, but she does know how to charm. My gaze lingers on the dancers at the gate, and with a sinking feeling, I imagine us down there with them. Too many memories of the Fortunata Court. *I only work with the worthy,* Magiano had said. If we can't survive tonight, then we aren't worthy.

Maybe the loyalty of Magiano *isn't* worth all this. Surely there are plenty of other Elites, lesser ones, who might join us without us risking our lives with the Night King. Magiano may be the most notorious of them all, but he is making us enter a snake pit in order to win him over.

Then I remember Teren's pale, mad eyes. I think back on

the massacre in the arena, Enzo's death, and Teren's taunts. With his versatile power, Magiano may be the only one capable of fighting Teren. If I'm going to return to Kenettra, I can't afford to go with a ragtag bunch of Elites. I need to have the *best.* This goes far beyond Magiano. This is about us taking the Night King's strength, of gathering our *own* power.

You have to be brave, the whispers say.

I start to weave a small illusion across the scarred side of my face. "Fine," I mutter. "I'll follow you."

There are six guards at the entrance when we arrive. I can tell immediately that most of them are seasoned soldiers, too experienced to be tempted by the pretty faces of dancers. I take a deep breath and adjust the silk wrap around my hair. Violetta does the same. By the time we approach the gate, the guards are inspecting each of the dancers. They kick several out of the group. One of them tugs on a girl's hair. She yelps.

"No *malfettos,*" he says to them, putting a hand on the hilt of his sword. "The Night King's orders."

His eyes fall on Violetta. My sister doesn't beg like the others; instead, she meets the soldier's gaze shyly, her expression full of innocence, and approaches him reluctantly.

The soldier pauses to take her in. "Ah, a new girl," he says, his gaze flicking to me before returning to my sister. "This one looks nice." He glances at his companion, as if looking for a vote of approval. "Too much golden hair surrounding the Night King tonight. What about this one?"

The other soldier studies Violetta in admiration. My sister

swallows hard, but gives them a small, demure smile. I've seen her win over many a suitor with that expression.

Finally, the first soldier nods. "In with you." He waves Violetta over.

"This is my sister," Violetta says, motioning to me. "We go together, please."

The soldier shifts his attention to me. I can see the spark of desire in his eyes as he recognizes my beauty, a sharper, more sinister version of Violetta. I step forward, then keep my voice firm and my shoulders straight. "You cannot take my sister in and leave me out here," I say. I remember the way Raffaele used to tilt his head, and I do that now, offering my own smile at them. My smile is different from Violetta's—darker, less naïve, promising other things. "We entertain the best when together," I add, looping my arm through Violetta's. "The Night King will not be disappointed."

The other soldiers laugh, while the first one watches me thoughtfully. "An interesting pair, you two," he mutters. "Very well. I've no doubt the Night King will have his fun."

I let out a quiet breath and we join the dancers who have been accepted. As the guards open the gate and let us walk past, I notice the soldier's eyes staying on us, his envy for the Night King obvious on his face. I lower my head and try to hide my thoughts.

Inside, the garden is lit with lanterns. Fireflies dance in the darkness, mingling with the low hum of laughter and movement. As we approach the center, the soldiers following us begin to fall back. Finally, the first soldier stops and turns to us.

"You know the rules," he says. Then he remembers us, the newcomers, and adds, "You go where you're invited, nowhere else. Stay in the courtyard grounds. Touch no wine or food unless offered to you by a guest. I'll not hesitate to escort out anyone who causes a scene." Then he gestures his permission for us to wander the garden.

"How do you think Magiano will get in?" Violetta whispers as we walk.

"I'm sure he's already here," I whisper back. Several guests walk by us, their eyes lingering on our faces. Violetta smiles sweetly at them, and their expressions relax. I watch her carefully, trying to follow her example.

It works well. We draw the right amount of attention for a pair of hired dancers. Men brush a little too closely to us, so that the silk of their sleeves touches our bare arms. We even attract the attention of the Night King's other scattered soldiers—one of them pauses long enough to rub my shoulder. I stiffen at his touch.

"They've let in some exquisite dancers tonight," he murmurs, nodding a greeting at both Violetta and me. Violetta blushes prettily at him, and he beams before continuing on his patrol of the grounds. I'm too surprised to do the same. The last time a soldier touched me, he cut a scar across my chest with his sword.

Seeing my expression, Violetta loops her arm through

mine and bends close to my ear. "You must relax, mi Adelinetta," she whispers. "Especially around the soldiers."

She is right, of course. I remind myself that no one here can see the true, scarred side of my face. All they see is the illusion of my beauty.

The crowd turns steadily thicker as the evening lengthens. Gradually, as we search for the Night King, I begin to relax. Violetta points out a pair of handsome noblemen and, when they notice us, she giggles and turns away. I laugh along with her, letting her guide us as questions swirl in my mind. Are any of the Night King's secret mercenaries here?

We wander the entire grounds of the garden before we finally stumble across the Night King's entourage.

A circle of silk-clad noblemen talk and laugh in a private corner of the garden, where colorful cushions line the grass and a cheerful fire burns in a central pit. A whole roasted pig turns over the fire. Large plates of fragrant rice, dates, and stuffed melon surround the pit. Several dancers have clustered here, enchanting their audience with drumbeats and swirling silks. Others sit and laugh with their patrons.

I know immediately which of them is the Night King.

He is easily the most adorned of the circle, his fingers decorated with thick gold rings and his dark eyes accented with black powder. A slender crown sits on his head. A nobleman to his right is muttering something into his ear. On his left is one of his soldiers, draining the last drops from a wine cup. Several others stand guard nearby, their gloved hands poised over sword hilts. My gaze goes to the collar of his silk shirt.

An enormous diamond-encrusted pin hangs there. Small wonder why Magiano is after such a monstrous thing—I can see the glimmer of it from across the courtyard. I glance around. Magiano hasn't made his move yet.

Violetta and I come upon the circle. When several noblemen glance up at us, I throw back my shoulders and give them my most dazzling smile. To my satisfaction, their eyes widen and they smile in return.

The Night King laughs as we approach. Then he gestures to a small space of cushions near him. "A night with the prettiest dancers in Merroutas," he says as we fold our legs beneath us and sit. "Midsummer is kind to us." His black-rimmed eyes linger on Violetta, then on me. It's always in that order. "What are your names, my beauties?"

Violetta just gives him a coy smile, while I let myself blush. If only he knew that we are both *malfettos*.

"No *malfettos* dirtying your estate," says the man sitting next to the Night King. "It's getting harder, sir. Have you heard the news coming out of Kenettra?"

The Night King smiles at him. "What is the new royalty doing there?"

"The Lead Inquisitor of Kenettra has handed down a decree, sir," the man replies. "All *malfettos* have already been removed from within the capital and set up in shelters outside the city walls."

"And what's to happen to them?" The Night King is still admiring both of us as he talks. He leans forward and offers us a platter of dates.

"Death, I'm sure. We've been turning away ships with *malfetto* stowaways."

"The Lead Inquisitor," the Night King muses. "The queen seems to be giving him quite a lot of power, isn't she?"

The man nods. His eyes shine from the wine. "Well, you must know he's always in her bed. He has been infatuated with her since he was a little boy."

The Night King laughs, while we smile along. "Well," he says, "congratulations to him on a royal conquest."

So, Teren does care for someone—not only is he a loyal soldier to Giulietta, but he is in love. Is that even possible? I keep my face frozen in a smile and store this information away, wondering how I might be able to use it later.

The nobleman talking to the Night King now turns his attention to me. It takes me a moment to recognize him. I don't know why I didn't see him earlier.

It's Magiano, and he stares at me with a lazy grin. His eyes don't look slitted tonight—his pupils are dark and round instead, and his mess of braids is neatly tied in a high knot on his head. He is dressed in luxurious silks. I have no idea how he charmed his way to the Night King's side, but there is no sign of his wild side here. He is as coiffed and charismatic as the wealthiest aristocrat, his appearance so different that I didn't even know it was him. I almost feel like I can read his thoughts.

Ah. There you are, my love.

"This dancer is new to the city, my friend," Magiano says to the Night King. He swings an arm good-naturedly around the other man's shoulders. "I've seen her before. She's very good—she is court-trained, I hear."

I hide my irritation and just continue blushing. He's taunting me, throwing little obstacles in my way. So be it. I smile back, wondering how I can lure the Night King away from his circle.

"Is that so?" The Night King claps. "Perhaps you can show us."

I exchange a quick look with Violetta, then rise to my feet. I stare once more at the glittering pin on his collar. Then I stand before the fire and start to twirl in time with the drums.

I draw upon everything I learned at the Fortunata Court. To my surprise, my body remembers it—I fall into a popular Kenettran dance and make an elegant sweep around the central pit. The other nobles stop to watch me. A memory of Raffaele appears unbidden in my mind, of him teaching me how to walk like a consort, how to flirt and dance. It distracts me, and suddenly, he *is* here—the illusion of his hand pressing lightly against the small of my back, the silk of his hair falling over his shoulders like a dark sapphire river. I can hear his laugh as he guides me in a circle. *Patience, mi Adelinetta,* says his beautiful voice. I see Enzo walking in as Raffaele prepares me for a night at the court, and I remember the young prince's deep scarlet eyes, the way he admired my glittering mask.

Violetta tugs on my energy in warning. I glance gratefully at her, then clamp down hard on my emotions. Raffaele's illusion wavers and vanishes. No one else seems to have seen what I created—perhaps I didn't create anything. I take a deep breath. Raffaele isn't here. He will never be here, so it is absurd of me to wish for it. I push the Daggers out of my thoughts and focus on the noblemen again. Violetta moves closer to the Night King, murmurs something to him, and laughs along. She's helping me distract him.

Magiano leans back and watches me as I dance. The look on his face is interesting. If I didn't know better, I'd think he was actually pleased by the way I move. "Court-trained," he murmurs, and this time he says it much too softly for the Night King to hear.

He has no idea that Violetta is very slowly whittling his power away right now, rendering him vulnerable to my illusions.

I make my way around the circle. As I do, I quietly weave a false diamond pin on the Night King's collar. Then I cloak the real pin, making it invisible. As I make my first turn around the central pit, Magiano whispers something to the Night King. Then I see the Night King applauding.

I smile. Magiano has taken the false pin with him.

The Night King is staring at me now. I think back to the way Raffaele would respond to clients captivated by his charms. I lower my lashes and tilt my head in a shy bow.

The Night King applauds. "Magnificent!" he says as I sit again. "Where in the city do you live, my beauty? I would like to see you again."

His voice makes my skin crawl, but I just laugh. "We are very new, sir," I reply, changing the subject. "And know very little about you."

This amuses him. He reaches for my hand and pulls me to him. "What do you want to know?" he murmurs. "I am one of the richest men in the world. Aren't I, my friend?" He pauses to glance at Magiano.

Magiano keeps his eyes on me, his smile cunning. "The Night King is no ordinary nobleman, my love," he says. There is an undercurrent of challenge in his words. "He sits on a pile of wealth and power that anyone would kill to have."

The Night King grins at Magiano's compliment. "Kenettra loves to trade with us. We enjoy her spoils more than anyone. Do you know how I earn that kind of trust in my power?" He puts an arm around me and nods at the soldiers with emblems on their sleeves. "I'll tell you how. The world's deadliest mercenaries always choose the most powerful to serve, and they choose to serve *me*. My city teems with them. So, if you ever want to see me, my dear, just whisper it into anyone's ear on the streets. Word will get back to me. And I will send for you."

Why are powerful men so stupid around a pretty face? Quietly, I begin to weave an illusion around the entire circle. It's a subtle one, of blurry lantern light and raucous cheering, the illusion of people intoxicated with wine. The Night King rubs at his eyes before smiling at me. "Ah, my beauty," he slurs. "I seem to have drunk too freely tonight."

The world's deadliest mercenaries choose to serve you, the whispers say, *because they have yet to meet me.* I lean over to kiss him on the cheek. As I do, I reach for his collar. Then I take the real diamond pin off and put it in the pocket within my silks.

"Perhaps you need to rest, my lord," I reply, rising to my feet.

His hand whips out without warning and grabs my wrist. I freeze—so does everyone else around him. Even Magiano stops, surprised at the man's speed. The Night King fights against his drunkenness and hardens his smile. "You do not leave until I say so," he says. "I hope my soldiers told you the rules within this courtyard."

Everyone around the fire exchanges nervous glances. I meet Violetta's gaze. She sees my cue, leans toward him, and whispers something in his ear. The Night King listens, frowning—then breaks into laughter.

I can see the relaxing of shoulders around the circle as the other nobles join in. The Night King softens his grip on my wrist, then stands. "So," he says, winding his arm around my waist while pulling Violetta up beside him. "A pair of adventurous sisters. Where did you say you were from, again?" He follows me as I lead us out of the circle and through the courtyard.

Behind us, several of his soldiers look at one another and follow along behind us. Magiano's stare stays on us, too, and for an instant, his eyes meet mine. He seems puzzled and curious.

I glance around the courtyard, wondering where the Night King's mercenaries might be. If they are as dangerous as everyone claims, then I know they must be watching us carefully. As I cast one last, casual glance over my shoulder, I see that Magiano has now disappeared from the circle.

I sustain the hazy, wine-like illusion around the Night King as we pass through the grounds and enter one of the open porticos lining the courtyard. Here, the shadows of the archways cover us, and we are swallowed by darkness. The soldiers following the Night King keep a short distance between us, giving him privacy while still keeping us in sight.

The Night King pulls me close, then pushes me against one of the portico's pillars. At the same time, I reach within for my energy, find it, and pull the strings close. I start to weave.

One by one, the lights along the portico flicker out. The soldiers startle, bewildered. They glance at the extinguished lanterns. Then one of them looks at us and lets out a shout as I pull a blanket of invisibility over myself and Violetta. We step away from the Night King, slipping out of his grasp.

The Night King opens his eyes to find us gone and stumbles backward.

I silently thank the night for hiding the imperfections of my invisibility. I keep weaving.

"Guards!" the Night King shouts, waving his men over. They hurry to his side. To my surprise, several figures also materialize out of the shadows in the portico. These men are dressed differently from the regular guards—they look like ordinary noblemen, except each of them has a dagger in hand. *His mercenaries,* I think.

"Where did they go?" one of them breathes, looking around and straight through us. Violetta and I stand perfectly still, pressed as tightly as we can against the pillars.

"How can you not have seen them?" the Night King snaps, trying to recover from his own embarrassment. *"Find them."*

I smile, amused by the fumbling soldiers. I grit my teeth and reach for the Night King.

Suddenly he gasps. He looks down. Then he lets out a scream, falls, and scrambles backward until he is pinned against the wall. A mass of red, disgusting sores have broken out across his legs, burning through his clothing as if a bucket of poison had just been poured on him. He screams again and again. Around him, his soldiers and mercenaries look on in horror. A wave of dark energy hovers over the crowd, and I drink it in hungrily, letting their fear fill my insides and strengthen me. The whispers in my head burst into a cacophony I can't understand.

The Night King's screams echo down the hall. Other spectators are now swarming over him. I catch glimpses of their shocked faces—their disbelief at seeing the all-powerful ruler of Merroutas crouched against a wall, paralyzed with terror. Good. Let them see.

Then, I stumble. One of the soldiers has accidentally staggered backward, right into me, and shoves me out of my place. The sudden jolt distracts me from my invisibility illusion—and suddenly, for a moment, Violetta and I are exposed. A dozen pairs of eyes are upon us.

On the ground, the Night King sees us—his lips curl into a snarl. *"You,"* he spits, looking at me and then at my sister.

I lift my chin and release the illusion from him. My heart pounds furiously in my chest.

"A demon. Damn *malfettos,*" he hisses. "Thieves, whores—" His voice has turned threatening and ugly. His eyes settle on Violetta, and within them, I see murder. My sister takes a step back and his focus shifts to me. "I'll cut you to pieces and burn you in the central square."

I look around at the others, letting my stare settle on the mercenaries. When we first came here tonight, I thought I would terrify the Night King in front of his men and mercenaries, so that they would realize how powerful I am—and come to serve me. *I did not consider killing anyone.*

But now, I stare at the Night King, hear his threats against my sister and me, and feel the full force of hatred in my heart. If my goal is to win over his ruthless mercenaries—to truly be a threat to Queen Giulietta and the Inquisition—then maybe I should do more than just terrify him.

"Seize her!" one of the guards shouts.

I glare at them. I am not sure what they see, but something in my gaze makes them hesitate. Their swords stay drawn, hanging in the air, unmoving. "How can you seize me," I say calmly, "if you cannot see me?"

One finally lunges for me. I vanish. The whispers in my head burst into chaos. Violetta shrieks for me to keep going, but a blur of thoughts is rushing through me with the speed of a howling wind. I grit my teeth and gather my energy. I reach out, seeking the darkness in those around us, the Night King's anger, the soldiers' fear, letting it strengthen me. I snap an illusion around the closest soldier like a whip.

He screams, faltering in his steps. To him, he is suddenly poised over a yawning cliff.

I reach for the Night King and wrap him in an illusion.

"What are you doing?" Violetta shouts. "This isn't part of—"

The Night King draws his sword, points it at Violetta, and lunges. The blade sings through the air, aiming straight for my sister's throat.

Too late, he realizes that his blade is an illusion. I vanish it in a puff of smoke. At the same time, I grab the real sword strapped to his waist. My limbs move of their own accord—I blink in and out of existence. The whispers in my mind burst from their cages, roaring, filling me with their hisses. I hold the sword straight out at him, right as he lunges into me.

His weight shoves me back. I feel the blade pierce through soft flesh. He lets out a gurgling scream as his own sword runs him through.

The man's eyes bulge, and he lets out a strangled cry, like how the roasting pig must have sounded in its final moment. Blood spills down the front of his fine silks. I immediately let go of the sword, and he staggers backward several steps, both hands clutched tightly around the sword's hilt in a vain attempt to pull it out. He looks back at me in confusion, as if he can't believe he's meeting his end at the hands of a young girl. He tries to say something, but he is too weak. He falls forward, going still as his side hits the ground, and blood spills around him in a widening circle.

For an instant, everyone—Violetta and I, the soldiers, the mercenaries—can only look on. *Save your fury for something greater,* she'd said to me.

When I was a little girl, I wanted to believe that my father would love me if I could just do the right thing. I tried and tried, but he didn't care. Then, after he died, the Inquisition Axis came and arrested me. I tried to tell them of my innocence, but still they weighed me down in chains and dragged me off to burn at the stake. When I joined the Dagger Society in my search for Young Elites like myself, I did everything in my power to become one of them, to please them, and to fit in. I opened my heart to them. I tried to free myself from the trap that Teren Santoro set for me, forcing me to betray my newfound friends. I made mistakes. I trusted both too little and too much. But, by the gods, I tried so hard. I gave everything I had.

I have always done the best I could, and yet, somehow, it has never been enough. No one cared what I did. They always turned their backs on me.

Why can't *I* be like that? Why can't *I* be the father who just shrugs off the love of his daughter? Why can't *I* be the Lead Inquisitor who enjoys watching his pleading victims burn at the stake? Why can't *I* be the one who befriends a lonely, lost girl and then casts her out? Why can't *I* be the one to strike *first,* to hit so early and with such fury that my enemies cower before they can ever think of turning on me?

What is so *great* about being good?

One of the mercenaries meets my gaze. "White Wolf," he whispers, barely able to get the words out.

I stare back into his wide eyes. The fact that he recognizes my power and knows my Elite name would have frightened me, once—some will know that I was here, many will be after me. But I am not afraid, not at all. Let them know who did this, and let word of it get back to Kenettra.

"I can give you more than he ever did," I reply, nodding once at the Night King's body.

A whistle sounds out above us. I jerk my head up to see Magiano perched on the top of the wall. He scowls, then throws a rope to us. I just manage to shield my face with my arms before the rope hits me.

"You're helping us?" Violetta calls up at him from her place by the wall.

Magiano puts something against the edge of the wall, then tightens the rope on top of it. "*Help* is a strong word for what I'm doing," he calls, before vanishing over the top. Some of the mercenaries have broken out of their trance—they draw their weapons and lunge for us. I react the only way I know how. I throw invisibility over us, then seize the rope. Violetta grabs hold as well. The instant we do, the rope yanks us up into the air. As the mercenaries pause below us, we fly to the top of the wall and pull ourselves over. Violetta gets her footing first and helps me scramble to the other side. We jump down, tumbling several times before staggering to our feet.

Outside the estate, more soldiers race toward us. I feel the sudden sag of lost energy now, and my curtain over us flickers in and out, leaving us exposed. An arrow sings past my shoulder, nicking my sleeve. We rush toward the shadows of the closest alleyway, but the soldiers pursue us. They're going to cut us off.

Suddenly, an illusion goes up behind us—a brick wall, as solid in appearance as something real. The soldiers send up bewildered shouts. Violetta glances back, startled, and then looks down at herself. We are invisible. Overhead, Magiano whistles at us again. *He is mimicking me,* I realize. *And he's protecting us.*

As we run through a maze of narrow alleys, Magiano continues to create rapid illusions behind us, slowing the soldiers down until they sound far away. We dash through corridors of smoke and spice sacks, listening to the call of merchants blur into one long note around us. People make startled sounds whenever our invisible figures bump into them. We run for a long time, until we finally turn from the narrow marketplaces onto a quiet street, with nothing but lines of damp clothing hanging above us.

Magiano is nowhere to be seen. I slide down the wall until I'm crouched with my knees to my chin. I lower my head into my hands. Violetta does the same. Sweat beads our foreheads, and our breaths come at rapid speed. I can't stop shaking. The terror that comes over someone before death is one of the sharpest surges of energy I can feel, and the death of the Night King now catches up to me. I want to lash out at something, anything, but I hold back and try to steady my breathing. *Calm down.* All I can do is picture the Night King's shocked expression, the blood pooling around him. The scene plays over and over. My thoughts are a blur.

Violetta's hand touches my shoulder. She tugs hesitantly at my power, asking permission to take it away if I desire. I shake my head. No, I must become used to this.

"You promised," she says to me.

I glance up at her in surprise. She has narrowed her eyes, and I can sense a tide of anger in her. "I broke no promises," I reply.

Violetta takes her hand off my shoulder and tightens her jaw so hard that I think it might break. "You said you wouldn't kill anyone. That you only wanted to frighten them and show off our powers."

"I said that *you* wouldn't kill anyone," I snap, wiping sweat from my forehead.

"You didn't have to do it." Violetta's voice sharpens. "Now we will be hunted all throughout Merroutas. They will seal the ports, I'm sure of it. How will we leave? Why do you do this?"

"You think they wouldn't have hunted us if we just intimidated the Night King and stole his pin? Did you see the way his mercenaries looked at me after it was done?"

Violetta looks sickly pale. "They are going to find us, and kill us for this."

"Not all of them. Some of them will be impressed by what we've done, and join us."

"This could have been done in a different way."

I glare at her. "Fine. Next time, you can ask them all nicely. Don't worry. You still won't have to dirty *your* hands with blood."

Our conversation halts as a figure steps into the alley, a dark silhouette with light from the market at his back. When he draws closer, I recognize the cat eyes looking at us from behind a half veil. A knot of braids sits high on his head.

"You came back," I whisper.

Magiano leans close. "Okay," he starts. The veil muffles his voice. *"Why did you do that?"*

"Because he was charging at us with a sword."

"But—" Magiano sputters. "You were doing just *fine*. You could have both run away. That was the other option, you know, aside from murder. You should consider it sometime, because it works splendidly."

"Did you even make sure that you got your diamond pin?" I ask. Before he can give us a haughty smile and reach into his pocket, I nod at Violetta, who takes out the real diamond pin from within her silks.

Magiano blinks. His brow furrows. Then he digs in his pocket for the false pin he thought he had stored safely away. As expected, his hands come up empty. He glances quickly back at us. A quiet moment passes.

"We win," I say, flashing the pin. My hand is still shaking from what happened, but I hope he doesn't notice.

"You have not told me of all your powers," he says. He glances at Violetta again, and I imagine that he must be reaching out, trying to mimic her power. His eyes open wider as she pulls on his energy. *He can't,* I realize. "You took my power away," he whispers. His eyes dart back to me. "No wonder I couldn't sense your illusions during your dance. You tricked me."

"Only for a moment," Violetta admits. "I can't hold it back for long."

I expect Magiano to be furious, or at least indignant. Instead, his pupils turn round, and a small grin plays underneath the fabric of his veil. "You tricked me," he says again.

I'm silent. Everything seemed so crystal clear in the middle of the action. Now that we are here, and my body is weak and spent, I'm having trouble remembering all that took place. The same dizziness washes over me that I'd felt after Dante's death, and Enzo's. I close my eye and lean against the wall, trying not to think about the Night King's blood spilling across the ground. If I'm not careful, I will conjure the illusion of him right here, his snarling face still pointed up at me.

After a while, Magiano folds his arms. "The Night King has ruled here for decades. I don't think you understand the true weight of what you've done." He pauses and lifts the veil to look more closely at us. "Or perhaps you *do* understand. By morning, every person in Merroutas will have heard your name. They will wonder and whisper over the White Wolf. They will fear you." He shakes his head again, and this time, it is in admiration. "You may have just earned yourself an army of mercenaries."

My heart starts to pound. No look of disgust from Magiano for what I did. No pitying gaze or wary expression. *Admiration. After I killed a man.* I don't know how to feel. A sense of horror? Pride?

Violetta hands him the diamond pin. "Take it. You're the one who wanted it."

Magiano turns the pin over in his hands with a look of reverence.

"Why did you come back to help us?" I ask. "Does that mean . . ." I can't quite bring myself to say it without hearing it first from him.

Magiano leans back against the wall and pulls his veil down. He gives us a wry look. "Do you know how much more notorious I could have been, if you were always close enough for me to mimic your power? Do you know what I could do, if we traveled together? And your sister, with her ability to take away an Elite's power?" He looks curiously at her, and she coughs uncomfortably under his gaze. "Very interesting," he murmurs. "Very interesting, indeed."

I stand there and listen, still lost in a haze. I find myself wondering what he aligns with. Ambition. Greed. Something wicked, perhaps, like me. Again, I find myself wondering what's going through his thoughts.

If you were able to kill a king, then perhaps you really can strike back against the Inquisition.

"Are you going to join us?" I ask.

He studies my face. Then he holds out a hand to me.

Raffaele Laurent Bessette

Raffaele sits atop a horse and enters the Estenzian gates behind Queen Maeve. With them are three of her brothers. Two of them, Augustine and Kester, ride beside her. Kester is an Elite, although Raffaele has yet to see his power in action. And the third brother is the youngest, the prince with the eerie energy, Tristan. Maeve's white tiger prowls in front of her horse.

Raffaele keeps his head high and eyes level. A long blue cape trails behind him and spills down the hindquarters of his steed. Gold shackles adorn his wrists and neck. Inquisitors have fenced off a wide path for Maeve and her companions. People have turned out in droves to see her. They bow their heads, but with Inquisitors lining the path, they seem too afraid to cheer or applaud the *malfetto* queen. When they do dare to look up, they take in the sight of her enormous white cat with awe.

Raffaele stares at Tristan's back. The entire two weeks they'd been at sea, the youngest prince had not said a word. Even now, whenever Maeve leans over to murmur something to him, he remains silent. His energy pulses in a strange, dark pattern. It distracts Raffaele. He shakes his head to clear it.

The prince is alive, he reminds himself. His strange energy is nothing to worry about. Enzo can live too. *Isn't that what I want?*

The procession finally reaches the sprawling main square of Estenzia, directly in front of the palace. Today, the square is decorated with a series of white tents, their canvases billowing in the wind, and flags of both Kenettra and Beldain fly side by side over each tent. Under the largest tent, Queen Giulietta is seated on her makeshift throne, a large, ornately carved chair. The tent across from her has a second, empty throne. Reserved for Maeve. Between them is a wide stretch of pavement, where two lines of Inquisitors stand as a guard between the two queens.

Raffaele's eyes fall on the Lead Inquisitor at Giulietta's side. Teren. He stares back. Raffaele knows he recognizes him.

They make their way through the path until they reach the tents. Teren approaches. His pale eyes flick to Raffaele, settling there for a moment. Raffaele forces himself to look back. Teren seems surprised to see him. The Inquisitor would probably kill him, if the Beldish queen were not here. Instead, Teren stops before Maeve's horse. He holds out a hand. Beside him, the white tiger growls but keeps his distance.

"Your Majesty," he says. "A little help?"

Maeve gives him a cold stare. Her black and gold braids are woven in a high blade down the middle of her head, trailing down in tassels over her back. Gold slashes decorate her face. She hops down in one easy swing and pushes past Teren. She strides toward Giulietta's tent as Raffaele and the others dismount.

"Your Majesty," Maeve calls out to Giulietta. Her hand rests on the sword hilt at her hip. She does not bow her head.

Silence in the square. Then Giulietta smiles and spreads her arms. "Your Majesty," Giulietta replies. "Welcome to Kenettra. Please, make yourselves comfortable."

At that, the crowd finally cheers. Raffaele looks to see many of them waving Kenettran flags. Giulietta's smile remains, but it is cold. Raffaele studies her face and imagines Enzo beside her. He shivers at how closely she and Enzo resemble each other, one the more delicate version of the other, both fiercely ambitious.

Maeve tilts her head in acceptance of Giulietta's greeting, then turns to take a seat on her own throne. Her brothers settle in chairs beside her, while Raffaele stands behind her. He folds his arms, and his gold wrist shackles clink against each other.

"It has been a long time since we hosted a Beldish royal," Giulietta calls across the distance. Raffaele notices it is far enough so that both young rulers can feel safe from each other.

"A Beldish *queen,*" Maeve corrects her, her smile vicious. "I've come to congratulate you." She bows her head low.

"Thank you," Giulietta replies. She nods at Teren, who turns to whistle at his men. "We will throw a great feast in your honor. I have a gift for you."

Teren waves at his Inquisitors. Raffaele sees them leading something out into the space between the two queens' tents. It's a stallion—a beautiful one, tall and powerfully muscled, with a glossy black coat and white mane. Feathered black hair adorns his lower legs. The horse tosses his head as the Inquisitors lead it out front and center.

Teren gives Maeve a bright smile as he shows off the horse. "A magnificent Sunland stallion," he announces. "Just one example of the beauty of our nation, generously given to you, Your Majesty, by our queen."

"He was my husband's favorite," Giulietta adds.

Raffaele listens carefully. This is a veiled insult—a hand-me-down gift from a dead king, a king Maeve knows was likely murdered by Giulietta. On either side of Maeve, Augustine and Kester exchange a dark look. But Maeve keeps her eyes on the horse. "A beautiful beast," she replies. "Thank you."

Then she nods at Raffaele to step forward.

Do not be afraid, Raffaele reminds himself. He walks slowly down the tent's steps until he stands in the center, between the two tents. Teren draws his sword. Other Inquisitors follow his lead.

"I have also brought you a gift," Maeve replies.

Silence. Not a sound is heard. Raffaele focuses his eyes on Giulietta, his long dark lashes sweeping his cheeks, and then falls into a graceful kneel. His blue robes pool around him in a circle. He lowers his head and brushes his shining hair across one shoulder so that Giulietta can see the gold shackle shining around his neck.

"I know this *malfetto,*" Giulietta says with ice in her voice. "He was a rumored Dagger, a friend to my traitor brother."

"He was once the greatest consort in your nation," Maeve replies. "He was found hiding in exile in my country."

Giulietta stares at her, suspicion plain on her face. Raffaele waits quietly. "I hope you are not starting our first meeting with lies," she says. "The Beldish love *malfettos,* while we do not. Why would you give one back to me as a prisoner?"

"You think I'm lying," Maeve says, her voice even.

"I think you may be playing me for a fool, yes."

"The Beldish believe that your *malfettos,* as you call them, are children of the gods, marked by their hands and blessed with their powers. But I know you have been hunting the Daggers," Maeve tells her. "When we found their leader in our midst, we wanted to bring him back to you. Know the sacrifice I make for you, our customs against yours, for the sake of our joint peace and prosperity."

Raffaele waits, marveling at Maeve's calmness.

"He has no powers that can harm you," Maeve continues. "He is the leader of a society that you despise, but he is alone here. Do you fear a defenseless boy, Giulietta, just because he is marked?"

Murmurs ripple through the crowd. Raffaele keeps his head down, but from the corner of his eye, he can see Teren's mouth twisting into a snarl. Giulietta doesn't seem to react to Maeve's words. When Raffaele turns his head up to look at her, he finds her looking back. She is admiring his face, and he feels tiny tendrils of attraction coming from her.

Maeve lets out an audible sigh. "I didn't come here as your enemy, Your Majesty," she calls out to Giulietta. "My mother has died, and I have taken the throne in grief. You and I are both new rulers. I know our nations have fought for hundreds of years, but I am tired of it. We have gained little from it. And the blood fever has hurt Kenettra deeply."

Maeve leans forward. "I've come here because I want us to develop a new relationship from which we can both benefit. Giulietta, let us talk of how we can open our nations to each other. How we can both prosper again. I am very thankful for the beautiful gift you've brought me." She nods at the stallion. "And I hope you see my gift to you not as something of suspicion, but as a gesture of my good faith." She motions to Raffaele. "In return, I do humbly ask that you give this *malfetto* the grace of a trial, if you choose to judge him, and a fair punishment. Or, Your Majesty, perhaps you can pardon him."

More murmurs from the crowd. Raffaele is awed by such excellent lying. Maeve's declaration in front of who she knows must be families suffering from the loss of their own *malfetto* loved ones.

Teren sneers at Maeve. "You cannot ask our queen to show respect for a disgusting dog of a demon."

At Maeve's side, Kester places a hand on the hilt of his sword. His Elite energy stirs. Raffaele's attention shifts first to him, then to Tristan, as he moves ever so slightly. It is the first time Raffaele has ever seen the youngest prince frown—and something in the expression chills Raffaele to his core. Maeve had said that bringing Tristan back from the Underworld increased his strength tenfold. For the first time, Raffaele believes it. Maeve waves a subtle hand, and Tristan stands down.

Teren looks as if he wants to continue, but Giulietta shakes her head once, stopping him. Raffaele takes it in—a small moment of disagreement between the two. He stores the image away.

Finally, Giulietta addresses Maeve. "I can promise you nothing. But I will consider your request."

Sudden movement distracts Raffaele. It is Teren, stepping away from Giulietta's side and marching toward him. A knot of dark, frustrated energy churns in the Inquisitor's chest, and Raffaele tenses. Behind Teren, Giulietta watches him with stony eyes. *She didn't tell him to move,* Raffaele thinks. *He's acting without her permission?*

Teren pauses a few steps from Raffaele. He smiles at Maeve. "Your Majesty, Beldain considers such marked survivors sacred, you say." He turns in a circle so that the entire crowd can hear him. "We are privileged to have a Queen of Beldain in our nation, and are thrilled to honor your stay here. But in Kenettra, we have different customs."

"Master Santoro." Giulietta's voice is not loud, but Raffaele hears the sharp warning in her tone. *She doesn't want to shout it, because she doesn't want to look like she has no control over her Inquisition.* Teren ignores her. "In Kenettra," Teren continues loudly, "a *malfetto,* gift or otherwise, is not to set foot inside Estenzia."

Good, Raffaele thinks. They had chosen to gift Raffaele precisely to anger Teren. *Is he angry that he didn't capture me first, or that his queen is looking at me instead of him?*

"In Kenettra," Teren says, "a *malfetto* who has committed treason against the crown must be executed. My Inquisition is grateful to Your Majesty for bringing this criminal back to us, so that we can carry out the appropriate punishment."

"Master Santoro." This time Giulietta's voice is a furious whip. Teren finally turns to face her, and she narrows her eyes at him. Her mouth is set in a firm line. "Cease."

As the crowd stirs restlessly, she holds her hands up for silence. "We have enough bloodshed in our past," she says. "Let there be none today."

Teren opens his mouth, then quickly closes it. He bows his

head to Giulietta, shoots Raffaele one last withering glare, and stalks back to Giulietta's tent. Giulietta doesn't look at him. While Inquisitors grab each of Raffaele's arms, Giulietta approaches.

"Do you always let your Lead Inquisitor speak for you, Queen of Kenettra?" Maeve asks in a low voice.

"Would you have stepped in to save your gift, Queen of Beldain?" Giulietta replies, a small smile playing at the edges of her lips. There is a coldness in her voice, a challenge, and suddenly, it seems the polite words exchanged only moments ago will be for nothing.

Then, Giulietta shakes her head. "Forgive my Lead Inquisitor's actions," she finally says in a loud, clear voice. "He defends his country fiercely, that is all."

Raffaele looks on as Maeve rises, bows a farewell to Giulietta, and takes the reins of her new horse. She leads the stallion down the path, toward the Estenzian palace, as the crowd watches her go.

Giulietta studies Raffaele awhile longer. Beside her, Teren notices the way she admires Raffaele's features. He scowls.

Raffaele's thoughts spin. Never has he heard of such conflict between the queen and Teren. More so, Giulietta's attitude toward *malfettos* seems to have shifted since the time when she wanted Enzo dead. Now that she has her throne, has she given up on her supposed war against *malfettos*? Had it all been part of her plan to both secure Teren's support and get rid of her brother? Raffaele studies her energy, wondering. *Will Giulietta punish Teren for defying her?*

Finally, Giulietta stands up. Her Inquisition gathers to escort her. She walks down the steps, stops before Raffaele, and walks once around him. She kneels down to his eye level. "Rise, consort," she murmurs, lifting his chin. Her touch is firm, even harsh. Raffaele trembles and does as she says.

"Come," she commands. Then she turns away, toward the palace.

Uncle Whitham, quickly out of bed!
Uncle Whitham, he's come for your head.
Hide under the stairs, hide anywhere,
Uncle Whitham, he wants you dead.

—"Uncle Whitham and the Ghost of Darby," children's rhyme

Adelina Amouteru

The next morning, I wake up in the Little Baths feeling strange.

I lie very still for a moment. It's not *pain,* exactly. Instead, there is a faint pressure in the air all around me, making everything blurry. I close my eye and wait. Maybe I'm just dizzy. I slept poorly, haunted by nightmares of bleeding kings, and now I'm exhausted. Or maybe it's the moisture in the air—when I glance up at the holes in the ceiling, the sky looks overcast, the clouds a dark gray. The whispers in my head are stirring again, active as usual after a night of vivid dreams. I try to understand what they're saying, but today they are incomprehensible.

When I open my eye again, the feeling has faded. The whispers quiet down, and I pull myself up to sit. Beside me,

Violetta is still asleep, her chest rising and falling in a steady rhythm. Magiano is nowhere to be seen.

I sit for a while, savoring the silence and the cool recesses of the bathhouse ruins.

Moments later, the leaves high above us rustle, and a figure appears through the holes in the ceiling, blocking out some of the light.

"We need to get you out of Merroutas," Magiano calls as he hops down. Violetta stirs at his voice. She pushes herself onto her elbows. I watch him, admiring how nimbly he skips from beam to beam until he finally lands on the marble floor in a plume of dust. His hair and face are obscured behind cloth, wet with rain. "Do you know what a mess you've made of this city?"

He doesn't sound very upset about it. "What's happening?" I ask.

He just grins and shakes water out of his hair. "A *wonderful* mess, that's what," he says. "The White Wolf's name is on everyone's lips, and rumors of what happened at the Night King's court have spread like fire. Everyone wants to know who managed to kill him." Magiano hesitates here, for the slightest instant. "Not a bad start, my love, although considering that you're now the most hunted person on this island, you might want to escape. Your stunts have forced the city to seal its port. As you can see, we may have some trouble getting out of here."

Violetta gives me a look, and I return it without reacting.

"Have you heard anything from the Night King's former mercenaries?"

Magiano undoes the cloth shrouding his face. "I'm sure you've earned yourself some enemies after last night. But you've also attracted admirers. Look." He tosses something at me.

It's a small scroll. "Where did you get this?"

"You don't think I have connections in this city?" Magiano gives me an indignant scowl, but when I keep waiting, he rolls his eyes. "A friend of mine works down at the ports. He passed it along to me this morning." He waves impatiently at me to open the message.

I untie the scroll's string, and the paper unfurls.

WW

I have a ship.

My heart races. I turn the paper this way and that, while Violetta looks at Magiano. "But this is useless," she says. "What ship? Where, when?"

Magiano takes the message from me and rubs the paper between his fingers. "Not useless," he corrects her. "Hold the paper up to the light."

Violetta does, moving the paper until it's directly under a sunbeam. I scoot closer for a better look. It takes me a moment to see what Magiano is talking about—under the light, the paper has a faint watermark on it. It resembles the Night King's mark, except that the blade cutting through the crescent moon is wide, with a deep blood channel down its center.

"The *Double-Edged Sword,*" Magiano says. "That's the name of the ship. It's a narrow devil of a caravel—it actually *looks* like a sword, if you squint at it properly. A part of the Night King's private fleet."

A part of the Night King's private fleet. That means that whoever runs that ship must have decided to turn his back on the Night King the instant he heard of his death. Or . . .

"It could be a trap," Violetta chimes in, finishing my thought. "How do we know they don't plan on getting Adelina aboard, only to kill her or drag her before the Night King's loyal men?"

"We don't," Magiano replies. He tosses both of us a bundle of clothes. "But we don't really have a choice. You both must realize that his loyal mercenaries and soldiers are combing the city right now. Merroutas is a small island. They *will* find you, if you don't flee."

It is only a matter of time before soldiers come searching ruins like these. I rise to my feet, take the message from Violetta, and tuck it inside my head wrap. "If we leave now, how will interested mercenaries find us? How will I round up my men?"

"You'll figure something out. Send a dove by sea," Magiano says, crossing his arms. "Now get ready. Think and move at the same time, my loves. I didn't choose to come along just to get captured. Can you at least cover us in invisibility while we head to the docks?"

"No," I reply. I'm so tired this morning. Invisibility,

already difficult, is the hardest to do in chaotic crowds. There is too much to imitate, and with that image constantly shifting, we would look like moving ripples. We would also bump into others, which would just startle and draw attention. Even with Magiano's help, we're better off saving our strength for when we might need it most.

"Fine. Whatever you can do. Even a song and dance would be better than nothing." Magiano pauses to grin at me. "And I've seen you dance, my love."

I blush and look away. It was the first time I'd ever danced for someone other than Raffaele. "Subtle disguises," I suggest, pushing his comment out of my mind. "I'll weave different features across our faces." He laughs at the color in my cheeks, but seems to decide against teasing me further and instead just motions for us to hurry.

By the time we're ready and heading into the city, the sun has burned away the gray drizzle and the sky blazes blue.

I ride with Violetta on the same horse. She has pressed herself tightly against me, and her warm, delicate body is trembling slightly. Her attention darts from the busy streets to the buildings and roofs, where soldiers are lined up with swords drawn. The Night King's blue-and-silver banners still hang from the balconies, but the streets are crowded with confused people and clusters of *malfettos*. It's a sight I'm familiar with—people who revere the power of the Young Elites, clashing with those who are calling out about how dangerous they are. *Malfettos*, hiding in the corners.

I look back at Magiano. He rides with his head held high,

his eyes constantly scanning the throngs. His lute sits in his lap, like he might decide to play it. He nods up at the Night King's banners on the balconies, then leans toward me from his saddle. "I don't know about those colors," he murmurs. "Don't you agree?"

"What do you mean?" I murmur back.

"Make your mark, Adelina," he urges quietly.

It takes me a moment to understand him. I look back at the banners. The Night King's blood still lines the inside of my nails in tiny flakes. In my mind, I see those same banners draped across the walls of his estate. If the Night King's mercenaries have any doubts about who killed their leader, let me reinforce my presence to the entire city. I gather my energy and start to weave.

People in the crowd startle. Their faces turn up to the balconies, and they lift their hands in the air to point. Above them, the tops of the blue-and-silver banners start to turn white, as if new flags were unfurling over them. The illusion tumbles down over each flag, one after the other, until it stretches all the way down the street, covering the Night King's emblems of the moon and crown, replacing them with solid white banners. I let the illusion of the fabric shimmer in the light, so that as the banners ripple in the wind, they change color from white to silver and back. The energy within me pulses, and the whispers in my mind coo with glee.

"Oh, Adelina," Violetta says behind me. Even she sounds awed by the sight. "They're beautiful." And I smile to myself, wondering whether she remembers when we used to attend festivities as children, and how we'd admire the king's banners on the buildings. They are my banners now.

Magiano doesn't say anything. A small grin plays at the corners of his mouth. He watches the reaction of the crowd—the startled murmurs, the whisper of a name across their lips.

The White Wolf. It's the White Wolf.

Finally, we are forced to a halt. Before us, there is a blockade of soldiers barring the width of the street, forcing people to turn around and take a new route. One of them sees me and nods apologetically. "I'm sorry, mistress," he says, making a circular motion with one hand. "You'll have to go back. You can't pass through here."

"What's going on?" Magiano calls out to him, gesturing at the white banners.

The soldier shakes his head. "I'm afraid that's all I can say," he replies. "Please turn around." He raises his voice to the rest of the crowd. "Turn around!"

Magiano makes a show of grumbling under his breath, but he puts a hand on Violetta's shoulder and steers us around. "There is always another door," he says, quoting *The Thief Who Stole the Stars* with a smile.

We make our way down the street until we reach a tiny, winding canal. Here, Magiano hands several coins to a boatman, and we hurry quietly on board his cargo boat. We float down the canal, listening to the bustle above, shrouded in shadows.

The strange feeling from earlier in the morning returns.

I frown, shaking my head. The world shifts, and the whispers in my mind leap forward, sensing a sudden chance at freedom.

Violetta turns to me. "Are you all right?" she whispers.

"I'm fine," I reply.

But I'm not. This time, when I close my eye and open it again, the feeling doesn't go away. The world takes on a strange yellow tint, and the sounds around me turn quiet, as if none of it were quite real. Am I creating an illusion? I glance at Magiano, suddenly suspicious. Is he mimicking my power?

That's it, the whispers hiss, eager to accuse. *All of this is a ruse. What if he's betraying you, mimicking your illusions so that he can hand you over to the Night King's men? To the Inquisition? This was all a trick all along.*

But Magiano doesn't seem to be using his power. He isn't even paying attention to me. His focus is entirely on the direction of the canal, and he has a concentrated frown on his face. Violetta doesn't seem to sense him doing anything, either. In fact, she's staring at me with a concerned expression. She takes my hand.

It feels numb and very far away.

"Adelina," Violetta whispers in my ear, "your energy feels strange. Are you . . . ?"

The rest of her words fade away, so that I can't understand her anymore. Something else has caught my attention. At the next bend of the canal, a man is sitting with his legs dangling over the edge. He turns when we approach.

It's my father.

He wears that dark smile that I remember all too well. Suddenly terror seizes my throat so hard that I can barely breathe. *He's here. He's supposed to be dead.*

"Heading the wrong way, Adelina?" he says. As we glide past, he gets up onto his feet and starts to walk the canal's edge along with us.

"Go away," I whisper up at him.

He doesn't respond. As we sail around a corner, he follows us—and even though we should be moving faster than he can walk, he manages to stay right behind us. I grit my teeth and turn around in my seat. Beside me, Violetta looks more alarmed. She calls out something—my name, perhaps—but it doesn't seem important to answer her. All I can do is stare at my father's silhouette as it follows us.

"Go away," I hiss again through my teeth. This time, I say it loud enough for both Violetta and Magiano to turn their heads.

"I beg your pardon?" I can hear Magiano say.

I ignore him. I turn away from my father's figure and try to catch my breath. I close my eye again. The world presses down on me. "It's just an illusion," I say, trying not to panic. *An illusion like always.* But my fear only fuels it, making it stronger. The lines of reality start to blur. *No, no, it's not an illusion at all.* My father has come back from the dead. When he catches up to me, he is going to kill me. I tremble all over.

When I glance behind me, my father is gone.

In his place is Enzo. *The Reaper.* His dark hood and

silver mask cover his face, but I know it's him, can tell by his tall, lean, lethal shape, the predatory grace of his walk. He holds a dagger in each hand, both blades glowing white hot with heat. For an instant, my heart jumps into my throat. The edges of my vision turn red, and I remember the way he used to train with me, how he'd touch my hand and mold my grip on my daggers to the correct shape. I want to run to him. I want to take his mask off and wrap my arms around him. I want to tell him that I'm sorry. But I don't. He walks with the stride of a killer. *He is hunting me.*

The Reaper flicks his wrists.

Lines of fire explode from his hands and rush down the canal toward us. Above, the edges of the canal burst into flames. The roar and heat drown out everything—my skin turns scorching hot. The fire closes in all around us. It licks at the buildings, climbing higher and higher until the flames consume the rooftops. I bury my head in my hands and scream. Somewhere, my sister is calling for me, but I don't care.

I'm back at my burning again, chained to the iron stake. Teren tosses a blazing torch onto the kindling at my feet.

I need water. I scramble to the edge of the boat. Magiano lunges for me, but I move too fast. The next moment, I feel the sudden splash of cold water and the fire crisping my skin extinguishes. All around me is darkness. Shapes glide in the depths. A haunting voice calls my name, beckoning me deeper. Claws loom in the eerie water around me.

A bony hand seizes my arm. I open my mouth to scream,

but bubbles rush out instead in a torrent. Something is trying to pull me under.

Adelina.

I'm in the Underworld. The angel of Fear is calling me.

"Adelina!"

The whispers of Formidite change into my sister's voice, and the bony hand on my arm turns into a boy's hand. Magiano pulls me to the surface. I suck in a lungful of air. Someone lifts me back into the boat, inch by inch—I think it is the boatman and my sister. I scramble to one side. My clothes cling heavily to my skin, as if still trying to drag me into the water and give me to the Underworld. I look around frantically.

The flames are gone. The odd yellow tone of the world has faded away, and the pressure in the air has disappeared. Enzo is nowhere to be seen. Neither is my father. All I see are Magiano, Violetta, and the boatman, all staring at me in bewilderment, while a few spectators have gathered along the canal's edge. Some of those spectators are soldiers.

Magiano acts first. He turns to the onlookers and waves his arms. "She's fine," he calls out. "Just afraid of dragonflies. I know. I worry for her too."

A few mutters of disbelief come from the crowd, but it works well enough that the people start to disperse, their attention turning back to the other chaos of the city.

"We have to go," Violetta says as she moves close to me. She puts a hand on my face. It takes me a moment to realize that the visions stopped only because she took my power away. Already, I can feel her slowly giving it back. Behind her, Magiano shoots me an irritated look as he talks to the boatman.

"You didn't see anything?" I stammer to Violetta. "The fire on the streets? Our father watching us from the canal bridge?"

Violetta frowns. "No. But we *did* make a scene."

I collapse backward against the boat and cover my face with my hands. *An illusion.* It was all an illusion I must have created. But I don't understand—no one else saw what I did. A *hallucination.* How is that possible? I think of the precision of the white banners I'd woven over the Night King's dark ones. I thought I was improving in my powers. Why couldn't I control them?

A moment later, I realize that because Violetta had to wrench my power away, I had also stopped holding the illusions over our faces. I quickly sit up.

Too late. Magiano's having some sort of argument with the boatman, who points his oar angrily at me. He doesn't want us on board anymore. I rise to my feet. The day had felt so hot earlier—now, the air nips at my wet clothes, chilling me.

The boatman pulls to a small dock along the canal, then ushers us off with a string of curses. Magiano skips ahead, bidding him a cheerful farewell. When the boat pulls away from us, he turns to me and holds up a purse stolen off the man.

"If he's going to be rude about it," Magiano says, "he might as well pay."

I'm about to respond when I recognize a soldier in the street. It's the same young man who had stopped us earlier and turned us onto a different route. He is now leaning over the canal's edge, listening intently to something our former boatman is yelling up at him. Then the boatman points in our direction. The soldier's attention turns to us.

Magiano grabs Violetta's hand and nods. "Follow me."

We break into a run. Behind us, soldiers shout something and start to push their way through the crowd in our direction. Magiano veers sharply onto a small side street, then darts back into a huge main square. I recognize it immediately as the square where the Night King's estate is located. We weave through the throngs that have gathered out here. Some mourn, although I can't tell how sincere they are. Others cheer. I don't have time to study the scene more closely. Behind us, we can hear the soldiers' hurried footsteps.

Magiano scowls. "An illusion would be really helpful right now."

I try, but my strength scatters as soon as I attempt it. I'm too exhausted from my strange hallucination to even pull a shadow from the ground. I shake my head at him. He curses under his breath.

"And here I thought you were powerful," he snaps.

For an instant, I think he's going to leave us behind to fend for ourselves, while he vanishes into the crowd.

Instead, he pulls at my energy. *He's going to try to mimic me.* I can feel the faint tug of his power against mine—his eyes dart to one side, and there in the crowd, I see him evoke the fleeting shapes of identical versions of us, running in a different direction through the square. At the same time, he pulls us into a thick cluster of people.

"There!" one of the soldiers shouts behind us. I turn to catch a glimpse of them between the milling bodies in the crowd. They are following the decoys' path.

Magiano lets the illusion drop. It's most likely all he can do, given my weakened state. We reach the end of the square. From here, the harbor comes into view between the streets' buildings. I run faster. Beside me, Violetta's breath comes in gasps.

"Keep going straight," Magiano calls over his shoulder. "Until you hit the piers. Hide when you get there. I'll find you." He takes an abrupt detour, veering sharply left of us.

"Stay with us!" I shout. I'm suddenly afraid he'll be captured. "You don't need to be a noble—"

"Don't flatter yourself," he shoots back. "You'd better wait for me." Then he's gone, vanished into the crowd before I can even think of what to say. Moments later, he reappears off in a corner of the square, where he hops up onto the stone railing overlooking a canal and pulls his lute from his back. He shouts something into the square that sounds like a taunt.

Behind us, half of the soldiers change their route to head in his direction. But the others continue pursuing us.

I try again to use my energy. Again, I fail. For a moment, I feel like I'm completely new to using my power, searching and reaching but never quite able to touch the threads of energy hovering inside me and all around us. What has happened to me?

Violetta tightens her grip on my hand. She points to where sailors are throwing ropes off one of the docks. She pulls me along.

An arrow whizzes past us from the roofs. It narrowly avoids hitting Violetta in the arm. Several screams go up from the people we pass. Others part the way as soon as they realize the soldiers are after us. Fear emanates from everyone around us—it feeds me, and I feel my strength grow. *Come on,* I urge myself. I reach again for my energy.

Finally. My mind closes solidly around it. I whip a blanket of invisibility over us, covering us with the brick and marble of the walls, the cobblestone and dirt of the streets, the crowds of people. It's an imperfect shield, in my tired state and with so many moving people around, but it's enough to throw off our pursuers. Another arrow comes from overhead, but this time it misses our moving ripple by a wide shot. I grit my teeth and keep the illusion moving as fast as I can. Another arrow lands somewhere behind us.

We reach the docks. Here, the commotion changes to the work of readying crowded ships, and we manage to find a place to huddle behind a cluster of barrels. Our invisibility solidifies, now that we're still, and we vanish entirely from sight. My breaths come raggedly, and my hands are shaking violently. Sweat beads on Violetta's forehead. She looks unnaturally pale, and her eyes dart nervously along the street.

"How is Magiano going to find us?" she asks.

I glance at the ships lined up along the pier, looking for one with a hull that resembles a double-edged sword. The water along the pier churns, frothed up by restless baliras that are still hooked to their ships, waiting as their sailors argue with soldiers who refuse to let them dock. A long rope as thick as I am tall now dangles low across the water behind the docked ships, preventing anyone from entering or leaving. My attention returns to the ships. Minutes drag on. Again, I find myself wishing the Windwalker was with us, knowing how easy it would be to get on board a ship with her help.

How *are* we going to find Magiano in all this chaos? What if there is no ship waiting for us?

Then a shadow falls over us. We look up into the faces of two soldiers.

Their hands close around my arms. They seize us before we can even utter a protest. The Night King's emblems sit prominently on their sleeves, and their faces are partially covered by veils. Violetta shoots me a terrified look. *Do something.* I reach again for my energy, trying desperately to grab it.

The soldier shoves me roughly before bringing his face closer. "Don't," he says quietly.

I suddenly still. Something in his voice stops me—a warning, a signal that they are not arresting us in the way we think. I glance back at Violetta, who stares in silence.

Two other soldiers approach us. One of them draws his sword and nods at the soldier holding me. "Is that them?" he asks.

"Could be," my captor says. "Go alert the captain. *Now.*" He says it with such force that the other two soldiers turn immediately and start running to send up the alert. Our two soldiers quicken their pace. "Move," the one holding me snaps from underneath his veil. And before us, I see what I've been looking for—a gangplank leading up to a ship that looks like a sword.

Together, we make our way toward the gangplank, carefully bypassing others as they hurry back and forth. One foot after the other. The gangplank creaks under our weight. We make it onto the deck of the ship right as another cluster of soldiers hurries by. They pause on the shore. I hold my breath, my hand wrapped so tightly around Violetta's that my knuckles have turned white. My sister winces. The sails overhead are unfurling, and two crew members are unknotting thick lengths of rope on the railing.

Finally, soldiers on the pier notice us. "Hey!" one of them shouts at the nearest crewmember on our ship. "You were supposed to be tying her in. Lower your mast, port's still closed!"

No one on board listens to him.

"I said, port's *closed*!" the soldier hollers again, and this time the other soldiers shift in our direction. "Lower your mast!"

Someone in the crew hollers, and the rest of them holler back. Violetta and I stumble a little as the ship pulls free of the docks, then slowly turns its bow to face the opening of the bay. The soldiers on the pier halt, while their leader signals frantically toward others to raise the alarm. Another points a crossbow in our ship's direction. Those closest to the railing fall into a crouch.

Our soldiers shove us. "Get down," one of them barks. We do, right as the ship gives a lurch that makes us all sway. From the ocean below come the haunting cries of baliras. I clench my teeth. Even if these men are all here to help us, how will they get us out of port with the soldiers onshore alerted? We'll have to get past the roped barrier, and even if we do, there will be ships sent after us—

"Adelina," a voice behind us says. I whirl around to see a young man crouched near us. Our two soldiers give him a respectful nod, and he nods back. His eyes turn to me. I stiffen.

He sees my expression and holds up his hands. "Easy," he says. "We didn't go through all this trouble just to hurt you." He glances at Violetta. "And your sister?" he adds.

"Yes," Violetta replies, right as the ship shudders again. We fall to one side, but the mercenary talking to us hops to his feet with little effort and rushes back to the stern. From where we are, I can see glimpses of the water—and that the rope suspended over it is now cut and floating uselessly. Shouts come from the pier as we pull farther away.

Magiano hops over the bow of the ship. He's almost completely soaked, and as the young mercenary approaches him, he shakes water out of his hair like a dog. The two exchange some words. I watch them carefully, my hand still clenched around Violetta's.

Seconds later, Magiano and the mercenary hurry back to us. Magiano bends down, helps us to our feet, and then stands with his arms crossed. He doesn't look concerned at all. At my suspicious expression, he just shrugs. "Relax, my love," he says. "If I wanted to make a quick coin by selling you to someone, I wouldn't have surrounded myself with people who don't stand a chance against you." The mercenary shoots him an irritated look, and Magiano holds up both hands. "I meant, you are all *fantastic* mercenaries. You just aren't—well, these are the two that I told you about. Trust me, you're interested in them because of how dangerous they are."

"You've brought a hell of a lot of trouble down on us," the mercenary replies. "I thought you were going to sneak them into the harbor, not bring the entire army down on us."

"Plans. They're fickle things." Magiano hesitates. "You *are* a mercenary for the Night King, yes? You *do* know how to get us out of this, right? Are we even on the right ship? Because—"

The mercenary ignores him, then shouts something at the

nearest crew and stalks away toward the middle of the ship. The crew bursts into action. As he goes, the color of the sky distracts me. I look up. It has suddenly turned a sickly shade of green and gray. Fat drops of rain have already started to fall. I frown at Violetta. Wasn't the day clear and blue just moments earlier?

But Violetta's eyes stay fixed on the mercenary's back. Her eyes are wide. "An Elite," she mouths to me.

Magiano hops onto the ship's railing to look back at the harbor. There, several thin *caravelas* flying the Night King's flag look ready to sail in our direction. I brace myself for a hunt.

But they don't get a chance to follow us. Because the skies open.

The ominous drizzle suddenly turns into a torrent of rain. It is a blanket that whips across the deck, stunning me with icy pellets. I shield myself with my arms; beside me, Violetta does the same. Enormous waves rock the ship. Somewhere, the mercenary shouts for Magiano to seek cover for us.

"Happy to oblige," Magiano mutters. He guides us to the stern, where we huddle beneath a cloth canopy draped over crates. Once we're settled, Magiano darts away again to the mercenary's side. We look on as the crew rushes to make sure the ropes latching us to our baliras are firmly in place.

The mercenary concentrates on the sky as it turns steadily blacker, until the harbor looks like it has been swallowed whole by midnight. The soldiers' ships seem to hesitate by the piers. There is no doubt that if they try to sail out into such a tempest, the ocean would splinter the boats to pieces. Still, one of them gives chase. Violetta and I hang grimly on to the canopy's ropes.

But the mercenary seems unconcerned. He focuses his attention on the oncoming ship, then looks up at the sky, as if searching for something. Rain pelts his face.

A bolt of lightning strikes the approaching ship. I jump. There is an earsplitting crack as the ship's mast splits in two, then erupts in flames. Shouts and screams come from on board, carried over to us by the wind even from our distance—and then the sheets of rain blanket the seascape again, obscuring the wrecked ship from view. I blink water out of my eye in shock.

The mercenary smiles a little, then sighs in relief.

As I watch him, a memory slowly emerges. It's of the day Raffaele first tested me, when he told me the story of an Elite who failed to prove himself worthy of the Daggers . . .

The storm rages on, until my sister and I have to flatten ourselves against the deck, still gripping the soaked sides of the canopy. I play the memory over again and again. I'd thought that the Daggers killed the Elite that Raffaele talked about, because he was unable to control his powers. And maybe I'm still right. Maybe this boy isn't who I think he is. But now, as we sail farther from Merroutas and the harbor behind us is lost within the storm, I wonder if Raffaele's story was about this boy.

The boy who could control the rain.

They tell me that you have been crying in your sleep. Do not grieve our separation, my love, for our reunion will come just as swiftly.

—Letter from unknown prisoner, convicted of treason, to fiancée

Adelina Amouteru

The worst of the storm dies down soon after we reach the open ocean. But the rain continues on, falling and falling until I start to wonder whether the clouds will ever go away. Violetta and I stay belowdecks, in a small but private cabin that the captain offers us, and dry off with clean towels.

Both of us are quiet. The only sounds we hear are the crash of waves outside the porthole, and the distant shouts of the crew overhead. In one corner of the cabin, a mirror sits on a vanity desk, and I can catch a glimpse of my unadorned features, my mask gone, my hair wraps removed and revealing my short silver locks. Right after Enzo's death, I'd cut off my hair with a knife—Violetta helped me trim the strands as neatly as she could, but my hair will stay short for a long time. I'm still not used to seeing it.

A sharp clap of thunder shakes the ship. From the corner

of my eye, I see Violetta jump, then settle down, embarrassed. Her eyes stay uneasily on the stormy seas outside our porthole. She wrings her hands unconsciously in her lap, as if trying to stop the shaking.

She catches me looking. "I'm fine," she says, but there is a tremor in her voice.

I realize how exhausted we both are. Where are we headed? Are this mercenary and his crew really trying to help us? When Violetta and I were little, I comforted her through thunderstorms by squeezing her shoulders and humming to her. I do that now, sitting beside her, wrapping my arms around her and picking a tune I remember our mother singing to me before Violetta was even born.

Violetta doesn't say anything. Gradually, her trembling lessens, though it doesn't go away entirely. She leans into my touch, and we sit together in silence.

"Adelina," Violetta finally says. Her voice startles me. She turns so that she can see me. "What happened to you out there in the city? When we were on the canal?"

I shake my head. The memory seems fuzzy now. I've always been plagued by illusions of our father's ghost, but what happened today was something new and frightening. I'd seen him so clearly that I believed he was there. I saw Enzo, engulfing the streets in flames.

Violetta's tone grows firm. "Tell me," she says. "I know you'll keep it bottled up if you don't, and that might be even more dangerous for all of us."

I take a deep breath. "I think I created an illusion by

accident," I reply. "Something that I couldn't control. I woke up this morning feeling a strange pressure against my head, and when we reached the canal, I . . ." I frown. "I don't know. I can't even remember creating the illusions. But I thought what I was seeing was real."

Violetta reaches a tentative hand out to touch mine. "Can you create something right now? Something small?"

I nod. I pull slightly on a thread of energy, and a ribbon of darkness winds its way up from the center of my palm.

Violetta frowns as she studies me. Finally, she releases my hand. I let the ribbon dissipate. "You're right," she replies. "There's something odd about your energy now, but I can't quite figure out what. Do you think it has anything to do with what happened at the Night King's estate?"

My temper rises at that. "You think this is my reaction to killing the Night King," I say, pushing off the bed and standing before her.

Violetta crosses her arms. "Yes, I think it is. Your energy flares out of control when you go to extremes."

I tighten my jaw, refusing to think back on Dante's death. On Enzo's. "It won't happen again. I mastered my powers when I stayed with the Daggers."

"You couldn't have mastered them as much as you think," Violetta argues. "You nearly got us all killed! How will you tell reality from illusion if you don't even know you're using your power? How do you know you won't feel that strange pressure on your mind again?"

"It won't happen again."

Violetta's expression is anxious. "What if it's worse next time?"

I run a hand through my short hair. The strands slide between my fingers. What if she's right? What if the consequence of letting my anger go unchecked, of twisting my illusions so hard that they kill, is that it feeds my energy so strongly it goes beyond what I can control? I let my thoughts wander. After I killed Dante and we walked the city in a haze, I could barely recall what I did. After Enzo's death, I'd unleashed my anger on the entire Estenzian arena. I fell unconscious afterward. And this time, with the Night King's death . . .

I sigh and turn away from her, then distract myself by fixing my hair in the mirror. In the corner of my vision, I think I see a glimpse of my father's ghost. He seems to smile at me as he walks along the length of the cabin. His eyes are shrouded in shadow, and his chest is torn open, just the way I remember it from the night he died. I glance at the illusion, but it vanishes before I can focus on it.

It's not real. I clamp down hard on my energy. "It won't happen again," I repeat, brushing Violetta's concerns aside with a sweep of my hand. "Especially since I'm aware of it now."

Violetta gives me a pained look—the same expression she once gave me as a little girl, when I refused to help her save the one-winged butterfly. "You don't have as much control over your power as you think. It shifts so wildly, more so than anyone else's I've felt."

My temper boils over into anger. I whirl on her. "Maybe if someone didn't force me to suffer alone as a child, I wouldn't be like this."

Violetta turns bright red. She tries to respond, but stumbles on her words. "I'm just trying to help you," she finally manages.

"Yes, you're always trying to help, aren't you?" I sneer.

Her shoulders slump. I feel a twinge of guilt for lashing out at her, but before I can say anything, there's a light knock on our door.

"Come in," Violetta says, straightening.

The door opens a crack, and I see Magiano's golden eyes. "Am I interrupting?" he asks. "It sounded a bit tense in here."

"We're fine," I say, sounding harsher than I mean.

Magiano gives me a look to let me know he doesn't believe me. He opens the door wider and steps inside. His long braids are matted from the storm, and streaks of water still glisten on his skin. He brings in the scent of rain and ocean. His gold hooped earrings shine in the light.

It takes me a moment to realize that the mercenary has followed him into the room. He closes the door behind him. Then he turns to us and nods a quick greeting. He's tall, his shoulders broad and his skin pale, perhaps from exhaustion.

"That was almost more effort than you're all worth," he says. "The ports are a mess today. Word has it that the new Beldish queen arrived in Kenettra today too. A great deal of water traffic is being diverted here to Merroutas." He raises an eyebrow at Magiano. "So, thank you for adding to the madness."

The *new* Beldish queen. I think back to the way Lucent occasionally talked about the Beldish princess, and how fond she was of her. What if the Beldish queen was a Dagger patron? If she's now in Kenettra, what are the Daggers up to?

"We may have some explaining to do when we reach port again," the mercenary continues. "I guarantee you word about the Night King's death will have spread to Kenettra by then, and Inquisitors will be checking every ship that docks today."

From under his shirt collar, I catch a glimpse of a faint gray marking. "I'm sorry for the trouble," I decide to answer. "Thank you for your help."

"Never thank a mercenary," he replies. He glances at Magiano, who is busy squeezing water out of his braids. "I was paid."

"You didn't really think I stopped by the Night King's court to only steal a single diamond pin, did you? I picked up some bags of gold on my way out."

The mercenary crosses his arms, then introduces himself. "Sergio."

"Adelina," I say.

Violetta smiles when he looks at her. "Violetta," she says. "The sister."

She manages to coax a smile, even a laugh, from him. "No need for humility," he replies. "Magiano mentioned your power." At that, Violetta blushes pink.

Magiano nods at him. "You must be one of the Night King's former men. Yes?"

Now I notice the many knives strapped to Sergio's belt, the dagger tucked into his boot. Battle scars on his arms. "Yes," Sergio says. "I was one of his mercenaries. You've heard the stories, I presume. Ten thousand of us, so they say, although we really number closer to five hundred." He smiles again. "We just manage to give an impression of many men."

"Why are you helping us?" I ask.

"No point in serving a dead man, is there? I'm sure several of his men are fighting over his vacancy right now, although I've no interest in ruling an island." He tilts his head in Magiano's direction. "He tells us you are the White Wolf, and you're looking for allies. Is it true that you ran the Night King through with his own sword?"

And you loved it so, the whispers in my head say without warning, their little voices full of glee. I swallow hard, forcing them down. Even though my powers are still weak, I answer by conjuring an illusion of a shadow before us, transforming it into a faint semblance of Sergio. I note the look of awe on his face before I pull the illusion away. "Yes," I reply.

Sergio regards me with renewed interest. "I'm not the only mercenary on board," he says. "A dozen others among the crew are as well. Some of them even think you are ruling Merroutas right now." He pauses and I notice a slight shift. "The Night King kept us in decent coin, though. What can you pay?"

Magiano looks on with a small smirk. "Ten times what he

gave you," I reply, making myself as tall as I can. "You've seen what I can do. I think you can guess at how powerful I can make my followers, how much I will reward them for their loyalty."

Sergio lets out a low, mock whistle, then glances sidelong at Magiano. "You never told me she was rich."

"I forgot." Magiano shrugs.

"And you think her words carry weight?"

"*I'm* following her, aren't I?"

The corner of Sergio's mouth tilts up. "So you are."

Beside me, Violetta is concentrating on Sergio in a way that can only mean she's studying his energy. "You're an Elite, too, aren't you?" I ask.

He nods once, casually. "Perhaps."

"You create storms."

He stands a bit straighter. "I do." He pauses to glance outside the tiny porthole, where the rain is still coming down. "It's proven useful enough to the Night King, stealing from stray vessels and in turn destroying pirates that try to take from him. Still, storms require time to begin and end. We'll have rough seas tonight."

The boy who could control the rain. It must be him. Raffaele had never explicitly told me what happened to him, only that the Daggers refused to keep him. I thought they killed him—but here he is, alive.

"I've heard of you," I say.

He snorts once. "I doubt that."

"I used to work for the Daggers too."

He stiffens immediately at the mention of the Daggers. My heart leaps a little. *I was right.* "You're the boy who could not control the rain," I press on.

Sergio takes a step back and regards me with a suspicious look. "Raffaele talked about me?"

"Yes, once."

"Why?" Sergio's entire demeanor has changed—all traces of amusement have disappeared from his face, replaced with something cold and hostile.

"He mentioned you as a warning for me to master my power," I reply. "I thought they killed you."

Sergio's jaw tenses as he turns to watch the storm. He doesn't answer me. A long moment of silence passes before he looks back to me again with a shrug. "Well, I'm here," he says stiffly. "So you thought wrong."

A sharp pain pricks my heart. Raffaele might have told Enzo to do the same thing to me. How can someone so gentle be so cold? Perhaps Raffaele was right on my count, at least—Enzo had refused to hurt me, and his decision destroyed him.

"Raffaele wanted me dead, you know," I say after a while. "In the beginning. He cast me out after . . . Enzo's death. I came here to Merroutas in search of other Elites, to put together a team of my own. I want to strike back at the Inquisition for all that they've put us through. We could be a team that far outpaces the Daggers. And together we can succeed."

"Are you saying you want to seize the throne?" Sergio asks.

I weave a brief illusion around me, trying to emphasize my height and stature, making myself as regal as I can. If I'm going to recruit more Elites, I'm going to need to start looking like a leader. "I told you that I could pay ten times what the Night King paid you. Well, this is my proposal. The Kenettran crown's treasuries would make the Night King's pale in comparison."

Sergio gives me a skeptical look. "The Kenettran crown is guarded by the Inquisition."

"And I killed the Night King with his own sword."

Sergio considers my words. The silence ticks by, eclipsed only by the sound of rain and howling wind. *He could have worked well with the Windwalker,* I find myself thinking. I wonder if Lucent was sad about his absence. I wonder if the other Daggers even know that Sergio is alive. I wonder about his history with the same people I once knew.

"I'll think about it," he finally replies.

I nod, but I already know his answer. I can see it in the gleam of his eyes.

Teren Santoro

"You sent for me, Your Majesty?"

"Yes, Master Santoro." Queen Giulietta sits on her throne and regards him with a calm look. He drinks in her beauty. Today she is in a loose sapphire gown, the train so long that it trails down the top of the stairs. Her hair is pulled high on her head, revealing her slender neck, and her eyes are large and very, very dark, framed by long lashes. Her crown reflects the morning light filtering through the windows, making tiny rainbows on the floor of the throne room.

She says nothing more. She's angry.

Teren decides to speak first. "I apologize, Your Majesty."

Giulietta considers him with her chin resting on her hand. "Why?"

"For my public disgrace of the Beldish queen."

She doesn't reply. Instead, she rises to her feet. She tucks one of her hands behind her back, and with her other hand, she waves forward one of the Inquisitors waiting along the walls. "You were unhappy with Queen Maeve's gift to me," she says as she walks.

Raffaele. Teren suppresses a jolt of anger at the reminder that the *malfetto* whore is now being held at the palace. "He's a threat to you," Teren replies.

Giulietta shrugs. When she reaches him, she looks down at his bowed figure. "Is he?" she says. "I thought you and your Inquisition had him properly chained."

Teren flushes at that. "We do. He will not escape."

"Then he's no threat to me, is he?" Giulietta smiles. "Have you found the rest of the Daggers yet?"

Teren's whole body tenses. The Daggers were the perpetual thorn in his side. He had cut off the funding of so many of their patrons. He had tortured *malfettos* affiliated with the Daggers. He had narrowed down their potential location to nearby cities. He knew their names.

But he hadn't succeeded in capturing them yet. They had scattered to the winds, until yesterday. Teren swallows hard, then bows lower. "I've sent additional patrols out to hunt them down—"

Giulietta holds up a hand, stopping him. "A dove came in this morning. Did you hear?"

Teren was too busy this morning with the *malfetto* slave camps to receive news. "I haven't yet, Your Majesty," he says reluctantly.

"The Night King of Merroutas is dead," Giulietta replies.

"Murdered, by an Elite called the White Wolf. Whispers about her have spread everywhere." She fixes Teren with a stare. "She is Adelina Amouteru, isn't she? The girl you've repeatedly failed to kill."

Teren stares at a vein in the marble floor. "Yes, Your Majesty."

Teren hears the Inquisitor return, and the telltale sound of metal blades dragging along the ground. "The Night King was our ally in Merroutas," Giulietta says. "Now there is chaos. My advisers tell me that the city is unstable, and we are vulnerable to a Tamouran attack."

Adelina. Teren clenches his teeth so hard that he feels like he might break his jaw. So, Adelina is in Merroutas, across the Sacchi Sea . . . and she had killed the city-state's ruler. Even as he seethes at the thought of her becoming a real threat, something about her ruthlessness calls to him. *Very impressive, my little wolf.* "I swear to you, Your Majesty," he says. "I will send an expedition there immediately—"

Giulietta clears her throat and Teren stops talking. He looks up to see the other Inquisitor approach the queen. He holds a nine-headed whip, each head tipped with a heavy, razor-sharp blade. This is Teren's custom whip. Teren sighs in relief at the same time that he winces.

He deserves this.

Giulietta folds her hands behind her back and takes a few steps away. "I was told you halved the rations of the *malfettos*, against my wishes," she says.

Teren doesn't ask how she found out. It doesn't matter.

"Master Santoro, I can be a ruthless queen. But I have no wish to be a cruel one. Cruelty is to hand out unjust punishment. I will not be unjust."

He keeps his head bowed. "Yes, Your Majesty."

"I wanted the camps as a visible punishment that the rest of our citizens can see, but I'll not have hundreds of rotting corpses outside my walls. I want submission from my people, not revolution. And you are threatening to undo that balance."

Teren bites his tongue to keep himself from speaking out.

"Remove your armor, Master Santoro," Giulietta says over her shoulder.

Teren does as she says. His armor clangs, echoing, to the floor. He pulls his tunic over his head. The air hits his bare skin, scarred from countless rounds of punishment. Teren's pale blue eyes glow in the chamber's light. He looks at Giulietta.

She gestures at the Inquisitor holding the bladed whip.

He lashes Teren's back with it. The nine blades strike him, ripping into his skin. Teren chokes down a cry as familiar pain explodes across his body. The edges of his vision flash crimson. His flesh opens before it immediately starts to heal. But the Inquisitor doesn't wait—he whips the weapon down again as Teren's skin struggles to stitch itself together.

"I'm not punishing you because you were disrespectful of the Beldish queen," Giulietta calls out over the sickening sound of blades slashing Teren's flesh raw. "I'm punishing you for disobeying me in public. For making a scene. For insulting the queen of a nation we cannot afford to fight again. Do you understand?"

"Yes, Your Majesty," Teren chokes out, as blood drips down his back.

"You do not make decisions for me, Master Santoro."

"Yes, Your Majesty."

"You do not ignore my commands."

"Yes, Your Majesty."

"You do *not* embarrass me in front of an enemy nation."

The blades dig in deep. Teren blinks back the unconsciousness creeping at the edges of his vision. His arms shake against the marble floor. "Yes, Your Majesty," he says hoarsely.

"Stand up straight," Giulietta commands.

Teren forces himself to do so, even as the gesture makes him scream. The Inquisitor whips the blades across his chest and stomach; his eyes fly open as they slash deep. This blow would have killed him instantly, if he were a normal man. For Teren, though, it merely brings him onto his hands and knees.

The whipping continues until the floor beneath Teren is slick with a film of his blood. The scarlet streaks across the marble make circular patterns, punctuated by Teren's handprints. He concentrates on the swirls. Somewhere, high above him, he knows he can hear the gods murmuring. Was this punishment from Giulietta, or from the gods?

Finally, Giulietta holds up a hand. The Inquisitor stops.

Teren trembles. He can feel the demonic magic of his body

laboriously bringing his broken flesh together again. These wounds will leave scars for sure—the cuts made too quickly over skin still not healed, over and over. His blond tail of hair hangs over his neck in sweaty strings. His body burns and aches.

"Rise."

Teren obeys. His legs feel weak, but he grits his teeth and forces them to steady. He deserved every last bit of that punishment. As he stands up straight, he meets Giulietta's eyes. "I'm sorry," he mutters, softly this time. The apology of a boy to his lover, not an Inquisitor to his queen.

Giulietta touches Teren's cheek with her cool fingers. He leans into her gentle grasp, savoring it, even as he trembles. "I am not cruel," she says again. "But remember this, Master Santoro. I only ask for obedience. If that is too hard, I can help. It is easier to obey without a tongue, and easier to kneel without legs."

Teren looks into her deep, dark eyes. This is what he loves about her, this side of her that always knew what had to be done. But why did she not immediately give the order to punish Raffaele? He should be executed.

She has not, Teren thinks, with a painful surge of jealousy, *because she wants something else from him.*

Giulietta smiles. She leans closer, then presses her lips to his cheek. Teren aches at her touch, her warning. "I love you," she whispers. "And I will not tolerate you disobeying me again."

The Cliffs of Sapientus are said to have formed when the god of Wisdom cut the world of the living from the world of the dead, sealing his sister Moritas forever away. The jagged edges look the most majestic during sunset, when golden light hits them and paints long shadows across the land.

–A Guide to Traveling through Domacca, *by An Dao*

Adelina Amouteru

Enzo visits me in my nightmare tonight.

It is evening, and the lanterns in the corridors of the Fortunata Court are already lit. Laughter floats from the Daggers' underground cavern, but Enzo and I make our way up the steps to the courtyard. Out here, the night is silent. *This is the night after the Spring Moons,* I remember through the haze of my dream. *After we attacked Estenzia's harbor.*

Enzo and I kiss in the courtyard, oblivious to the light rain falling all around us. He walks me back to my chambers. But in my dream, he doesn't bid me good night and then leave. In my dream, he comes inside with me.

I don't know if my power is at work . . . but I can *feel* his locks of dark hair against my cheeks, can *sense* the ripples of heat that his touch sends through my body. His lips brush past my ear, then touch my jaw and my neck, working their way steadily downward. I sit on the bed and pull him closer until we are a tangle of limbs. This is where we first met, after all, when he came to sit beside me and offered me a chance to join the Daggers.

Now his face stays buried against my skin. Currents of heat rush through me until I think I might burn alive. His shirt slips to one side, exposing his shoulder. Is he really here? Am I really in the Fortunata Court, in all its former glory? My finger traces the ridge of his collarbone. He sucks in his breath as I tug off his shirt, then run my hands down his chest. He pushes against me. *This is real. It must be.*

This is what could have happened that night.

"I love you," he whispers in my ear. And I am so enveloped in my dream, so lost in his trail of kisses, that for a moment I let myself believe it.

Enzo pauses. He coughs once. I turn my head enough to see the angles of his face in the darkness. "Are you all right?" I ask with a smile. My arms reach up to wrap around his neck and pull him closer.

Enzo stiffens, then coughs again. His brows twist into a knotted line, and he frowns. He pushes away from me and sits in a hunched position on the bed. His coughs come again and again, until he can't seem to stop. Spots of blood stain the sheets.

"Enzo!" I cry out. I scramble to his side and put a hand on his shoulder. He waves me away and shakes his head, but he's coughing so hard that he cannot speak. There's blood on his lips, glistening in the night. His face contorts in pain.

One of his hands comes up to grip his chest, and when I look, I notice with horror that a deep, scarlet wound is growing in the center, right over his heart.

He needs help. I leap out of bed, run to the door, and throw it open with all my strength. All of my limbs feel like they're dragging through the darkness, struggling through some invisible current. Behind me, Enzo's breathing turns desperate. I stare wildly down the hall.

"Help!" I scream. Why are all the lanterns dimmed now? I can barely see through the shadows of the corridor. My feet pound silently against the floor. I can feel the coldness of the marble. "Help!" I cry again. "The prince—he's hurt!"

The hall goes on and on. *Raffaele will know what to do.* Why can't I find the way back to the underground cavern? I keep running until I remember that Raffaele isn't at the cavern with the others. He doesn't come back on this night, because he has been captured by the Inquisition.

The hall is endless. As I run, the paintings lining the court's ornate walls begin to peel away, burnt and ashen, the corners ruined by fire. There are no doors or windows. Somewhere in the distance comes the sound of pouring rain.

I pause to catch my breath. My limbs burn. When I look behind me, I can no longer see my own chambers. The same hall stretches in both directions. I continue forward, walking now, my heart pounding against my ribs. New paintings begin to appear on the walls. Perhaps they've been there the entire time, and I've just noticed them. None of them make any sense. One of the paintings shows a girl with large, dark eyes and a rosy mouth—she sits in the middle of a garden and holds a dead butterfly in her hands. A second painting is of a boy dressed in white Inquisition armor, his mouth stretching from one ear to the other, his teeth scarlet red. He crouches inside a wooden box. A third painting runs from the ceiling to the floor. It is a girl's face, and half of it is gruesomely scarred. She does not smile. Her brows are knotted in anger, and her eyes are closed, as if they might open at any moment.

Fear begins to gnaw at my stomach. There are whispers here, the familiar whispers that plague me. I start to run again. The hall grows narrower, closing in on me from all sides. Up ahead, it finally reaches an end. I pick up my pace. *Help!* I call out again, but it sounds strange and distant, like an underwater cry.

My steps now make a splashing sound. I stumble to a halt. Water is pouring down the hall, black and cold. I start to back away, but the current sweeps me off my feet, and the water swallows me whole. I cannot think, I cannot hear, I cannot see anything except for the swirling darkness all around. The cold numbs me. I open my mouth to scream, but nothing comes out. I look for the light of the surface, but the same darkness yawns all around me.

The Underworld.

Black shapes swim through the depths. Through the darkness, I finally see a set of stairs that I instinctively know leads back to the hallway. Back to the living world. I try to swim toward the stairs, but they never seem to get any closer.

Adelina.

When I look over my shoulder, a shape materializes out of the blackness. It is a monstrous form, with long, bony fingers and milky, sightless eyes. Her mouth is open in a snarl. The fear in my heart turns to terror.

Caldora. The angel of Fury.

I struggle toward the stairs, but it is no use. Hissing fills my ears. When I look behind me again, Caldora's hands reach for me, fingers curled into claws.

I jolt awake at the ominous blare of a horn from above deck. Sunlight streams in from our porthole. The storm has passed, although the waters are still choppy. I swing my legs over the side of the bed and try to still my pounding heart. The whispers are stirring, but their voices are muted, and after a few seconds, they fade away entirely. My fingers shake as they run along the fabric of my pillow. This feels real. I hope it is. A part of me yearns to go back to the Fortunata Court, to throw my arms around Enzo and will him back to life—but another part of me is afraid to blink, lest I return to the Underworld's waters. Even glancing out the window sends a ripple of fear through me—the water is a dark, opaque blue, eager to swallow a ship.

I look to Violetta's bed. She's not there.

"Violetta?" I jump to my feet and hurry to the door. I make my way through the dark, cramped passageway of the ship's belly. My sister. She's gone. My nightmare comes back to me—the scorched, endless hall—and suddenly I'm terrified I'm still lost inside it. But then I reach the ladder leading to the deck, and I climb it gratefully.

When I peek over the top of the ladder, I see Violetta at the bow of the ship, leaning over the rails and talking in a low voice to Sergio. My limbs turn weak with exhaustion. I take a deep breath, calm myself, and pull myself up onto the deck. Several other crewmembers give me long looks as I pass by. I wonder which of them are also mercenaries, and whether Sergio has told any of them about our conversation from yesterday.

As I draw near, Sergio puts a hand on Violetta's arm. He laughs at something she says. A feeling of jealousy runs through me. It's not that I want Sergio's attention—but rather that he is attracting Violetta's. *She is* my *sister.*

"What was the horn for?" I ask. I purposely push between them, forcing Sergio to take his hand off my sister and assume a more distant stance. Violetta shoots me a sullen look. I blink innocently back at her.

Sergio points toward the outline of land on the horizon, still faint through the morning mist. "We're nearing the city of Campagnia. Have you been there before?" When I shake my head, he continues, "It's the closest port city to Estenzia. My guess is that we're not going to be greeted with open arms in the capital. It'd be impossible to dock."

Violetta nods in agreement. "Adelina's illusions are good," she says, "but she can't protect all of us forever from the number of Inquisitors in that city."

Estenzia. Somehow, it feels as if we left the capital a lifetime ago.

Sergio just shrugs it off as we watch the outline of a city gradually appear on the shore. "We'll dock in Campagnia soon," he reassures us. "They haven't passed any mandates outside of the capital that I know of. It'll be safer."

I nod. Sergio falls back into a conversation with Violetta. As they talk, I look around the deck. "Where's Magiano?" I ask.

Sergio's eyes roll skyward. "In the crow's nest," he replies, pointing up. "Gambling away his life's work."

On cue, a perfect imitation of a crow's caw sounds out. We all glance up to see Magiano above us, leaning so far forward that I'm afraid he'll topple right out. He's shouting something at the other sailor in the nest.

"I'll make that *twenty* gold talents, then," he calls out, leaning back into the nest and out of sight.

"Is he . . . winning?" Violetta asks, squinting up at the sky.

We look on as Magiano mutters a train of words to himself. A half-mad thief and a rejected Dagger—I'm certainly off to a good start in building my Elite society.

Sergio shrugs. "Does it matter? If he loses, he'll just steal the poor bastard's winnings, anyway."

Suddenly, the sailor Magiano is playing hops up to his feet. He points out at the water. Magiano cranes his neck toward land too, then shouts something down to Sergio that I can't make out.

Sergio bites his lip. I watch him, noting the tiny sparks

of fear coming off him. I stare hard into the mist. For a long moment, none of us can see anything. Only when the morning sun burns away more of the mist do I detect the faint outline of golden sails, the curving hull of a ship sailing out of Campagnia's harbor. The sound of horns floats toward us again. This time, they're deafening.

Overhead, Magiano grabs the rope attached to the crow's nest and glides down the mast. He lands with a light thump. His hair is in wild disarray, and the salty smell of ocean permeates his clothes. He gives us a passing glance. "An Inquisition ship," he says when he sees my questioning expression. "Looks like they're heading straight for us."

"You saw the Inquisition's flag on them?" I fold my arms and try to swallow the fear building in my throat. "But we're a completely common-looking ship."

"We're also the only ship passing the bay right now," Magiano replies. He frowns out at the water. "Why would they care if a cargo ship's making its way to Campagnia's port?"

The Inquisition's ship is getting closer. Something about the sight of its familiar emblems stirs the whispers in my head, and they shuffle their little claws, restless. The fear in my throat gives way to something else—a wild courage, the same thing I felt when I confronted the Night King.

A chance at revenge, the whispers say over and over. *Adelina, it's a chance at revenge.*

"Teren may be expanding his operations into Kenettra's other cities," Violetta says, casting me a sideways look. *Are you all right?* her expression says.

I tighten my lips and push down the whispers. "Do you think they're going to board us?" I ask Magiano.

Magiano points to how the small ship is now positioning itself behind us. "It's a small team, but they're going to steer us into the port," he replies. "And then they're going to inspect every nook and cranny of this ship." His expression darkens as he turns to me. "If I'd known you were going to cause this much trouble in the first three days since our little agreement, I would've left you to the Night King without a second glance."

"Good," I shoot back. "I'll remember that the next time I see you in danger."

My answer makes Magiano let out a surprised laugh. "You're charming." He grabs my wrist before I can stop him, then nods at Violetta to follow him. "It looks like we're stuck together now, aren't we?" he says. "I recommend we hide."

We hurry back belowdecks, where a nervous and sweaty crewmember hisses at Magiano to take us down to the ship's belly. Our footsteps echo hollowly across the narrow wood floors.

We make our way down three ladders before finally reaching a closet where crates are stacked haphazardly from floor to ceiling. Here, he ushers us into its dark recesses. The space is nearly pitch-black, except for a dense iron grating high overhead that lets in slivers of dim light.

Magiano gives me a pointed look. "Stay quiet," he whispers. He glances at Violetta. "Keep a lid on your sister's power. It'd be in all of our best interests for it not to careen out of control like it did in Merroutas."

"She's going to be fine," Violetta answers, a note of irritation in her voice. "She knows how to control herself."

He looks unconvinced, but still gives her a nod. Then he's gone, closing the door behind him and leaving us in darkness.

I can feel Violetta's faint trembling. She doesn't do as Magiano suggested—take away my power—but she doesn't seem entirely comfortable with me, either. "You're feeling okay, right?" she whispers to me.

"Yes," I reply.

We wait without saying another word. For a while, the only thing we can hear is the familiar sound of waves outside the ship. Then, we hear new voices. Footsteps.

"Don't lose control again," Violetta whispers. After such a long silence, her words sound deafening. She doesn't even look at me. Instead, her eyes stay fixed on the grating above us.

I turn up to stare at it too. I keep waiting for that strange, hazy pressure to hit me again, like it did in Merroutas—but this time, my strength holds steady, and I keep a firm grip on my powers. "I won't," I whisper back.

The voices are very faint. Through two layers of wooden floors, all I can make out are muffled human sounds and the subtle vibrations of boots on the deck. I sense a general unease in the energy of the ship's crew. Violetta's head turns as the voices travel from one end of the deck to the other.

"They're going to come belowdecks," she whispers after a while. And sure enough, no sooner have the words left her mouth than we hear the stomp of boots on the ladder leading downward. The voices abruptly become louder.

Now I can hear the soldiers speaking to one another. My fear rises as they draw steadily closer overhead.

In the mix, Magiano's animated voice suddenly appears. "And, why, the last time I was in Campagnia, I fell in love with your wines. Do you know I've never been drunker? I—"

An Inquisitor cuts him off with an exasperated sigh. "When did you leave Merroutas?"

"A week ago."

"A lie, boy. No ship takes a week to reach our shores from Merroutas."

Sergio's more reasonable voice now sounds out. "We docked in Dumor first, to drop off some cargo," he says.

"I see no Dumorian stamps on your ship. You left Merroutas recently, I wager. Well, some new laws have come into effect here in Campagnia. The Inquisition deems all arriving ships subject to search. *Malfettos* from other countries are no longer allowed in this city, you see." He pauses for a moment, as if to peer closer at Magiano. His eyes must not be slitted, because the soldier steps back again. "So if anyone in your crew is a *malfetto,* I recommend you tell us now."

"We have none that I can think of, sir."

"And you wouldn't happen to have any stowaways?"

"You're welcome to search," Magiano pipes up. "*Malfettos*—a pile of trouble, aren't they? I still count us lucky that we'd already left Merroutas by the time the incidents down at their pier happened. You heard about that by now, haven't you?"

I glance at Violetta in the darkness. She stares back. Her mouth puckers into a word. *Ready?*

Slowly, I weave a web of invisibility across us, changing us into the slants of light on an empty closet floor, the dark grooves of an empty closet's walls. The voices and footsteps draw steadily closer, until they sound like they're right on top of us. I peer at the grating through the darkness.

The bottom of a boot suddenly appears over it, then another. They're directly overhead now. I hold my breath.

"Anyone else on board this ship?" the Inquisitor asks. He's turned toward who I assume must be Sergio. "Is the entire crew here?"

"All accounted for, sir," Sergio replies. "Supplies are on the lowest deck."

More muttering between the soldiers. I stiffen as footsteps now sound out from our deck. Moments later, the door to the dark supply room opens, and someone approaches our closet. I tighten our invisibility illusion. The door flies open.

An Inquisitor squints straight at us. *Through* us. He looks bored. One of his hands taps restlessly against the hilt of his sword. Violetta's hand shakes harder, but she doesn't make a sound.

He peers through us and around the closet for a moment before leaving the door ajar and wandering around to search the rest of the room. His cloak billows past us. I continue to hold my breath. If he tries to step inside this closet after the rest of his search, and he bumps into our bodies, I will have to kill him.

Above us, Magiano's voice pipes up again. "You're searching the wrong ship," he says. His tone has changed from lighthearted innocence to something ominous. "How do I know this?" He digs around in his pocket for a moment before pulling something out and holding it up to the light. Even from down here, I can see the object glinting. It is the pin he stole from the Night King. "Do you see the crest engraved on the side of this beauty? This is the Night King's very own emblem. We are a crew of his protected fleet from Merroutas, and none are more aggrieved than us by news of his death. But even in death, he is a wealthier and more powerful man than any of you could ever hope to be. If you dare kill one of our crew, just in the futile hopes of finding a fugitive that's probably making his way as far from Kenettra as possible, I can guarantee you that you will be answering to your Lead Inquisitor and your queen."

A taunting note enters Magiano's voice. "After all, think for a moment, if your mind is capable of that. Why would a fugitive who fled Kenettra hide on board a ship that's now trying to dock *back* in Kenettra?" He holds his arms out in an exaggerated shrug.

I can't help feeling a certain gratitude to Magiano for defending us like this. He could have turned us in for a good price. I shake my head. *He's not doing it for you. He's doing it for himself, for money and survival. Not for you.*

For an instant, I think that the Inquisitors will take Magiano's words to heart. My stare stays on the Inquisitor studying our hiding spot.

Then Sergio's boots shuffle across the grating. I look up, hoping my illusion doesn't waver. One of the other soldiers has grabbed Sergio around the neck and pressed a knife to his waist. In a flash, Sergio slips out of the grip and whips out a blade of his own. From down here, I can see the edge flashing in the light. The other Inquisitors draw their weapons. Magiano lets out a groan and an incoherent curse as he takes out a dagger too, and together, they stand off against the Inquisitors.

"A good story," the leader of the soldiers says. He takes a step closer to Sergio, blade pointed at him. "But we have a description of the ship that the Night King's soldiers believe their fugitives sailed away on. It is undoubtedly yours. Congratulations." The soldier raises his voice. "Show your face, illusion worker, or some up here may start losing their heads."

Violetta looks at me. Her dark eyes shine. If only we'd stayed above deck with the others, I could have disguised our faces and attacked the soldiers before they ever boarded the ship. But now there is an Inquisitor standing right in front of us, the closet door still ajar, staring through us as if he might see something any moment.

The Inquisitor standing in front of us looks up and draws his blade. In doing so, he bumps Violetta hard. Violetta stumbles back with a grunt—it is all the Inquisitor needs to look sharply back at us. He narrows his eyes. Then he lifts his sword to chop at the air in the closet. At *us*.

Thoughts flash through my mind like lightning. I could just stop this Inquisitor and save Violetta and myself. If we flee this ship without uttering a sound, we could leave Sergio, his crew, and Magiano to handle the Inquisition. When we dock, we could simply sneak off the ship and make our way undetected into the city. Forget about my newfound Elites and protect ourselves.

But instead, I clench my teeth. Sergio is one of mine now. And if I hope to have allies at my back, I'll have to stand up for them.

Violetta shoots me a wide-eyed look as the Inquisitor's blade flies toward us. That is all the encouragement I need to unleash my energy.

The Inquisitor suddenly stops his attack in midair. His eyes bulge. He trembles, then opens his mouth into a silent scream as I reach for him and weave around him the illusion of a thousand threads of pain. His sword clatters to the floor as he falls to his knees. I erase our invisibility—I see the shock in his eyes as we suddenly appear before him.

Violetta crouches down to grab the sword. As she points it at him with shaking hands, I turn my attention to the standoff above us. My energy whips out at the Inquisitors there. The threads latch on to them, painting the illusion of hooks digging deep into their skin, yanking them down into the ground and beyond.

They scream in unison. Sergio seems stricken for a split

second—but then he snaps out of it right away. He hops over their writhing bodies and attacks the closest Inquisitor who has headed down the passageway at him. The clang of blades rings out. Magiano crouches down to the fallen Inquisitors and starts to tie their hands as quickly as he can.

"Let's go," I say through gritted teeth. We step out of our hiding place. The Inquisitor on the ground makes a weak attempt to grab Violetta's ankles, but she yanks herself out of the way, then turns the sword around in her hands and brings the hilt of it down on the soldier's jaw. He goes limp.

"Nicely done," I say, giving my sister a tight smile. A year ago, I would never have expected her to be bold enough for that. Violetta takes a deep breath and gives me an anxious look.

We hurry out of the cabin and into the dark corridor, then up the steps leading to the next level. When we finally reach the others, I skid to a halt. Several of the crew are inspecting the Inquisitors tied up on the ground, while Sergio and another man are securing bonds on another one. He looks up at us. There is wariness in his eyes as he regards me.

"I never witnessed what you did to the Night King," Sergio says. "But I saw the looks on these Inquisitors' faces when you attacked them. That *was* you, wasn't it? What did you do?"

I swallow, then explain what my illusion over them had been. My voice is calm and steady.

The other crewmember helping Sergio now looks at me. "We were all a bit skeptical of you when you first came on board." He regards me carefully. "I've never seen such fright on grown men's faces."

This must be one of Sergio's fellow mercenaries. I nod, returning his stare, unsure of what it means. Now I notice that several of the others are staring at me too, as if seeing me for the first time. I glance around, searching their expressions, then let myself dwell on the Inquisitors moaning on the ground. If they hadn't recognized me earlier, they all seem to know who I am now. My gaze shifts from one to the next, settling finally on the one lying closest to me, a young soldier who still has some bewildered innocence left in his eyes. My energy feeds on their fear, strengthening and replenishing itself.

If the Inquisition is searching Campagnia like this, they must have expanded their efforts out from Estenzia. Does that mean Teren will be here, looking for us too? Does that mean that he is starting to round up all *malfettos* here?

"Where's Magiano?" I finally say.

Sergio nods to the ladder. He waves for us to follow him. We make our way up the ladder and onto the deck of the ship, where Magiano is waiting for us. The Campagnia harbor draws close, while behind us, the Inquisition's ship stays where it is, quiet.

Magiano has his hands tucked into his pockets. When he hears us approach, he leans toward me and gives a casual nod toward land. "We will continue to sail into harbor," he says, "and leave the Inquisition's ship to drift at sea. By the time anyone onshore figures out that something has gone wrong, we'll have long dispersed into the city."

"What about the Inquisitors tied up below?" Violetta asks.

Magiano exchanges a glance with Sergio, then looks at me. His eyes are serious for a moment. "Yes, what *should* we do about them?" he asks. "No matter what, we'll undoubtedly bring the Inquisition's wrath down on us. They'll hunt us relentlessly."

His words ring in my mind, echoing in the wrong way, and the echo awakens the whispers in my mind again. I can feel their little claws against my consciousness, eager to hear my answer. Down below, I can hear some of the Inquisitors still moaning and struggling. It sounds as if they are ready to beg for their lives. Without answering Magiano, I walk back over to the ladder leading down and stare into the shadows.

At first, I think I'll spare them.

But then the whispers say, *Why worry about the Inquisition's wrath? You came back to this country to exact your revenge on them. You shouldn't be the one to fear them anymore. They should fear you.*

There is a moment of heavy silence. Magiano watches me with an unreadable expression. I think back to the Inquisitors' faces. Some of them had cringed away from me, while others had tears streaking their cheeks. Their white uniforms all blend into one in my thoughts. All I can see are the same men who had once so unceremoniously tied me to the stake and thrown fire at my feet. How many have they killed? How many will they go on to kill?

Strike first.

And with that, a dark cloud starts to fill my insides again, and my heart hardens. I look at Magiano. "I'm not afraid of the Inquisition," I say. Then I nod at Sergio. "Tell your men to kill them. Make it quick and clean." Violetta shoots me a sharp glance. I wait, perhaps defiantly, for her to say something against my decision . . . but she doesn't. She swallows hard and looks down. After a while, she nods her agreement. As I talk, I can hear the whispers saying the words with me, so we are in chorus. Their voices remind me of my father's.

"Let the youngest one live," I finish. "When the Inquisition finds him, he can tell them who did this, and how I made them feel."

Magiano's eyes slit a little at me. There's something admiring in his gaze that mingles with something . . . unsettled. I can't quite figure out the expression. He glances back at the nearing harbor. He lets out a sigh, then leaves us to walk toward the bow.

Sergio is still smiling. "In that case, we'd better be careful in Campagnia. You have taken on a challenging adversary."

"And are you and your men going to help us take on that adversary?" I ask.

It's the question that has been lingering between us since we stepped on board this ship. Sergio looks at me, then around at some of the other crew on deck. Finally, he leans over. "We help whoever can get us the most gold," he whispers. "And right now, that's you, isn't it?"

That is a yes. Something soars in my chest. I don't want to ask what happens if we fail to take the throne and overthrow the Inquisition. Instead, I decide to revel in his words.

I turn my back as Sergio walks over to the ladder and shouts a command down to the other mercenaries. The Inquisitors below let out muffled sobs behind their bonds. Their fear bubbles up to the deck in a thick cloud. It makes me tremble.

Then, the sound of blades against skin, the gush of blood.

The whispers cheer in my head. I keep my mind on the burning stake, the *malfettos* I've seen suffering right in front of Inquisitors who turn a bored eye, the breaking glass and screaming people. I should feel some sense of disgust, some recoil or horror at the thought of the carnage down below. But I don't, not for those Inquisitors.

I strike first from now on.

We watch in silence as the harbor approaches, until our hull bumps dully against the piers and a worker on the ground ties us in. He casts a glance over at the quiet Inquisition ship behind us, but he doesn't act on it. Instead, our crew prepares the gangplank, and we gather near the railing. Down on the harbor's main street, clusters of Inquisitors cut lines through bustling crowds. I wonder how long they will take before they investigate the floating ship.

As the crew haul crates down the gangplank and hook up thick ropes to hoist larger cargo, we follow Magiano and Sergio off the ship. "This is exactly why I left this forsaken country in the first place," Magiano mutters to me as we go. He still seems like he is in an odd mood. "Damn Inquisition, always swarming about. Come on. And keep your face disguised."

I straighten my head wrap and check Violetta's, then

strengthen the illusion over my face. It's not hard to blend in with the throngs wandering the harbor. I keep a steady illusion over my face, and my hair stays hidden inside its wrap. Behind us, several other crewmembers also make their way off the ship and scatter into the crowds. I watch them go. I recognize a few of their faces now, men I saw tying up the Inquisitors on the ship. I also see the man who had spoken briefly to me on board. All mercenaries. All loyal to me. For now.

Dead men belowdecks, sightless eyes, bloody chests. The whispers excitedly remind me of what had happened on the ship. *Dead men, dead men.*

Violetta makes a small sound, breaking my stream of thoughts. When I look at her, her brow has tensed. She starts to drag her feet, as if something had caught her interest. I frown, then look into the crowd.

"What is it?" I ask.

Violetta just nods silently into the milling people.

It takes me another second to spot what she's noticed. Not far from us, walking along the edge of the street, is a girl I recognize. She seems like she's in a hurry. Still, even in her rush, she pauses to smile and pet a stray dog. The dog starts to follow her.

"Gemma?" I whisper to myself.

The Daggers are here.

And so they huddled together,
waiting, hoping for a savior
that would never come.
–Tides of a Midwinter War, *by Constanze De Witte*

Adelina Amouteru

Already, I'm starting to lose her in the crowded street. A traveling cloak hides the top half of her face, and her figure is almost lost amid the horses and wagons.

"That girl," I murmur to Magiano. I tilt my head in Gemma's direction. "She's one of the Daggers. I know it."

"Are you sure?" Magiano gives me a skeptical look.

"Adelina's right," Sergio interrupts, his eyes following Gemma down the street. We look on as she stops to talk to one of the sailors from a ship. "That's the Star Thief."

I start to move. "If they're here, I want to know what they're up to. I'm going to follow her. Don't let her know we're here."

Ahead of us, Gemma reaches the end of the harbor and turns onto a winding street. Sergio leans close to us, his eyes fixed on her as if she'd vanish any second. "We'll trail her," he says to me in a low voice. "I'd like to see what those Daggers are up to here." I expect him to start pushing his way through the crowd without hearing my reply—but to my surprise, he looks at me expectantly.

It takes me a moment to realize that he's waiting for my approval. "Yes," I reply, stumbling over the word.

It is all he needs to hear. He exchanges glances with a couple of the other crew from the ship, those who must be his fellow mercenaries.

"Count me as curious too," Magiano mutters, then nods once at me before vanishing into the crowd.

Violetta leans over to me. "Look," she says, subtly motioning to the general direction where Gemma is heading. "The sailor we just saw her talking to. He's heading that way as well."

My sister's right. I pick out the back of his head among the people. He smiles and laughs at a few children that cross his path, but there's no doubt about it—he must be following Gemma too.

I touch Violetta's arm. "Don't stay too close," I say as I start walking. I weave a subtle illusion over her face, changing her features enough to make her unrecognizable should Gemma ever look back.

Off in the crowd, Magiano flickers in and out of sight. When I look to my right, Sergio's hair peeks out from the throngs. We move together, unorganized yet coordinated. I'm reminded of the first time I ever saw the Daggers go on a mission—and a ripple of excitement runs down my spine.

We head down the same street that Gemma entered. As we do, I see her turn around to look down at the dog still trailing faithfully behind her. She smiles, bends down, and rubs its ears. Even though I know her power, I'm somehow still surprised to see the dog turn obediently around, as if led by an invisible hand, and walk away from her without another backward glance. I slide between two clusters of people and look on, awed for a moment. There is something quiet and warm about this tiny, temporary bond between the girl and the dog. What must it feel like to harness joy and love, instead of fear and hate? What kind of light does that cast?

I lose her a few times in the thick of the crowds. She makes her way out of the busy sections of the port, then heads up a small hill to what looks like a tiny tavern at the end of a street. I look behind me, wondering where Magiano and Sergio are. Violetta walks several paces behind me, stopping now and then to weave her way through pockets of people.

Finally, up ahead, Gemma turns where the tavern's main entrance is. She doesn't try to go through the front—instead, she steps into a side street and disappears from view. I hurry along, trying to stay in the shadows along the edges of the buildings. Not many people wander here. No Inquisitors to be seen. I wait until I'm fairly alone on the street, and then I wrap myself in threads of energy. I blend into the shadows, and then I become the shadows, until no one notices my invisible figure heading up to the tavern.

I turn onto the street where I saw Gemma go, then stop at the corner to watch.

She's standing at a back entrance of the tavern with several others, a space so narrow and shadowed that no one would think to turn back here. I recognize Lucent immediately—her copper curls are tied back into a bushy tail, and she has a frown on her face. Michel is there, but Raffaele is not, and a bald boy I don't recognize is talking in low voices with Gemma. The sailor we saw down at the pier is here too, along with a couple of others. Are these new Dagger recruits? It seems as if everyone has gathered here to wait for Gemma. I make sure my invisibility is intact, and then I walk forward. I keep going until their voices drift to me and I can understand what they're saying.

Gemma's voice comes to me first. She's arguing with Lucent. "At least Raffaele is safely there," she says.

Lucent lifts a brow and shakes her head, as if this were the first time she's hearing the news. "He's going to get himself killed," Lucent replies, "the instant they leave him alone with Teren. Why couldn't we have just asked for an audience directly with the queen?"

I hold my breath. Raffaele is back in the Estenzian palace, by his *own* choice? What are they planning now?

"Giulietta would never hold an audience with us and risk her life," Gemma says. "Trust your queen, Lucent—Maeve knows what she's doing. Giulietta will be forced to dine with her and celebrate her arrival, which should give Raffaele time to deliver what he wants to say."

Maeve. Queen. I think back, remembering after a moment that Lucent is originally from Beldain. If Maeve is her *queen,* then Maeve must be the Queen of Beldain. Beldain is working with the Daggers.

"Maeve will act in three nights' time," Gemma now says. "That's when the festivities will end in a night of raucous performances. It will help to hide what we're doing."

"She will make her way to the arena at midnight," Lucent says to the others whom I don't recognize. "She needs to be in the exact place where he died. During the process, she will be entirely defenseless. We have to make sure she is safe and untouched."

Lucent's words send a prickle down my spine. *The exact place where he died.* What is she talking about?

"We'll ensure it," the men reply. I wonder whether they are Queen Maeve's own soldiers in disguise.

"And Raffaele must be there, yes?" asks another.

Gemma nods. "Yes. The dead cannot exist in this world on their own. Enzo must be bound to someone in order to have the strength to live again. Maeve already has her brother bound to her. She will bind Enzo to Raffaele."

Enzo.

Suddenly, I can't seem to catch my breath. The world shifts around me, and my invisibility is in danger of flickering out. I struggle to hang on to it, then stumble back until I hit the edge of the tavern wall. I must not have heard Gemma say the name correctly—this must be some misunderstanding, a different name. It cannot be Prince Enzo. *My* Enzo.

The bald boy shakes his head and gives Gemma an

apologetic look. "I don't understand. Raffaele never informed me of this. Why are we bringing him back?"

Lucent shoots him an annoyed glare, but Gemma gives him a pat on his shoulder. "You are a new Dagger," she replies. "You'll be brought up to speed soon enough. Kenettra lost a leader when Prince Enzo died at the hands of the Lead Inquisitor. Maeve had counted on him to be the one to bring trade and prosperity flowing again between our two nations. When she brought her little brother back from the Underworld, he returned with strength unheard of in mortal men. If she can also bring back Enzo—an Elite—he may return with his powers strengthened in ways we cannot even fathom. She can place him back on the throne, where he belongs, as her Kenettran ambassador."

I close my eye. Blood roars in my ears. *The dead cannot exist in this world on their own.*

I cannot possibly be hearing their conversation correctly. Because if I am, then that would mean that the Daggers are planning on bringing Enzo back. My mind spins. Maeve, Maeve . . . *she will bind Enzo to Raffaele.*

Hadn't Raffaele once mentioned rumors of an Elite who could raise the dead?

That's what the Daggers are here for. The realization finally makes my invisibility break down, and for a second, I'm exposed.

Instantly I fix it, melting myself back into the scene around me. Gemma's eyes dart in my direction—she looks confused for a moment, but then she seems to shrug it off and return to the conversation. I swallow hard and try to ignore the thundering of my heart.

The bald boy narrows his eyes. "But—I have seen the queen's brother. He is not of the living. Will the same not happen to Prince Enzo?"

Gemma sighs heavily at that. "We don't know. Perhaps. Perhaps not, as he is an Elite. The queen has never brought back anyone else, aside from her brother. But he will walk the world again, with Raffaele at his side."

Lucent addresses the bald boy. "Leo," she says. "We need to get Enzo out of the city once he returns. None of us have any idea how he will be—not even Maeve. He may not have his powers at all, or he may be exactly as he used to be. Regardless, he will cause a scene. Maeve said that her brother's revival caused a whirlpool in the lake where he'd"—she pauses for a moment, and I detect a hint of guilt in her voice—"where he'd originally drowned. Then he was bedridden for a week. Do you think you know your power well enough to distract the Inquisitors at one of the gates?"

The boy named Leo sounds nervous, but he still lifts his chin. "I think so," he replies. "My poison is temporary, but it will last long enough to weaken them."

"Maeve will be weak as well," Gemma adds, turning her attention to the others standing beside Leo. "You need to get her to safety as quickly as possible."

One of them steps forward. He lifts a hand, and a tiny flash of blinding light sparks in his palm. *Another Elite.* "We are the queen's personal Elites," he says, as if insulted. "We know how to protect her. Just handle your prince."

"And her navy?" Lucent asks.

"They will arrive soon. Mark my words—it will be a massive siege."

They exchange a few handshakes and some more words, but I stop listening in order to take in what I've already heard.

Raffaele is working with the Beldish queen to bring Enzo back. Meanwhile, Beldain's navy is coming. In fact, Beldish soldiers—Elites—are already here, perhaps all hiding in plain sight. Pieces are all moving into place to force Giulietta from her throne.

Enzo. *Enzo.* I place a hand on the tavern wall and guide myself around the corner. I find a dark spot in the next alley. There, I finally shed my invisibility and lower myself into a crouch, then rest my head in my hands. Threads of energy inside me start to rise out of control. The scene changes from a hilly street in Campagnia to a dark hallway back at the Fortunata Court. I'm crouched in one corner, hiding, listening to Dante talk to Enzo. I hear how little the Daggers trust me—how even Enzo hesitates when Dante talks about my disloyalty. The scene vanishes, replaced by a bed and Raffaele sitting beside it, holding my hand and telling me I am no longer one of them.

Adelina.

I look up to see a vision of Enzo standing there. His face is as beautiful as I remember, his eyes scarlet and piercing, his dark red hair tied back in an unruly tail. He leans down, and his ghostly fingers brush my cheek. I want to reach up to him, but I know he's too far away.

I should be happy to hear all this. This is what I want too—to see Giulietta overthrown and *malfettos* safe under the rightful ruler of Kenettra. Why am I unhappy? I want Enzo back, don't I? And yet, the memory returns to me of the child sitting along the stairs, fantasizing about the crown of jewels on her head.

I know exactly why I am unhappy. The Daggers have given themselves to another country. They have put Enzo—and Kenettra's throne—in the hands of a foreign nation. The thought makes my stomach lurch violently.

This is wrong. Enzo wouldn't have wanted this, handing Kenettra over to Beldain. How can the Daggers agree to be Maeve's lackeys? Beldain treats their *malfettos* well, certainly—but they are not our allies. They have *always* been Kenettra's rival.

They shouldn't be on your throne, the whispers in my head snap, suddenly awakened. They stir in a restless whirlwind, irritated. *That is why you are angry. The Daggers don't deserve to rule, not after what they did to you. Don't let them have something that is yours. Don't let them take that revenge from you.*

"My revenge is against the Inquisition Axis," I whisper, my voice so quiet that even I can't hear it.

It should be against the Daggers, too, for throwing you into the wild. For putting their own prince in Beldain's hands.

The whispers repeat their words until I can't understand them anymore, and then, gradually, they fade away. The illusion of Enzo disappears, returning me to the street. To reality.

The sound of footsteps snaps me out of my thoughts. My head jerks up from my hands. Violetta? She's probably nearby, perhaps listening in on the conversation from somewhere else. But something about the footsteps seems off. There is a certain familiarity between those who have known each other for an entire lifetime—I would recognize the sound of Violetta approaching from anywhere. This is not her.

Even though I'm already exhausted from the invisibility I'd been holding up, I take a breath and weave the net around me again, hiding myself away. Then I move from the edge of the alley, just in case the approaching person accidentally bumps into me.

I see the shadow of a person first. It yawns across the opening of the alley, hesitates, and then moves forward. A girl. *Gemma.* She stops in the entrance of the alley and looks around. A slight frown sits on her face. I stay completely still, not daring to move or breathe. She'd noticed my illusion flicker earlier, after all.

Gemma doesn't call out for the others. Instead, she steps slowly into the alley. Now I can see her face clearly—the purple marking across her face is hidden behind a layer of beauty powder, and her waves of dark hair are woven back into a long braid over her shoulder. The cloak's hood still shades her face. She looks suspicious, though, and moves gradually closer to where I crouch.

She stops barely a foot away from me. I can almost hear her breathing.

Gemma shakes her head. She smiles a little at herself and rubs her eyes. I think back to when she'd ridden a horse in the qualifying races for the Tournament of Storms. To how I'd decided to save her.

I have a sudden desire to lift my illusion of invisibility. I imagine myself getting up and calling out her name. Perhaps she'll look at me, startled, and then break into a smile. "Adelina!" she'd say. "You're safe! What are you doing here?" I imagine her hurrying over to take my hand, tugging me to my feet. "Come back with us. We could use your help."

The thought leaves me warm, rosy with the feeling of a friendship that once was.

What a fantasy. If I were to show my face to her, she'd back away from me. Her expression of confusion would change into one of fear. She'd run to the others, and they would hunt for me. I am not her friend anymore. The truth of this brings a surge of darkness up in my stomach, a smattering of the whispers that call for me to lash out at her. I could kill her right here, if I wanted. Hadn't I so easily ordered the deaths of those Inquisitors on the ship? I have never known the mind of a wolf hunting a deer, but I imagine it must feel a little like this: the twisted excitement of seeing the weak and wounded cowering before you, the knowledge that, in this instant, you have the power to end its life or grant it mercy. In this moment, I am a god.

So I stay where I am, looking on while Gemma turns one

more time in the alley, holding my breath, wishing I could talk to her and wishing I could hurt her, suspended between light and dark.

The moment passes—a warning horn blares out across the harbor, jolting both Gemma and me out of our thoughts. Gemma jumps a little, then turns sharply in the direction of the piers. "What was that?" she mutters.

The horn blares again. It is the Inquisition; they've discovered the Inquisitors' bodies on board our ship at the docks, as well as gone to investigate their floating ship out in the water. They know I'm here. Somehow, the thought brings me a small smile.

When the horn sounds a third time, Gemma turns away from me and hurries out of the alley, then makes her way back to the street she was on. I don't move for a few minutes after she leaves. Only when Magiano drops down from a balcony ledge to land nearby do I slowly unravel my illusion. At the other end of the narrow alley, Violetta and Sergio come around toward us.

"I hope you heard everything I heard," Magiano whispers as he helps me up. The sheer length of time I've had to hold the invisibility over myself has taken its toll, and I feel as if I could sleep for days. I sway on my feet.

"Hey," he murmurs. His breath is very warm. "I've got you." He glances at Sergio. "Sounds like the hunt for the White Wolf is on now, isn't it? Well, let's not make it too easy for the Inquisition."

I find myself clinging to his shirt. From the corner of my

eye, I can still see an echo of Gemma fluttering in and out of the world, barely translucent enough to exist, as if her shadow hadn't quite caught up with her. Ideas churn in my mind, connecting.

"We have to get to Estenzia," I whisper back. "Before the Daggers make their move."

Loyalty. Love. Knowledge. Diligence. Sacrifice. Piety.

–*The Six Pillars of Tamoura*

Adelina Amouteru

After maintaining my invisibility illusion for so long, I'm exhausted. I am half carried to the outskirts of Campagnia while the Inquisition floods the city's streets. We finally set up camp some distance inside the forestland along the edges of Campagnia. Here, Violetta unhooks our cloaks and rolls them up for me to use as pillows, then sets about wetting cloths from a nearby creek and placing them carefully on my forehead. I stay quiet, content to let her fuss over me. Sergio takes up watch along the border. Magiano counts out our gold, placing them in meticulous little piles on the ground. Even though his lute stays on his back, he taps the ground with his fingers as if in mid-play.

I watch him halfheartedly, distracted by my own thoughts. By nightfall, papers with my name and description on them will be pinned to the wall of every street corner. Word will get back to the capital before long. I picture Teren crumpling a parchment in his hand, sending out more soldiers to hunt me down. I imagine Raffaele getting word of my presence in Kenettra, of him with the other Daggers, plotting my downfall.

As time goes on, several others from our ship's crew find us. They come creeping in on silent feet, exchanging nothing but quiet stares with Sergio before acknowledging me. Sergio talks in low voices to a few of them. None are pretending to be mere sailors anymore. I catch glimpses of blades at their belts and boots, and notice the way they move. Not all of them stay. Eventually, they disperse back into the forest, as quietly as they'd come. I want to address them, but something about their interactions with Sergio tells me I might be better off letting Sergio guide them, rather than trying to command them myself.

"There are others in Merroutas who want to join you," Sergio says to me after a while. "Some have already made their way to the lands around Estenzia. You should know that Merroutas is in turmoil at the moment, as no one is sure who will replace the Night King." He smiles a little. "Some already think that *you* rule there, even if no one can see you."

"Not with this little pile of gold, you don't," Magiano grumbles from where he sits counting. "I'm impatient to swim in the Kenettran royal treasury."

"It seems the Beldish queen is a patron of the Daggers," Sergio says as he sits beside me.

"Beldain has always celebrated *malfettos*," Violetta replies. "Adelina and I considered fleeing there for a while."

Magiano taps absently at the ground. "Make no mistake—Beldain's not here to help *malfettos* out of the goodness of its heart. Maeve is a new, young queen. She's itching to conquer, and she's probably had her eye on Kenettra for a long time. Watch. If they kill Giulietta and bring Enzo back, Enzo will be their puppet king. The Daggers will be a new branch of their army." He winks at me. "And that means no crown for you, my love. A shame for all of us, I would think."

The mention of the Daggers brings their faces into my thoughts again. I hesitate, then look at Sergio. "How long did you know the Daggers?" I ask. "How did you leave them?"

Sergio pulls out one of his knives and starts to sharpen it. He ignores me for a while. "At the time, they'd recruited only Gemma and Dante," he finally says. "I was their third. Raffaele found me working on a ship as a rigger after he returned from visiting a duchess in southern Kenettra. I refused him, at first."

My eyebrows lift. "You refused him?"

"Because I didn't believe him," Sergio replies. He finishes with the blade he's working on and moves on to another. "At that point, I was eighteen and still had no knowledge of my powers. I thought of the Elites as rumors and legends." He pauses to laugh a little. He tilts his head at Violetta. "It *is* ridiculous, isn't it, what we can do?"

In this moment, there is little of the mercenary in him, and he seems like a kindhearted boy. A remnant of who he once was, perhaps. His blade sharpening speeds up. "It took Raffaele inviting me to a dinner to change my mind. Afterward, Enzo demonstrated his ability with fire. They gave me a heavy bag of gold. I suppose I became a mercenary first through them, eh?"

Violetta fiddles with a hunk of dry bread. "And so you joined them," she coaxes him on.

Sergio shrugs, unwilling to repeat the obvious. "I learned that I was drawn to the sky, to the elements that make storms. I learned how to fight from Enzo and Dante. But six months passed, and still I could not call upon my power." He stops sharpening his knife abruptly, then plunges it deep into the soil. Violetta startles. "Their training turned urgent, and the way they talked to me changed. After another year, I could tell that Raffaele was having private conversations with Enzo about what to do with me. Gemma and Dante had both displayed their powers so early on that they expected the same from me too."

Sergio sighs at this point. He takes a swig of water from his canteen and regards me with gray eyes. "I don't know what Raffaele told you. I don't even know myself all the details of what was said. All I know is that, one evening, Enzo took me aside to train, and cut me with a poison-tipped blade. The next thing I knew, I woke up in the belly of a ship heading south, out of Kenettra. He left a note tucked into my shirt. It was sparse, to say the least."

In the silence that follows, Magiano sits back and admires his piles of coins before gathering them all up again. "So . . .

what you're saying is that you wouldn't be too happy with the idea of the Daggers ruling Kenettra."

I stare at a spot over Magiano's head. I'm thinking about Enzo, the way he used to be. The hard look in his eyes as he trained me, and then the vulnerability I saw in him whenever we were alone. I don't need to push Sergio to know that Raffaele had asked Enzo to kill him, just as he did to me. Enzo had spared us both. He had been such a strong leader, such a natural crown prince. He would have been an admirable king.

But if he does come back, he will be tethered to Raffaele. And based on the little that Gemma said, Raffaele will control him. They will let Beldain use him as a puppet king for Maeve, a shadow of what he would have been. The thought sends a shudder through my chest, awakening the whispers again. *No, I will not let it happen.*

Magiano gives me a sidelong look. "You're thinking about him again," he says. Something flashes in his eyes, narrowing the slits of his pupils. "You think of him a lot, and not just for your political ploys."

My gaze darts away from the woods and to him.

"The prince, I mean," Magiano says, when I don't reply. He pulls the lute off his back and plucks a few sharp notes. "Enzo—"

"He's not anything of the sort," I interrupt. The darkness in me flares. Violetta touches my hand, trying to subdue me. I squeeze it back instinctively.

Magiano stops playing his lute to hold his hands up in

defense. "Just interested is all, my love," he says. "There's still much I don't know about your past."

"I've known you for the grand total of a week," I snap back. "You know nothing about me."

Magiano looks like he's ready to say something back, but he thinks better of it. Whatever barbed words he meant for me, he now swallows. He smiles a little and goes back to his lute. There's a strange twist hiding at the corner of his lips, a hint of something unhappy. I stare at him for a while, trying to puzzle it out, but it quickly disappears.

Violetta puts a hand on my shoulder. "Careful," she murmurs, frowning as she looks me over.

"He's not," I say again, softer this time. Violetta shrugs away my response, but as she does, I can tell that she has noticed something I haven't. She doesn't say anything, though.

Sergio speaks up again, and this time, his voice holds a grave note. "If they succeed in bringing Enzo back," he says, "he will not be the same. That's what the Daggers said in their conversation, isn't it? It's what apparently happened to Maeve's brother. Who knows what kind of monster he may be, with what kind of power?"

A monster, a monster, the whispers in my head chime in, parroting him.

And suddenly, I know what to do.

"They *will* succeed in bringing him back," I say. "And perhaps he will come back forever changed, a . . . monster, with fearsome powers." I pause here, then look at each of them in turn. "But in order to live, Enzo must be bound to Raffaele."

Violetta's eyes open wider as she understands my plan. She starts to smile. "How will Maeve tell the difference between the real Raffaele and a false one?"

Magiano lets out a bark of laughter, while Sergio smiles wide enough to show a glimpse of teeth. "Brilliant!" Magiano exclaims, clapping his hands together once. He leans toward me. "If we can meet them in the arena at the same time they arrive, you can disguise yourself as Raffaele."

Sergio shakes his head in admiration. "Maeve will tether Enzo to *you*. And *we* will have a reborn prince on our side. It is a good plan, Adelina. A very good one."

I smile at their enthusiasm. But deep down, something still tugs at my conscience. Memories flicker through my thoughts. I am the White Wolf, not a Dagger, and they are no longer my friends. But then I saw Gemma, and the old pull returned. I hadn't felt it since I left them. No matter how they betrayed me, I still remember Gemma offering me her necklace in friendship. No matter how often my father abused me, I still remember the day he showed me the ships at the harbor. No matter how Violetta abandoned me in childhood, I still protect her. I don't know why.

You're so stupid, Adelina, the whispers say with disdain, and I want to agree.

"You're still loyal to the Daggers," Magiano murmurs as he studies me, his joy subdued. "You miss the way things used to be. You're hesitant to break them apart like this."

My jaw tightens as I stare back at him. I hesitate. There's no question that I want revenge against the Inquisition. The burning whispers return, their hisses sharp and disapproving. *You want the crown,* they remind me. *It will be your ultimate revenge. It is why your new Elites follow you, and you cannot let them down. So why do you keep protecting the Daggers, Adelina? Do you really think they will accept you again, that they will let you have your throne? Can you not see that they are even willing to use and abuse their own former leader?*

Enzo can take his place properly on the Kenettran throne—at your side. You can rule together.

Violetta speaks up. "*Malfettos* in this country are still dying every day," she adds quietly. "We can save them."

In the silence that follows, Sergio leans forward to rest his elbows on his knees. "I don't know what you experienced when you were with the Daggers," he says. He hesitates, as if not sure whether to share this with us, but then he scowls and goes on. "But I considered them my friends, until they weren't."

Until they weren't. "How are we different?" I say, meeting Sergio's eyes. "You are a mercenary." My gaze shifts to Magiano. "What happens to our alliance if we fail to get the throne?"

Sergio gives me a bitter smile. "You think too far ahead," he says. "This is nothing personal. But at least we're not pretending with you. You and I both know what we're doing, and why. I gather mercenaries for you, and you put us to good use. You reward us as you have promised. I have no reason to betray you." He shrugs. "And I have no desire to work with the Daggers. It gives me great pleasure to know that we will take their prince from them."

"And where will your mercenaries be, when we need them?"

Sergio gives me a sidelong look and takes a swig of water. "They will be waiting for us in Estenzia. You'll see when we get there."

I lower my head and close my eye. Why shouldn't I have as much of a right to rule Kenettra—as much as Giulietta, or Enzo, or Maeve and the nation of Beldain? Raffaele is a gentle soul, but he has his darkness too. He can be a traitor, just like me, and untrustworthy. Should *he* be the one controlling Enzo? My old affection for Raffaele starts to bend, fueled by Sergio's story and my own memories, curving until it turns into bitterness. Into ambition. Into *passion*.

I think of Enzo back in the world of the living, of what it will be like to see him again. To rule, side by side. The thought of such a future makes my heart ache with longing. This is right, the two of us. I can feel it.

I pull myself upright and lean forward from my pillows. My stare lingers first on Violetta, then Magiano and Sergio. "The Daggers failed because I didn't trust them," I say. "But I have to trust *you*. We have to trust one another."

Sergio nods. There is a brief silence. "Then perhaps we need something to solidify our plans. We are a force as much as the Daggers are."

"A name, then," Magiano adds. "Names give weight, reality, to an idea. Sergio, my friend, what did the Daggers call you when you stayed with them?"

Sergio frowns a little, reluctant to remember, but still decides to answer Magiano's question. "They called me the Rainmaker."

"Ah, the Rainmaker." Magiano plucks a note in reply. "I suppose it's as good a name as any."

The Rainmaker. A beautiful name, actually, one that makes me smile. Magiano is right. Knowing Sergio's Elite name somehow makes him feel like a true Elite, a force to be reckoned with. *My* Elite. "A good name," I agree. "And what about you, Magiano?"

He shrugs, plucking a few final notes before putting his lute down. His eyes meet mine, and there, again, is that mixture in his gaze of admiration and wariness. "Magiano is already my Elite name," he says after a while. "I don't think any of us doubt the effect it has on people." Then he gives us his savage smile, and doesn't add anything more about it. He may think he knows little of my past, but I know even less of his. I want to ask him more, about where he came from, and what his real name is, but he looks away, and I let it drop again.

"What about you?" Sergio says to Violetta. She blushes a little at his expression. "No one has ever given you an Elite name."

"I . . . I was never trained in anything," Violetta replies.

She turns her eyes down in a way that only I recognize, a look that can melt hearts.

"You are a puppet master," I say to her. "For taking life, and then gifting it back." For knowing how to use and gain the affections of others.

"Puppet Master," Magiano repeats, laughing. "I like it, our sweet mistress of strings." His smile fades as his expression turns serious. "And our little wolf, who will lead us all to glory. Tell us, Adelina, how we should take an oath of loyalty. You're right. We must trust one another. So, let us do that here. Now."

I blink at him. Of all of us, I'd least expected Magiano to be the first to pledge his loyalty to my cause. Why he's followed us this long already, I'm not sure. He must see something in me—in all of this. When he notices my expression, he leans forward and brushes my chin with his fingers, tilting it up. "Why so surprised, White Wolf?" he murmurs, smiling a little. There is something in the way he says my Elite name, a secret sweetness.

Why so surprised that you are worthy?

I lift one hand and hold my palm out. A black stem gradually weaves into existence, sprouting dark thorns and spiked leaves. The stem grows until it blossoms into a dark red rose. It hovers in the center of us, not quite a solid object, still shimmering from the newness of its own creation.

"A pledge," I say, looking at each of them in turn. My stare settles on Violetta. She stares silently at me, looking straight through the rose and into my heart, as if seeing something that no one else can see. My voice hardens. "A pledge," I say again. "To drive fear into those who will confront us."

Violetta hesitates—only for a moment. "To bind us together."

"I pledge myself to the Rose Society," I begin. "Until the end of my days."

One by one, the others call out the same thing, murmurs at first that turn into firm words.

"To use my eyes to see all that happens," says Sergio.

"My tongue to woo others to our side," says Magiano, with his savage smile.

"My ears to hear every secret," Violetta continues.

"My hands," I finish. "To crush my enemies."

"I will do everything in my power to destroy all who stand in my way."

Right now, what I want is the throne. Enzo's power. A perfect revenge. And all the Inquisitors, queens, and Daggers in the world won't be able to stop me.

Raffaele Laurent Bessette

The first time Raffaele ever set foot inside the royal palace of Estenzia was when he turned eighteen. The palace had hired the Fortunata Court for a Spring Moons masquerade in their gardens. He could still remember the gardens lit by twilight, the fireflies and laughing guests, the masks, the whispers he drew wherever he went, the flood of client requests that followed.

But Raffaele has never been inside the palace itself, until now.

The first three nights in the dungeons, Raffaele sits alone against a cold, damp wall, shivering, and waits for the Inquisition to come. His manacles clink against each other. He can barely feel them against his numb hands.

On his fourth night as prisoner, the queen finally sends for him.

He goes in chains. Shackles clang together as he keeps his wrists in front of him. Inquisitors hold his arms and walk beside him. Raffaele knows the limits of his powers, but the Inquisition doesn't, and he feels a faint sense of satisfaction at their unease around him. They make their way from the dark, dank corridors of the dungeons to the ornate bath halls. Servants bathe him until he smells of rose and honey, and his hair is once again a sleek, shining river of black and sapphire.

Memories of the court come back to Raffaele, flashes of nights and mornings filled with the scent of rich soaps. As much as he despised being a helpless consort, he still finds himself thinking about the court with nostalgia, missing the golden afternoons and the musk of night lilies.

Finally, the servants dress him in a velvet robe. The Inquisitors lead him on. The halls grow more intricate as they go, until they finally reach a set of double doors blocked by four guards. The doors are painted with an image of Pulchritas emerging from the sea in all her pristine beauty. Raffaele trembles as the guards push them open now, ushering him inside the royal bedchamber. The doors close behind him with the finality of a coffin.

High, intricately carved ceilings. A canopy bed draped with sheer silks. Candlelight illuminates the entire space as Raffaele looks around the walls of the bedroom. Inquisitors stand shoulder to shoulder along each wall, their white cloaks blending into one another's. All of them have swords at their belts and crossbows hoisted in Raffaele's direction.

As he steps slowly into the chamber, the arrowheads follow his every movement.

His gaze pauses on the Inquisitor standing at the head of them all, closest to the canopied bed. Teren. The Lead Inquisitor's face tightens as he meets his eyes. Raffaele lowers his lashes, but he still notices Teren's energy stir with anger, and the way his hand grips the hilt of his sword so strongly that his knuckles turn white.

An uneasy tingling runs down Raffaele's spine. Will these soldiers stay in here all night? Will Teren stand by and watch his queen?

"You look well." Giulietta's voice comes from where she sits at a small writing desk. She rises, then walks over and stops before him. The fabric of her robes glide behind her in smooth trains of silk. *She is paler than Enzo,* Raffaele thinks.

She looks him up and down. Then she makes a spinning gesture with one finger. "Turn around," she commands. "Let me see you."

Raffaele lets a faint blush touch his cheeks, and does as she says. His velvet robe sweeps the floor, the candlelight revealing swirls and slashings of gold. His hair flows over one shoulder, straight and glossy, tied past his shoulder with a thin gold chain. A few of his sapphire strands glitter in the low light. He looks at her through eyes rimmed with black lines and shimmering silver powder.

Raffaele feels the queen's energy stir. He reaches out to tug gently on her heartstrings. He studies the shift of her emotions. He can sense her distrust and suspicion of him . . .

but underneath it, he also senses something else. A note of something calculating. And beyond that . . . a small, singular touch of desire.

"Is Her Majesty pleased with me?" he says when he turns back to her again. His eyes stay downcast.

Giulietta smiles. Her eyes roam over him. She touches his chin with one cool hand. "Hard to say. You haven't done anything yet."

He holds his breath, drawing on his familiar exercises to block out a client's unwanted advances, to escape from his body and do his duties as if he were someone else. Numbing his mind. He goes by the motions, returning Giulietta's smile with his own trained one, leaning into her touch as if he ached for more, tugging gently on her energy until her pupils dilate. He can almost fool himself.

Beside the bed, Teren looks away.

"You had quite the reputation at the Fortunata Court," Giulietta says, retracting her hand abruptly and stepping away again. She gives him a curious look. "I can see why. Rumor has it that when my brother was alive, he visited you frequently. He was fond of you, wasn't he?"

She is baiting him, toying with his emotions. *Careful.* Raffaele keeps his lashes down and his grief tightly at bay. "He enjoyed my singing and wit," he replies in a calm, humble voice.

"Your singing and wit," she echoes, a small smile on her lips. "Is that what the pleasure courts call it now?" A brief pause follows before she continues, "I've heard about your power, Messenger. That you can find other Elites like yourself. Is this true?"

"Yes, Your Majesty."

"What else can you do?"

She fears me, Raffaele thinks. He lowers his eyes and his voice. "I bring comfort and calm," he replies simply. "I soothe."

"Then give me some peace of mind, Messenger, and answer me this," she says. Her eyes harden. "Where are the other Daggers?"

Raffaele doesn't hesitate. "In Beldain."

At that, a spark of pleasure lights in Giulietta. She smiles a little and makes a sympathetic sound in her throat. "Ran away after your prince died, didn't you? If I spared your life, would you betray your fellow Daggers and lure them here?"

Raffaele keeps his eyes downcast, and doesn't answer.

Giulietta gives him a cold smile. "I didn't think so," she murmurs. She nods at her Inquisitors, and they hoist their crossbows higher. Raffaele stays very still, careful not to make a move that will set off one of the Inquisitors. His heart pounds. The queen tilts her head at him. "Are you afraid of death, Messenger?"

Raffaele can hear the breath of string against wood, the tightening of the Inquisitors' grips on their crossbows. "Of course, Your Majesty," he answers in a tight voice.

"Then tell me why I shouldn't execute you right here. What do you want, Messenger? Or did you really become so incompetent as to be captured like this? Why did the Beldish queen bring you here?"

Raffaele stays silent for a moment. "I let myself get captured," he says, "because I knew you would never agree to an audience with me otherwise. You are too clever a queen to meet Elites out in the open. This is the only way to talk to you and make you feel safe in the process."

Giulietta raises an eyebrow. "How considerate of you. And what do you need to tell me that is worth risking your life?"

"I came to ask your mercy for the *malfettos* in Kenettra."

Teren stiffens at that. Raffaele can feel the surge of his temper. *This is a good test.* How will Giulietta react to his request? What will Teren do?

Giulietta gives Raffaele an amused smile. "*Malfettos* were traitors to my crown. They tried to put my brother on *my* throne."

"But now your brother is dead," Raffaele replies. He moves closer to Giulietta and leans toward her, letting his lips brush her cheek. His eyes dart briefly to Teren. "And the leader of your Inquisition is an abomination. You are a practical queen, Your Majesty, not a radical one. I can see this quite plainly."

Giulietta searches his face, looking for evidence that Raffaele feels pain at talking about Enzo's death. She doesn't find it.

"The Daggers have always fought for security," he continues. "For survival. It is the same thing *you* fight for." His eyes harden for a moment. "Your husband was the one that the Daggers wanted gone. He was a fool—we all knew this. If you show mercy to *malfettos* in your kingdom, then what reason would we have to fight you?"

"Mercy," Giulietta muses. "Do you know what I do to those who betray me?"

"I have seen it, yes."

"So, what makes you think I will grant the Daggers or the *malfettos* mercy?"

"Because, Your Majesty," Raffaele replies, "the Dagger Society is a group of powerful Elites. We can bend the wind to our will, can control the beasts, can create and destroy." He doesn't take his eyes off her. "Wouldn't you like to have that power at your command?"

Giulietta laughs once. "And why would I trust you to pledge me your powers?"

"Because you can give us the one thing we want, the only thing we have ever fought for," Raffaele replies. "Spare your *malfettos*. Let them live peacefully, and you may gain for yourself a society of Elites."

Giulietta looks serious now. She studies Raffaele, as if searching to see whether or not he's lying. A long silence passes. Behind them, Teren's energy churns, a dark blanket across the room. He stares at Raffaele with eyes full of hate.

"This whore is a liar," Teren says in a low voice. "They will turn on you the instant—"

Giulietta holds up a lazy hand to stop him. "You told me you would find the White Wolf and bring me her head," she says over her shoulder. "And yet, I received word this morning that Adelina Amouteru overpowered a ship of my Inquisitors in Campagnia. Left them dead. Rumor has it that she has gathered supporters, that she is sending us a message of her approach. So, does that not also make *you* a liar, Master Santoro?"

Teren flushes a dark scarlet at the same time Raffaele frowns. For a moment, Raffaele's careful demeanor cracks. "Adelina is here?" he whispers.

Giulietta looks at him. "What do you know of the White Wolf?"

A hundred memories flash through Raffaele's mind. Adelina, scared and furious at the burning stake, uncertain during her testing, timid and sweet in their afternoon training sessions . . . cold and hateful in their final farewell. What is she doing back in Kenettra, and what does she want? "Only that she has betrayed enough of us," he replies. He hides the twinge of guilt in his heart. *And that I once betrayed her too.*

Teren bows his head to Giulietta. "We are hunting for her relentlessly, Your Majesty. I'll not rest until she's dead."

It is Teren who is spearheading the hatred of all malfettos, Raffaele realizes. *He is the executioner, while she is the politician. Giulietta has no reason to annihilate them now that she is queen. This is the wedge between them that can drive them apart.*

Finally, Giulietta shakes her head. She steps closer to Raffaele. "I do not grant mercy easily," she whispers as she admires his jewel-toned eyes. Raffaele hears the clicks of crossbows around the room. One wrong move from him, and he will die. Giulietta studies him a moment longer, and then turns away and waves a hand. "Take him back to the dungeons."

Inquisitors seize his arms. As Raffaele leaves the chamber, he reaches out one more time for Giulietta's energy. She is suspicious of him. But at the same time, his words have stirred a new emotion from her, something that Raffaele had not sensed earlier.

Curiosity.

Only the beautiful young Compasia dared to defy Holy Amare. Even as he drowned mankind in his floods, Compasia reached down toward her mortal lover and changed him into a swan. He flew high above the floodwaters, above the moons, and then higher still, until his feathers turned to stardust.

–"Compasia and Eratosthenes," a Kenettran folktale, various authors

Adelina Amouteru

Getting to Estenzia will require traveling by land. We can't afford another round of inspections while on board a ship, and from what we're hearing, the harbor at the capital is teeming with Inquisitors and workers, all preparing for the celebration in honor of Maeve's arrival.

Early the next morning, we set out on horseback along the road from Campagnia to Estenzia. *Two days,* says Magiano. He plays his lute the entire way, humming as he goes, and by nightfall he has composed three new songs. He creates with an intensity I haven't seen since I first met him. He seems preoccupied, but when I try asking him what's on his mind, he only smiles and plays a few measures of music for me. Eventually, I stop asking.

The first night, Sergio sits away from us. I watch him as

he looks up at the night sky, studies the sheet of stars, and closes his eyes. Only Violetta stays at his side, her attention riveted on him. Occasionally, she asks him a question, and he answers her in low tones, keeping his body turned toward her in a way that he doesn't do for us.

After a while, Violetta rises and makes her way back over to us. "He's calling the rain," she says as she approaches. She sits next to me, her side pressed against mine. I lean against her. She used to do this when we were little, I recall, as we rested together underneath the shade of trees. "Weaving it, you might say."

"Can you imitate that too?" I ask Magiano, my stare still fixed on Sergio.

"Not well, but I can strengthen him," Magiano replies. He glances over his shoulder to where Sergio still sits, then up at the sky too. He points to one glittering constellation. "See that? The shape of a swan's neck?"

I follow the curve of stars. "Isn't that Compasia's Swan?" There are dozens of folktales about this constellation. My mother's favorite was about how Amare, the god of Love, brought endless rain to the land after mankind burned down his forests, and how Compasia, the angel of Empathy, saved her gentle human lover from drowning by turning him into a swan and then putting him in the sky.

"It is," Magiano replies. "It aligns with the three moons—which I assume helps him know which direction to pull from."

Violetta's attention stays on Sergio as he works, her eyes riveted on his still posture. "It's fascinating," she says, not to anyone in particular. "He is actually gathering individual threads of moisture in the air—mist from the ocean, ice crystals high in the sky. It requires so much concentration."

I smile as I watch Violetta. She has grown more sensitive to the energy of others, to the point where Raffaele would have been proud of her. She will be a powerful weapon against the Daggers when we meet them again.

I'm about to ask her to explain how she has managed to figure out so much about Sergio's powers, but then Sergio stirs for a moment, and his movement prompts Violetta to get up and hurry back over to him. She asks him something else I can't hear, and he laughs softly.

It takes me a moment to notice Magiano watching me. He leans back on his elbows, then tilts his head curiously at me. "How did you get your marking?" he asks.

Familiar shields go up over my heart. "The blood fever infected my eye," I reply. That's all I want to say. My gaze goes to his eyes, the pupils now round and large in the darkness. "Do you see differently when your eyes slit?"

"They sharpen," Magiano says. Right after the words come out of his mouth, he contracts his pupils, giving them their catlike appearance. He hesitates. "That's not my main marking, though."

I turn my body to face him. "What *is* your main marking?"

Magiano looks at me, then leans forward and starts to pull up his shirt. Underneath the coarse white linen is smooth, brown skin, the lean lines of his stomach and back. My cheeks start to redden. The shirt slides higher, revealing all of his back. I gasp.

There it is. It's a mass of red and white flesh, scarred and raised, that covers almost his entire back. Rough ridges outline the mark. I stare at it with my mouth open. It looks like a wound that should have been fatal, something that never healed right.

"It was a large, red, flat marking," Magiano says. "The priests tried to remove it by peeling off the skin. But of course that didn't work." He smiles bitterly. "They only replaced one marking with another."

Priests. Did Magiano grow up as an apprentice in the temples? I cringe at the thought of them cutting into his flesh, tearing it back. At the same time, the whispers stir, drawn to such a painful image. "I'm glad it healed," I manage to say.

Magiano tugs his shirt down and goes back to his leaning posture. "It never really heals," he replies. "Sometimes it breaks open."

The shields on my heart start to lower. When I look back up at him, he is staring at me. "What brought you into this life?" I ask. "Why did you become . . . well . . . Magiano?"

Magiano tilts his head to the stars. He shrugs. "Why did you become the White Wolf?" he says, tossing the question back at me. Then, he sighs. "In the Sunland nations, *malfettos* are seen as links to the gods. This doesn't mean anyone worships us—it only means that the temples like to keep *malfetto* orphans in their care, believing that their presence will help them speak to the gods." He lowers his voice. "They also liked keeping us hungry. It's the same reason why a nobleman might keep his tigers on a lean diet, see? If we're hungry, we're alert, and if we're alert, we are a better link to the gods. I was always hunting for food in that temple, my love. One day, the priests caught me stealing food that was meant to be offerings to the gods. So they punished me. You can bet I ran away after that." He gestures at his back, then grins at me. "I hope the gods forgave me."

His story is so familiar. I shake my head. "You should have burned that temple to the ground," I say bitterly.

Magiano gives me a surprised look, then shrugs again. "What good would it have done?" he says.

I don't argue, but silently, I think, *It would have warned them all of what happens when you defy the children of the gods.* I shift, drawing an idle line in the dirt near my boots. "We must have different alignments," I mutter, "to think such opposite thoughts."

Magiano tilts his head again. "Alignments?"

I wave a hand in the dirt to ruin the line I'd drawn. "Oh, it's just something that Raffaele used to talk about," I reply, irritated with myself for thinking of the Daggers again. "He studies the energy of every Elite he comes across. He believes that we all align with certain gemstones and gods, and those alignments influence our powers." I take a deep breath. "I align with fear and fury. With passion. And with ambition."

Magiano nods. "Well, I can certainly see that." He smiles a little. "What do I align with?"

I look at him. "Are you asking me to guess?"

His smile widens, turning playful for an instant. "Yes, I suppose so. I'm curious what you think you know of me."

"All right." I straighten and lean back, taking in his face. The fire gives his skin a golden glow. I pretend to squint at him. "Hmm," I murmur. "Prase quartz."

"What?"

"Prase quartz. For Denarius, the angel of Greed."

Magiano throws his head back and laughs. "Fair enough. What else?"

His laughter brings a trickle of warmth to me, and I find myself savoring it. I smile back. "Kunzite. The healing gem. For the god of Time."

"Holy Aevietes?" Magiano raises an eyebrow and gives me a sly look.

"Yes." I nod. "A thief must be both patient and impatient to be good, must have impeccable timing. Right?"

"Solid reasoning." Magiano leans closer, then gives me a teasing look. His hand brushes against the edge of mine. "Go on, then."

"Diamond," I continue, unable to stop smiling. "For the goddess of Prosperity."

He draws closer. There is no hint of wildness in his eyes. His lashes shine in the light, then lower. Suddenly I am aware of his breath warm against my cheeks. "And?" he murmurs.

"And . . . sapphire." My voice fades into a whisper. "For the angel of Joy."

"Joy?" Magiano smiles, gently this time.

"Yes." I look down, overwhelmed by sudden sadness. "Because I can see so much of it in you."

A warm hand tilts my chin back up. I find myself looking into Magiano's golden eyes. He doesn't reply. Instead, he leans toward me. I hear nothing around us but the crackle of the fire.

His lips touch my cheek. It is a soft, careful touch, one that brings a lump to my throat. His lips shift to brush against mine. Then his kiss deepens in earnest, and the strings of my heart pull taut. His hand shifts from my chin to cup my face, pulling me into him. I go willingly. One of his arms encircles my waist. The kiss goes on, as if he were reaching for something within, turning firmer until I'm forced to steady myself against the ground, lest he makes me fall over. A low, sweet sound comes from his throat. I bring a hand up to the back of his neck. Aside from the deep warmth of passion, my energy stays very, very still, and for the first time, I don't miss it.

His lips finally break from mine. He brushes them against my cheeks once more, then against the line of my jaw, and then, finally, he pulls away. For a moment, all we can do is breathe. My heart thuds in my chest. The complete stillness of my energy is something I have never felt before. I am full of light. I am confused. A strange mix of guilt and wonder swims inside me.

The thought of ruling Kenettra with Enzo at my side—Enzo, who had saved me from certain death, who brought my powers out with a mere touch of his hand on my back, whose own fire awakened my ambitions—thrills me. So why am I here, this close to a boy who is not my prince? Why am I reacting in this way to his touch?

On the other side of the fire, Violetta's eyes flick momentarily away from Sergio and toward me. She catches my gaze, then tilts her head once in Magiano's direction before winking at me. She smiles a little. Suddenly, I realize why she left me alone with Magiano like this. I can't help sharing in her smile. When did my little sister become so sneaky? I'll have to ask her later how she knew that Magiano would take advantage of our moment alone. Hiding a laugh in my throat, I turn back to Magiano.

He is observing the ruined half of my face.

A cold wind hits me, and I suddenly blink away the haze of warmth and amusement that had enveloped me just moments earlier. My defenses go up. I lean away, and an edge returns to my voice. "Why do you look?" I mutter.

I half expect Magiano to tease me, spitting back one of his sarcastic phrases. But he doesn't smile. "We are drawn to stories," he says in a soft voice, "and every scar carries one." He lifts a hand and places his palm gently against the ruined side of my face, covering the scar.

I look down, embarrassed now. Instinctively, I reach up to brush some of my hair over my face—only to remember that I no longer have long locks.

"Hiding it makes you more beautiful," Magiano says. Then he takes his hand away, exposing my scar again. "But revealing it makes you *you*." He nods at me. "So wear it proudly."

I don't know what to say to that. "We all have our stories," I reply after a moment.

"You are the first I've ever met who is willing to take on the Inquisition," he continues. "I've heard plenty of idle threats in my lifetime against those soldiers, and made plenty myself. But you *meant* what you said, when you wanted revenge against them."

For an instant, I see an illusion of blood dripping down my hands, staining the ground. It is Enzo's blood, and it is bright scarlet. "I suppose I'm just tired of them being the ones standing over us, as we beg in vain for our lives."

Magiano gives me a smile that looks sweet . . . and sad. "Now you are the one who can make them beg."

"Do I frighten you?" I ask softly.

He seems to think about that. After a while, he leans back and looks skyward. "I don't know," he replies. "But I do know that I may never meet another like you again."

His expression reminds me of Enzo, and all of a sudden, that is who I see before me, my prince who mourned his own lost love. He is close enough now that I can see the slashes of color in his irises.

He is not Enzo, I remind myself. But I don't want him to be. With Enzo, my energy yearned for his power and ambition, all too happy to let him take me into the darkness. But with Magiano . . . I am able to smile, even to laugh. I am able to sit here and lean back and point out the constellations.

Magiano glances at me again, as if he could tell who is on my mind. That strange little twist reappears at the edge of his lips, an unhappy note that mars his joy. It is there, and then it is gone.

I want to say something to him, but I don't know what. Instead, he smiles, and I swallow, mimicking him. After a while, we both return to admiring the stars, trying to ignore the kiss that lingers in the air between us.

Dear Father, did you receive my gift? Please let me come home.
I no longer recognize this place, and my friends
have become my enemies.

—Letter from Princess Lediana to her father, the King of Amadera

Adelina Amouteru

The next day, clouds start to gather in low blankets along the horizon. They build in height as the day goes on. By the time afternoon starts shifting to dusk, and the dirt and grasses of the Kenettran countryside make way for the first rivers of outer Estenzia, the sky is covered in a thick layer of gray, making twilight look more like midnight. There is a spark of lightning in the air, something sharp and tense that promises a storm. The tension grows as we approach the city, until the sky finally opens and a cold, heavy rain starts to drench the land.

I pull the cloak lower over my head. Wind whips at my back.

"How long will this storm last?" Violetta calls out at Sergio through the rain.

Sergio rides up beside us. "At least a day. I can never really tell. Once I set them in motion, they take on a life of their own that not even I can stop."

We all pause as we reach the first small village clustered outside the walls of Estenzia. Our chances of running into Inquisitors after this point are high. I swing down from my horse, pat its neck, and lead it toward the buildings. Behind me, the others do the same. Time to give up our steeds and go on foot.

Or, more specifically, go by canal.

We leave our horses tied in front of a tavern, and then continue on our way. The village gives way to another, bigger cluster of homes, and then soon the walls fencing in Estenzia loom out of the mist of rain, black silhouettes against a gray sky. Lanterns start flickering to life in the villages behind us. My weathered boots squish against the soaked ground. My hooded cloak is already useless against the rain, and we keep them on only to hide our features. I'd rather save my energy for when we are close enough to the city itself.

Here, the land starts splintering into fragments, disjointed islands clustered close together and connected by canals. Already, the storm has started to flood some of the canals, washing untended gondolas up to the shores. Magiano stops us here, where several gondolas have piled on top of one another at a canal's corner. Dark canvas covers their tops, and their oars snap back and forth haphazardly in the current, absent their gondoliers.

"Lately, Estenzia has kept her canals locked in order to control the passage of cargo," he says in a low voice. "But in a storm this bad, the canals in the city will flood too quickly if they don't pull up some of their gates. They have to help the water drain." He nods to the piled gondolas.

This is our chance to get into the city.

As the boys flip the first gondola over and Sergio helps Violetta into it, I stare at the city walls. The rain blurs them so that they look like little more than a fog of gray—but even in this downpour, I can make out the dense rows of dilapidated shelters huddled underneath the walls.

"What is that?" I ask Magiano, nodding toward the shelters.

He wipes water out of his eyes. "*Malfetto* slave camps, of course," he replies.

My heart seizes. *Malfetto* slave camps? The camps wrap all the way around the wall, disappearing only when it curves out of our line of sight. So, this is what Teren has been busy doing. I wonder what kind of slave labor he has forced upon the *malfettos,* and how long he will allow them to live. There is no question that he is only biding his time. A dark tide swells in my stomach, bringing a scowl to my lips.

I will fix this, once I rule Kenettra.

"Come on," Magiano urges me, snapping me out of my thoughts. He beckons me into the back of the gondola with Violetta. As I accept his outstretched hand, his eyes meet mine and hold me there for a heartbeat, unsure. His hand tightens. I cling to him, the heat rising fast in my cheeks. The kiss that had lingered between us last night is still here, and I don't know what to do with it.

Magiano leans closer, as if about to take that kiss again. But he stops a hairsbreadth from my lips. His eyes lower, gentle for a moment. "Watch your step," he says, guiding me into the boat.

My response is an incoherent murmur. I lower myself in carefully. The boat dips in the water as I crawl underneath the dark canvas and lie in the boat's belly. It is already rapidly filling with water, but I'm able to keep myself up enough to breathe. Violetta's boots are a foot away from mine, so that both of our heads are facing the ends of the gondola.

"When we get close enough," I say up to him, "I'll veil us. Stay close and keep an eye out for the rest of us."

Magiano nods. Then he and Sergio give my gondola a push, and the boat jerks forward, taking me with it.

The storm intensifies as we draw closer to Estenzia. I stay low in the boat, keeping my head out of the water. I can barely see anything but the stone lining the edges of the canals, but now and then I get a glimpse of the approaching walls. Ahead of us is the start of the camps. Now we are close enough to see the dots of white scattered throughout the rows of crumbling tents—Inquisitors, their cloaks weighed down in the storm, hurrying back and forth along the camps' dirt paths. I risk a glance behind me. There is a long distance between our gondola and the one behind us. If everything went well, Magiano and Sergio should be following us. I reach out with my energy, searching for the beating hearts of excitement, anticipation, and fear in them.

I find them. And I pull.

A net of invisibility weaves across me first, erasing me from the gondola and melting me into the wet wood, the pooling water in the boat's belly, and the dark canvas. I do the same to Violetta, and then I grit my teeth and reach for the others behind me. It is an imperfect illusion. I can't know exactly what the inside of their gondola looks like, and as a result, I can only make an estimate. If Inquisitors look too carefully into their gondola, they will see the figures of two hiding Elites underneath the texture of the boat's bottom.

It's the best I can do.

As we draw near the camps, Inquisitors come into sharp view along the banks of the canal. One of them notices our gondolas floating with the current toward the city walls. "Sir," he calls to one of his companions. "More stray boats. Should we pull them ashore?"

Another Inquisitor peers at my gondola first. I cringe, reminding myself to keep a tight hold on our illusions.

"Empty," the second Inquisitor says. He makes a distracted gesture with his hand and starts to turn away. "Ah, just let them float by and come help me with these *malfettos*. The gondoliers can find their boats piled somewhere in the canals after this storm's over."

I can't move much without risking detection, but as the

Inquisitors turn away, I lift my head enough to see down a path among the shelters. At the far end, I catch a glimpse of disheveled, frightened *malfettos* lowering their heads as the soldiers pass them. The sight of them makes my stomach churn. For a moment, I wish I could do what Raffaele does.

We keep moving. The walls loom closer, until I can see their individual stones washed dark by the rain. By now, night has fallen completely. Aside from the few scattered torches and lanterns holding up against the rain, I can hardly see anything. In front of me, Violetta stirs underneath our shield of invisibility.

"The gate is up," she says back to me.

I look ahead. The gate is indeed drawn up, allowing the canal to swell, and beyond it I can see the start of inner Estenzia, the cobblestone streets and archways of buildings. The city's celebrations are subdued by the rain, and broken paper lanterns litter the streets. Brightly colored flags hang limp and soaking from balconies.

Two Inquisitors walk where the canal meets the gate, their eyes trained on the water, but aside from them, we are alone.

We are not as lucky with this second pair of Inquisitors. One of them leans over the edge of the canal as we sail by. His boot stops our gondola with a jerk. I bite my tongue in frustration. In the darkness and rain, he can't see that the gondola looks empty. He nods to his partner. Behind us, the second gondola carrying Magiano and Sergio comes to a stop.

"Check that one," the first says to his partner. Then he

turns back to ours, draws his sword, and points it down into the boat—right at Violetta's crouched body. He lifts the blade. Violetta tries to press herself away, but it will be useless if he stabs down all along the length of the boat.

Behind us, the second Inquisitor lifts his blade at the other gondola.

I yank back my blanket of invisibility. We suddenly come into view.

The Inquisitor pauses for an instant as he sees eyes blinking back at him from where moments ago there had been nothing. "What in—" he blurts out.

I narrow my eye and lash out at him. Threads of energy whip around his body, the illusion hooking into his skin and pulling taut. At the same time, Violetta leaps out of the boat and knocks the Inquisitor's sword from his hand. It clatters to the ground. The man lets out a half shriek, but I cut it off as my threads tighten around him. The energy in me surges with delight as the man's confusion changes into terror. His eyes bulge, filling with pain.

Behind us, Magiano leaps out of their boat to attack the second Inquisitor.

The first Inquisitor clutches his chest and falls to his knees. He reaches for the sword on the ground, but I grab it first. As I move, I catch a glimpse of Violetta's face. Her lips are set in a grim line. I half expect her to cower in the darkness, or reach out with her powers to stop me, but instead, she stoops down and grabs the Inquisitor's cloak. She yanks it, forcing him to topple backward. He gasps in pain.

The world around me closes in—for a moment, all I can see is midnight and my victim. I grit my teeth, lift his sword, and plunge it into his chest.

The man trembles on the blade. Blood sprays from his mouth. I glance to my side to see Sergio with his arm wrapped tightly around the second Inquisitor's throat. Sergio squeezes hard. His Inquisitor's arms grapple frantically for him, but Sergio hangs grimly on. I breathe in the terror of the struggling man.

The Inquisitor I stabbed stops trembling. I close my eye, lift my head, and take a deep breath. The metallic scent of blood fills the air, mixing with the wetness of the rain—it is all so familiar. When I open my eye again, I'm no longer looking down at the Inquisitor. I'm looking down at my father's ruined corpse, his ribs smashed in by his horse's hooves, his blood staining the cobblestones—

And I'm not horrified. I look at it, indulging in the darkness around me, feeding me, strengthening me, and I realize that I'm happy I killed him. Truly happy.

A hand touches my shoulder. My face jerks around to see who it is, and my energy surges, eager to hurt again.

Violetta jumps back. "It's me," she says. She holds a palm out, as if that might stop me. Her own power touches mine, and I can feel it pushing me back hesitantly, threatening to take my power away. "It's me, it's me."

The snarl gradually fades from my lips. I look back down at the body before me, now no longer my father but the Inquisitor I killed. Magiano and Sergio hurry to my side, leaving their Inquisitor lying lifeless in the shadows. Violetta stares at the two dead men. Her expression is numb.

My moment of bloodlust has passed, but the darkness it brought lingers, feeding the little whispers in my head that have suddenly become deafening. *Quiet,* I hiss back at them, until I realize I say the word out loud.

"We'd better move. Now." Magiano glances over his shoulder, then hops over the Inquisitor's body to glance down both sides of the canal. "We won't be alone here for long."

I pull myself up to my feet. I wash my hands in the rising waters of the canal. Then I hurry after them. Up in the pouring sky, a haunting cry echoes over the city, followed shortly by another. A pair of baliras are passing over the city, although in the night, all I can see are their silhouettes, their massive, translucent wings covering up the sky. If Gemma were with us, she could have gotten us onto their backs—we could have flown over the city and found a way down somewhere. I could have avoided killing those two men. It's not that I wanted them dead, after all. It's that we had no other way. I repeat this over and over again to myself. Had it been this easy for me, when I ended Dante's life? When I killed the Night King? When I watched Enzo die? When I nodded my approval to Sergio to execute the Inquisitors on the ship?

No. *But this time, it was.*

I look at my Roses, then step forward so that I lead the way. I start to weave a curtain of invisibility over us again. As the baliras pass overhead, I turn us in the direction of the Estenzian palace. My thoughts transition from the Inquisitors' deaths to the task before us. If the Beldish queen makes her move tonight, then I have to find Raffaele before she does.

Already, I'm starting to forget the face of the man I killed.

Raffaele Laurent Bessette

It takes another week before Queen Giulietta sends for him again. This time, when he visits her private chambers, Teren and several of his guard stand outside the doors instead of within. Raffaele looks briefly at him as he walks past. The energy churning in Teren is black with rage and jealousy, and the feeling makes Raffaele dizzy. He turns his eyes back down, but he can still feel the Lead Inquisitor's stare burning into his back as the chamber doors open and close for him.

Inside the chambers, Inquisitors still line the walls. Queen Giulietta sits at the edge of her bed, her hair down in long, dark waves, her hands folded neatly into her lap. The sheer drapes hanging on each side of the bed are also down tonight, half drawn in anticipation of sleep. She watches him as the soldiers guide him into the center of the chamber, then leave him to stand there alone. He hesitates, then steps closer and lowers himself into a kneel before her.

For a moment, neither of them says anything. *The queen's emotions are different tonight,* Raffaele thinks. Calmer, less suspicious, more calculating. *She wants something.*

"They say that you were the greatest consort ever to grace the courts of Kenettra," Giulietta finally says. "You fetched a virgin price that had the courts talking for weeks." She leans back on her arms and regards him thoughtfully. "I've also heard that you are something of a scholar, that your patrons frequently gifted you books and quills."

Raffaele nods. "I am, Your Majesty."

Giulietta's lips curve into a smile. When he looks up at her, she motions for him to rise. "You certainly look and speak as beautifully as they say." She straightens then, and approaches him. Raffaele stays very still as she draws near. Her fingers go up to the gold string near the collar of his robes, then tugs it loose, exposing a bit of his skin.

Raffaele's eyes dart to the Inquisitors lining the walls, their crossbows still fixed on him. When Giulietta sits down on the edge of the bed again and pats the spot beside her, he steps closer. "I've already told you what I wish for, Your Majesty," he says in a gentle voice. "Tell me, then, what *you* desire. What can I do for you?"

Giulietta smiles again as she lays her head down on her pillow. "You say that if I grant mercy to all *malfettos,* you and your Daggers will do my bidding as a part of my army."

Giulietta nods. "I've decided I will grant you that, as long as I am satisfied with what you can do. Tomorrow, I will order my Inquisitors to begin bringing our *malfettos* back into the city. In return, I want you to summon your Daggers. And I want you to fulfill your end of the bargain." Her stare hardens for a moment. "Remember that I can easily bring my wrath down on the *malfettos* of this city if you fail to follow through on your word."

Raffaele's smile returns. So, it is as he suspected. Giulietta's "hatred" for the *malfettos* is not the same as Teren's. Teren despises *malfettos* because he believes them to be demons. Evil, cursed. But Giulietta . . . Giulietta despises *malfettos* only when they are in her way. She will use them as much as they can benefit her. *Very good.* He bows his head in a perfect imitation of submission. "Then we are yours to command."

Giulietta nods at his expression. She stretches out on her bed and looks at him through a halo of dark curls. As beautiful as Enzo was handsome. Raffaele sees for a moment what must have drawn Teren to her. It is hard to believe that, behind the dark lashes and small, sweet, rosy mouth, is a princess who had once tried—even as a child—to poison her brother.

"Well, my consort," she murmurs. "Prove your reputation to me."

In the early hours before dawn, Raffaele emerges from the queen's chambers and into the long shadows of the hall.

Inquisitors still stand guard on either side of the door, and two of them move away to walk alongside him.

"The queen has ordered you moved to more comfortable quarters," one of the Inquisitors says as they walk.

Raffaele nods, but his eyes stay on the shadows in the hall. Teren is still here—he can feel his Elite energy seething in the darkness, waiting for him to approach. Raffaele slows his walk. Although the shadows cover nearly everything, he can sense that Teren must be standing just a few feet away.

He will attack you. Raffaele's instincts suddenly flare up—he knew this would happen. He whirls in the direction of the queen's chambers, then calls out, "Your Majesty!"

It's all he manages to say before a blur of white materializes from the shadows and seizes him by the collar of his robe. Raffaele feels himself lifted nearly off his feet—his back slams so hard against the wall that the impact knocks all the breath from his chest. Stars explode across his vision. Somewhere comes the sound of a blade through air, and an instant later, cold metal presses hard against his throat. A hand clamps over his mouth.

Teren's face comes into focus before him. His pale irises seem to pulse in the darkness. "Pretty little peacock," he snarls as Raffaele struggles for breath. He gestures for the other two Inquisitors to pin him against the wall. "What lies did you tell the queen this time? What demonic spells are you weaving?"

Raffaele returns Teren's glare with his own quiet one. "I am no more a demon than you are."

Teren's gaze hardens. "Let's see how often the queen will ask for you after I carve the skin off your face."

Raffaele smiles back. His smile is sharp, a blade of silk and grace. "You fear me more than I fear you."

Teren's eyes flash. He nods to the Inquisitors to hold him tightly, and then he hoists his dagger higher. He smiles in a way that prickles Raffaele's skin.

"*Stop.*"

The queen's command rings out sharply down the hall, and Teren freezes. Raffaele turns to see Giulietta heading out of her chambers with soldiers at her back, her face cold and distant. She narrows her eyes at Teren. Immediately, the two Inquisitors pinning Raffaele to the wall release him, and everyone falls into a hurried kneel. Raffaele gulps as pain continues to lance down his back.

"Your solution to everything, Master Santoro," she says when she reaches them, "is to bite."

He opens his mouth as she approaches him, but before he can say anything, Giulietta reaches out for the gold clasp holding his Inquisition cloak in place. She flicks the clasp open, then gives the cloak one vicious yank. The cloak falls from his shoulders, pooling at his feet.

The sign of a demotion.

Teren's eyes snap open in shock. "Your Majesty—" he begins.

Giulietta just gives him an icy look. "I warned you what would happen if you ever ignored my commands again."

"But I—"

"I ordered Raffaele to be taken back to his new chambers. Why did you disobey me?"

Teren bows his head in what looks like shame. "Your Majesty," he replies. "I apologize. I—"

"I've heard enough of your apologies," Giulietta interrupts. She folds her arms. "When dawn arrives, you are to take a patrol and report to the southern cities immediately."

"You . . . ," Teren says, his words trailing off as realization hits him. "You are sending me away? Out of Estenzia?"

Giulietta arches an eyebrow at him. "You are asking me to repeat myself?" she says.

"Your Majesty, please." Teren takes a step closer to her. "Everything I do—*everything* I have ever done—is to protect your crown. You are the one true queen. There are times I may act rashly, and I deserve to be punished, but I do it in the name of the crown."

"I expect you to relinquish your quarters and your armor by tomorrow." Giulietta gives him a look of disinterest. This, Raffaele thinks, more than anything, makes Teren wince. "You will set out with several patrols by tomorrow evening, to secure my rule in the south. If you truly care for me, you will obey this order. Do you understand?"

Teren's voice hardens. "Your Majesty," he says. "I am your best fighter. I am your *champion*."

"You are useless if you ignore my commands."

Teren grabs Giulietta's hands. His voice lowers, turns tender. "Giulietta," he murmurs. Raffaele watches in fascination. Addressing the queen by name? He has heard plenty about their affair, but this is the first time he has ever seen it on display. Teren bends down toward her, close enough for his lips to brush her cheek. "You will kill me if you send me away."

Giulietta turns her face and pulls away, separating herself from him. She tilts her chin up. Her eyes are ice cold. Raffaele watches Teren's expressions shift on his face. The young Inquisitor is realizing, for the first time, that he may be unable to sway her mind. Teren stares at Raffaele, then turns desperately to Giulietta.

"I *love* you," he suddenly says, his voice urgent. "I've loved you since I was a boy. I would kill a thousand men for you."

"I don't need you to kill a thousand men, Master Santoro," Giulietta says. "I need you to listen to me." She gives him a look that borders on pity. "But you were always an abomination. You always knew, Master Santoro, that this could never last."

"It's him, isn't it?" Teren snaps, pointing in Raffaele's direction. "He has hypnotized you. It is his *power*, don't you understand?"

Giulietta's eyes harden at that. "Do you insult me?"

Teren swallows, then continues, "It's true that I am unworthy of you. But you forgave my abomination in return for my loyalty—and I will carry that loyalty with me to my grave. Please, Giulietta—"

Giulietta holds up a hand, and the Inquisitors behind her tighten their grips on their crossbows. Teren stands with his shoulders hunched. "You have until tomorrow night to leave Estenzia. This is a command. Do this, Teren, if you truly love me."

Tears well in Teren's eyes. Raffaele grimaces, feeling the Inquisitor's dark energy twist in the familiar pain of heartbreak. "Giulietta . . . ," Teren whispers, but he says it this time in defeat.

Finally, he bows his head. He falls to one knee before her. "Yes, Your Majesty," he says. He stays there until Giulietta dismisses him, and then he storms out. His cloak remains on the floor.

Giulietta watches him go for a moment before she turns back to Raffaele. "Go," she says. "Gather your Daggers. Remember that if you go back on your word, I will make sure the *malfettos* suffer for it."

Raffaele gives her a bow. *The capital weakens. We close in.* "Yes, Your Majesty."

Sometimes, love can bloom like the tiny flower hidden in the tree's shadow, found only by those who know where to look.

–The Courting of a Prince of Beldain, *by Callum Kent*

Adelina Amouteru

Enzo died in the capital's arena. That is where the Daggers will go to revive him, and so that is where I now go with my Roses.

Violetta and I wait in the shadows of the arena's lowest pits, where the underground tunnels let baliras into and out of the arena's center lake. Here, where enormous wooden gates and levers cast strange shadows down the tunnel, we can hear little more than the hollow churning of water and the occasional squeaking of rats. Sergio and Magiano stay elsewhere in the arena, on alert for any signs of approaching Daggers. A full day and night pass. Lightning forks over the sky, and the storm continues on, raging relentlessly in a tirade that Sergio doesn't have the ability to stop.

On the second night, Magiano drops in and shakes water

out of his hair before he sits down beside us with a sigh. "Not yet," he mutters, tearing into a wet piece of bread and cheese.

"What if the Daggers don't come?" Violetta whispers to me as she blows her warm breath against her hands.

I don't answer right away. What if they don't? They are already late, according to the plans we'd overheard from Gemma. Perhaps Raffaele failed in his mission at the palace, and the queen had him executed. Perhaps the Daggers were captured. But then we would have heard something, I'm sure of it—news like that would never stay secret for long. "They'll come," I whisper back. I untie my cloak, drape it around both of us, and we gather it around ourselves as tightly as we can. My toes feel cold and damp inside my boots.

I wish you were here, Enzo, I add to myself. A memory returns of the heat his touch could bring, the warmth that he could send bubbling through me on a cold night. I shiver. Soon, he *will* be back. Can I bear that?

Magiano sighs loudly and leans back against the canal wall. He sits close enough to me that I can feel the warmth coming off his body, and I find myself savoring it. "Sergio says you have more mercenaries gathering behind you. Why don't we retreat to somewhere outside of Estenzia and mobilize whatever allies you've gathered? Then we can figure out a way to strike at Teren and the queen when they least expect it." He gives me a wry look. "Do we *really* need to be here?"

I huddle deeper into my cloak so that Magiano can't see

me blushing. He has been uncharacteristically moody today. "Enzo is an Elite," I say to Magiano, something I've repeated several times in the last day.

"Yes. And also the former leader of the Daggers. How do you know this will work? What if something goes wrong?"

A part of me wonders whether he is acting like this because of what Enzo used to mean to me. What he *still* means to me. And Magiano—does he stir those same feelings? Even as I lean in the direction of his warmth, I'm not sure. "I *don't* know," I reply. "But I'd rather not risk letting a chance go."

He tightens his lips for a moment. "The Beldish queen has no ordinary power," he says softly. "This is tampering with the gods themselves, bringing the dead back to life. You are putting yourself directly in that path, you realize."

It's almost as if he's trying to tell me, *I'm worried about you.* And suddenly I want so much to hear those words that I almost ask him to say them. But my desire is quickly replaced by irritation at his concern. "You've gone this far with us," I whisper. "We'll get you your money, don't worry."

Surprise flashes in Magiano's eyes . . . followed by disappointment. Then he shrugs, leans away from me, and goes back to eating his bread and cheese. "Good," he mutters.

I make myself smaller. It was a spiteful thing for me to say, but so is his open doubt over whether or not we should be here for Enzo. I watch him from my cloak, wondering whether he will glance in my direction and give me a hint of what his thoughts are, but he doesn't look my way again.

Beside me, Violetta stirs. She blinks while facing the arena's center, then tilts her head. Magiano and I both still as we watch her. "Is it them?" I whisper to my sister.

Before Violetta can respond, a silhouette drops down behind us with a silent thud. I jump to my feet. It's Sergio.

He hefts a blade in one hand. "I spy our favorite Dagger," he says with a smile.

Raffaele Laurent Bessette

As he leaves the palace, Raffaele presses his hands together over and over, but he can't seem to stop their trembling. A wide hood covers him, partially shielding him from the storm. He looks over his shoulder. Inquisitors escorted him as far as the palace gates, but now that he has reached the main streets, they stay behind and allow him to have his freedom.

He blinks water from his eyes, then hurries down the streets until he melts into the shadows. Teren will leave the palace tomorrow, no doubt about it—exactly the goal Maeve had set for him when bringing him into the palace. Now the city loses their near-invincible Lead Inquisitor, and the queen loses a powerful bodyguard. The Beldish navy draws closer.

Still, Raffaele frowns as he walks. Teren is not gone yet, and now he is as furious as a wounded beast. No doubt there are still soldiers watching him right now. He walks in a wide arc, far from the arena where he knows he must end up. *I have to hide quickly.* Out here, the queen cannot protect him from Teren's wrath. If the Lead Inquisitor finds him, he will kill him. Raffaele searches for any signs of Teren's energy nearby, then changes his course, careful to leave the signals he had agreed upon with the other Daggers.

A deep line in the mud with his boot, clearly visible from the air. A whistle, nearly lost in the storm's roar, mimicking a lonely falcon. A glass ring on his finger that reflects the lightning whenever it flashes.

He hopes Lucent is watching from somewhere high, and that she has raised the alarm.

Moments later, he calls on his memory of the underground maze of catacombs beneath the city. He makes his way through a labyrinth of alleys before finally vanishing through a small, unmarked door.

The sound of pouring water echoes everywhere down in the tunnels. Raffaele keeps one hand gripped tightly around his cloak, and the other against the wall. Water soaks his boots and keeps the steps dangerously slick.

"North, south, west, east," he murmurs to himself as he goes. "The Piazza of Three Angels, the Canterino Canal, the statue to Holy Sapientus." The landmarks appear in his mind in a map. He inches along in the blackness, completely blind. Glittering threads of energy flicker all around him, connecting everything to everything else, however faintly. He reaches out and tugs gently on them, feeling the way the energy of the air connects to the walls, to the aboveground. If there were even a bit of light, he knows he would see his breath rising in clouds before him, warming the icy air.

"Left. Right. Right. Straight."

The labyrinth continues to branch as he goes farther down. He has never been here during such heavy rain before. Sometimes, water sloshes up to his knees. *If parts of the tunnels are flooded, I might trap myself in a corner and drown.* Raffaele forces the thought away and replaces it with a still surface, a calm to keep the panic at bay. He keeps moving, relying only on his hand on the wall and the map of threads in his mind. How did such a storm like this come so suddenly?

Left. Left. Straight. Right.

Abruptly, Raffaele pauses. Frowns. It lasts only an instant, a fleeting moment of someone's energy from the surface. He waits for a second, reaching tentatively out with his own power. *Strange. And familiar.*

But the feeling has already faded away, and the storm returns in full force.

Raffaele hesitates awhile longer, until the water forces him to continue moving again. He shakes his head. The threads of energy in the storm are overwhelming in their power—they must be distracting him. Or perhaps it is the thought of what he is about to participate in, what may happen in mere hours.

The thought of Enzo returning.

Raffaele pauses again, steadying himself against the wet

walls, and closes his eyes. Again, he thinks of the calm surface. He stills, then continues on.

Finally, he reaches a spot in the darkness where the tunnel ends in a wall. Beyond it is an overwhelming pressure, the unmistakable energy of countless drops of water all tied to one another, the lake in the center of the Estenzian arena. Raffaele pauses, then heads back several paces until he finds an uneven set of stones, the hands of Moritas posted at the end of every catacomb path, and then the tiny, winding steps beside them that lead up to the surface.

He emerges into the dark recesses of the arena's enormous canals, but after so long in complete blackness, the night almost seems bright. The sounds of the storm are suddenly deafening again. Raffaele gathers his soaked cloak tighter, then walks on silent feet up the canal's steps to the surface.

He is alone here. The other Daggers are nowhere in sight. He folds his hands into the sleeves of his cloak, shivers, and reaches out with his energy to sense whether or not other Elites are close.

Then, he frowns. Something stirs in the air, strings pulled taut.

They *are* here. At least, someone is.

The energy draws closer. It is a dark, familiar energy, and Raffaele finds himself resisting the urge to pull away from it. He had cringed when he first felt Maeve's energy on the day he met her, had shuddered at the connection she drew to the Underworld. He looks down the arena's dark tunnels that lead to the center's lake, then out into the storm. She must have just arrived. Now Raffaele can hear footsteps. They are faint and light, the steps of someone slender. He turns all the way to face the approaching energy, then folds his hands before him. The footsteps echo faintly down the tunnel. Gradually, he makes out the silhouette of a figure approaching him. The energy grows stronger. Now he can tell that the figure is indeed a girl.

She stops a few feet away from him. Along with the scent of rain, he also detects the copper smell of blood. Raffaele eyes her warily. In the darkness, he can't quite make out her face. Her energy is strange, too, familiar in its darkness. *Too familiar.* It is the unmistakable alignment to the Underworld, to Fear and Fury, to Death.

"Are you hurt, Your Majesty?" he says in a low voice. "Did anyone follow you?" If Maeve was injured in the process of getting here, she might not have the strength to pull Enzo from the Underworld. Worse, she might have been attacked by an Inquisitor, and word of her presence here has leaked out. Where are the other Daggers?

But Maeve doesn't say a word. She reaches up to her hood, lifts it, and pulls it back. The shadows disappear from her face.

Raffaele freezes.

The girl is not Maeve. She has a scarred half of her face where her eye should have been. Her lashes are pale, and the locks of her hair are bright silver tonight, cut short and scraggly. She stares at Raffaele with a bitter smile. For a moment, it seems as if she were glad to see him. Then the emotion disappears, replaced with something wicked. She holds a hand out toward him, weaves a web of threads around him, and twists hard.

"I'm sorry, Raffaele," Adelina says.

Once every ten years, the three moons all fall under the world's shadow and turn scarlet, bleeding with the blood of our fallen warriors.

—The New Atlas to the Moons, *by Liu Xue You*

Adelina Amouteru

There are no moons tonight to fill the Estenzian arena with silver light. Instead, the lake in the arena's center, fed by canals, is black and churning with the storm's fury.

The last time I stood in this arena, I was a spectator in the audience, looking on as Enzo stepped forward to challenge Teren to a duel. They fought here. And it ended with me hovering over Enzo's dying body, sobbing, trying over and over again to hurt Teren in any way I could.

Now the arena is empty. No cheering crowds in this midnight storm. The Kenettran flags up above flap frantically in the wind—several of them have been ripped completely away by the force of the rain. And I am here not as myself, but as Raffaele.

The expression of agony on his face.

The sweat beading his brow.

His anguished cry, erased by the storm's thunder.

The whispers echo in my mind, delighted at what I've done.

I follow Maeve along the stone path. Water crashes against either side of the walkway, soaking the hems of my robes. My heart pounds furiously—the energy of the storm is full of darkness, and when I look up, I can almost see the weave of threads glittering between the clouds, connecting the rain to the black sky, the threat of approaching lightning. Somewhere in the arena, Sergio and Magiano are poised to strike. From down in the arena's lake come the occasional, muffled calls of baliras. An enormous, fleshy head emerges from the churning water for a moment, then goes under again, as if the creatures of the Underworld have come to watch us too.

Maeve doesn't look back at me, which is just as well. A gust of wind blows the hood of her cloak back, revealing black and gold hair before she pulls the hood back on again. I admire her marking. In fact, I've done nothing but obsess over her energy. She is the first Elite I can actually *sense*—there is a darkness in her power that reminds me of myself, something deep and black, connecting her to the world of the dead. I wonder whether she ever has nightmares about the Underworld in the way that I do.

The feeling of being watched hits me, and the hairs on the back of my neck rise. I remind myself to stay focused on my disguise. Even though I can't see them, the other Daggers must be scattered around the arena, watching, along with anyone else who came with Maeve. So far, no one has raised an alarm over my appearance.

Raffaele's pained face.

Images flash before me of my confrontation with Raffaele. He didn't even try to fight back. He knew he was defenseless against me alone, that his power was useless against mine. He resisted well, I have to admit, much longer than most—he can see the reality behind my games. At least, for a little while.

But I didn't kill him. I couldn't bear to do it. I'm not sure why. Maybe a part of me still wishes we could be friends, still remembers the sound of his voice when he sang my mother's lullaby for me. Maybe I couldn't bear to kill a creature as beautiful as he is.

Why do you care? the whispers sneer.

"Stay close, Messenger," Maeve calls over her shoulder. My steps quicken. The damp edges of my robes catch on my feet, threatening to trip me. *You must stay calm,* I tell myself. I slow to a more dignified walk, something more befitting a high-class consort. Raffaele's old lessons run through my mind.

We reach the center of the platform. I find myself staring numbly at the ground here. It had once been covered in Enzo's blood, dripping a pattern on the ground from Teren's sword, the dark stain spilling out around the prince—*my* prince—as he lay dying. I can still feel my hands coated with it. But the bloodstains are gone now. Rain and the churning lake have washed the stones clean again, as if no death had happened here.

He is not your *prince,* the whispers remind me. *He never was. He was only a boy, and you'd do well to remember that.*

Maeve stops in the center. She turns to face me for the first time. Her eyes are cold, and her cheeks are streaked with water. "Did he die here?" she says, gesturing to the ground beneath her boots.

Strange, how I can remember the exact spot, right down to the stones. "Yes."

Maeve looks up and around the arena's top row of seats. "Remember the signal," she tells me, holding two arms up and out to her sides. "If you see any of the others give this signal, you must take me out of the arena. Do not waste your time waking me from my trance."

I bow my head in the best imitation of Raffaele I can do. "Yes, Your Majesty," I reply. I pause to look at both ends of the arena's stone path. Maeve's brothers are watching me down here too. I can see them now, barely noticeable in the night, and now and then I can see the gleam of their arrow tips fixed on me.

Maeve pulls the hood from her face. Rain soaks her hair. She takes a deep breath, almost as if she were afraid of what will happen next. She *is* afraid, I realize, because I can feel the fear building in her heart. In spite of everything, I recall that she has only ever brought her brother back from the dead. We are all venturing into strange territory.

"Come closer," she commands me.

I do as she says. She gives me a long look for the first time, her eyes lingering long enough that I start to wonder whether she can see through my disguise. She pulls a knife from her belt.

Maybe she does know. And now she will kill me. I lean hesitantly away, ready to defend myself.

But Maeve instead beckons me forward again. She reaches out and grabs a lock of my soaked hair. In one deft move, she slices a length of the lock off.

"Give me your palm," she says next.

I hold one hand out at her, palm facing up. She murmurs for me to brace myself, digs the blade into my flesh, and makes a small, deep slice. I flinch. My blood wells against her skin. The pain sparks something inside me, but I force it back down. Maeve lets my blood drip on the strands of my cut lock.

"In Beldain," Maeve says, her voice steady and low, "when a person lies dying, we send a prayer to our patron goddess, Fortuna. We believe she goes to the Underworld as our ambassador, to speak with her sister Moritas and vouch for the life she wants to take. Holy Fortuna is the goddess of Prosperity, and Prosperity requires payment. This is what I did when I brought my brother back—a ritual prayer." Maeve's brows furrow in concentration. "A lock of your hair, drops of your blood. The tokens we give to bind a dead soul to a living one."

She bends down on one knee, then presses the bloody

lock against the stone. The blood smears against her fingers. She closes her eyes. I feel her energy grow, dark and pulsing. "Every life I pull back to the surface takes a piece of my own life," she mutters. "A few lost threads of my own energy." She turns her eyes up at me. "It will take a piece of yours too."

I swallow. "So be it."

She falls silent. All around us, the storm rages on, whipping at Maeve's cloak and throwing fresh rain into my eye. I squint against it. Up on the arena's top row, a silhouette with curls of hair turns toward us. The Windwalker, perhaps? She makes a subtle gesture, and a moment later, the wind around us dies down, pushed back by a funnel of wind that shields us in its center. The storm's gusts rage in vain against the Windwalker's shield. Maeve's cloak drapes back down behind her, soaking in the rain, and I wipe water from my face.

Maeve bows her head. She stays still for a long moment. As I watch, a faint blue light starts to glow from under the edges of her hand. I can barely see it at first. But then the light begins to pulse, growing in strength from a faint, narrow outline to a soft glow that stretches all around her hand. Overhead, a streak of lightning brings with it an instant clap of thunder. It echoes around the arena.

A surge of fear emanates from Maeve now. I feel the change like water to a parched man, as intense as the storm. In order to reach the Underworld, one must gain the permission of she who walks the Underworld's surface, Formidite, the angel of Fear, the same deity I've seen before in my nightmares. Somehow, I know that Maeve must be at that surface now, seeking a way in.

Something starts to *pull* from the depths of the arena's lake. No, deeper than that. Deeper than the ocean, something that stretches all the way down, past the world of the living and into the realm of the dead. A darkness, something I have only sensed before in dreams. Threads of energy in the mortal world are infused with life, even the darkest, most twisted threads. But *this* new energy . . . it is something else altogether. Threads that are black, through and through, lacking the pulse of life and ice cold to the touch. My mind coils away from it—but at the same time, I hunger for it in a way I've never felt before.

This energy feels like . . . it belongs to a part of me.

Maeve shifts to press both of her hands against the ground. Out in the lake, the waters turn choppier. The waves crash against either side of the path, sending white foam up into the air. The energy from deep in the ocean starts to surge upward. It pushes past the barrier between death and life, and I gasp as the darkness permeates the water around us, staining the water with something not of this world.

A balira surfaces from the depths of the lake. It gives a cry of distress, then pushes itself up out of the water and launches into the sky. Its wings soar over my head, sprinkling a trail of ocean water across us. I shield myself. Salt water mixes with fresh rain on my tongue. Another balira follows after it, and their absence sends the water churning violently. A large wave crashes against the path, spraying us both.

The glow under Maeve's hand now wraps all around her body. The energy in the water has changed too . . . to something familiar. *So familiar.* I recognize the touch of these threads. There is fire in them—that which aligns with diamond—an intense, ferocious heat that I've only ever associated with one person.

Maeve's eyes open. They look glazed, as if she were not really here. She leans forward to where the stone path meets the lake, and dips her arms down into the water. Water drips from her chin. She cringes, from pain or fear or strain. Her teeth clench harder.

Then her arms surge out of the water, pulling on something invisible.

And the ocean bursts open.

The waves of the lake explode, sending a jet of water high into the sky, level with the top of the arena. Thunder roars overhead in the same moment. As I look on in awe, the jet of water bursts into flames. Water rains down on us.

The water is hot.

Fire races all across the surface of the lake. It rages in whirlwinds, funnels of flames twisting and turning to meet with the wind and sky. The arena, so dark a moment ago, is now alight with scarlet and gold, and heat pulses across the surface, scalding my skin. I shield myself against the brightness.

The flames form a circle around the water before where

we stand. *There is too much fire.* I feel an overwhelming urge to run away, but instead I force myself to keep concentrating. *It won't be long now.*

A silhouette rises from the surface of the water.

The water parts for him, and fire rushes in, engulfing his body. He tilts his head up to the sky, taking a deep gasp of air, and then bows, his shoulders hunched, kneeling over the water. Flames lick at his limbs, but don't burn his skin. Slowly, he rises to his feet in the middle of the water. Flames rush around him, as if eager to be reunited with their master. His dark hair is wild and unruly, hiding his face from view. His clothing is still the same, exactly what he wore when he died. Blood stains the front of his doublet. Flames engulf his hands, curling around him in spools of golden heat.

When he opens his eyes, they are pools of blackness. *Leader. Prince. Reaper.*

"Enzo," I whisper, unable to look away.

It is Enzo, truly him, here.

Maeve turns to me from where she crouches, and holds out a hand to me. A net of threads whips around my heart, ice cold, linking me to Enzo. I stagger forward, then dig my feet into the stone path and push back. I feel as if these new threads would yank me straight into the water.

"Do not resist it," Maeve commands.

The threads twist, growing tighter and tighter until they seem like they will suffocate me. My own energy responds to the darkness in Enzo. Then something cleaves together. A new bond has suddenly formed, made of threads from the Underworld, a tether that links *me* to *him*.

We are bound. I know it as instinctively as I know how to breathe.

Enzo walks toward us across the water. His face is turned toward me now, recognizing our bond, and I cannot bear to look anywhere else. He is exactly how I remember him . . . all except his eyes, which stay as black as empty sockets. *Concentrate,* I continue to repeat to myself, but it becomes a constant drone in the back of my mind. I wait as he draws closer, until he steps from the surface of the lake onto the stone path. Fire surrounds us. The heat coming from Enzo goes straight through me, scorching my insides. What a familiar feeling.

I can't believe how much I've missed it.

Enzo stops a foot away from me. Fire loops around us, closing in and rising higher until it forms a funnel up into the air, so that it seems like we are the only two people in a world of flames. He looks down at me.

It takes a moment for me to realize that the water running down my face is no longer from the rain, but from my tears.

Enzo blinks twice. The black pools in his eyes swirl and fade, until they reveal the whites of his eyes, the familiar dark irises and scarlet slashes. Suddenly, he seems less like a phantom risen from the Underworld, and more like a young prince. His strength leaves him. He falls to his knees. There he crouches, shaking his head. The flames surrounding him vanish, leaving a circle of smoke, and the arena comes back into view, the lake returned to dark, stormy waters, the rain still pouring down in sheets.

I kneel too. I reach out with slender hands to touch Enzo's cheeks. Enzo lifts his head weakly to look at me, and suddenly, I can no longer hold back. I pull Enzo toward me, then touch my lips gently to his.

A second. No more than that.

The kiss ends. Enzo searches my gaze. Somehow, he sees straight through the illusion.

"Adelina?" he whispers.

And that is all it takes to undo me. Raffaele's face disintegrates into my own, revealing silver and scars. My shoulders hunch in abrupt exhaustion. It feels like all the energy in my body has been sucked away, leaving nothing but the strange, otherworldly threads that now bind me to my prince. I'm exposed before the entire arena, and I don't care at all.

"It's me," I whisper back.

They waged war for decades, never realizing that

they were fighting for the same cause.

–Campaigns of East and West Tamoura, 1152–1180,

by Scholar Tennan

Adelina Amouteru

The Beldish queen reacts first. She has never met me before, but somehow, she knows who I am.

"White Wolf," she says. She tries to get up, but she's still too weak from using so much of her power. She spits out a curse, then glances at the young man standing beside her. *Her brother.*

"Tristan!" she shouts.

The boy turns to me. I can sense the dark energy building in him, something far more terrifying than anything I have ever felt within me. My darkness is a blanket that shrouds the patches of light in my heart. But this boy—his darkness *is* his heart. There is no light anywhere.

His eyes turn black. He bares his teeth and rushes at me.

The speed at which he moves is dizzying. One moment he stood a dozen feet away—the next, he has reached me and holds a flashing blade over his head. *I'm going to die.* No one will be able to rescue me in time. I glance at Enzo, but Enzo has hunched over on the ground, barely conscious.

Tristan slashes at me. The blade cuts deep into my shoulder. I shriek—pain blossoms in me and I stagger back. My illusions ache to lash back. But I am so weak, drained from my disguise as Raffaele, that all I can do is throw a thin black veil at him. It vanishes into smoke.

"Enzo!" I reach for him. He stays crumpled in a heap on the platform.

Tristan reaches me. His hands close around my neck. I fall backward and hit my head hard on the platform. Stars burst across my vision. He's choking me, pushing down hard with blind, *blank* rage.

The only thing that saves my life is Maeve. As I struggle, Maeve's voice reaches my ears. "Do not kill her!" she shouts. There is a frantic note in her words, and in a flash, I realize why.

If they kill me, Enzo's only link to the living world, then Enzo will return to the Underworld.

Tristan stops immediately at Maeve's call. Instead, he whirls, his attention shifting to where Enzo lies. The sudden realization that my life isn't in danger hits me. My advantage. As Tristan turns to pick up Enzo, I stagger to my feet, clutching my bleeding shoulder, and flee off the stone path.

I'm only halfway when a blast of wind hits me hard, then lifts me high into the sky. I struggle in vain. The Windwalker's work. The world around me spins—I think I see flashes of dark robes among the arena's seats, the Daggers moving against me and heading down to where Enzo and Maeve are. Where are my Roses? My mouth opens in a scream as the wind suddenly cuts off, sending me plummeting down toward the arena's rows.

A new current of wind stops me several feet from the stone seats. It flings me to one side, leaving me to tumble along the stairs. I stop there, breathing hard. As my vision clears, I see a Dagger approaching me, her curls tied back high on her head, her face hidden behind a silver mask that sends a ribbon of fear slicing through me. The only part of her face I can see are her eyes, flashing in fury at me. Lucent.

"*You,*" she snarls. "What have you done with Raffaele?"

I can't think. Visions flash before me—I'm not sure if they are real or if they are illusions. Memories of Enzo kissing me in the rain shift into an image of him with his black eyes, staring through me as if searching for his soul. I tremble like a leaf in the wind. *He recognized me through my illusion.* How did I give myself away? How did he know?

Another figure hops nimbly down by my side. He puts a protective arm out in front of me. It's Magiano.

He flashes his savage smile at Lucent. "Sorry for that rough landing," he says, tilting his head close to me. "But I have a prince to steal for you." Then he braces himself and hits Lucent with a blast of wind.

Lucent's eyes open in surprise, but she manages to catch herself in time. She leaps backward, then rides a current of her own wind to the bottom of the steps. She prepares to attack us—but Violetta stands up from where she's crouching nearby. My sister narrows her eyes.

Lucent gasps. She steadies herself, then blinks in confusion. She tries to pull together a curtain of wind, but nothing happens. Fear sparks in her, and I reach hungrily for those threads. They shimmer in a halo around her.

Magiano laughs a little. A dagger gleams in his hand. "Why so surprised?" he taunts. He lifts a hand down toward the arena, where Enzo is still kneeling on the platform, and calls the wind to pick him up. Then he lunges at Lucent with the blade drawn.

I scramble to my feet. Just standing up feels like an overwhelming task. My head spins, and cold sweat covers my forehead. Below, Enzo lifts onto the wind, and I feel the bond between us move with him. It pulls at the insides of my stomach, making me simultaneously nauseated and excited. What does our new connection do?

Lucent pulls two short swords from her belt. She crosses them as Magiano hits her, and the clash rings out over the storm.

A black shadow falls over me. Overhead, Gemma appears on the back of a balira. The balira lets out a sharp, furious cry. I've never heard such a sound before from these gentle creatures. Its eyes gleam in the night, and it lunges down toward me. A sharp stab of anger surges through me at the sight of Gemma. *I chose to spare you earlier. How dare you turn on me.* If I had my power right now, I would attack her. The balira's rage feeds me, returning some of my strength.

The balira spins so that its giant wings swing down toward us, threatening to send us flying through the air. A hand clamps down on my arm. It's Sergio. "Get down!" he shouts, then shoves me aside. I throw my hands over my head and curl up as small as I can. Above me, Sergio sidesteps enough to let the tip of the fleshy wing swing past him. He grabs its edge. It yanks him into the air, and as the balira starts to soar up again, Sergio glides up from where he dangles from the wing.

I yank out the dagger at my belt. Almost immediately, though, the weapon unfurls right before me and vanishes into thin air. *The Architect.* Michel's here. I whirl around, looking for him. At the last second, I see him rushing down toward me from the top of the arena's stairs, my dagger now in his hand.

Energy builds in my chest again. I reach for him and lash out.

I don't have enough strength to envelop him in pain, but I *can* fool him with my tricks. A quick replica of myself materializes and lunges at him with a scream. I scramble out of the way as Michel skids to a halt on the stairs, startled by the illusion of me. I rush up to him, take advantage of his hesitation, and grab my dagger out of his hands.

Then I wrap my arm around his neck and hold the blade to his throat. "Move, and I'll kill you," I snap at him. Then I raise my voice over the storm. "*Stop!*" I shout.

Farther down the stairs, Magiano and Lucent break from their duel for an instant. Lucent glances up at me through the rain. She's breathing heavily, and one of her wrists looks bent at an unnatural angle. She has her powers back now, but she's not using them.

Violetta makes her way up toward me. She holds a hand up to the sky, where Gemma's balira soars by. She clenches her jaw and makes a fist. The creature shudders. Gemma lets out a faint cry as my sister yanks her power away. Her balira shudders—she struggles with Sergio. Then she loses her grip altogether on the balira. I can tell the instant it happens, because the beast suddenly starts to dive toward the water.

Gemma seems to regain control at the last instant. The balira pulls up. It slides one of its wide wings underneath Enzo. Water sprays as the balira's long tail hits the lake.

"Let him go," Lucent shouts at me.

I tighten my grip around Michel. Michel stays still. I hold the dagger far enough from his throat so that I don't accidentally hurt him. The storm overhead shifts into a steady downpour.

"Where's Raffaele?" Lucent shouts. "What did you do with him?"

I can feel the fear emanating from her. She thinks I killed him, perhaps that I slit his throat the way I'm threatening to do right now to Michel. I find delight in that, her fear of what I am capable of doing. "Find him yourself," I snap back.

Lucent grits her teeth. She makes a move toward me, but stops when Magiano clicks his tongue in disapproval. He flashes his teeth in a grin. "Careful," he says to her. "I keep my blades very sharp. It's a nervous habit."

She gives him a look full of dislike before turning her attention back on me. "Where'd you get your new crew?" she calls over the rain. "What do you *want*?" She spreads her arms. "We parted ways! You want your darling Enzo back? Is that what this is all about?"

Her taunt about Enzo hits home. I clench my teeth, then throw an illusion of fire around her. It circles her, mimicking the heat of a real fire, and closes in. She shields her face for a second as the scorching heat hits her. I let her think that the fire singes her, then pull it away. The flames vanish.

"I came to take the throne away from you," I reply. "From Beldain. How dare you all think you can hand our country over to a foreign power! A foreign queen!"

Lucent looks genuinely confused. "You hated the Inquisition! You wanted to see the *malfettos* saved as much as we do. You—"

"Then why aren't we allies, Windwalker?" I yell. "If we all want the same things, why are you my enemy? Why did you cast me out?"

"Because we couldn't trust you!" she yells back. Her anger returns. "You *killed* one of ours! You betrayed us to Teren!"

"I had no *choice*."

The tide of rage over her rises. "Enzo died because of *you*."

"He died because of *Teren*," I snarl. "Your precious Raffaele wanted me dead too! Have you forgotten that?"

"The throne doesn't belong to you," Lucent spits out. She clenches her sword tighter. "It belongs to the rightful king."

My energy builds with my own fury, surrounding me

in a cloud of darkness. "No—it will belong to your Beldish queen, not Enzo," I snap. "There *is* no rightful ruler of Kenettra. Can't you see that?"

I can be the rightful ruler. I can be the greatest ruler there ever was.

Something in my words hits Lucent hard. I feel a sudden rush of darkness in her, a deep hatred for me, and her lips curl up into a snarl. She makes as if to lunge at me, but her broken wrist suddenly jolts in pain, and she winces, clutching it. I keep my stranglehold on Michel.

A movement in the shadows of the arena behind Magiano catches my eye. It's the bald boy, the new Dagger recruit named Leo. He darts forward toward Magiano, blade drawn, right as I scream out a warning.

Magiano whirls in time to block the sword—but Leo clenches one hand down on his arm. Magiano lets out a shout of pain. He kicks Leo backward, sending him reeling, but then staggers, falling to his knees. I freeze in terror. Magiano turns pale, then leans over and retches.

Leo scrambles up. He points to the top of the arena, where someone I don't recognize crouches against the stone. He's making a gesture with both arms out. "The Inquisition's here," Leo shouts. "We have to hurry!"

In unison, we all look to the horizon. There, a fleet of balitras is heading toward us.

Magiano manages to glare up at both me and Lucent. "I'm fairly certain none of us like them, yes?" he gasps, wiping his mouth.

Lucent looks torn for a moment. My stare goes to the top of the arena too. I could slit Michel's throat right now—take one of the Dagger's Elites away from them permanently. It'd be so easy.

But the Inquisition is coming, and Magiano is hurt. We don't have time to fight one another and hold off the Inquisitors.

I make a disgusted sound, let go of Michel, and shove him forward. He trips on the stairs and almost falls, but Lucent manages to catch him on a gust of wind. As she rushes to him, I go to Magiano's side. Together, Violetta and I manage to hoist him up between us. He sways on his feet, his eyes rolling back, but forces himself forward. "Poisoned, I think," he chokes out. "That little bastard."

"We're getting you out of here," I reply. Up in the sky, Sergio circles back on his balira. The Daggers turn their backs on me again, and we make our way out of the arena, the tenuous bond between Enzo and me still tugging at my chest.

Maeve Jacqueline Kelly Corrigan

In the alcove off a lonely stretch of Kenettran cliffs, several Beldish ships rock in the choppy waters. The dawn has arrived overcast and windy, the remnants of last night's storm still on the horizon.

On board and belowdecks, the Daggers gather around Maeve and Raffaele. The normally bold queen is subdued today, slumped against a stack of pillows and impatiently waving away her brothers. Tristan sits some distance from everyone, looking on at his exhausted sister with a straight face, as if not quite seeing her. Still, every time she winces, he twitches, ready to defend her and helpless to do so.

Maeve's eyes are fixed on Raffaele, who has just woken. His skin is deathly pale, and his hands still tremble. Michel wrings out a warm cloth from a basin, and Gemma places it gingerly on his head. She squeezes his arm.

"What do you remember?" she asks him.

Raffaele doesn't answer for a moment. His attention shifts to Lucent, who sits beside Maeve, gritting her teeth as a servant binds her broken wrist. Raffaele's thoughts seem to be far away. "Adelina," he finally says. "She has progressed rapidly in her illusions of touch." His voice turns quiet. "I've never felt pain like that in my life."

Michel's hands tense. He squeezes out another cloth until his knuckles look ready to burst. "I'm surprised she didn't kill you," he mutters.

"She let me live," Raffaele replies, his stare fixed on Lucent's wrist. "She wanted me to know, so that we are even."

Maeve's eyes narrow. "This is your White Wolf, then," she says. "Your traitor. You told me she had fled the country with her sister. Why is she here? What is she trying to prove by tethering Enzo to herself?"

Raffaele's eyes stay fixed on Lucent's wrist. "She's here for the throne," he replies. His voice is distant and calm. "The alignment in her to ambition has grown far stronger than I remember. It is a storm in her chest, poisoned by her other alignments. She will have her revenge, or she will die trying."

"She also seems to have strengthened her relationship with her sister," Gemma adds. "I've never experienced someone wrenching my power away like that. Violetta is learning fast."

Leo, who leans against the wall and rubs a healing cream

into a jagged cut on his arm, looks up. "Not to mention their mimic. Magiano."

"Good thing you stopped him before he could try to copy you," Lucent mutters.

Maeve grabs her mug and flings it at the wall. Gemma jumps. It nearly breaks the porthole, but instead hits wood and clanks to the floor. "The bond between Adelina and Enzo is weak," she snaps, "but like a vine, it will grow rapidly. She will learn to control him—and then she will have another formidable ally at her side. That, along with her sister and her Elites?" She takes a deep breath to calm herself. Her eyes close. The rush of bringing Enzo back returns to her now, and she trembles at the memory. When she closed her eyes and pulled Enzo's soul from the ocean of the dead to the living, she had felt the darkness seeping out of his chest, threatening to taint everything around him. He is no longer just a Young Elite. He is something else entirely. Something more.

Lucent curses under her breath as the servant secures the splint of her broken wrist. "What a strange break," the servant remarks, shaking his head. "The wrist is broken as if twisted from within, rather than caused by some outside force."

"We should be hunting down Adelina right now," Lucent snaps at Maeve. "Should've followed her instead of running away with our tails between our legs."

"Is there any way to undo Enzo's bond to her?" Michel asks.

Maeve scowls at Lucent, then shakes her head. The beads

in her hair clack against one another. "Adelina is now Enzo's only link to the living world. If we sever that bond, he will die immediately, and there will be no bringing him back a second time." She pauses to glance at Tristan. "But there is one difference," she says in a quieter voice. "He is an Elite. I am able to control Tristan at my whim, because Tristan was a normal boy, with an innate energy of a normal man that cannot hope to rival mine. I can therefore overpower his energy with my own. But *Enzo* is an Elite. Whatever powers he once had, he now has tenfold." She nods toward Raffaele. "Adelina may be able to control Enzo . . . but Enzo is so powerful that he may also control Adelina."

Raffaele's eyes dart away from Lucent's wrist for the first time. He looks at Maeve. "You want Enzo to turn his power against Adelina?" he says. Again, that calm voice.

"It is our only way to win him back to our side." She nods. "I heard the way her voice broke at the sight of him. Adelina is in love with the prince—"

"What haven't you told us about your brother?" Raffaele suddenly interrupts. Beneath the calm is an undercurrent of anger, something Maeve has never heard in him. She blinks, surprised.

"What do you mean?" she asks, narrowing her eyes.

Raffaele nods at Tristan, who stares out the porthole with his soulless expression. "He has deteriorated since you first brought him back, hasn't he?" he says, his voice turning raw now. "I should have known it from the instant I first sensed his energy. He is *not alive*—he is just a shadow of what he once was, and the Underworld will slowly claim him until he is nothing but a shell."

Maeve's eyes have turned into dangerous slits. "You forget your place, consort. He is a prince of Beldain."

"We should not have brought Enzo back!" Raffaele suddenly snaps. All of the Daggers freeze. "He is *not* of the living—*not* one of us! I did not even have to *see* him emerge from the arena—I could *feel* the unnatural state of his energy from where I was in the tunnels. I felt that abhorrent, *dead* energy in him, the taint of the Underworld coating him. It does not matter if it amplifies his powers tenfold—it is not *him.*" His face contorts in fury and anguish. "Your brother is a *true* abomination, a demon of the Underworld. And now you have turned Enzo into one."

Maeve rises from her resting place. She gathers her furs around her neck, turns away in stony silence, and walks toward the door. When she reaches it, she glances once over her shoulder. "Your White Wolf happens to be in love with that abomination," she replies. "And it shall be her undoing."

Raffaele's jaw tightens. "Then you don't know Adelina, Your Majesty."

Maeve glares at him for a moment. Then she throws open the door and strides out of the room. Behind her, Lucent hops to her feet. "Wait," she calls out. But Maeve ignores her. Everything seems muted, the world blurred, and the young queen suddenly needs to get off this ship.

Her soldiers step hastily out of her way as she storms across the deck and down the gangplank. Her horse stands ready and waiting near the shore. She unties its reins from the post, then puts a foot in the saddle and swings up onto its back.

"Maeve," Lucent calls out behind her. "Your Majesty!" But Maeve has already guided the horse around and tapped its hindquarters with her heels. She doesn't turn around at Lucent's voice. Instead, she leans down to the horse's ear and whispers something. She kicks its hindquarters again. The horse startles to life and takes off down the path.

Behind her, Lucent hurries to her horse and swings up. Then she hunches down over its back and takes off down the path in close pursuit. Her copper curls stream out behind her, whipping in the wind in unison with its mane. Maeve pushes her horse faster. She used to ride like this with Lucent when they were young, when Maeve was just a little princess and Lucent one of her guard's daughters. Lucent always won. She would push her horse until the two of them became one, and her laughter would ring out across the Beldish plains, teasing Maeve to ride faster in order to catch her. Maeve wonders now whether Lucent remembers those moments. The wind whistles in her ears. *Faster,* she urges the horse.

Lucent calls the wind. A sudden gust seems to hit Maeve, and the gap between their horses narrows. They race up the path until it leads them to the top of the cliffs, then race along the edge of a plain, hugging the edge of the land where the canals open into the sea. Maeve shifts her attention from the path ahead to where it curves along the cliff side.

Suddenly, Lucent steers her horse off the course and races to cut off Maeve. Maeve looks over her shoulder. It's a familiar move, and somehow, it brings a slight smile to Maeve's lips. *Faster, faster,* she urges her horse. She bends so low over its neck that it seems like they blend together into one.

The world disappears into streaks. Lucent's shouts pierce the tunnel, until it seems like they have gone back in time to the day when Tristan first drowned. *Help him!* Lucent had screamed that fateful night. She shook Maeve with a tear-stained face. *I didn't mean it—the ice was too thin! Please—help me get him!*

Maeve lets out a startled shout when Lucent suddenly cuts into the path beside her. The childhood version of her voice vanishes, replaced by the voice of the woman she has become.

"Stop!" Lucent shouts.

Maeve ignores her.

"Stop!"

When Maeve still doesn't listen, Lucent pushes her horse one more time. She tries in vain to steer her horse away. Maeve glances over. "Your wrist—!" she starts to shout, but the warning comes too late. Lucent forgets her broken wrist, and flinches away with a yell. For a moment, her concentration breaks—right as her horse leaps. She loses her balance. Maeve has no time to reach out as she sees Lucent topple from her stallion and vanish from sight.

A rush of wind cushions her fall, but she still rolls once.

Her stallion gallops on. Maeve looks over her shoulder to where Lucent lies in the dirt, then pulls her own horse to a halt. She dismounts and runs over to her side.

Lucent pushes her away when she tries to help her up.

"You shouldn't have come after me," Maeve snaps. "I just needed to think."

Lucent looks up at Maeve with flashing eyes. Then she pushes herself up from the ground and starts to walk away. "Never in my life have I seen Raffaele raise his voice like that to anyone. We all knew that Tristan would never be wholly like how he was before . . . but it's worse than that, isn't it? He is *dying*, all over again."

"He is *not* dying," Maeve calls angrily to her. "He is exactly the way he's supposed to be." She runs a hand along her high braids. "Don't tell me I should have done differently."

"Why didn't you tell us?" Lucent shakes her head. "Tell *me*?"

Maeve scowls at her. "I am your queen," she says, lifting her head high. "Not your riding confidant."

"You think I don't know that?" Lucent blurts out. She extends her arms, as if she can no longer feel the pain in her injured wrist. "We haven't been riding partners for a long time, Your *Majesty*."

"Lucent," Maeve says quietly, but the other girl goes on.

"Why didn't you write more?" she says, stopping in her tracks. She shakes her head in despair. "Every time you wrote, it was business and politics. Tedious matters of the state that I never wanted to know."

"You needed to know," Maeve replies. "I wanted to keep you updated on the affairs of Beldain, and on when I thought you could return from your exile."

"I wanted to hear about *you*." Lucent takes a step closer to her. Her voice sounds anguished now. "But you just went along with your mother, didn't you? You know what happened with Tristan was an accident. I dared him to walk out on the ice—he fell through. I never meant to hurt him! And you just stood by and let your mother decide my fate."

"Do you know how hard I begged my mother to not execute you?" Maeve snaps. "She wanted you dead, but I insisted that she spare your life. Do you ever think about *that*?"

"Why didn't you ever *tell* me about Tristan?" Lucent says. "*Why?* You let me live with the guilt of thinking that my actions almost caused his death! You never even told me about your power!"

Maeve narrows her eyes. "You know why."

Lucent looks away. She swallows hard, and Maeve realizes that she is trying to hold back her tears. She starts to walk away again, back in the direction that they had come. Maeve follows beside her. They walk in silence for a long time.

"Do you remember when you first kissed me?" Lucent finally murmurs.

Maeve stays silent, but the memory comes back to her, clear as glass. It was a warm day, a rarity in Beldain, and the plains were covered in a sheet of yellow and blue flowers. They had decided to follow an old, mythical trail through the woods that the goddess Fortuna was rumored to have once taken. Maeve remembers the sweet smell of honey and lavender, then the sharpness of pine and moss. They'd stopped to rest by a creek, and in the middle of their laughter, Maeve had suddenly leaned over and gave Lucent a kiss on the cheek.

"I remember," Maeve replies.

Lucent stops in her tracks. "Do you still love me?" she asks, her face still turned toward the sea.

Maeve hesitates. "Why do we even try?" she replies.

Lucent shakes her head. The wind blows strands of hair across her face, and Maeve can't tell if the wind is of Lucent's creation or of the world itself. "You are queen now," she says after a moment. "You will have to marry. Beldain needs an heir to the throne."

Maeve takes a step closer to her. She touches Lucent's hand softly. "My mother married twice," she reminds her. "But her true love was a knight she met much later. We can still be together." In this moment, Lucent looks so much like the girl Maeve used to go hunting with in the woods, with reddish-gold curls and a straight stance, that she pulls her forward. She kisses her before Lucent can stop her.

They linger for a long moment. Finally, they break away.

"I will not be your mistress," Lucent says, meeting Maeve's eyes. Then she looks down again. "I cannot be so close to you and know that a man will have you every night." Her voice turns quiet. "Don't make me bear that."

Maeve closes her eyes. Lucent is right, of course. They

stand together in silence, listening to the distant roar of the waterfalls. What would happen after all of this ends? Maeve would take Kenettra's throne with the Daggers at her side. She would return to Beldain. And she would have to birth an heir. Lucent would stay with the Daggers.

"It cannot be," Maeve agrees in a whisper. She turns her eyes toward the cliffs from which they'd come. The two stand together, not talking, until the wind changes directions and the clouds overhead start to move away.

Lucent breaks the silence first. "What do we do now, Your Majesty?"

"I'll send my men out to hunt down Adelina," Maeve replies. "Nothing changes. Raffaele has damaged Teren's relationship with his queen, and my navy shall arrive soon." Her eyes harden. "We *will* have this country."

Raffaele Laurent Bessette

The others pound on Raffaele's door that night, asking if he is all right, and Leo tries to bring him a plate of soup and fruits. But Raffaele ignores them. They will talk about Enzo. Raffaele's heart aches at the thought. He cannot discuss the prince yet. Instead, he pores through his old parchments, his years of careful study on how threads of energy work in each new Elite he comes across, his meticulous recording of Elite history and science to be left for future generations, his journals attempting to understand all there is to understand about Elites, where they had come from and where they will go. All that he had managed to save from the Fortunata Court's secret caverns.

His notes are full of sketches: long, delicate lines of the thread patterns he sees woven around each Elite in a halo, the countless ways that they shift as the Elite uses her energy; then, the Elites themselves, fleeting, hurried sketches of them in motion. He now lingers in particular on notes he took during Lucent's training, peering closely at what he had written beside his sketches of her.

> *The Windwalker's energy pulls from her bones. She has a marking invisible to our eyes—her bones are light, like a bird's, as if she had never meant to be human.*

It was a single note, one he never touched upon again, and a detail that he had largely forgotten about. Until today. Raffaele leans forward in his chair, thinking back on the tangle of energy he had been observing around Lucent's broken wrist earlier.

What a strange break, the servant wrapping Lucent's wrist had muttered. *As if twisted from within.*

A cold dread seeps into Raffaele's mind. Outside his door, Gemma calls for him, asking whether he wants any supper, but he barely hears her voice.

Lucent's bones are not just light anymore. They are brittle, more so than they should be for someone her age . . . and they are *hollowing out.*

He wanted to live in a house built on delusion,
would rather believe in a million lies than face one truth.
–Seven Circles Around the Sea, *by Mordove Senia*

Adelina Amouteru

Enzo looks the same. I can't stop staring at him.

Magiano watches us from the doorway while he tunes the strings of his lute. The house we're staying in sits somewhere in the Estenzian countryside, an old, crumbling barn that roving bands of thieves must have started using as a stopping place. True to Sergio's word, other mercenaries have secured this place for us. I can hear them talking in low voices downstairs, taking stock of the horses they have. A few soft neighs float up to us.

From the window, I can see the beginning of the *malfetto* camps. Sergio's storm has finally cleared, and what clouds remain are painted a brilliant red by the setting sun.

"How long is he going to sleep like this?" Magiano finally mutters, plucking a few strings. His song sounds agitated, the notes harsher than usual and oddly off-key.

Violetta, seated on the other side of Enzo's bed, frowns. She rests her chin on one hand and concentrates harder on Enzo's energy. "He's stirring," she replies. "It's hard to tell, though. His energy is nothing like any of ours."

We settle into a long, silent wait. Magiano props himself up by the door again and plays a little song, then wanders out into the hall right by the door. Time drags on.

"Adelina." I look up at my sister as she rises from where she's sitting and comes to my side. She crouches down and leans toward my ear. I sit back. "Enzo's link to you is growing stronger by the minute. Like he is strengthening himself by tying himself closer and closer to you." There is uneasiness in her voice as she says this. "Can you feel it?"

I do, of course. It's a pulse that rises and falls, pulling and pushing at my chest. It makes my heart feel like it's beating in an uneven rhythm, and it makes me short of breath. "What is his energy like?" I whisper.

Violetta bites her lip in concentration. She tilts her head at Enzo's sleeping figure. I can tell that she is reaching out toward him, testing him. She shudders. "Do you remember when we learned needlework together?" she says to me.

Violetta had learned it faster than I did. She'd once switched our two pieces so that our father would praise mine for once. "Yes. Why?"

"Do you remember one time when we each picked out a color of thread, then sewed a pattern together, and our two colors were so interwoven that they looked like a completely new color?"

"Yes."

"Well, the way Enzo's energy is tied to yours, the link between you two . . . it feels like that." Violetta turns her frown on me. "A new form of energy. His threads are so tangled with yours that it's almost like you two have become one. For example, I cannot take away his power without taking yours, nor yours without his." She hesitates. "His power feels like ice. It burns me."

How ironic. I return to staring at Enzo, trying to get used to the new link between us.

"He's not the same, you know," Violetta adds after a while. "Don't forget that. Don't . . ."

"Don't what?" I reply.

Violetta purses her lips. "Don't be blinded by your old love for him," she finishes. "It might be dangerous for you to get too caught up. I can tell."

I cannot sense what Violetta senses. I know I should believe her, and take her warning. Still, I can't help staring at him, imagining him awake. When I first met Enzo, he was the Reaper, and I was tied to a stake and left to burn. He had materialized out of smoke and fire as a whirlwind of sapphire robes, a long dagger gleaming in each of his gloved hands, his face hidden behind a silver mask. Now, he looks more like he did on the night we kissed in the Fortunata Court. Vulnerable. Waves of dark hair framed by light. Not a killer, but a young prince. A sleeping boy.

"You're right," I finally say to Violetta. "I promise I'll be careful." She doesn't look like she believes me, but she shrugs anyway. She gets up and returns to the other side of Enzo's bed.

From the corner of my eye, I can see Magiano returning to hang out in the doorway. I don't know if he heard any of what was said between us, but he keeps his eyes turned away. The song he plays sounds sharp, jolting.

More minutes pass.

Then, finally, Enzo shifts. My own energy twists at the same time, and I can feel our new bond turning with him. The tether is buried deep in my chest, entwined around my heart, and when he moves, his energy flares to life, feeding me as mine must feed him.

His eyes flutter open.

They look just like how I remember.

He's not the same, Violetta had said. But now he's *here.* Saved somehow from the waters of the Underworld. Suddenly, all I can think is that perhaps nothing has changed at all—that we can go back to the way we once were. The thought forces a smile onto my face that I haven't worn in a long time, and for a moment, I forget my mission and anger. I forget everything.

His eyes turn to me. It takes a moment for the light of recognition to appear in them—when it does, my heart leaps. With it leaps the tether between us. The spark that the new energy gives off makes me want to draw closer to him, as close as I possibly can, *anything* in order to further feed this new energy.

He tries to sit up, but winces immediately and settles back down. "What happened?" he says. A shiver runs down my spine at the deep, velvet voice that I know so well.

Magiano lifts an eyebrow as he plucks away at his lute. "Well. This may take some explanation." He pauses when Sergio calls out his name from the barn's lower floor. I turn to say something to Magiano before he leaves, but he purposefully avoids my stare. I hesitate, knowing what's bothering him, and feel guilty again. Violetta shoots me a knowing look. Then Enzo utters another groan of pain, and my attention returns to him.

I reach for Enzo's hand. They are both gloved, as always, and underneath the leather I know I will see the hideous layers of burned, scarred tissue. When I touch his hand, the tether sings. "What do you remember?" I ask, trying to ignore it.

"I remember the arena." Enzo falls silent for a moment. He stares up at the ceiling. Again, he tries to sit up—this time, he does so easily. I blink. Just a few minutes ago, he seemed as if he would take weeks to recover. Now he looks nearly ready to stand up and walk. "I remember a dark ocean and a gray sky." He's quiet. I imagine the Underworld as he describes it, thinking back to my nightmares. "There was a goddess, with black horns twisting out of her hair. There was a little girl walking on the ocean's surface." His eyes turn back to me. The link between us soars again.

"Give me some space," I murmur to Violetta, before

fixing my gaze back on Enzo. "I have something I need to tell you."

Violetta tugs once on my energy. I suck in my breath. I know Violetta meant nothing by it, nothing more than a gesture to comfort me—but something about her tug feels like a threat, a reminder to me that she is now more powerful than I am. She gets up and walks out of the room.

"Tell me what?" Enzo asks quietly.

He looks so natural, as if he had never died at all. Perhaps the ominous things we overheard from Gemma about the dangers of bringing him back were unfounded. His energy is darker, true, a strange and tumultuous mix, but there is life under his brown skin, a glow to the bright slashes of scarlet in his eyes.

"Teren stabbed you at the arena," I say. "When you dueled with him."

Enzo waits patiently for me to continue.

I take a deep breath, knowing what to tell him next. "There is an Elite who has the ability to bring us back from the dead. To pull us straight from the Underworld. That Elite is the Queen of Beldain."

The scarlet lines in his eyes glow brighter. He hesitates, then says, "You are telling me that I died. And that I was revived by an Elite."

Here is the moment I've been dreading. I made a promise to myself that if Enzo came back from the Underworld, I would have to set things right between us. And to do that,

I must tell him the truth. I lower my gaze. "Yes," I reply. Then, in the silence, I add, "It is my fault that you died."

Suddenly, the weight of the air in the room feels unbearable. Enzo frowns at me. "No, it's not," he replies.

I shake my head and reach out to brush his hand. "It is," I say, more firmly this time. The confession pours out of me. "In the chaos of that final battle, I mistook you for Teren. I had disguised you as him and I couldn't tell the difference. I lashed out at *you* with my powers, and I brought *you* to your knees, thinking you were him." My voice turns soft, meek. "I am the reason Teren was able to deliver a killing blow, Enzo. It *is* my fault."

Telling the story makes me revisit it, and revisiting it stirs my energy enough that I start to unconsciously paint the arena around us—the blood under our feet, the image of Teren standing over Enzo, his sword dripping scarlet.

Enzo straightens. He leans forward. I forget to catch my breath as he touches my hand, returning my gesture. I search his eyes for anger and betrayal, but instead find only sadness. "I remember," he finally says. "But our powers are dangerous, as is what we do." He gives me a grave look, one I know well. The same look that cuts through every shield I can put up, that weakens me at the knees. Immediately I am reminded of our old training sessions together, when he surrounded me with walls of fire and then stood over me as I cried. *Broken so easily,* he'd said. That was the push I'd needed to keep going. "Do not blame yourself."

The complete lack of doubt in his voice makes my heart beat faster. Before I can respond, he looks around the room and settles on the door. "Where are the others?"

This is the second piece of what I must tell him—the harder piece. The one that cannot be all truth. If I tell him what I did to Raffaele at the arena, if I reveal to Enzo that I had twisted an illusion of pain around Raffaele that left him unconscious on the ground, I will never be forgiven. *He'll never understand that.* So instead, I tell him this. "The Daggers aren't here. It is only me, my sister, and several Elites you may have heard of."

Enzo narrows his eyes. For the first time, he looks wary. "Why are the Daggers not here? Where am I?"

"Everyone thought you were dead," I say softly. This, at least, is the truth. "The entire country mourned you, while the Inquisition rounded up all *malfettos* and began a massive hunt for the Daggers." I pause again. "Raffaele and the Daggers blamed me for your death. They cast me out," I say. The memory of my last real conversation with Raffaele haunts me. "Raffaele thinks I helped Teren and the Inquisitors, and that I betrayed the Daggers."

"And did you?" Enzo's voice is quiet, the calm before a predator's strike. His trust in Raffaele runs so deep that he knows there must be a good reason why Raffaele cast me out. I think of the way he'd once tilted my chin up with his gloved hand, how he'd told me so firmly not to cry. That I was stronger than that. I remember the way he once pushed me against the rocky wall of the training cavern, and how, when he left, a scorched handprint remained on that wall. I tremble. *This is my Enzo.*

"No," I reply. "I wish I could convince the Daggers of that." I sound more certain than I feel. The lies come more easily now. "I don't know where the Daggers are now, or what they plan to do next. All I know is that they will certainly strike the palace." I steady my trembling voice and I give Enzo a determined look. "We can still take the crown."

Enzo studies me for a moment. I sense him searching for buried truths in my story. His gaze wanders from the scarred side of my face, to my lips, then to my good eye. How strange that I should be the one sitting here now, and he is in bed. I think of when he had first come into my chambers on the day we officially met, how he'd smiled and asked me if I wanted to strike against the Inquisition. What does he see now?

Can we rule together?

The whispers in my head hiss at me. They are upset, I realize, with Enzo's presence. *There is no rightful heir to Kenettra's throne. You deserve it, as much as anyone.* I try to silence them, annoyed.

At last, Enzo sighs and softens his gaze. "When I mentioned what I remembered from the Underworld," he says, "I left something out." His hand closes around mine. This time, I jump at his touch. His fingers are scalding hot, the energy underneath them overwhelming. A delicious, familiar heat rushes through me. His ability with fire churns under his skin, stronger than I remember it ever being. He leans toward me.

"What?" I whisper, unable to turn away.

"I saw *you*, Adelina," he whispers. "Your energy wrapping around me, pulling me through the black ocean and up to the surface. I remember looking up and seeing your dark silhouette in the water, framed by the quivering glow of the moons through the ocean's surface."

The moment when Maeve tied him to me, forever.

"And do you remember me well?" I ask. "Do you remember all that has happened in our past?"

"I do," he replies. And I wonder whether he is remembering the last night we spent together, when he told me of his darkest fears, when we slept side by side for comfort.

"I've missed you," I say, my voice hoarse, and the truth in those words burns me until I'm raw. It takes me a moment to realize that my cheek is wet. "I'm sorry."

Enzo tightens his fingers around mine. Heat rushes from his hand and through me in a current, and for a moment, I'm helpless. The whispers' protests fade away into nothing. The tether wraps tightly around us both, entangling us as surely as if a rope had tightened around our hearts, and I lean toward him, unable to resist the pull. This is something different altogether, the strength fueled by the history between us, the passion I once felt for him, that I *still* feel. Did Enzo ever love me? He must have. He looks at me now with a strange hunger in his eyes, like he can feel the pull of the tether too.

"What is this?" he whispers. His lips are very close to mine now. "This new tie between us?"

But I can't think straight anymore. My energy lurches, and my passion sparks wildly out of control, fed by the strength of our connection. I had not expected this. All I know is that the tether is hungry to join its two ends together, and that it pulls us tighter and tighter together, the energy growing more and more powerful the closer we get. Violetta's warning echoes in the back of my mind.

"I don't know," I whisper back. I put one hand against his face. He doesn't pull away. A small sound comes from his throat, and before I can do anything else, he puts a hand against the back of my neck and pulls me forward. He kisses me.

I cannot breathe. It is a frightening, savage energy—my power lashes out at Enzo, pulling him forward and trying to overpower him. For a while, it does. I can feel the threads of my energy whipping around his, washing over them and swallowing them whole. They act as if I were not even here. Like I have no control.

I can feel his fire coursing through me, wrapping around my heart, wanting more. This is nothing like the gentle kiss I'd shared with Magiano. I cannot let go—I'm not sure I want to. My energy darts through our tether, coiling itself around his heart and whispering for him to come closer. I realize that I am the one coaxing him on. Commanding him.

Then, suddenly, something pushes back against my power. It pushes hard.

The sound in Enzo's throat turns into something dark, a rumble, a growl that doesn't sound human. Without warning, he shoves me back against the wall, pinning me there with his weight. I gasp. His energy blankets me. *This shouldn't be possible.* An illusion of mine flings out from us and spirals around the room, erasing the dilapidated barn and replacing it with a night forest covered in snow, illuminated by the glow of the moons. The ground beneath us is soft with bright green moss. The wall behind me turns into the trunk of an enormous, twisted tree. And Enzo . . . when I get a glimpse of his eyes, I see that they have gone completely black, the darkness filling every corner. I choke out a gasp of horror. I realize vaguely that the string at the top of my tunic has come undone, exposing my skin and the curve of my shoulder. He arches against me as I pull him toward me.

No. My energy suddenly explodes against him, forcing his power back.

His lips leave mine. He forces himself away, pushing back even as our joint energy protests. The darkness leaves his eyes, returning them to normal, and the hunger that had been on his face moments earlier dissipates, leaving confusion. We stare at each other, trying to figure out what just happened. The tether between us still protests, even now, each of our Elite powers whispering and clawing for the other.

"This doesn't feel right," Enzo whispers, taking a step back.

It feels horribly wrong, like a slick of oil coating the inside of my stomach. But with the nauseating feeling had come that unimaginable heat. When I look at Enzo's face, I can tell that he desires it too, even as it unsettles him. He tightens his jaw and turns away from me. When he looks back at me again, his face has settled into something cold, distant, and calculating. The Reaper's face.

Is it him? I try to force down a shudder of frustration. I'd thought that the darkness pooling in his eyes was something that happened only in the arena, while he was being revived. But here it is again, turning him into something inhuman in the moment that it invades his eyes, in the moment when we touch. There is something *very* wrong.

The tether between us pulses, disturbed, and I tremble, remembering the way his power had nearly overwhelmed mine, pushing me down and down until I would have been just a tight ball of energy, trapped inside myself. What had truly happened? According to Gemma, whoever Enzo is tied to should be able to control him. But I had not felt in control in that moment. I'd felt threatened, felt *him* trying to overpower *me*.

That should not be right. But Enzo is an Elite, reborn—he is something that has never existed before. Perhaps Maeve did not predict the extent of Enzo's powers as well as she should. I shiver, trying to understand what this means.

You are his link to the living world. You can control him. Try it.

I reach out through the link now, searching for him. My threads seek out his heart as if they have a mind of their own.

Enzo shudders and closes his eyes. When he opens them again, blackness pools into the whites of his eyes. I try to breathe—but I realize that when I hold his heart in my hands like this, I cannot. It's as if the action of controlling an Elite requires every last bit of my energy. An irrational boldness takes hold of me.

"Paint a wall of fire behind me, Enzo," I whisper, taking a step toward him. My gaze stays locked on the blackness in his eyes.

Enzo doesn't say a word. He lifts one hand, then brings it back down in an arc. Heat explodes behind me. I break my stare for an instant to look—and there, exactly as I'd commanded, burns a wall of flames roaring from floor to ceiling, so hot that it threatens to scald my skin. I turn back to Enzo with my lips slightly parted. I'm so surprised by his obedience that I lose my concentration.

Enzo shakes his head violently. Suddenly his power lunges back at me again, taking advantage of my moment of distraction. I stumble once as the force of his energy overwhelms me. An illusion sparks around us, gray mist and rain, only to vanish again. My mind struggles for control, pushing back against his, trying to contain him. It is like pushing against a wall. I grit my teeth, shut my eye, and hurl my energy through our tether.

Finally, he backs down. Enzo shudders as my power forces his away. The flames behind me vanish in a trice, leaving only Enzo pressing a hand against his forehead, his eyes squeezed tightly shut. My energy snaps off from his heart and comes rushing back to me. The room falls back into silence. I'm breathing hard.

This. This is the power that Maeve, Raffaele, and the Daggers had wanted by bringing Enzo back. None of them care about him—they only want to do with him what they once did with me: to use him to get the throne. But even they must not have anticipated this strange phenomenon, that Enzo can fight back against his bonded partner. I blink rapidly as the realization sets in, and it sends a knife through my heart.

Just as I can control him . . . if I am not careful, he will be able to control *me.*

"What happened?" Enzo whispers, looking up at me from where he crouches. I realize that he does not remember what he did—when the darkness takes over, he loses himself. My shock at what happened sinks into despair. How can we rule side by side like this, always fighting each other for dominance? How can we return to where we once were?

You will have to crush him, the whispers answer me. *Either he will be your slave, or you will be his.*

The door bursts open. Both of us jerk our heads to see Magiano standing there, mouth already open to tell us something. He pauses when he sees our faces. His slitted eyes go to Enzo first. He hesitates, then looks back at me. His gaze lingers as I turn a bright red. Hastily I try to weave an illusion to cover up my flush, but it's too late—suspicion appears on Magiano's face, along with something else. Fear.

I will tell him later how I was able to call on Enzo's powers.

Enzo straightens and pulls out one of his daggers. Magiano's eyes dart back to him. The two glare at each other.

"Who are you?" Enzo says in a low voice.

Magiano blinks, then holds up his lute. "I'm the entertainment," he replies.

"He is an Elite," I say, when I see Enzo's threatening stare. "Magiano, the thief. He's joined us."

"Magiano." At that, Enzo lowers his dagger slightly. He gives him a curious look. "We'd all started to think that you were a myth."

Magiano gives him a half smile. "I guess I must be real, Your Highness."

"Why is he here?" Enzo turns back to me. "What are you planning?"

"To take back the throne," I reply. "To destroy Teren and the Inquisition Axis."

Before I can say more, Sergio and Violetta come to the door.

For a moment, Sergio looks as if he might address the prince, even thank him for sparing his life all those years ago. But he doesn't. Enzo watches him with a quiet, careful stare. Sergio opens his mouth, then closes it again. He clears his throat, and walks over to the window instead. He points out at where the *malfetto* camps start dotting the field. "You can see the commotion from here." He waves us over. His eyes settle on Enzo again, as if he's not quite sure what to do around him. "You'll want to see this too, Reaper," he adds.

Enzo walks over. The tether tugs between us, leaving my heart beating and my breaths short. I even recognize his walk—elegant, predatory, careful. *Regal.* My thoughts scatter as I walk over to the window. If I gain the throne, will I match that kind of grace? Can I persuade Enzo to follow us, find a way I can reliably control him?

Sergio points as we gather. "The camps. They're burning." He doesn't have to gesture much for us to see what he means. A dark cloud of smoke and ash rises over the land where the camps are set up. Even from here, we can see patrols of Inquisitors making their way through the camps' rows. Their white cloaks are a stark contrast against the green and brown of the land. There must be dozens of them.

"Do you know what's happening?" I ask Sergio.

He nods. "The rumors have been flying through the city and the villages," he replies. "The queen has demoted Teren from his Lead Inquisitor title. He is to leave tomorrow to inspect the southern cities."

"Demoted?" Violetta exclaims. "The queen relies so heavily on his power. Why would she send him away?"

Magiano shrugs, but his eyes glow bright. "He either upset her, she finds him unreliable, or she has no more use for him."

"Teren has angered my sister," Enzo says. "Disobeyed her. He will do it again."

"But he's the queen's lackey," Magiano says. "He—"

Enzo raises an eyebrow. "I remember that rumor. He has been in love with my sister since he was a boy. He would give his life for her, but he will not be sent away from her side. Not even by her. He is convinced that her well-being is in his hands."

Even though I don't know the details of what happened, I know immediately who must have come between them. Raffaele. He is working his power, and the Daggers are closing in. That means Beldain's navy may make their move soon. I look down at the scene. Why are they burning the camps?

And then it comes to me. If the queen has sent Teren away, he must be furious. If the queen has rejected his wish to destroy all of Kenettra's *malfettos,* then he might have turned his back on her. *He is going to carry out his plans, one way or another. He will kill the* malfettos *today.*

He will burn them all.

"We have to save them," I whisper. "And I think I know a way."

Pale eyes suddenly flash in front of my face, directly on the opposite side of the glass—as if Teren were right there, floating in midair, lunging for me. I choke on a scream and stagger back from the window. I lash out to shield myself. *Teren, he's here, he's going to kill me.*

"Adelina!" It's Violetta, and her cool hands have grabbed my wrists. She's pleading with me. "It's okay. You're okay. What happened?"

I blink as I look at her, then back at the windowpane. The pale eyes are no longer there. Sergio and Violetta stare at me in concern and confusion. Enzo's lips are tight. Magiano has a serious look that I rarely see on him.

One of my illusions, run rampant. It's happening more frequently now.

Enzo approaches me first. He offers a hand, then helps me to my feet with one effortless tug. I tremble at his touch. "Steady, little wolf," he says gently. The words are so achingly familiar that I want to collapse against him. Behind him, Magiano looks away.

I shake my head and let my hand fall away from his. "I thought I saw something," I mutter. "I'm fine."

"Are you sure—?" Sergio starts to ask.

"I'm *fine*," I spit back. He blinks, startled at the venom in my voice. I'm startled too. Immediately I tone it down, then sigh and run a hand through my short hair. Beside me, Enzo watches me carefully. I know he felt the way my energy lurched through our tether. He knows. But he doesn't say anything.

I can't stand everyone looking at me. "I'm fine," I repeat, as if saying it enough times will make it true. The image of the pale eyes appears again in my mind. I shudder. Suddenly, the room feels too small, the air too thin. I turn away from everyone and hurry out into the narrow hall leading down to the stairs.

"Hey."

Magiano catches my arm and spins me around. His pupils are round now, and his eyes a soft honey. He frowns. "Another illusion out of control, wasn't it?" he says. "Has this always happened with your powers?"

"It's not unusual," I grumble, even though I know it's not true.

"When did it start?" When I don't answer right away, Magiano's voice hardens. "We have pledged ourselves to putting you on the throne. We deserve an answer. *When did it start?*"

I'm silent.

"Was the time in Merroutas your first? In the gondola?"

I feel as if illusions were lying in wait right outside my line of sight, ghosts waiting to appear. I can't hide it from Magiano. "It happens after I kill," I whisper.

After I killed Dante, my uncontrollable illusions caused Enzo's death. After I killed the Night King, I saw my father in Merroutas. And after I killed the Inquisitor that night in Estenzia . . . this. I shiver uncontrollably.

"I'm fine," I say over and over again. I glare at Magiano, daring him to question me.

He steps closer, then reaches down to touch my cheek. "Adelina," he murmurs, then hesitates. I think he's going to tell me to be more careful, that I shouldn't stay on this path. Instead, he sighs. As always, I find myself drawn to his warmth. He is truly alive, and this moment feels real. I'm still trembling. Why can't I stop my illusions anymore? Behind him, the others emerge from the room and look on.

Finally, he nods back toward the window. "You said you know a way for us to save those *malfettos*," he says. "Well, what? What's your plan?"

I squeeze my eye shut and take a deep breath. *Calm yourself,* I command. Magiano's presence steadies me. I look up at him. "Teren is down there right now, in the *malfetto* camps," I say. "We can trick him to work in our favor."

"In our *favor*?"

"Yes." I look from Magiano to the others. "If Teren is at odds with the queen, he'll want retaliation. He's doing it right now. He can be our way into the palace, and to the throne."

Enzo approaches and a surge of anger travels through the tether that links us. "And what makes you think you can bend Teren to your will?" he says. "His disobedience to my sister will not make him our ally."

"Enzo," I reply, "I think I know why Teren has been banished. I think I know who came between them."

At that, Enzo's expression changes instantly. His anger becomes confusion, then realization, all in the blink of an eye. "Raffaele," he says.

I nod. "I think Raffaele is in the palace. I don't know what he has done, but if the Daggers are working to break the two of them apart . . . then we might be able to find the Daggers by going to the palace. In order to do that, we'll need to trick Teren into working with us. He will be able to get us in faster than we can do it ourselves." I hold up my hands. "I can only disguise so many of us, and only for so long."

"We don't have much time," Magiano adds, looking in the direction of the burning camps.

Enzo considers my words. The thought of reuniting with the Daggers and with Raffaele has given him some spark of life, and I can feel it burning within him. Someday, he will figure out what I did to Raffaele at the arena. What will happen then?

The whispers surface. *Then you must exert your control over him.*

After a moment, Enzo straightens and walks past us. "Let's hurry, then."

Teren Santoro

I'm not supposed to be here.

Still, Teren marches down the rows of the *malfetto* camps. "There," he says, pointing, leading a squadron of Inquisitors behind him. Giulietta may have stripped him of his Lead Inquisitor title, but he still has patrols at his command. Now he motions for his men to head to each of the longhouses where the *malfettos* are. "Get them all inside."

Inquisitors push frightened *malfettos* back into their assigned quarters. Their shouts ring out across the camps. Teren waits until each longhouse is filled, and then he nods again at his men. "Lock the doors."

As Teren marches down the row of longhouses, the Inquisitors lock each door behind him, metal scraping against metal as the doors are bolted shut.

Giulietta's words ring in Teren's head over and over

again, becoming a cacophony of betrayal. *You are no longer my Lead Inquisitor.* He pledged his entire life to her, but she no longer wants it.

He remembers the way he used to make her smile, how she would let him unpin her hair and it would tumble down past her shoulders. He imagines kissing her again, wrapping her in his arms, waking up in her bed.

How could she push him aside in favor of the Daggers? Teren shakes his head. No, this is not the princess he grew up knowing. This is not the queen he pledged to serve. He had made a promise before the gods that he would cleanse this land of abominations, and he'd thought that the queen wanted the same thing.

And now she wants to free the *malfettos*, after all the hard work he has done?

"Light the torches," Teren commands, and his men rush to do his bidding.

No, he cannot allow the Daggers to win like this. If he has to leave the city, he is going to take the *malfettos* down first.

He pauses at the end of the row, then turns to face the longhouses again. He takes a torch from one of his men, walks up to the first longhouse, and holds it up to the thatched roof. It catches fire.

As the smoke builds, and the people trapped inside begin to panic, Teren walks to the next longhouse, shouting a command over his shoulder. "Burn them all."

It is better to have an enemy who will fight you in an open field than a lover who will kill you in your sleep.

–Kenettra and Beldain: An Ancient Rivalry, *various authors*

Adelina Amouteru

I sense what's happened in the *malfetto* camps before we even arrive there. An aura of terror and pain hovers over the entire area, blanketing the land as surely as the smoke fills the air. I shiver at the feeling.

Violetta rides with me. Behind us, Enzo flanks our left, his face masked behind a cloth veil in case Teren sees us, and Sergio flanks our right, one hand on his horse's reins and the other on the hilt of his sword. Somewhere nearby, Magiano watches us. I imagine his eyes narrowed, focused on me as we go.

By the time we reach the edge of the camps, the smoke is thick. Screams fill the air. The longhouses used to house the *malfettos* are on fire, the flames licking at the roofs, crackling and roaring, red splinters floating through the air. *Malfettos* are trapped inside. Their terror feeds my darkness so much that I can barely see. I lean over in my saddle, struggling to keep my own fear at bay. The screams coming from the longhouses are familiar to me. They remind me of my own. Where are the Inquisitors? The paths are empty, the soldiers having long since passed through and moved on to the other camps in the area.

The fires closest to us flicker—as if a great wind had just whipped past—and then they vanish into curls of black smoke. I glance to my side, where Enzo gallops. He gives me a single nod, his eyes the only part of his face that are exposed, and then urges his horse onward. He raises another hand. Other fires along the path flicker out. Each time he uses his energy, the tether between us vibrates, sending shudders through my chest. Tendrils of his power seep into me, the threads scalding my insides. I try to keep it under control.

Screams continue from inside the longhouses. The whispers in me jump, excited by their overwhelming fear. I grit my teeth as we reach the first of the houses. I jump down from my saddle and rush to the closest door. Even though fire has eaten away at it, and the wood is charred black, I can't seem to pull the wood apart. I yank at the metal lock. The sudden rush of helplessness angers me. I am the White Wolf, capable of creating the most powerful illusions in the world—but they are just that. Illusions. I cannot even break a lock with my own hands.

Enzo appears beside me. His gloved hand closes on my frantic ones. "Allow me." He wraps his fist around the lock. The metal turns bright red, then white, and the wood around it chars. It bursts apart in a shower of splinters. The lock comes free.

We pull the door open, and a plume of smoke rushes out.

I don't wait to see how many survivors are inside. Instead, as Violetta and Sergio call for people to get out of the house, I move on to the next door. One by one, we break open each locked house.

A few Inquisitors run straight into us right as we turn a corner. They startle at the sight of us—and Enzo is on them before they can even react. He whips out a blade and stabs the first, then puts his hands around the collar of the second. The soldier's eyes bulge as they burn from within. He falls without a sound, his mouth still open, smoke pouring out. Enzo steps over him in one stride, then lunges at the third. Flames alight beneath his feet with each step that he takes. He throws him roughly to the ground before the Inquisitor can even properly draw a weapon, then pins him down. I blink at the sight. Enzo had attacked all three in a blur of motion. I have not even seen the full extent of his new power, but I can feel it burning under his skin and through our tether.

The Inquisitor on the ground whimpers beneath Enzo's grip. "Teren Santoro," Enzo says, tightening his hand around the man's neck. "Where is he?"

The Inquisitor waves one arm frantically against the ground, pointing in the direction of his head. My stare travels down the burning camps, then settles on one of the temples lining Estenzia's outer walls.

In the short time that I knew Teren, I learned several things about him. He is in love with the queen because she is pure of blood and wants the *malfettos* destroyed as well. But one thing he honors more than the queen: his duty to the gods. If Teren has lost her love, then he may have turned to the gods for comfort.

Farther down the path behind us, Sergio throws knives into the throats of two other Inquisitors who happen upon us. They fall from their steeds, gurgling. Sergio swings down from his horse and joins us, while Violetta rides up behind him. He notices my line of sight. He nods, then mounts his horse again and taps the creature's hindquarters with his heels. Enzo has already returned to his own steed. He holds a hand down to me, and I take it, swinging up behind him.

Behind us, a few *malfettos* take up a cry.

The Young Elites!

They're here!

We dismount when we reach the temple. A horse is already outside, nervously stamping at the ground. Enormous statues stand on either side of the entrance—Laetes, the angel of Joy, and Compasia, the angel of Empathy. I exchange a look with Violetta. "I will go in first," I whisper to Enzo. "If Teren is here, then I need him to see me alone."

"Go ahead," Violetta tells me. She tightens her riding gloves. "I'll be waiting in the shadows. I won't let him use his strength against you."

Enzo turns his horse around and looks toward the horizon, where other *malfetto* camps have started to burn.

Sergio rides up beside him. "My other men are ready to move, should we give the signal," he says to Enzo.

"No need," Enzo replies, his eyes still fixed on the rising smoke. "I've seen you fight—I trained you myself." It is the first time he has acknowledged their past. He hoists a blade in one hand, and it gleams in the light. "This will be quick, and quiet."

Sergio nods in agreement.

Enzo glances at him before he moves. "The Rainmaker," he says.

Sergio narrows his eyes. "I've not forgotten, you know," he replies. He kicks his horse in its hindquarters. "But we have more important things to settle first."

Enzo's eyes flick back to me. He does not ask if I will be okay. His silent approval makes me stand taller. Then he turns away and rides with Sergio toward the smoke in the distance. I turn to Violetta, and together, we head up the steps.

The sun has almost completely set. There are no Inquisitors near the temple, as there is nothing to guard, really, no valuables or jewels—only daily flowers laid at the marble feet of the gods. For once, I have no illusion of invisibility over myself. I walk in plain sight.

The temple is nearly empty. Shafts of evening light penetrate the space from the high windows, painting the air with blue and purple stripes. At the very front of the temple, with his back turned to me, is Teren, crouched low before a statue of Sapientus, the god of Wisdom. I stop at the door, then carefully remove my boots. My bare feet make no sound against the floor.

Teren doesn't seem to notice my presence. As I draw closer, I can tell that he's muttering something under his breath. Louder than muttering, actually. He is talking in earnest, his voice angry and rushed. My tether to Enzo hums. I can still feel him nearby. The others must be too. Magiano must be somewhere in the shadows. But if Teren were to move against me right now, would Magiano save me in time? I'm close enough to see the silver lines engraved on his armor. He's not wearing his Lead Inquisitor cloak.

The last time I saw him, Enzo lay dead at my feet. *You don't belong with them,* Teren had said. *You belong with me.* Perhaps he's right.

I'm close enough now to hear what he's saying.

"This is not my mission," Teren insists. He shakes his head and looks up at the statue. His thin blond tail trails down his upper back, the gold bands on it shining in the light. "You put me in this world for a purpose—I know that purpose, have always known it. But the queen—" Teren pauses. "The Daggers have poisoned her against me. Raffaele—he's working his demonic magic on her."

An image appears in my mind of Raffaele seducing the queen. Even Giulietta is no match for his charms.

"I can't leave her like this," Teren snaps. His voice echoes through the temple, and I freeze. "She is my superior in every way. I have pledged my entire life to obeying her. But now she wants to send me away, Lord Sapientus. How can I leave her with *them*?"

He sounds confused now, like he is arguing with himself. His voice changes from grief to confusion, then back to anger. "She's listening to him. She used to listen to *me*. She used to hate the *malfettos*—but now he's talking her out of our goal. Would she really give up our entire mission of cleansing this country, just to have those abominations fight for her? They are liars and whores, thieves and murderers. They are tricking her, and she is allowing it. Do you know what she said to me when I tried to defend her?" Anger again. "She said I am an abomination, *like them*." His voice takes on a frightening tone now, somewhere between the borders of fury and madness. *"I am not like them. I know my place."*

Suddenly he stiffens. I hold my breath. The temple is so silent now that I can hear the rustle of my sleeves brushing against the sides of my robes. For an instant, I think he might not have heard me.

Then, in the blink of an eye, Teren whirls from his crouched position, draws his sword, and points it straight at me. His eyes are chilling, his black pupils floating within them like drops of ink on glass. His cheeks are wet, to my surprise.

His eyes widen a little at the sight of me, then narrow again. "You," he murmurs. Gradually, his grief fades away, hidden behind a shield, until all I can see is the cold, calculating smile I remember, his eyes still dancing with the light of madness. "Adelina," he says, his voice turning silky smooth. "What's this?" He takes a step toward me, his sword still pointed at my neck. "Has the White Wolf finally decided to stop hiding? Did the Daggers send you?"

"I am not a Dagger," I reply. My own voice sounds even colder than I remember. I take a step toward him, forcing my head to stay high. "And it sounds to me like you can't seem to remove their thorn from your side."

Teren's smile deepens so that I can see his canine teeth. It is a furious smile. He pauses, then lunges at me with his sword.

"Violetta!" I shout.

Teren stops mid-attack. He lets out a terrible gasp, then stumbles backward and clutches his chest. It takes him an instant to catch his breath. He lets out a weak laugh, then points his sword at me again. In the shadows, I see a glimpse of Violetta moving. "I knew your sister must be here somewhere," he says. "She seems to have grown bolder since last we met. Fine, let's play. I could slit your throat even without my strength."

He lunges at me again. Old lessons from Enzo flash through my mind—I sidestep, then lash out at him with an illusion of pain. The threads wrap tightly around his arm. I pull, and he shrieks as he thinks his arm is being ripped clean of his body. But almost immediately, he recovers and slashes his sword at me.

"Stop," I call out. "I've come to talk with you."

"All an illusion with you," he shouts through gritted teeth. I can feel him pushing back against my power. If he doesn't believe me, I can't hurt him.

I concentrate, throwing all my strength into my pain illusion. This time, the threads slice deep into his belly—when I pull, I conjure the illusion that I am ripping apart his organs, that I am cutting him from the inside out. Teren screams. Still, he comes at me. His sword catches my skin this time. It slashes a scarlet mark on my upper arm.

Something flickers in the darkness—and an instant later, Magiano appears before me, drawn out by the sight of my blood. His pupils become slits as he looks at Teren. "Keep your filthy blades off her," he snaps. "It's rude."

Teren's eyes widen again, surprised by Magiano's sudden appearance—but then he strikes at Magiano with his blade, cutting deep across his chest. Instinctively, I reach out to protect him.

Magiano stumbles backward. Before our eyes, the bloody cut on his chest heals almost immediately, stitched together by invisible threads. He laughs at Teren. "I believe she told you to *stop*, so that we can all talk," he says, crossing his arms. "Don't you like talking? You seemed to be doing a great deal of it a moment ago."

Teren can only stare at Magiano's healed chest in disbelief.

"Don't fight me," I shout as the Inquisitor whirls, his blade aimed at me again. I barely avoid it in time. "I know what you're really up against."

Teren laughs. "Brave little wolf," he taunts. "The queen wants your head, and I shall give it to her."

"Raffaele has taken your place at the palace," I say, toying with Teren's temper. "And he has also cast me out of the

Daggers." I nod at Magiano. "Not that it has stopped me from finding allies."

"You've been busy," Teren says with an icy smile. His pale eyes cut me to the bone, then shift to Magiano, who gives him a winning grin.

"Do you really believe Queen Giulietta deserves the throne, now that she has thrown you away?" I ask. "Now that she is willing to have other Elites in her army?"

Teren watches me carefully. I can feel his darkness rising again. "What do you want, mi Adelinetta?" he says.

Suddenly, I stop where I am. I weave an illusion over my entire face . . . transforming myself into Giulietta. Same rosy cheeks, same heart-shaped face and tiny, puckered lips, same deep, dark eyes so reminiscent of Enzo's.

Teren stops so quickly that he loses his grip on his sword. The weapon clatters to the ground. Even though he must know that it's just an illusion, he cannot seem to control his reaction. "Your Majesty," he whispers, staring at my face in wonder.

"This is what you want, isn't it?" I murmur, stepping closer to him.

Teren stares at me. This time, he falls completely for the illusion—he has forgotten about me. Instead, he takes a step forward and holds my face in his hands. He is surprisingly gentle.

"Giulietta," he whispers. "Oh, my love. It's you." He kisses each of my cheeks. "How could you send me away?"

Then, his hands tighten on my cheeks, grabbing at the

flesh. "You sent me away," he says again, harder this time. A spark of fear jumps in me. Something in his voice reminds me of my father, that hard-hearted fury. "I did everything for you, and you *sent me away*."

I decide to play along. "I am the Queen of Kenettra," I say. "Pure of blood. If I want, I'll send you away. If I wish, I'll kill you. Shouldn't I?"

"But you are taking counsel from a Dagger," Teren spits out. His grip hardens against my face until it hurts. "You are letting a *malfetto* tell you it's not worth it to cleanse this country."

I force down my fear. "I have no interest in destroying *malfettos*. I never have. Why should I? It's useless."

Teren brings his face so close to mine that his lips brush mine. Nearby, I can hear Magiano's sharp intake of breath. "I *loved* you," he hisses. His voice shakes with rage, and I drink it in, terrified at the power behind it, yet hungry for more. My illusions strengthen. "And now, you love *them*?" His lips brush mine again, in something that can only be called a kiss. But there is nothing but hatred in it, something deep and hard and revolting that makes me want to shrink away. His fingers are like claws against my face. "Tell me, My Queen—how can I love a *traitor* to the gods?"

I unravel my illusion again, until Teren is holding *my* face in his hands, staring into my broken features. He stares at me a moment longer. Gradually, his energy calms as he recognizes me. He bares his teeth, releases me in disgust, and turns away. I'm shaking from how close I was to his rage. He wanted to crush me in his hands. Enzo had said that Teren was madly in love with the queen . . . but this . . . this is not love. This is obsession.

"You once said that I belong with you," I call out. "Instead of with the Daggers."

Teren pauses to turn his head slightly in my direction. In the waning light, all I can see of his features is an outline of his profile. It reminds me of how I saw him in the very beginning, his profile framed by light on the day of my burning, how he came over to me and threw a burning torch at my feet.

"The only way to get what you want in this world," I say, "is to do it yourself. No one else will help you in this. The only way is if *you* are on the Kenettran throne."

Teren laughs a little. "And why, my dear Adelina, would *you* want that?" He ignores Magiano and steps toward me. "I almost killed you. I killed your *lover*."

An image of Enzo dying on the ground, of me crying over his body, flashes at me. *I hate you, Teren,* I think as I stare at him. *I hate you, and someday I will kill you. But first, I will use you.*

"Because," I say, tilting my head up, "the Daggers also wanted me dead. Because they would have killed me." I step closer. "How can I love a traitor?" I say, echoing Teren's words. He raises one eyebrow in surprise. I have unsettled even him. "I would sooner *die* than see them take the throne." I raise my hands then, and call the threads around us. The darkness in Teren's heart feeds my power, giving me the fuel I need.

Flames erupt all around us. They explode from my body, rush along the ground, roar up the walls and the statues of the gods, up to the ceiling, eating up the dim blues and replacing them with searing gold and orange and white, leaving no space untouched except the spots where each of us stand. The entire temple is ablaze. The illusion of heat burns the edges of Teren's clothes and threatens to peel away his skin.

"The Beldish queen has already sent for her navy," I call out above the roar of fire. "There will be war. She has been working with the Daggers this entire time." I nod at Teren. "You were right to suspect Raffaele."

"How do you know this?" Teren snaps.

"I overheard the Daggers." I narrow my eye. "And I would like nothing more than to see their plans turn to ash." Around us, the insides of the temple turn black and charred.

Teren smiles at me. He takes a step closer. "Ah, mi Adelinetta," he says. His eyes soften in a way that surprises me. "I have missed you. You, more than any other abomination, understand what we truly are." He shakes his head. "Had I known you when I was a young boy . . ." He lets that sentence die, leaving me curious.

My hatred for him rises like bile and I grit my teeth, letting my illusion of fire die out, and we're left to stand in the charred remains of the temple. Then that, too, disappears, returning our surroundings to normal.

Teren's eyes glow with an unstable light, and I know that I have reached his tipping point, that any doubt he might have for helping me will be overshadowed by his desire to strike back against the Daggers. "What are you planning, little wolf?" he says. "The Daggers have already wedged their way to the queen's side. She has already sent for them for tomorrow morning."

My hands tremble at my sides, but I press them harder against my legs. "Then lead us into the palace, Master Santoro. Tomorrow morning." I look beside me, where Magiano watches with slitted eyes. "And we will destroy the Daggers for you."

Maeve Jacqueline Kelly Corrigan

The lookout in the crow's nest is the first to give the signal. He rushes down from the mast to kneel in front of his queen. "Your Majesty," he says breathlessly before Maeve. "I saw the signal far out at sea. Your ships. They're here."

Maeve gathers her furs around her neck and puts a hand on the hilt of her sword. She walks to the edge of the deck. The ocean looks like an expanse of black nothingness from here. But if her lookout is to be believed, he saw two bright flashes out in the midst of that darkness. Her navy has arrived.

She looks to her side. Aside from her brothers, the Daggers are also up on deck. Lucent bows her head, while Raffaele folds his hands into his sleeves. "Messenger," Maeve calls to him. "You say Giulietta has asked for your audience tomorrow morning?"

Raffaele nods. "Yes, Your Majesty," he replies.

"And Master Santoro?"

"He should already have left the city, Your Majesty." Raffaele gives her as level a look as he always has, but underneath it, Maeve senses his distance. He has not forgiven her for what she did to Enzo.

"Good." The wind whips Maeve's high braid over her shoulder. Her tiger utters a low growl at her side, and she pats his head absently. "It's time for us to strike." She hands Raffaele a tiny vial. At first glance, the vial seems to contain nothing but clear water and a tiny, insignificant pearl. The Daggers draw near for a better look. Maeve gives the bottle a light tap.

The pearl transforms in an instant, shifting from its round shape into a writhing, dozen-legged monster hardly an inch long. Maeve can see its needle-like claws raking against the glass, and the way it swims through the water in a jagged, furious motion. The Daggers back away. Gemma puts a hand over her mouth, while Michel looks sickly pale.

Raffaele meets Maeve's gaze. His lips tighten into a tense line.

"It can burrow underneath the skin," Maeve explains. "It does so with such speed and precision that the victim will not even realize it until it is too late." She hands Raffaele the vial carefully. "Giulietta will be dead within the hour."

Raffaele stares at the wriggling creature, then places it carefully in a pocket of his robes. "I will find a way tomorrow morning," he says.

Maeve nods. "If we time this correctly, Giulietta will die as my navy invades her harbor. The throne will be ours before Master Santoro can turn tail fast enough back to the capital, and before the Inquisition can push back."

"And what of Adelina?" Raffaele says. "What of Enzo?"

Maeve's attention shifts. She reaches for her belt, pulls out a parchment, and unfurls it. It is a map of Estenzia and its surroundings. She points toward a spot in the forests near the city's outskirts. Beside her, Augustine toys with the hilt of his sword, while her brother Kester's eyes glow bright. "We are going to fetch him tonight."

"Turn it one way," said the merchant to the girl,
"and you will see where you want to go. But if you turn it
the other way, you will see where you are needed the most."
–The Other Side of the Mirror, *by Tristan Chirsley*

Adelina Amouteru

The rains come tonight.

Lightning forks across the sky, and thunder shakes the windowpanes. I watch Sergio's downpour from the court's old entrance. The haunting cries of baliras fill the black sky overhead. The shores near Estenzia are churning furiously, and the chaos must have stirred the enormous creatures into the skies. Violetta tosses in a fitful sleep in the next room, the thunder working its way into her nightmares. Enzo sits out in the hall and sharpens his blade. He doesn't interact with anyone else here. I know what he's waiting for—I can almost feel it through our bond. He is looking forward to reuniting with the Daggers. I dwell on it with a sinking heart. Sooner or later, he is going to find out what really happened, and that my story to him is not the whole story at all.

From downstairs come low voices and the shuffle of

boots. My mercenaries. They are restless, now that we will storm the palace tomorrow. Earlier, I'd walked among them to count how many of the Night King's former men had decided to follow me. There are forty of them. A small number, to be sure, but they are deadly, each the equivalent of ten soldiers. Sergio tells me there are more, scattered across the land and waiting for our strike. "They won't show themselves until you look like a sure bet," he'd said earlier. "Then they'll come out of the woodwork to help you finish the job."

A light tap comes from the door. When I look over, I see Magiano walking toward me. He comes to stand beside me and watch the baliras haunting the wet skies.

"If the Star Thief were near us," he mumbles, "I could control those baliras. We could fly right over the palace and land on its roofs."

I stare at the sky, listening to their cries. "The storm has stirred them from their waters," I reply. "Not even Gemma can control more than one, not in this agitated state."

Magiano leans against the windowsill. "Do you really think Teren will help us?" he says. "I don't remember him being great at keeping his word."

"I know how he keeps his word," I reply. A fleeting memory comes back to me of his pale eyes and twisted smile, how he'd watch me beg for more time whenever I went to see him in the Inquisition's tower. I tense at the recollection. "He hates the Daggers more than he hates us. It's all the advantage we need."

Magiano nods once. His eyes seem distant tonight.

Behind us, we both hear Enzo rise in the hallway and make his way downstairs. His boots hit ominous notes against wooden floors. Magiano looks over his shoulder, then back to me when the footsteps fade away. "The prince is a moody one, isn't he?" he says. "Was he always this way?"

"Enzo has always been quiet," I reply.

Magiano looks at me. Whatever taunts he might have had on the tip of his tongue now vanish, replaced with a grave expression. "Adelina, you keep waiting for him to become what he once was."

My hands tighten against the windowsill. Even now, I can feel the tether between me and the prince pulling taut, calling for me. The whispers stir restlessly in the back of my mind. "It will take time," I reply. "But he will come back." My voice drops to a whisper. "I know it."

He frowns. "You don't believe that. I can see the truth on your face."

"Do you say this to hurt me?" I snap, turning a fiery glare on him. "Or do you actually have a point to make?"

"I'm trying to say that you are living in a world of illusions," Magiano says, reaching a hand out to touch my arm, "of your own creation. You are in love with something that no longer exists."

"He is one of *us* now."

Magiano leans closer. His eyes flash, his pupils black and round. "Do you know what I saw when I passed him in the hall? I looked down at him, and he up at me—I looked into those eyes and I saw . . . *nothing*." He shivers. "It was like staring straight into the Underworld. Like he aches to return to where he came from. He is not really here, Adelina."

"He is right here, in this building, with us," I say through clenched teeth. "He is tethered to *my life*. And I will use him as I see fit."

Magiano throws up his hands. His eyes turn distant, and his pupils turn again into slits. "Yes, I know," he growls sarcastically. "That's all you see. Your victory. Your prince. Nothing else."

I blink, confused for a moment, and then I realize that he's talking about himself. He is standing before me, confessing something, but I am not hearing it. I've forgotten our moment under the stars, when his kiss brought me calm like nothing ever has. I do not *see* him. I hesitate, torn between my anger and confusion, and say nothing.

When I don't reply, Magiano shakes his head and leaves the room. I watch him go before turning back to the window. The anger continues to churn inside, blackening my heart. I don't want to admit it, but I find myself aching in his absence, missing the light that he brings. *We shared a moment,* I remind myself. *Nothing more.* Magiano is here because he wants his gold, not because he's in love with me. He's a trickster and a thief, isn't he? The familiar feeling of betrayal wells up in me, memories of how others have turned their backs on me in the past, and I recoil, folding away my thoughts about Magiano. Caring for a scoundrel is a dangerous thing.

When I look down at the soggy grounds below, I can see

Enzo standing near the entrance. Behind him, small fires still dot the scorched earth of the courtyard.

Magiano's right about this, at least. There is a distance about Enzo that has not faded since he returned. Tonight, it seems as if he were not really here at all—like his thoughts don't linger with the Daggers, or with us, but with something far, far away, in a realm beyond the living. I watch his dark figure in the night, then push away from the windowsill and head out of the room. I head down the hall, then the stairs. I ignore the mercenaries chatting with one another in the house's crumbling entryway. I make my way outside, where the rain is still soaking the air. I stop a few feet away from Enzo. It is quiet out here, and I can see only the two of us. I wrap my arms around myself in the cold, then approach him.

He turns to look at me. The tether between us pulls tight.

"What's wrong?" I ask him.

He doesn't answer right away. Instead, he turns back to the storm with a frown, the distance still plain on his face. It takes me a moment to realize that he has turned in the direction of the ocean. I feel a deep ache in my chest.

He is here, but he doesn't want to be.

He nods once as I come to stand beside him, acknowledging my approach. Even now, he still has the air of nobility, an unspoken sense of authority. It gives me a glimmer of hope. "I am thinking of an old tale," he says after a long silence. His voice is deep and quiet, the voice that I remember. Why, then, does he seem so different? "'The Song of Seven Seas.' Do you know it?"

I shake my head.

Enzo sighs. "It is a ballad about a sailor who spent his entire life and fortune sailing the oceans, searching for something he'd never actually seen, someone he'd never actually met. Eventually, he reached a place far in the north where the sea was frozen solid. He spent a month wandering through that dark wasteland, before he finally collapsed and died." He stares off into the forest. "All that time, he was searching for a girl he'd loved in a past life. He had been searching in the wrong lifetime, and he would never be in the right one again. So it would go, until the end of time."

I stay silent. The rain stings my face with its cold fingers.

"I feel as if I were out to sea," Enzo says quietly. "Searching for something I don't have. Something only the sea can give."

He is searching for the Underworld. Just as Magiano had said.

I'm suddenly angry. Why must I lose everything that I care for? Why is love such a weakness? I wish, for an instant, that I didn't need such a thing. *I can win the same things in life with fear, with power. What is the point of searching for love, when love is nothing but an illusion?*

I reach through our tether, and he shudders at my touch. *Do you remember, Enzo?* I think sadly. *You were the Crown Prince of Kenettra. All you ever wanted was to save the* malfettos *and rule this nation.*

Magiano's words haunt me. *Did Enzo ever love me? Or do I love something that never existed?*

When we stand this close, our tether pulses with life. Enzo turns to me, then takes a step closer. The power between us leaves me dizzy. The threads of my energy dart out and seek him, and he seeks back. It is as if he were clinging desperately to the spirit of life inside me, clawing on top of it as a drowning man would push his rescuer underwater in an attempt to save himself. His soul is alive, but it is not living.

Still, I can't break myself away from the twisted feeling of this union. I want it too. So when he wraps his arms around my waist and pulls me closer against him, I let him. His hands run through my short hair, tugging at it. I struggle for air, but he pulls me back down by meeting my open lips with his own. Panic shrouds my mind, my illusions burst free, and my alignment to passion roars in my ears. I am caught in the maelstrom. I can feel him overpowering me now, the tendrils of his unnatural energy, tainted by the Underworld, wrapping around my heart and covering it with black threads. This is the danger of our tether, as I always knew. He is too strong.

My energy soars, pushing back against the rush of his. I shove him off me with a violent strength I didn't know I had. My darkness wraps around his heart and digs its claws in. Enzo shudders, and the whites of his eyes turn black.

Then I blink, and it is no longer Enzo before me. It is Teren.

I open my mouth to cry out, but Teren puts a hand over my mouth and shoves me against the wall. He presses a sharp knife against my chest. The blade digs in, hurting me. *This is an illusion,* I tell myself over and over. *But why does the blade hurt?*

"I will help you," Teren whispers in my ear. "And when we are done, I will kill you."

The dagger digs into my flesh. My skin breaks. Blood comes out. I force myself free from Teren's grasp, clutching the bleeding mark, and run across the courtyard through the rain. Behind me, Teren rises from his crouch and starts to walk forward. Where did Enzo go? I stagger into the court's corridors, calling for Magiano. For Sergio. For Violetta.

No one answers. I squeeze my eye shut and tell myself to snap out of my illusion. But when I open my eye again and look behind me, Teren is rushing toward me, his blade drawn, his lips pulled back in a demonic smile.

And then it is not Teren anymore, but my father, and I am running through the halls of my old home, trying to escape my father and his knife.

I start to cry. I reach a set of stairs and stumble down them. I trip on one, nearly twist my ankle, and fall a few steps to the lowest level. Up at the top of the stairs, my father's silhouette appears in the darkness, blood staining the ribs of his ruined chest. His knife flashes in the night. I am ten years old, and he is drunk with wine, out to cut the skin from my body. He calls my name, but I keep running.

"Violetta!" I sob. My voice breaks. "Violetta!" And then I remember that on the night this happened, my sister hid under a staircase and did not make a sound. I see her crouched there, huddled with her knees tucked up to her chin, her eyes glittering in the darkness. She waves me over, but there isn't enough space for me to hide with her. We exchange a helpless look. I glance desperately up at the stairs. My father lurches down them toward me. I have no choice. I have to run.

"Adelina!" Violetta screams for me, reaching her arms out. "Hide! He will catch you!" She starts to scramble out of the hiding place in order to give it to me, but I whirl around and bare my teeth at her.

"Stay where you are," I cry.

Break the illusion, Adelina. You have to. None of this is real.

I tell myself this, but I don't know how to escape my mind.

I stagger out of my father's house and into the rain. Silverware glistens on the wet ground all around me. I am sixteen, and I am trying to run away. Behind me, my father emerges from our home's entrance with a bloodstained knife clutched in his hand. His eyes meet mine. I whirl, looking wildly around for my horse, but there is none. I stagger forward, then trip over the silver candelabras and dishes cluttering the ground. I fall, making a thunderous clatter. I start to crawl on my hands and knees. My father gets closer. My breaths come in ragged sobs.

I just want to get away. I just want to escape. I just want to be safe. *Somebody help me.*

A rough hand grabs my ankle. I kick frantically, but it's no use. Another hand grabs my soaked shirt and yanks me up, then slams me against the wall. My arms fly up in defense. My father's snarling face appears before me, rain carving rivers down his cheeks and chin, water making his teeth slick. He grabs my hair tightly in one fist. There is fire around us, distant shouts.

"No—" I cry out. *Break out of the illusion break out of the illusion it's not real tell me it's not real.*

My father's knife presses against my chest. He stabs down, hard. I can feel the knife slice into my flesh. It hits deep. My eye widens—my mouth opens in horror. I try to stop him, but my arms are weak and useless. The blade hits my lungs.

I take a deep breath and scream.

"Adelina! Adelina!"

Hands are trying to pull my arms down. I scream and scream, unable to stop. *Stop saying my name.*

And then, everything leaves me in a rush. I crumple in sudden exhaustion.

It takes me a long moment to realize that the person calling my name is Magiano, and it is his arms wrapped around me. Beside him stands Violetta. She has taken my power away. Our old home, my father, the silverware littering the ground, the knife, Teren—they've all vanished, leaving me huddled at the entrance of the Fortunata Court, drenched in rain. I cling desperately to Magiano. How had my illusions felt so real this time? How can I be sure that Magiano and Violetta are not an illusion? What if they aren't here at all?

"It's okay," Magiano whispers into my hair as I cry. He kisses my face. "You're okay. I'm sorry."

I try to say that I'm grateful he's here, that I hope he's real, but my words are lost in my sobs. Violetta watches me helplessly, then turns away and looks at Magiano.

"What happened?" she calls out over the rain.

"A group of attackers," Magiano replies. "They ambushed us."

Violetta gasps. "Inquisition?"

"No. These were foreign soldiers, with foreign accents." One of his arms loops under my legs, while the other presses against my back. He lifts me effortlessly. I huddle against his warmth, balling his shirt into my fist. "I don't know where Enzo's gone. Some of the other mercenaries have given chase." He raises his voice. "Hey! A little help here!" A couple of our men run toward us.

I realize, slowly, that the fires and shouting around us are real. Someone had attacked us. The tether between Enzo and me is pulled tight, stretched thin. I reach out through it, but he is too far away for me to control him. The distance sends a sharp pain through me, and I wince, trying to choke that pain down. He's gone. I blink through the rain, fighting to see the difference between illusion and reality. *Am I truly here?*

"Get a warm cloth," Magiano is saying over me. We head inside and up the stairs, where he places me gingerly on the bed. The rain dripping from my hair soaks the sheets. From here, I can see out the window toward the black sea.

"Who were they?" I whisper. I'm still not entirely sure that any of this is happening.

"The Beldish, I think," Magiano mutters. "They must have sent a hunting party out after us."

I shudder. The knife stabbing into my chest had felt so real—my father had been right there, Teren had slammed me against the wall. My wild illusions, like my powers, are starting to take on more facets than just sight and sound. They can touch me, make me think they are hurting me. I think of all the times I have used this against others. Then, the thought of it turning against *me*.

I look up at Magiano. He stares at me with a worried expression. His eyes are not slitted. His pupils are black, and his gold eyes are warm and bright. "This is your tether making things worse," he says. "I know it. You told me you aligned with passion. It calls to you when you're tied to him, doesn't it?"

My alignment to passion. He's right, of course. Enzo has returned from the dead, and with him has come all of my old passion, the same passion that caused my powers to leap out of control, that had made Raffaele so distrusting of me in the first place. Now, with this tether between us, my instability has only grown.

"Why . . ." I fight to clear my head. "What did they want?"

I know the answer before Magiano even replies. "The Daggers came for Enzo," he says.

No. The pain returns to my chest as I realize that the Daggers will tell him everything about me—both lies and truths. He will find out what I did to Raffaele.

The distant rumble of explosions makes us both freeze. At first, I think it must be the thunder. Then I see something on the horizon, filling the dark, furious oceans around Estenzia as dawn slowly creeps forward. The light of fire.

Magiano sees it too. We freeze where we stand, and together we see a trail of fire arc through the air, then send up a burst of flames.

I try to see what is going on through the rain and darkness. "Is that . . . ?"

Then a fork of lightning cuts through the sky, illuminating the clouds and land and sea, and my question dies on my tongue. Yes, it is. Warships dot the horizon, their blue-and-white banners unmistakable even from this distance, an endless trail of beads on a necklace, stretching as far as the eye can see. Their hulls curve high, and their sails loom tall. The Beldish navy has arrived.

Such blinding dreams of white ice and spinning dice,
I watched them all vanish in a trice.
What will be your sacrifice?
–Leven Night: A Collection, *by Enadia Hateon*

Adelina Amouteru

Never in my life have I seen so many ships. They cover the sea like a swarm of insects, and from here I feel as if I could hear the buzz of their wings. The sound of horns and the deep rhythm of war drums float to us. Estenzian horns answer back. From the Fortunata Court's vantage point, I can see the Inquisition spilling into the streets, swarming in the direction of the palace. Kenettran warships cover the ocean closest to our harbor. But our ships are outnumbered.

There is no time for me to recover from my illusion. I shake my head violently, trying to force the terrifying images away. "We have to go," I breathe, forcing myself up off the bed. "Now."

To my grateful surprise, Magiano doesn't argue. Instead, we rush to join the others. They are already waiting near the court's side door. Sergio has horses for us, while my other mercenaries have already melted into the forest. I go to the stallion Violetta is astride, and she reaches a hand down to help me. I take it and swing up behind her.

"We will be surrounded by Inquisition forces," Magiano reminds me as we turn our horses in the direction of the palace. He raises an eyebrow at me. "Are you strong enough?"

He is concerned for me, but he doesn't stop me either. "Yes," I say, and he nods. It's all he needs to hear from me. Without another word, we set off in the rain. Off in the distance, the Beldish war horns blare again.

I feel a faint tug on the tether linking me to Enzo. The feeling makes my stomach seize painfully. The Daggers had come to sabotage me. They are making their move with their Beldish queen, and now Enzo will be at their side instead of mine. I grit my teeth. *But not for long. They cannot control him like I can.* By the end of this day, someone shall take this country.

As a bleak, rainy dawn breaks, we draw closer to the harbor. The canal where Teren told us to meet already has a line of gondolas waiting for us. The boats are painted a deep black so that they blend right in with the dark, stormy waters. I hold my breath as we rock along, the sides of the gondolas buffeted by waves.

As we sail closer to the plaza bordering the palace, a vision of white cloaks comes into view—a patrol of Inquisitors, all with their attention pointed at us. At the front of the patrol of Inquisitors stands Teren. He catches sight of me, and I hold my breath. Magiano's doubts echo in my mind.

If Teren goes back on his word now, then we will have to fight here.

But then I remember the anguish in his voice, the force of his hands clutching my face, and I know that his fury in the temple was real. He does not move as we approach. Instead, when we dock, he commands his Inquisitors to pull our gondolas forward and secure them. He holds a hand out to me.

I step out of the gondola without taking it. Behind me, Violetta follows. Magiano hops out with a nimble leap, his eyes fixed warily on the former Lead Inquisitor. A low rumble of thunder echoes across the sky. I know Violetta is trembling behind me.

I stare at Teren too. For a moment, neither of us says a word. I realize that this is the first time his eerie eyes are trained on me like an ally, and the feeling turns me cold. *All I need is for him to take us into the palace,* I remind myself.

"Do your work," he says, and turns in the direction of the palace gates.

Teren cannot set foot inside the gates if he looks like himself. He has been banished by the queen, after all, and if he reveals himself too soon, the palace's soldiers will stop him. So I weave an illusion over him, changing his nose and the tilt of his eyes, the lines of his jaw and the arc of his cheekbones. His eyes shift from ice to something dark and murky. His patrols look on as I transform their leader into a complete stranger. Their fear is directed at me, and I cherish it. It will be useful later.

I finish disguising Teren. "Well done, illusion worker," he says to me. Magiano steps closer to me at Teren's words, but Teren only smiles at him. "Don't fear for her," he goes on. "We are allies, remember?"

Magiano does not smile back.

We head toward the palace. Above us, a flash of lightning punctuates the darkening dawn. The closer we get, the stronger the tether pulls between me and wherever Enzo is. We must be drawing near to the Daggers too. The feeling makes me restless, impatient for us to move faster.

The Inquisitors at the main gate don't stop us. Neither do those in the palace's front courtyard, or those lining the palace's main entrance. We fool guard after guard. I walk beside Violetta, our steps in sync, the illusion of white cloaks trailing behind us. Teren does not turn around, but his Inquisitors press close beside us, ready to stop us if we give the faintest sign of moving against him. I stare at his back, fantasizing that I could reach out and twist him, that I could let pain wash over him. The thought fuels my powers further. We make our way down long corridors and halls lined with windows from floor to ceiling. The storm clouds gathering outside have thickened now into blankets so that I can no longer see the sky through its gaps.

Finally, we reach the hall leading to the throne room. The number of Inquisitors here would not be able to stop us now. So I reach out for Teren's disguise and slowly unravel it. The illusion of his dark, murky eyes gives way once again to his pale ones; his blond hair and cold, chiseled face return.

The Inquisitors standing at the throne room's door stiffen at the sight of him. I smile at their confusion. They must be wondering where Teren suddenly appeared from, and how he had gotten past all of the other soldiers in the palace.

Teren stops before them. "Stand aside," he orders.

The guards hesitate for a moment longer. Teren had been the Lead Inquisitor for long enough that it is hard for them to break the habit of obeying him. But then one shakes his head nervously. "I'm sorry, sir," he says, standing as straight as he can and putting his hand on his sword's hilt. "I don't know how you got this far, but we'll have to escort you out of the palace. The queen has ordered you—"

Teren doesn't wait for him to finish. He draws his own sword, steps forward, and slashes it across the man's throat. The man's eyes bulge, and his jaw drops. The second guard starts to raise the alarm, but I lash out with my illusions. A thousand imaginary hooks dig into his flesh, yanking hard, and he collapses to the floor. Teren crouches down and stabs him before he can scream. The man convulses, gurgling, on the ground. I stand and watch, remembering the Inquisitors I'd sentenced to die on the ship.

Teren steps over the bodies, pushes open the throne room doors, and goes in.

The first person I see is Queen Giulietta.

I have only caught glimpses of her from afar, but I recognize her immediately because of her resemblance to Enzo. On this dark morning, she has shed her long silk robes and replaced them with traveling gear—a heavy cloak drapes from her shoulders, and the hood covers her head, revealing only a sliver of her dark locks and the glint of a thin crown. My eye goes to the balcony. The shadow of an enormous ray-like wing glides past, and I realize that baliras are circling the palace, waiting to take the queen and her personal Inquisition guard out of the palace. They are preparing to escort her out of dangerous territory.

Raffaele is out on the balcony. He has already boarded a balira, and several Inquisitors are climbing upon the creature's back with him. His eyes dart to me—he is the only one in the room who I know realizes who we really are. I can feel the wave of fear surge from him, and a burst of anxiety. *The other Daggers.*

Where is Enzo? I search frantically. No. The bond is still too far away. He isn't here.

Giulietta turns in our direction as Teren strides toward her, Inquisitors trailing in his wake. She focuses her eyes on us menacingly. "What is this?" she says. "*Guards.*" Even the tenor of her voice, rich and deep and mysterious, reminds me of Enzo's.

A beat later, her eyes dart to the chamber doors. She catches sight of the dead guards' blood pooling on the floor. Her stare shifts to me. A faint recognition sparks there. Even though she has never met me, she *knows* who I am—and I want to drink the trickle of fear that appears over her. "The White Wolf," she murmurs.

Teren smiles a broken smile at her. "Hello, Your Majesty," he replies. He stops before her and drops into a deep bow.

Giulietta frowns, then tenses. She glances at me again before turning her attention back to him. "You shouldn't be here, Master Santoro."

Teren seems unconcerned with her words. "I live to serve your crown," he says. He glances behind her—his eyes, gleaming with hatred, settle on Raffaele. "But you turned me away, Your Majesty, and let these other abominations near you."

Giulietta lifts her head. "You do not serve me by being here," she snaps. She starts to move in the direction of the balcony, where one of the baliras has slowed its circling to hover outside. She glances at Raffaele. "See to it that your Daggers take care of this."

But Raffaele doesn't make a move. Of course he doesn't. Instead, he takes a step back and folds his arms into his sleeves. Overhead, several baliras are flying in the balcony's direction. I recognize the tiny spot of copper hair on one of the riders. It's Lucent.

Giulietta gives Raffaele a harsh look. She narrows her eyes. Realizes the danger she is now in. She glances at the Inquisitors behind Teren. "Seize him," she calls out. One of her Inquisitors shouts at her to board a balira, and she starts rushing in its direction.

A tingling begins in my fingers and travels up my arms. My power is so strong now that the edges of my vision are starting to blur, illusions of memories and people flashing in and out of my periphery. *I could kill the queen myself, right now.* The thought rushes through me with exhilarating speed. Teren and his Inquisitors have gotten us into the palace, and now I stand a mere few feet from the ruler of Kenettra. I could twist her so hard with pain that she could die, writhing, here on the floor. This is what we came here to do. Beside me, Magiano gives me a quick glance. He expects it too.

What are you waiting for, Adelina?

But a better idea occurs to me. I came here for revenge, didn't I? So, instead, I let *Teren* move forward. Then I reach out with my threads and coil them around Giulietta's wrist. I yank hard, weaving.

Giulietta lets out a shocked cry of agony as a sudden, searing pain twists her wrist. She looks down in horror as she sees blood dripping down her hand. I smile, strengthening the illusion. She looks up at me. My illusion wavers as she realizes what I'm doing, but she is not strong enough to see past it.

The Inquisitors behind Teren do not move at Giulietta's command. For the first time, I sense a flicker of uncertainty in her. Giulietta gathers her strength. "I said, *seize him*!"

Still, the Inquisitors do not move.

Teren lifts his bowed head to look at Giulietta. I expect him to smile, but instead his eyes are filled with tears. "You sent me away," he says. "I loved you. Do you know how much I *loved* you?" His voice trembles. I shudder at the blackness that has started to rise within him.

"You are a *fool*!" Giulietta retorts back. "Do you still not understand why I sent you away? It is because I am your *queen,* Master Santoro. You do not disobey your queen."

"Yes, you are my queen!" Teren shouts. "And yet you no longer act like one! You are supposed to be chosen by the gods. Pure of blood, *perfection.* But look at whom you surrounded yourself with!" He gestures to Raffaele. "You commanded that abomination to touch you? You accepted the Daggers as part of your army, in exchange for halting the cleansing of *malfettos*?" Teren's words turn uglier, his voice harsher and louder. He is entirely oblivious to the hypocrisy of what he is saying.

"And what are you?" Giulietta snaps. "You, my *malfetto* Inquisitor? Have I not forgiven you for your abomination? You know nothing about how to rule! I would do the same for your fellow *malfettos,* as long as they recognize their abomination, and serve me as my humble subjects."

I reach for Teren, feeding his anger with threads of my own darkness. My energy wraps around him, adding to his, weaving an illusion around him. I paint a fleeting image before him of Giulietta wrapped in Raffaele's embrace, with her head thrown back, Giulietta turning away from Teren and toward Raffaele. Giulietta standing on a balcony, pardoning *malfettos* of all crimes. I paint all of these images before Teren, flashing them one after another, until he is lost in them.

Teren's fury lurches higher. The whispers in my head grow and grow, until they are deafening.

Your revenge your revenge your revenge.

Do it, now.

I reach for Giulietta, and I start to weave.

Suddenly, Teren pauses. His eyes widen. They focus on something in Giulietta's hair . . . a wide, shining lock of red and gold, prominent against the rest of her dark strands. Teren frowns, confused. In the midst of his rage, swirling in the storm of illusions I've created around him, he cannot tell that this is an illusion I've just created.

I smile. *Look, Teren. Why, how did you miss this marking on her, after all these years?*

His eyes dart back to Giulietta's. "You," he whispers, blinded by my illusion. "You have a marking?"

"A marking?" Giulietta's expression shifts for a moment in confusion.

Teren's focus returns to the unnatural color in her hair. I conjure whispers in Teren's ears, and they speak to him of betrayal. "You've hidden it from me, all this time," he mutters. "Covered by an apothecarist's work, hidden by black powder. A marking. I know it."

"What are you talking about?" Giulietta's anger is bitterly dark now, a rising tempest. "You have lost your mind, Master Santoro."

"You are no pure royal. You were tainted by the blood fever, like your brother." His mouth curls into an ugly sneer. His eyes are glazed, delirious with the illusions I've woven around him, and he can focus on nothing but the false marking I've painted into Giulietta's hair. "You are an abomination, a filthy *malfetto,* just like me. And I gave you my *love*. And you *fooled me*."

"*Enough,*" Giulietta snaps. She looks again to her Inquisitors and draws herself up to her full height. "This is an *order*. Seize him."

Still, the Inquisitors don't move. Teren stares at Giulietta as if his heart were icing over. "Now I know why you always had such sympathy for those damn *malfetto* slaves," he chokes out hoarsely. "Asking for them to be properly fed. Asking for them to return to their homes." His voice trembles with rage now. "Now I know why you give yourself away to other abominations."

"You are a madman," Giulietta says. I shiver at how her voice reminds me of Enzo's. "You cannot tell sympathy apart from strategy."

Teren shakes his head. "You cannot be a pure-blooded queen chosen by the gods." He holds out a gloved hand and gestures at the Inquisitors. They shift their crossbows from Teren to the queen.

Giulietta narrows her eyes at Teren as she takes a step back. "What have you done to my men?" she demands.

"They are *my* men," Teren says. "They have always been mine. Not yours." He raises his voice. "You are under arrest, for corrupting the crown."

My powers surge out of control. The world turns black, then scarlet. The whispers claw to the surface, seizing my mind. I feel my rage and fear surge forward in unison.

Giulietta lets out a strangled cry as the pain in her wrist spreads to the rest of her arm, then to her entire body. At the same time, I wrap my illusions harder around Teren, caressing his subconscious thoughts, reminding him of everything Giulietta has done to betray him.

Look, Teren. She is a malfetto *queen. You cannot let this go on.* The whispers turn into a roar in his ears. *End this now.*

End this. End this!

Teren draws his blade. His eyes pulse with madness, hypnotized. He steps toward Giulietta. She backs away, puts her hands out in defense, calls his name, calls once again for her traitorous Inquisitors to listen to her—but it is too late. Teren seizes her by the arm, pulls her toward him, and stabs her straight through the heart.

"Now, are you happy? Have you finally achieved all you set out to do? What will you do next, little assassin, with no one left to see you?"

–One Thousand Journeys of Al Akhar, *various authors*

Adelina Amouteru

I flinch, even though I knew it was coming. The whispers in my head burst into delight.

Teren grits his teeth and plunges the sword deeper into her chest. My threads of energy tighten around him, blinding him, continuing to feed his frenzy. I'm not sure whether I'm even controlling my energy anymore. "I do this for Kenettra," he says through clenched teeth. Tears stream down his face. "I cannot let you rule like this."

Giulietta clings tightly to him. Her knuckles turn white, the color of his cloak that she clutches in her fist—and then, gradually, she starts to slip, sliding toward the floor like a flower meeting the frost. Teren keeps his arms wrapped around her. He lowers her gently, until she crumples to her knees beneath him, blood soaking her traveling cloak.

Only then do I unravel the illusion I'd woven into Giulietta's hair. The red-gold lock shifts back to dark brown. I pull back the curtain I'd woven over Teren's eyes. The throne room comes back into clear focus for him—gone are the images I'd painted of Giulietta with Raffaele, of Giulietta pardoning the *malfettos*. I pull all of it back, leaving Teren alone with his thoughts again.

Teren breathes hard. He blinks twice, then shakes his head as the fog clears. He seems suddenly unsure of himself. He stares at the darkness of Giulietta's hair, as if finally regaining some semblance of his sanity. I feel his energy shift violently from one extreme to another, his hatred and grief transforming into rage, and then fear. Sheer terror.

He finally realizes who it is that trembles on his blade, bleeding and dying.

Teren looks sharply at her. "Giulietta?" he says. Then he lets out a wrenching cry. "*Giulietta.*"

Giulietta's grip on his cloak softens. I can sense the energy shimmering around her, the strings of light fading, going dim, leaving her and returning to the world, seeking the dead ocean. Her face twists for a moment, but she is too weak to speak now.

The energy within her fades then, and she goes limp.

Teren shakes her shoulders. His head stays bowed over her, and his voice cracks. "We were supposed to fix the world together," he says. I can barely hear him. He sounds confused, still shaking off the remnants of my illusion. "What have you made me do?"

Giulietta just stares back at him with empty eyes. Teren lets out a choked sob. "Oh gods," he breathes as he finally realizes what he has done. My darkness swirls, and the whispers in my mind coo at the sight. From the corner of the room, my father's ghost laughs, his shattered chest heaving in amusement. He keeps his stare focused on me. I see for an instant what Teren might have been like when he was younger, a little boy in love with an older girl, watching her dance while he hid in the palace's fruit trees, infatuated with an idea that he could never become. My smile turns savage.

I could have killed Giulietta myself . . . but this is better.

"I suppose she is a pure-blooded royal, after all," I say aloud. I give Teren a bitter smile. *"Now you know how it feels."*

In the midst of his grief, he lifts his head to look at where Raffaele is now on a hovering balira's back. A spark of fury burns in him. No, not fury. Madness. The madness in him is growing. It fills him until it threatens to spill out. *"You,"* he snarls. He turns back to me. "You did this to her." His rage grows and grows, until it seems to blind him. I gasp at the rush of it.

He shouts for his Inquisitors to attack me. Magiano whips out a dagger and braces himself. But we stand our ground. I glance at the Inquisitors walking behind Teren, then smile and gesture to them.

Some of the Inquisitors aren't Inquisitors at all. They are my *mercenaries,* in disguise.

They break rank with the real Inquisitors, draw their

weapons, and attack. Two Inquisitors fall, screaming, clutching at their throats.

Raffaele reaches for the balira's reins. The creature shudders, startled, and before the few Inquisitors with him can react, the balira surges forward, hitting its back against the balcony's marble railings. It crushes two Inquisitors against the railings with a sickening crunch of bones and flesh. Another is flung, screaming, out into the air. The last one tries gamely to hang on to Raffaele, but I see Raffaele reach down in one fluid motion, pull a dagger from the Inquisitor's belt, and stab it grimly through the man's neck. At the same time as the man falls, the balira pushes its fleshy wings down and shoots up.

I suddenly realize that Gemma must be nearby, calling Raffaele's balira forward. *Enzo must be nearby too.* I rush forward.

Outside, heavy drops of rain have started to fall. I nearly slip on the balcony's slick surface. A blast of icy cold air hits me. As I reach the edge of the railing and look down, I see a sight that lifts my heart. Magiano is riding on the back of one balira, while Sergio and Violetta are on another. Magiano whistles to his, and the creature rushes upward toward me.

"Jump!" Magiano shouts at me.

I don't think. I just act.

I push myself up onto the railing until I'm straddling it. The fall down to the courtyards below makes me dizzy, and I teeter for a moment, lost in a sudden haze of fear. My power floods my chest and mind. I clench my teeth, then swing my other leg over and fling myself out into the open space. I fall.

The balira glides up to meet me. I land against cold, slick flesh. I almost slip off, but Magiano's warm hand seizes my arm and yanks me up. He pushes me forward until I can grasp the edge of the saddle next to him. I pull myself into a sitting position, then grab the reins with him.

He turns the creature sharply in the direction of Raffaele's balira. Now I can see others in the air, dozens of them, some ridden by the Daggers, others by my own mercenaries. I focus my energy on the Daggers and the Beldish queen: my next targets.

Behind us, baliras carrying Inquisitors stop to hover at the balcony, and Teren and his men board. Magiano whistles at ours, and it surges forward. Rain whips against my skin.

"We have to keep up with your Star Thief," he shouts. "I can't mimic her if I can no longer see her."

I squint against the rain and look over my shoulder. Teren and his Inquisitors are on our tail.

Black clouds have now completely covered the sky, blocking any sign of the sun from view, and the rain comes down in torrents. Lightning forks ahead. Sergio's storm is building quickly now, likely out of his control. The baliras fly low, as unnerved by the charge in the air as we are. I can feel a steady pulse of unease from the balira beneath us, and the sheer intensity of its fear makes me light-headed.

Beside us, Violetta shouts at me. I turn instinctively in her direction, as if I've always known where she is. She points to a balira some distance before us. "Star Thief," she calls out over the storm.

My attention darts to where she gestures. Now I can see a rider on the balira's back, her hair whipping behind her in a long sheet. It's Gemma. For an instant, I think back to the day I'd seen her race a horse, her head thrown back in sheer joy, hair streaming out, and I realize that even if I cannot see her face, I can recognize her by the life in her movements. She urges on her balira. Arrows sing toward her from Inquisitors flying nearby, but her creature turns in a spin, narrowly avoiding the weapons.

Magiano whips our reins, guiding our own balira. It speeds up.

We soar over Estenzia's piers, and suddenly we're out over the bay. The entire siege comes into view below us. A line of Beldish warships blockade the entrance of the bay, while others are engaged in battle against Kenettran ships—cannon fire looks like orange and white balls of light against the dark ocean. I can barely tell the sounds of their explosions from the roar of thunder overhead. Above them, baliras armored with silver plates glide through the air, their white-cloaked riders gleaming against the dark sky.

The tether hums, tugging at my chest. We are drawing

very near to Enzo now. I can feel him turning his attention in my direction, too, sensing me in the same way that I sense him.

Even in the melee, I can see the Beldish queen riding on one of the baliras, her high braid in plain sight, her face protected behind a metal guard. She fires arrows one after another, taking down every Inquisitor rider in her path. Another rides with her—one of her brothers—no, *Lucent*. As I look on from a distance, Maeve leaps to her feet as an Inquisitor suddenly drops onto their balira, trying to throw them off course. Her sword flashes through the air. A spray of blood follows it, and the Inquisitor plummets from the balira's back.

Then they veer away sharply, until they're lost in the midst of riders.

"Adelina!" Magiano's shout jolts me back. Gemma's balira flies straight into our line of sight. We pull closer behind her. She glances over her shoulder at us—we are near enough that I can make out the familiar purple marking stretched across her face. Our eyes lock.

She recognizes me. And suddenly my power wavers.

Why am I hunting her down? She has always been kind to me, and perhaps she would be kind to me even now. A strange, wild hope grows in my chest—out of everyone, Gemma would accept me despite what I've done.

Gemma turns back around in her seat. For an instant, I think she's going to slow her balira so that we can fly along side each other, so that she can talk to us. I open my mouth and start to tell Magiano to pull aside and give her room.

Then she turns back to face us—and a crossbow is in her hand. She lifts it and fires.

I'm too shocked to dodge.

"Move!" Magiano snaps at me. He shoves me hard, and the arrow sings past my neck. I fall flat against our balira's back. My ears ring.

Gemma fires a second arrow, this time toward Magiano, but Magiano ducks low and pulls our balira sharply left. The arrow shoots past us and disappears into the darkness.

Magiano grits his teeth and urges our balira to speed up. "We need to work on your reflexes, my love!" he shouts.

My fear changes to bewilderment, then betrayal, then anger. White-hot, searing anger, burning the whispers in my head and forcing them out of their cages. They flitter around my mind like a cloud of furious bats until I can barely see. *You would have gladly seen me dead, Gemma.* A part of me tries to urge that, no, perhaps Gemma had only fired a warning shot, had purposely missed us—but the whispers in my mind shove this thought away. My teeth clench, and my fists tighten so hard against the reins that the rough ropes cut my palms.

How could you? I spared your life in that alleyway. Don't you know?

I should have killed you.

I can hardly breathe. I don't even care if what I'm

thinking is fair. I should have killed her right there, it would have been so much easier. It would have sped up our goals. Why didn't I? My power churns with my fury, and I push myself back upright on the balira's back. I lean toward Magiano.

"Chase her *up*," I shout. Perhaps it is a whisper in my voice that shouts, because in this instant, I no longer have a voice of my own.

Magiano pushes against the balira's back. The creature lets out a haunting cry that shudders through our bodies. Then it dives. It dives so sharply that I have to steady myself against the saddle so that I don't slide off completely. Almost immediately, Magiano pulls it back up, and the balira jerks its head up toward where Gemma flies.

She senses us. Suddenly our balira shudders off course—she is trying to manipulate our ride's mind. Magiano grits his teeth. He pushes back. Our balira steadies. Magiano pulls it until its head is turned back up, and then he whispers something to it.

Gemma sees what we're about to do, because she pulls hers up too. We charge forward, hurtling higher, leaving the warring bay below us. Rain flies in my face and I feel that old panic again, the fear of not being able to see, and I hastily wipe the water away. Gemma's balira swings its tail in an arc. Its needle-like endpoint swipes at us, threatening to cut us—Magiano pulls us away at the last second. He forces us to move slower, out of the tail's reach.

I grit my teeth and reach out with my energy. The threads shoot toward her, wrap around her like a cocoon, and then, as I concentrate, *tighten*. I feel her shrink away, her terror jump. From her point of view, it seems as if the world had suddenly rushed up to her, the sky become the sea, and she is upside-down, hurtling into the ocean and submerged in water. She can't breathe. From where we are, I see her hunch over in her saddle in panic. Her balira veers sharply off course as she tries to turn them around in their illusion of an ocean.

I grit my teeth and tie my strings tighter and tighter around her. Gemma twitches violently again as she feels like her lungs are filling with water. She's drowning, and she claws at the air, trying to swim.

"Adelina." Magiano's voice cuts through my concentration like a knife. My illusion wavers, and for a moment, Gemma can see. "We have to pull back!" he shouts. "We're too close to the storm!"

I hadn't even noticed. The black clouds loom far too close, an endless blanket of black that stretches in every direction—and we are about to plunge right into it. I blink, breaking out of my anger. Above us, Gemma shakes her head and realizes the same thing. But her concentration has been thrown off, and her balira struggles against her, refusing to listen. Magiano pulls our own balira so that its nose points down again. The black clouds leave our view, and I find myself staring once more at the bay dotted with fire and warships. We start to dive back down.

I look, once, over my shoulder, to see Gemma still struggling with her balira. It lets out a shriek of protest.

Then the dark world lights up, and we all go blind.

A bolt of lightning—a crack of thunder that splits the sky. The sound explodes all around us. Heat sears us from above. Magiano and I both throw ourselves against our balira's back as it continues to plummet down. I can't see anything but light. Something burns. My eye tears up. Magiano somehow manages to pull our balira up as we near the bay—I feel my weight drop down against the creature's back. I'm trembling uncontrollably. All I can do is turn my face to one side, and through the blur, a streak of light shoots past us.

It is Gemma, burning, falling to the ocean. Her balira's enormous, lifeless body hurtles beside her. Struck by lightning.

I watch her. She falls forever, the shooting-star thief, her light fading from a streak into a dot, then into nothing, then, finally, into the sea with her balira. From the ocean's surface, I know the impact must look like a tidal wave, pushing all the ships around it outward in a ring. But from up here, it looks like an insignificant splash, like she was here and then she was gone.

And the world continues as if she had never existed.

My heart twists, but we have no time to dwell on it. Even as we sit, stunned and suspended in midair, Magiano turns his head toward where a cluster of ships have gathered around a single one. Baliras dotted with white-cloaked figures head toward it. Immediately, I know this must be Queen Maeve's

Beldish ship. Magiano shouts something at me. I nod in a daze. Below us, an anguished scream comes from a voice I recognize all too well as Lucent's. She is screaming Gemma's name.

Magiano turns our balira away, even though all I want to do is stare at the spot where Gemma had hit the water, where ripples have covered her flaming light.

Mankind has been fascinated with baliras for thousands of years.
Countless stories have been written about them,
and yet we are still no closer to understanding
the secrets of their flight, kin, and life in the deep.
–A Study of Baliras and Their Closest Cousins, *by Baron Faucher*

Adelina Amouteru

We are close enough now to the ocean that the cannon fire sounds deafening. Rain whips sideways against us. Some of the Kenettran warships nearest the royal Beldish ship blow sharply off course, and I realize that Lucent must be somewhere nearby, pulling and pushing at the winds to throw the Kenettran army into turmoil. Others fire at the Beldish ships—only to see their cannons unwound right on the decks of their ships or their cannonballs vanish in midair. Michel at work. I keep expecting to see Gemma reappear on the back of one of the baliras zooming through the skies, but she doesn't. The rain streaks lines on my face. I remind myself that we were enemies.

There are so many Beldish ships. One quick glance is all it takes for me to see that this isn't a battle the Kenettran navy can win. How can we ever push them back? I look down to where the royal ship sails. It is surrounded on almost all sides by reinforcements, and the Kenettran navy is throwing itself forward in vain. Baliras in armored plates soar around the ship, protecting it from the air. Other Elites ride on some of them—one is wearing the royal gold of Beldain. Perhaps he is one of Queen Maeve's brothers. As I look on, he makes a sharp gesture with his arm toward a Kenettran soldier. The enemy rider rocks wildly backward, as if hit hard, and falls from his balira.

"Get closer," I call to Magiano, pointing to a clearing in the sky.

"If you have any clever ideas for how to do this without killing ourselves, I'm happy to listen," Magiano shouts back.

I look harder at the Beldish formation. *The royal ship is protected on almost all sides.* A half circle of warships. Beyond them is another ring, and then another, until all of the ships look like a honeycomb.

"Look out!"

I throw myself flat against the balira at Magiano's warning call. A cannonball explodes near us, sending a surge of sea spray high up in the air. I duck. Our balira jerks sideways with a roar, one of its wings singed. I catch a brief glimpse of the Beldish warship that fired at us. My energy churns madly within me, feeding off the fury and fear from the thousands of soldiers in the bay. It builds and builds, until the flesh right underneath my skin tingles from it, as if it might rip me completely apart.

The tether between Enzo and me trembles. I look around

instinctively. My heartbeat races. *He's here.* The bond trembles violently—as if he has realized I am near too—and an instant later, I see him. He is on the back of a balira, and a stream of fire bursts from his hands, aimed down at the Inquisition ships below. Inquisitors follow closely on his tail. A Beldish rider near Enzo screams as he weaves fire right out of the air and hurtles it toward the soldier. Fire consumes the soldier—he falls from his balira's back, and the balira, now without a rider, dives toward the water.

Enzo, I call through our bond. He turns to face me. His energy hits me hard, right as I try to exert my own power. Magiano shoots me a look and tightens his grip on me. For a moment, Enzo meets my gaze, and his stare is hard and dark. I know right away that the Daggers have told him everything.

He turns in the direction of an Inquisition warship. He opens his hand, then closes it into a fist. The simplest, smallest movement.

A line of fire explodes across the surface of the water with a deafening roar. The flames race toward the ship at terrifying speed, then burst and curl as they strike the ship's mighty hull. The fire swallows the wood. Flames shoot high into the sky, engulfing the entire ship. The blast blinds me. I throw an arm across my face, trying in vain to shield myself from the heat and light. My bond pulses violently, his energy feeding mine, the heat scalding the insides of my body. I tilt my head back and close my eye as anguished screams reach us from the Inquisitors on board the burning ship.

The fire hits something—the gunpowder of the cannons. A fierce explosion shudders on the ship's deck. Burning splinters of wood fly into the air, some rocketing toward us, smashing into the water in giant plumes.

I need to control him. Enzo's energy is finite, and making such a big move will almost certainly take something away from him. But suddenly it is all I can think about. If I can gain control over him, then we can win this battle.

"Get us closer to Enzo," I say.

"As you wish, my love." Magiano pulls hard on the reins, and our balira veers off our course to fly beside Enzo. On our other side flies Sergio and Violetta. Magiano pushes us forward until we are a triangle, and then he takes us down hard.

We skim along the ocean surface. Cannon fire explodes around us, but Magiano pushes on. I feel the balira shudder underneath us. It is injured, and it will not fly us for much longer.

We sail past the burning ship, and as we do, the Beldish queen's vessel suddenly comes into view, startlingly close. Enzo's balira draws near, and my heart soars, our bond screaming for us to be closer.

Then, suddenly, Magiano yanks us to one side. An arrow hurtles right over our heads. I only have time to let out a startled cry before I see another balira pull up close to us. Maeve's hard eyes bear into mine. She hoists her crossbow at us.

I fall flat against our balira's back. Behind Maeve, Lucent

lifts an arm—a blast of wind hits Magiano and me. I squeeze my eye shut and hang on for dear life. Our balira screams in protest. It flips in midair. When I open my eye again, Maeve has pulled right next to us. She crouches against her balira and makes a flying leap toward ours.

Her sword is in her hand the instant she lands. She lunges at me. I'm so surprised that all I can do is throw my hands up in defense. My powers lash out desperately at her, seeking to wrap her in an illusion of pain. For an instant, it seems to work—Maeve shudders mid-attack, then drops to her hands and knees. Magiano whips out a blade of his own and slashes at her. But another blast of wind from Lucent forces him back. At the same time, Maeve glances up at me with clenched teeth, fighting to tell herself that the pain she's experiencing isn't real.

"You little *coward,*" she spits at me. Then she manages to come for me again. Her blade glitters.

Another cannon explodes near us, hitting our balira's other wing, and it careens wildly out of control. Suddenly I feel nothing beneath me but rain and air, and all I can see is a blur of sea and sky. I reach out blindly to grab for Magiano's hand, but I don't know where he is.

I hit the ocean hard. The icy water knocks the breath out of me, and I open my mouth in a vain attempt to scream. My hands grapple for the surface. Cannonballs and arrows streak through the dark water, leaving trails of bubbles in their wake. The muted sound of explosions sends tremors through my bones. My lungs scream. This is the

Underworld, and I will meet the gods on this dawn. The fear trapped inside me bursts free, and my powers veer wildly out of control. For an instant, I remember what it felt like to stand within an inch of the burning wood at the stake, an inch from death. I feel my power intensify and the whispers ignite in my mind.

Then I see the flicker of fire and light overhead, and turn my face in its direction. I kick out as hard as I can. The sky draws closer.

I break through the surface of the sea. The muted sounds around me turn deafening. I turn my face up to the sky to witness the terrifying illusion I've painted across the stormy night—a monstrous creature made of ocean and storm grows, covering nearly the entire expanse of sky, its eyes burning crimson, its fanged mouth so wide that it stretches from one end of its face all the way to the other. It lets out an earthshaking shriek. I feel the call from deep in my bones. On board the ships closest to me, Inquisitors and Beldish soldiers alike drop to their knees, shielding their faces in horror.

Suddenly, a curtain of wind pushes me up out of the water. *Lucent?* No, there is an arm around me, strong and sturdy. It's Magiano, mimicking her. I see wood debris, then the massive hull of a ship. The queen's ship. He sends us surging over the side of the ship. His arm wraps tightly around my waist.

We soar over the railing and land hard against the ship's deck. The impact knocks me down. I roll a few times, then come to a stop. Immediately I try to struggle to my feet. I fight for air. Nearby, Magiano pushes himself up onto his hands and knees, then leaps to his feet. Soldiers and sailors are everywhere, manning the cannons and firing flaming arrows in the direction of Kenettran ships. My tether trembles. Enzo is already here, crouching on the ship's deck. Michel is up in the rigging, and Raffaele stands at the bow, his eyes turned right on us.

Another balira soars over our heads. An instant later, Teren lands in a flurry of white armor and robes, his Inquisition cloak fanning all around him in a soaked circle. His eyes glint with the light of insanity, madder than I've ever seen.

A curtain of water splashes down on us, and I look up to see Maeve leap from her balira and onto the deck in a graceful crouch. Lucent follows behind her, carried on a curtain of wind.

"Surrender," Teren shouts at Maeve. "And give your navy the order to retreat." It is a strange sight, seeing the Inquisition standing with us. Rain drips down Teren's chin. "Or this bay will be your grave, Your Majesty."

Maeve laughs. She nods toward the ocean, where Beldish warships continue to push steadily forward. "Does this look like we should surrender, Master Santoro?" she shouts back, her voice raw and harsh. "We'll sit on your throne by noon." Then she nods at her youngest brother, and Tristan lunges forward. He moves with terrifying speed. One moment, he is rushing toward us with sword drawn—the next, he has reached Teren and slashes at him with the blade. I'm suddenly reminded of Dante, the Spider, my first kill, and the memory sends energy rushing through me. *He will cut Teren in half.*

But Teren wastes no time. He draws two blades from his belt, lowers his head, and smiles at Tristan. He blocks the prince's attack—the sound of metal against metal rings out.

Beside me, Magiano whirls and launches into the air. His braids are swept behind his shoulders by gusts of wind, soaked through and glittering with rain and ocean, and in this instant, I do not see a mortal, but the angel of Joy, his wild ecstasy permeating everything around him, his power overwhelming. I can see him taking in a deep breath of air. He is surrounded by Elites. His power has reached its height.

He sends a blast of wind hurtling at Maeve. It knocks her clear off her feet. At the same time, he sends a column of fire racing toward her. Lucent manages to move in time, carrying Maeve on another curtain of wind out of danger—but only barely. Magiano rushes forward at them, daggers drawn, and hurls one at Maeve.

The dagger unwinds before it can ever reach her. It reappears in Michel's hand.

He sends another dagger hurtling in Raffaele's direction. This one nearly hits him straight in the throat. Enzo is the one who saves him this time—the prince is a blur of motion, leaping into the path and deflecting the dagger with his own sword. He shoots Magiano a deadly glare. At the same time, Raffaele hurls something in my direction that glints in the darkness. A glass vial. It shatters at my feet.

I jump back just as a creature darts from between the

broken shards. It's a tiny thing—flesh-colored, with what seems like hundreds of legs. Its jaws seek my feet. I jump again as it lunges forward.

When the creature snaps at me a third time, I stamp on it hard with the heel of my boot. I manage to catch its back half. It writhes, trying to bite me, but I pull out my dagger and stab it, crushing its body against the floorboards.

My energy roars in my ears. The battle all around us has fed me to an uncontrollable level. The color of the ocean around us shifts, turning from dark gray to bright silver and then to a brilliant turquoise, lit from within, the illusions fed by my growing power.

I look up to see Michel, swinging from the rigging toward me. I weave an illusion of pain around him. He shudders for an instant—but then I feel him push back with his own strength. *He is an artist. He taught me illusions.* And now he seems able to see through mine.

"You *monster*!" he shouts at me. And I know from the pain in his voice that he has already learned of Gemma's death.

Magiano lands near the helm. He points a dagger up at Michel. The rigging rope Michel is swinging from suddenly unwinds, vanishing, only to reappear on the deck's floor. Michel's swing turns into a fall. He plunges towards the deck. Lucent catches him at the last second.

In anger, I lash out toward Lucent with all my strength. My gaze flicks to her hurt wrist—I focus on that, weaving an illusion that increases her pain tenfold. Lucent falls, uttering an anguished cry.

Maeve leaps down between us, and my illusion wavers for a moment from the distraction. The queen's glare is one of ice and fury. She draws her sword and her gaze intensifies. *"Leave her,"* she snaps, then rushes toward me.

Sergio's blade saves me—he appears from nowhere and meets the queen mid-swing. I stagger backward, then look up at the sky. There, Violetta continues to circle on the balira's back. She meets my stare for an instant.

The distant boom of cannons distracts all of us. The Beldish warships have drawn closer, and Beldish soldiers have us surrounded. Maeve leaps away from Sergio suddenly and calls down at Teren.

"You are outnumbered!" Her eyes fix on me. "The Beldish do not believe in abominations," she says to me. "We revere your *malfettos* in the Skylands. You are an Elite, the children of the gods. Just like me. There is no reason for us to fight."

A long time ago, I might have listened to that. Not an abomination. An Elite. But I am the White Wolf, and I am too powerful to be swayed by the Beldish queen's words. I look up at her, suddenly disgusted by her olive branch. What a trick. She doesn't want peace—she nearly killed me. She wants to *win*, and she will take over Kenettra under the disguise of friendship. Not all Elites are the same. Not all Elites can be allies.

I don't answer her. Instead, I tilt my head in Enzo's direction. "Enzo," I shout. My power surges with his.

"He will not bow to you, White Wolf," Maeve barks at me.

Still, I can hear the uncertainty in her voice. "He knows the truth. He is one of the Daggers, one of *us* now."

Not if I can help it, I think, clenching my jaw. Through our tether, I reach out with my threads of energy and seek out his heart. *I* will *control you.*

Enzo approaches me. Daggers are in both of his gloved hands, and his face is a mask of anger. "You are a traitor, Adelina," he growls.

My strength wavers under his words. My heart—my bond, I can no longer tell the difference—cries for his nearness, yearns for him. "I kept myself alive," I call out over the chaos.

"You kept so many lies," Enzo seethes.

The energy of the tether between Enzo and myself now shifts, pivoting the balance of power. The tendrils of my energy that had been wrapped so securely around Enzo's heart a moment earlier now start to loosen. Something pushes back against it. I claw for control, but suddenly Enzo's energy surges back at me, seeking *my* heart. It is the same surge I'd felt when he'd first returned, when we were alone together and his strength overwhelmed mine.

"I *love* you," I cry out at him. "I didn't want to see an enemy nation use you for their own gain. They are taking your throne—can you not see that? Your Daggers are traitors!"

I stop when Enzo's power hits me again through the tether. It makes me cringe in pain. His fists tighten. An anguished expression haunts his face. "You nearly killed Raffaele at the arena," he shouts back. "You killed Gemma.

Are you not using others for your own gain? Your new Elites? This war, your aim for the throne? Me?" His voice breaks a little, and beneath his rage is a deep pain. "How could you?"

His words stir the whispers in my mind. They are angry now, and so am I. "And who did I learn that from?" I snap. *"Who taught me to use others for my own gain?"*

Enzo's eyes fill again, pooling with darkness. "I loved you once," he shouts. "But had I known what you did to Raffaele in the arena—had I known what you'd do to Gemma, I would have killed you myself when I had the chance."

The words stab me, one by one. I feel a wave of grief, even as my anger continues to beat against my heart. How easily he turns away from me. How quickly he forgives his own Daggers' betrayals. I grit my teeth through my tears. *"I'd like to see you try!"*

Enzo's eyes are fully black now. I feel his energy overpowering mine, wrapping me in heat. I try to move my limbs, but I can't. *No.*

He lunges at me.

I fling my illusions at him, wrapping him in a net. He staggers backward for an instant, clawing at his face—he thinks there is a white-hot blade stabbing him in the eyes. But somehow, through our link, Enzo is able to discern which threads are real and which are illusion. He pushes it aside. Then he shakes his head, fixes his eyes on me again, and sends fire searing toward me.

Enzo, no. I throw my hands up and scream. So, after

everything, this is how I will die—burned alive, the way I should have gone all along.

The flames sear my skin. But then, an instant later, an ice-cold blast of rain strikes me hard, quenching the fire. The force of the wave knocks me to my knees. When I look up, Sergio clings to the back of a balira right over our heads, the creature's enormous wings spraying water across the deck as it turns in a spiral.

Enzo looks up too. His moment of distraction is all that I need. I take the opportunity to reach out and hurl my threads of energy through our tether. Enzo winces as my claws rake back into place, returning control into my hands. Enzo shudders. He fights me once more, but then stops. I fall to my knees on the deck, breathing hard. Nearby, Enzo crouches onto one knee too. His head is bowed. We are both exhausted.

"You live because *I say so,*" I hiss, my teeth clenched together. My rage builds, filling every corner of my body. I can no longer see the boy I once loved. I can hardly see anything at all. The whispers take over, wrenching away my control over myself. My voice is no longer mine, but theirs. "And you will *do as I command.*"

Once more, I reach through our bond and pull hard.

Set this world on fire, Enzo. With everything you have.

Enzo turns his head to the sky. He takes a deep, ragged gasp of breath.

Raffaele steps forward. "No!" he calls out, but it's too late.

Fire explodes from Enzo's hands.

It leaps over the railing of our ship and races across the water in all directions. The closest ring of warships catches fire instantly. From each of them, the flames radiate out, one ring expanding after another, setting alight the honeycomb of ships. Every Elite on board our ship freezes to watch it unfold. Screams echo from the burning ships.

Enzo's power flows endlessly, engulfing everything in its wake. Explosions deafen us as the fire finds cannons on board the ships. The blasts throw us all to our knees. I can feel the tremor of it through the deck's wood. Farther and farther burns Enzo's fire, until all of the Beldish warships are ablaze, connected to one another by lines of fire as far as the eye can see. The flames lick high into the sky. I lift my head and let the rain fall on me, soaking in the feeling of his darkness. I am taken back to the night at the Spring Moons, so long ago, when the Daggers had set the Estenzian harbor on fire.

Finally, Enzo lowers his head. His shoulders hunch, and he falls to his knees. He lets out a moan, and when I look closer, I realize that the horrible burns that have always plagued his hands are now as high as his elbows, his skin destroyed, crisped black. His eyes remain dark pools, and a small ring of fire still encircles him.

All around us, the Beldish warships burn. Maeve looks on, stricken with disbelief. It is the first time I have ever seen her stunned into silence.

Teren motions his Inquisitors forward. A triumphant smile is on his face. It takes me a moment to realize that perhaps he thinks I did all this *for him*. "I want her head!" he commands, pointing his sword at Maeve.

But the Beldish queen is already on the move. Lucent exchanges a quick look with her, then calls a curtain of wind to send her soaring into the sky. One of her brothers flies by. He reaches out for her arm, grasps it, and then pulls her up onto the back of his balira.

But my eyes are fixed on Raffaele. He walks toward where Enzo stands, the prince's eyes still liquid dark, his face frozen in fury, the ring of fire burning near his feet. I don't know why I pause to watch Raffaele. Perhaps I have always done so, so captivated am I by his beauty. Even now, in the midst of death and destruction, he moves with the grace of someone not of this world. His attention is focused entirely on Enzo. The sight breaks my heart, and a small, lost part of me sparks with light.

Raffaele reaches Enzo. Flames still burn on Enzo's hands, but for some reason, he doesn't move to attack. Instead, he waits as Raffaele reaches up to curl a hand around the back of his neck, then pulls him close so that their foreheads touch. Tears streak Raffaele's face. Suddenly I remember how he had looked on the day he turned his back on me, the way he had closed his eyes when I begged him to let me stay. It is the same expression he wears now.

Enzo narrows his eyes. He moves as if to grab Raffaele's wrist with his burning hands, to burn him alive from the inside out.

"Don't," Raffaele whispers to Enzo. And even though

Enzo's eyes stay black, Raffaele does not flinch away. He remains where he is, surrounded by fire.

Enzo's eyes flicker. He blinks at Raffaele, confused, and then lowers his face toward him. Raffaele leans forward, closes his eyes, and rests his head against Enzo's shoulder. I do not need to touch them to know that Raffaele's energy is coursing through Enzo now, healing and soothing, calming, pushing against the fury of his own.

For a moment, Raffaele looks at me. His jewel-toned eyes are breathtaking in the light of the fire.

"Don't," he says again, this time to me.

Teren snarls. He steps forward now, ready to lunge for Raffaele.

"Violetta!" I scream. And up in the air, she answers. She reaches out and pulls.

Teren lets out a shriek as his power vanishes and Violetta takes over. I pull grimly. The threads of darkness tighten around him, strangling his nerves and making them scream. I pull as hard as I can, trying to redo what I did to Dante. To someone who deserves to die. The whispers take full control. "You do not command me," I snap. Teren shudders on the floor of the ship as the battle rages on behind us.

My attention turns to Raffaele for a moment. There is no fear in him for what I could do. Not even after the way I'd tortured him at the arena. All I feel from him is sadness and, beneath it, a firm resolve.

"If justice is what you seek, Adelina," he says, "you will not find it like this."

I feel my own resolve waver. How can I find in my heart the coldness that I need for all else, but I cannot bring myself to move against Raffaele? Against the other Daggers? How does he soften my heart, after all he has done to me? I realize that I am crying now, too, and I don't bother to wipe my tears away. As Teren writhes on the floor beside me, Raffaele takes Enzo's hand and pulls him toward a balira. I don't have the strength to reach out and stop them. All I can do is look on.

Teren struggles to his feet on the deck. I'm forced to tear my gaze away from Raffaele and Enzo. Violetta continues to hold Teren's powers at bay, but he still manages to give me a glare full of hatred. "I'm going to cut you open, little wolf," he snarls.

He attacks me. I barely manage to avoid his sword—he swings past my shoulder by a hair, then whirls in midair to send the blade cutting back toward me. I dart away. My hands clench into fists, and with my powers heightened, I fling an illusion across the entire harbor, making the water churn as if boiling. Then I look back at him and tighten my threads of energy as harshly as I can.

At this level of pain, Dante had already turned delirious. But Teren is still able to look at me. I blink, taken aback for a moment by how much he can withstand—even without his powers.

"Kill her," he chokes to his Inquisitors. "*Now!*"

The Inquisition draws swords against me, but I am not afraid of them anymore. They are done being useful to me.

Sergio steps forward, taking over the scene. He whips out two daggers at his belt and throws them with punishing speed. Each lodges in the chest of a soldier. Magiano mimics Enzo's power, sending tall lines of flames surging toward a dozen others. They alight like fresh tinder in a fire. The men scream as their armor heats instantly from the flames, burning them alive. I watch the scene, letting my revenge happen.

"Stop!" I command.

Dead Inquisitors litter the deck. Those who are still alive cower as I approach. Teren stays where he is. Violetta has released his powers already, but he is still recovering from the pain I wrought upon him. I look on as he coughs, pushing weakly against the floor in an attempt to sit up. Then I glance at the surviving Inquisitors.

"You have hunted me and tortured me," I say to the soldiers. "Now you have seen what I can do. And you have seen the power of my Elites. I have mercenaries at my back, seizing control of the palace. I have power that you cannot hope to defeat. I can be your enemy, and look on as you die." I raise my arms at them. "*Or,* I can be your *ruler,* and bring you glory you could never have imagined."

Silence. The Inquisitors look warily at me, and for the first time, I see expressions on their faces—reminders that behind their fearsome armor and white cloaks are just men, still capable of being terrified and conquered. I blink, startled by this realization. I have spent my entire life thinking of the Inquisitors as *things,* soulless creatures. But they are just men. Men can be swayed, and I have the power to do it.

"Why are you fighting me now?" I say. "Because your Lead Inquisitor tells you to? He is no better than an abomination himself." I smile bitterly at them. "More importantly, he has met his match."

The Inquisitors shift, hesitant and fearful, exhausted.

"Follow me," I continue, "and I will lead you to Beldain. We will take their country and have our revenge. We can seize Tamoura, in the Sunlands, and far beyond. We will expand our empire in ways no one could have imagined. Give up this pointless campaign against *malfettos*. You fear our powers. And I know you want to live. If you follow me, I will shower you with everything you've ever desired." My expression hardens. "It is that, or death. You don't have much time." I nod at Magiano, and he twirls a dagger in one hand. "So. What will it be, my Inquisitors?"

They do not move against me. And I know, in this moment, that I have their answer.

I gesture to Teren. "Chain him well," I command. "He is no longer your Lead Inquisitor. He is not your king." I lift my head. "*I* am."

For a moment, I think they will ignore me. I'm so used to it.

But then, they move. And they—the Inquisition, the white cloaks, the enemies of all *malfettos*—obey me and move against Teren.

Teren seizes the cloak of the first Inquisitor in his fist, but he is still too weak to stop him. They pull his hands roughly behind his back. "What are you doing?" he spits at them as they tie him down. "You cowards, you believe her—you *fools*." He snarls a string of curses at them, but they ignore their former leader. I smile at the sight.

Fear motivates, more than love or ambition or joy. Fear is more powerful than anything else in the world. I have spent so long yearning for things—for love, for acceptance—that I do not really need. I need nothing except the submission that comes with fear. I do not know why it took me so long to learn this.

Inquisitors drag Teren to his feet. Even now, in his pain and exhaustion and heavy chains, he pulls and strains against them, causing the multiple iron shackles binding his limbs to pull taut. To my surprise, he smiles at me. It is a bitter, anguished smile, full of heartbreak. His cheeks are wet with tears and rain. His eyes still shine with madness, and now I realize that the madness is because of Giulietta's death.

"Why don't you kill me, my little wolf?" he says. His voice is strangely calm now, hoarse with a sorrow I have not heard before.

"Yes, I suppose I could."

"Then do it," he snaps. "And end this."

I just watch him. Why *don't* I? My eye wanders back to where Raffaele had been beside Enzo only moments earlier. He is already gone. So are the other Daggers. I search the sky for them, but I no longer see them anywhere. They are retreating with what is left of the Beldish navy.

I walk over to Teren, then bend down so that my gaze meets his. I watch the rain pour down his face. When was the first time I saw this face? When I was chained to the stake, of course, and he had come over to bend down before *me*. How poised he had been, then, with his handsome, chiseled face and his mad, pulsing eyes. I smile, realizing that we have switched places now.

I bend close to his ear, in the same way he had once done to me. "No," I say. "I will keep you, until the day I *choose* not to. You have destroyed and harmed all that is dear to me. In return, I want you to know what that feels like. I will not kill you. I will keep you alive. I will torture you." My voice drops to a whisper. "Until your soul is dead."

Teren can only stare back at me. I cannot describe the expression in his eyes.

The strength of battle finally leaves me. I stand on the deck, letting the rain continue to soak me. All around us, Beldish warships burn low in the stormy waters. Magiano, Sergio, and Violetta look on in silence. Inquisitors stand still, waiting for my next move. The Daggers are defeated, and Teren is my captive.

Enzo inherited a throne. Giulietta relied on her royal blood. Queen Maeve rules Beldain because she was born to it.

But true rulers are not born. We are made.

A cruel queen does not mean an unsuccessful one.
Under her guidance, Kenettra changed from a glittering gem
into a clouded stone, and her empire became one to rule all others,
a darkness that stretched from sun, to sea, to sky.
–The Empire of the Wolf, *translation by Tarsa Mehani*

Adelina Amouteru

The first time I met an Inquisitor, he dragged me out of the hay in a barn and arrested me for the death of my father. They threw me into their dungeons for three weeks, and then shackled me to an iron stake. They have hunted me for months, chased me between the borders of nations, murdered those I love.

How strange that they now see me and keep their swords sheathed. As I walk down the halls of the palace with Violetta beside me, they step aside and lower their eyes. I keep my head high, but I still stiffen at the sight of so many white cloaks. My mercenaries wander the halls, their blades drawn in loyalty to me. Behind us walk Magiano and Sergio. When I glance over my shoulder, I see Magiano staring out the windows toward the burning harbor, his gaze distant. Sergio stops to talk to one of the mercenaries. I tighten my jaw and remind myself that with them as my allies, I shouldn't fear the Inquisition as much as I still do.

Their queen is dead. Their Lead Inquisitor is in chains, unconscious. Their palace is overrun, and, most of all, they are afraid of what I can do to them. I can sense the fear in their hearts. Word had spread of how Enzo lifted his hands and set fire to the entire Beldish navy. Even now, they whisper of the way I made Teren crumple in agony. The way my Roses hunted down a Dagger riding on the back of her balira, how a lightning strike had killed her.

I sense their fear, and use it to build my strength back up.

Thousands have gathered around the palace. As morning arrives in earnest, sunlight slicing through black clouds in thin patches, lighting up the rain, we make our way to the royal chambers. I need to address my people, and I need to look the part. I will walk out onto the balcony with my head held high, fulfilling the fantasy I'd had as a little girl in my father's home.

You all live in a new era now. From this day forth, ill treatment of any malfetto *shall be punishable by death. None shall live in fear, as long as loyalty is sworn to this crown. I will be your queen, and I will restore Kenettra to glory.*

"Your Majesty," Magiano says as we enter the room. When I turn to him, he gives me a quick bow. His eyes are still distant. "I'll leave you to prepare, then. No need for a thief on the royal balcony."

"No more need for you to be a thief," I say.

Magiano smiles and, for a moment, the old flame returns

to his eyes. He takes a step closer to me. It seems as if he wants to reach out for my hand, but then he decides not to, and lets his arm fall back to his side. It sends a stab of disappointment through me. "A stunning victory," he murmurs.

I can see a reflection in his eyes of the final moments of battle, can hear in his voice an echo of his shouts from when we were on board Queen Maeve's ship. Somewhere out there, Enzo calls through our tether, and I shiver at his pull. I want to reach out for Magiano's hand too, as if he could pull me back.

But those thoughts are quickly replaced by the memory of Enzo's final words to me during the battle. Of his black eyes. *I would have killed you myself, if I'd had the chance.* He's right, of course. If I were him, I would have said nothing different. There is no question that we are enemies now. Shields go up over my heart, and my alignment to passion flickers lower, dying. It is the only way to protect myself.

So I don't reach out for Magiano's hand.

"I couldn't have done it without your help," I say instead. "And without Sergio's."

Magiano just shrugs. He studies me for a brief moment. What does he see? Then he utters a small laugh. "Just point me in the direction of the royal treasury, Your Majesty," he says, waving a hand in the air. He turns away as he speaks, but not before I catch a hint of sadness on his face. "Then you'll always know where to find me."

I return his smile with my own bittersweet one. I nod at an Inquisitor to show him, and the soldier gives me a nervous bow. Magiano follows, but pauses for a moment to look back at me. His smile wavers.

"Adelina," he says. "Be careful."

Then he leaves us, and I miss him instantly.

Once he's completely disappeared down the hall, I dismiss everyone except for Violetta and order the doors closed. The Inquisitors don't dare hesitate at my command. How strange, to be able to say something and watch them obey. It almost makes me laugh. The room falls into silence, and all we can hear now is the roar of people outside.

We are quiet for a long moment.

"How are you feeling?" Violetta finally asks in a quiet voice.

What can I say? I feel everything. Satisfaction. Emptiness. I feel confused, unsure of where I am and how I arrived here. I take a shuddering breath. "I'm fine," I reply.

"He cares for you, you know." Violetta turns her head briefly in the direction of the closed doors. "Magiano. I've seen him standing guard outside your door, making sure you aren't having another nightmare or an illusion."

Her words sink in, and I find myself looking at the closed doors too. I wish I hadn't sent him away to the treasury. I would have asked him why he told me to be careful, what he sees when he looks at me. Why his expression had seemed so sad.

"I know," I say.

"Do you care for him?"

"I don't know how to," I reply.

Violetta gives me a sidelong look. I know she can hear in my voice the evidence that he means more to me than I'm revealing. She sighs, then waves for me as she walks toward the steps leading up to the throne. Our footsteps echo in unison. She sits down on the bottom step, and I join her.

"Let him in," she says. "I know you're holding back." She stares out at the long, empty expanse of the chamber. "Keep him close. His love is light, and it calls out the light in you." Her eyes come to settle on me.

Something whispers in irritation at the back of my mind, resisting the advice. "You're telling me this because you think I love him?"

"I'm telling you this because he calms you," she says, her tone uncharacteristically sharp and biting. "You're going to need it."

"Why?"

Violetta doesn't say anything more. I watch her tiny movements—the tightening of the skin around her eyes, the way she squeezes her hands together in her lap. There is definitely something she's not telling me. Again, the whispers in my mind hum their disapproval.

"What's wrong?" I say, firmer this time.

Violetta's fidgeting hands separate from each other. One of them tucks into a pocket in her skirt. She swallows, then turns to me. "There was something I found on board Queen Maeve's ship," she begins. "I thought it wise to tell you later, when we had a moment alone."

"What is it?"

"It is . . . from Raffaele, I think." Violetta hesitates. "Here." She reaches down into the pockets of her skirts, then takes out a wrinkled parchment. She unfurls it and holds it before both of us. Our heads lean in together. I squint, trying to make sense of what I'm seeing. It is a smattering of sketches, interspersed with words written in Raffaele's unmistakably beautiful calligraphy.

"Yes," I agree, taking the parchment from Violetta. "This is his writing, without doubt."

"Yes," Violetta echoes.

I run my hand along the parchment, imagining Raffaele's deft quill gliding across the surface. I remember him writing pages and pages of notes about Elites back at the Fortunata Court, how he would always record everything he saw in my training. He is the Messenger, after all, tasked with immortalizing us and our powers in writing. I begin to read the parchment.

"He talks about Lucent," Violetta says. "Do you remember the night at the arena, when Lucent broke her wrist?"

I nod. My hands start to tremble as I read each of Raffaele's notes.

"Raffaele says . . . that her wrist did not break because of combat. It broke because her powers . . . her ability to control the wind, to move the air . . ." Violetta takes a deep breath. "Adelina, Lucent's wrist broke because her power has started to eat away at her. Wind is hollowing out her bones. It seems the more powerful we are, the faster our bodies will crumble."

I shake my head, unwilling to understand. "What is he suggesting? That we . . ."

"That, in a few years, Lucent will die from this."

I frown. That cannot be right. I stop and start again at the top, analyzing Raffaele's sketches, reading his writing, wondering what I'm missing. Violetta must be misinterpreting this. My gaze lingers on the sketches Raffaele has drawn of threads of energy in the air, his observations about Lucent.

Wind is hollowing out her bones. *Lucent will die from this.*

But that means . . . I read further, looking at a brief note about Michel at the bottom of the parchment. The faster I read, the more I realize what he is saying. He is saying that, someday, Michel will die because his body will bleed from pulling objects through the air. That Maeve will succumb to the poisons of the Underworld. That Sergio's body will starve from being unable to retain water. That Magiano will go mad from mimicking other powers.

"This is impossible," I whisper.

Violetta's voice trembles. "Raffaele is saying that all of us, *all* Elites, are in danger."

That we are doomed to be forever young.

I'm silent. Then I shake my head. The parchment's edges crinkle in my grip. "No. But that makes no sense," I say, turning my back on Violetta and walking close to the windows. From here, we can make out the commotion down below, the noise of thousands of uncertain civilians and anxious *malfettos*, none of whom know what rule under an Elite will be like. "Our powers are our *strengths*. How can Raffaele possibly know such a thing, just from one broken wrist?"

"It *does* make sense. None of our bodies were ever designed to wield powers like this. We may be the children of the gods, but we are *not gods*. Don't you see? The blood fever left us tied to the immortal energy of the world in such a way that our fragile, mortal bodies cannot possibly hope to keep up."

As Violetta speaks, the sound of her voice changes. The sweetness of it, which reminds me so much of our mother's voice, is transformed into something eerie, a chorus of off-pitch voices that send a shiver down my spine. I lean away, wary. The whispers in my head shove a memory forward at me—I remember my sister and me, alone in a chamber, her power used against mine.

I think of Enzo's burned hands. Then, of my uncontrollable illusions. My hallucinations and bursts of temper. My trouble recognizing familiar faces around me, twisting them into strangers. I know it is true, with chilling certainty. My power of illusion is destroying my mind as surely as Lucent's power is breaking her bones.

No, something hisses in my mind. The hiss sounds urgent, the whispers more agitated than usual. *She is lying to you. She wants something from you.*

"We will all die," Violetta says, again in her new, frightening chorus of voices. It sends a jolt of fear through me. Why does she sound like this? "We were never meant to be."

"This cannot be happening to all Elites," I murmur. My gaze goes back to her. "What about you? You've felt no effects."

She only shakes her head. "I am not powerful, Adelina," she replies. Her teeth flash. Did I see that? It seemed for a moment as if she had fangs. "Not like you, or Lucent, or Enzo. I take power away. I don't even have markings. But someday I may manifest something too. It's inevitable."

I move away from her. *She is dangerous,* the whispers in my mind say, louder now. *Stay away from her.* "No. We will find a way," I whisper. "We are chosen by the gods. There *must* be a way."

"I have thought about this. The only way will be to remove our powers permanently," Violetta says.

The whispers let out a deafening howl in my mind at that. The fear crawling along my spine turns from a trickle into a river. It roars through me.

What kind of life will that be, the whispers say to me, *without powers?*

I try to imagine my world without my ability to change reality. Without the addictive rush of darkness and fear, the sheer power to create anything at will, anytime I want. How can I live a life without that? I blink, and my illusions spark out of control for a moment, weaving for me an image of what my life once was—the helplessness I felt when my father held my finger between his hands and snapped it like a twig; the way I pounded weakly at my locked door and begged for food and water. The way I cowered under my bed, sobbing, until my father's hands would seize me and drag me out, screaming, to face his bloody fists.

That is life without power, the whispers remind me.

"No," I say to Violetta. "There must be another way."

It takes me a moment to realize that Violetta is looking at me. Her face suddenly terrifies me. I push myself up from the steps and back away from her. "You will not touch me," I whisper.

"Adelina, I've seen you deteriorating over the past months." Violetta speaks now with tears in her eyes. Why do her tears look tinged with blood? I blink. *My illusions. They must be getting away from me again . . .* but the whispers in my mind force my thoughts away, filling my head instead with more of my own fear. "I've held back many times, I haven't said nearly everything I wanted to say, all because I don't want you to be angry with me. I've seen your powers spiral wildly out of control, have seen you terrified by illusions that aren't really there." Violetta glances to one wall of the chamber, where the gold of the pillars reflects our image. "Just *look,* mi Adelinetta," she whispers. "Can you see yourself?"

I barely recognize the girl reflected back at me in the pillar. The scarred side of her face is hollow with anger. Dark circles line the skin under her good eye. There is a savagery in her expression, a hardness, that I do not remember being there before. Behind me float ghosts, fanged creatures with glittering eyes. I know immediately that these are the whispers in my head. They crowd the reflection in the pillar, until they start to claw their way out of it and onto the floor.

I look away from them and back to Violetta. Her eyes are still bloody.

"Those moments are fleeting," I snap at her, widening the gap between us. *I have to get out of here.* "Nothing more. I always recover. What Raffaele has learned is a mistake."

"It's *not* a mistake," Violetta snaps back desperately. "It's truth, and you don't want to accept it."

"He's *lying*!" I shout, trying to drown out the whispers that have turned into a roar. The fanged creatures continue to crawl their way along the floor toward us. I try to erase them with my mind, but I can't. "He has *always* been a manipulator!"

"What if he's not?" Violetta replies, throwing her hands in the air. "Then what? Should we all stand by and watch one another fall apart?"

I turn away from her, then whirl back around. *She is your sister,* the whispers growl at me. *How can she understand you so little?* "Do you realize what my power means to me? It is my *life*. There is *nothing* more important to me than it. It has given me all of this." I gesture around us at the opulent chamber, the gold-lined marble, the beautiful curtains. The reward for my revenge. "Are you trying to say that you want to take it away from me? Have you forgotten our promise to each other?"

"Our promise was *always* to protect each other," Violetta says. "You protect me with your illusions. You comfort me from thunderstorms, you weave illusions around me to protect me from the horrors of war. Our promise was to never use our powers *against* each other." She steps toward me. Bloody tears run down her face. "I am not against you!"

"Stay away from me," I say through clenched teeth, holding one trembling hand out before me.

"You've *won*, Adelina!" Violetta snaps at me. Her anger contorts her face as if in a nightmare. Maybe this *is* a nightmare. Why does everything seem so hazy? "Just *look*! You have everything now—you control your prince, you control Teren, you control your Roses and your mercenaries, you control an entire Inquisition army. You rule a nation."

My breathing turns rapid. "They follow me because of my power."

"They follow you because they *fear* you." Violetta tightens her lips. "Other kings and queens are human too. They rule with fear and mercy. So can you. You don't need your power to lead this country."

No. I want more than that. I want real weight behind my fear, I want the reassurance of—

"You want to keep your ability to hurt, don't you?" Violetta suddenly says. "You want your power because you genuinely enjoy what you do to others."

The tone of her voice turns me cold. The whispers swarm inside me and along the floor. Darkness appears in the corners of the chamber. "Well, Violetta?" I taunt. My words come out all on their own, vicious in a way I cannot control. "Tell me what I do to others."

Violetta hardens her expression. In this instance, my gentle, beautiful sister is unrecognizable. "You destroy people."

You see? The whispers roar. *She has turned her back on you. She has always planned to betray you.*

"And what do *you* do?" I shout. The whispers take over my words. It is as if I were watching myself speak. "*You,* my *righteous* little sister? You left me to suffer our father alone. Do you know what it was like for me, to lie bleeding on the floor, while he showered you with dresses in the next bedchamber? Do you know what it was like for our father to threaten to kill me, and then for me to murder him in return? No, *you don't.* You stand on the sidelines and wait for me to do your dirty work. You hide in the shadows so that I can *bleed* for you. You give me your pitiful look when I kill, but you do not stop me. And now you judge me for that?"

Scarlet tears spill from Violetta's eyes. "I *am* a coward," she says. "I've been one all my life, and I am sorry for it. I never thought I had a right to stop you, after what you did for us. For freeing us from our father."

"We are *never free* from our father," I—the whispers in my head—spit at her. "Do you know that, even now, I can see his illusion in the corner of my eye? He is there, behind the banister." I shove a finger in the direction of where my father watches us, his mouth curved into a dark smile. He holds out his hands, as if encouraging the swarming creatures on the floor to draw nearer to us.

"Then let me free you!" Violetta cries. Her cry sounds like a shriek. I cover my ears.

"I would rather *die* than let you take my power away from me," I snap.

"You *will* die, at this rate!"

Get out of here! You are in danger! the whispers scream at me. I turn away from her.

And then I feel it. Violetta reaching for my threads of energy. Pushing them away, out of my grasp. For an instant, I can't breathe. I claw at the air in front of me, grabbing for the threads, but they are already gone, out of reach. I whirl, staggering, to look at Violetta. No. She wouldn't.

Our promise.

She is crying in earnest now. Her tears form a puddle of blood on the floor. "I can't let you keep doing this," she says. "You have killed so many, Adelina, and it is destroying you. I cannot watch you deteriorate."

You see? the whispers say. The creatures crawling on the floor finally reach me, and before I can shove them off, they lunge up at me and enter my mind. Their thoughts replace my own. I shudder.

Yes, of course.

Now I know why she did it. She wants my place. *She* wants the throne, she must have wanted it all along—with her power, she can control any Elite she wants, make them do anything at her beck and call. I always knew she would turn on me like this, and now that I have done all the work for her, dirtied my hands with blood and grief, she is going to take her turn. Most of all, *she broke our promise.* We are never, ever to use our powers against each other.

How could you? *How could you?*

I can no longer think. Fury fills every crevice of my mind. Even without my power, I can feel the force of the whispers, calling me on. I pull out the dagger at my belt and lunge at Violetta.

She manages to grab my wrist, but my impact throws her off her feet, and she lands with a thud. All the air rushes out of her lungs. Her eyes widen, and she flounders for a moment like a fish out of water, gulping for air. I raise my dagger over my head, even as a part of me screams for me to stop, and I bring it down.

She dodges to one side. Somehow, my fragile sister manages to throw me off her, but I just scramble to my feet and lunge for her again. I grab a fistful of her hair. She cries out as I yank her back toward me. Already, the absence of my power is making me panic. I can barely see straight. The world crushes in around us. I pull her to me and press the dagger to her throat.

"Your promises mean *nothing*—you—I trusted you! You were the *only* one!" I shout. "Give it *back! It is mine!*"

Violetta sobs desperately. "Adelina, *please*!" If I could sense her emotions right now, I know I would feel a tide of terror unlike anything I've ever felt from her. But in this moment, she is not my sister. She is only another enemy. *A traitor,* the whispers remind me. And I listen.

"Give back my power," I say in her ear. My dagger presses hard enough to cut her skin. "Or I swear on all the gods that I will slit your throat right here."

"Then take it," Violetta suddenly hisses. "And let it take *you.*" And just like that, I feel my power rush back over me in a flood of darkness, filling the empty crevices of my heart and mind with its familiar, poisonous comfort. I drop the dagger and let go of Violetta. I fall backward to the ground, close my eye, and curl into a ball, clutching the threads close to me. I'm breathing hard. The world spins. My anger churns in me, pulsing, fading.

It takes me a moment to realize that Violetta has already struggled to her feet and is running for the door. Even now, she seems so far away.

"Where are you going?" I snap at her, but she has just thrown the door wide open. She doesn't look back at me.

"Violetta!" I call out from where I still crouch on the floor. "Wait!"

What happened? What did I do to her? I shake my head, squinting my eye shut. The whispers in my head swirl, fading. The chamber seems to fall back into silence. When I open my eye again, the world is no longer spinning. There is no puddle of bloody tears on the floor. There are no fanged creatures swarming the ground. My sister is not here, pulling away my powers.

Gradually, the haze over me clears. I crouch there as bits

of what had just happened come back to me. The dagger. Her hair. Her throat. Her trembling, weeping body.

My stomach clenches.

"Violetta!" I call again. "Violetta, wait. Come back!"

No answer. I'm alone in the chamber.

I try again, turning more frantic. "Violetta!" I repeat. How could my illusions get away from me again like that? "I'm sorry! I didn't mean—I wouldn't have hurt you! Come back!"

But she's already gone.

I press my hands against the marble floor and lower my head. I'd yanked her hair with the same viciousness that my father did on the night he died. My dagger had flashed down—I'd aimed for her, aimed to hurt, to *kill*. My vision had been so blurred and tinted with scarlet. How did I not stop myself?

"Violetta, Violetta," I cry, my voice hoarse, too quiet for her to hear. "Come back. I'm sorry. It was a mistake. Don't leave me here."

Silence.

You're all I have. Please don't leave me here.

I call and call, until Inquisitors come in to check on me. I realize that I'm crying. Through my blur of tears, I see Magiano's concerned face, Sergio's surprised one. He looks at me with a wariness I remember all too well. It was the way Gemma last looked at me, before she died. The way the Daggers looked at me before they cast me out.

"Get out!" I shout when they close in around me. They stop, and then their shadows step back. They turn their backs and leave me alone in the room. I sob. My broken finger claws and claws against the marble floor. My dagger lies where I threw it, a tiny dot of my sister's blood on its blade. This blood is no illusion; it is real.

Please don't leave me, don't leave me, I've changed my mind, take this power away, the whispers won't stop.

The sunlight through the windows shifts. I stay on the ground.

I have no idea how much time passes. Or how long I cry. I don't know where Violetta might have gone. I don't know where Magiano went, or what he might be thinking. After some time, I finally cry everything out of my chest, and there are no more tears left in me. I stay on the ground. I watch the lattice of shadows from the windows move slowly along the floor. The light changes, turns golden. The shadows and highlights stretch until they reach me, bathing me in light. Even the warmth of the sun cannot make the darkness in my stomach go away.

Gradually, my thoughts start to turn. And slowly, slowly . . . the whispers start to come back. They caress my mind.

No, Adelina, this is better.

You don't need to care about her leaving. Haven't you already learned that love and acceptance are less important than the power of fear? The control over those you know?

I nod, letting the thought strengthen me. I don't need to lean against my sister in order to stand up. I can do it on my own. Without anyone.

I slowly push myself onto my feet, wipe my face with my sleeve, and run trembling fingers along the monstrous, eyeless side of my face. My expression settles into something numb and hard. I turn to face the throne at the top of the steps. My illusions start to spark again, and darkness blurs into the corners of my vision, leaving the throne as the only thing I can see.

I walk up the steps toward it. Around me, ghosts of those I have once known fade in and out, those I have left behind. Who left me. I make my way up each step. The whispers in my mind roar, filling every crevice, shoving out the light and letting the darkness flood in.

This is good, Adelina. This is the best way.

I have earned my revenge on everyone who hurt me. My father, who tortured me every day—I crushed his chest and his heart. Teren, sick and twisted and mad—I took away his beloved just as he took away mine. Raffaele, who betrayed and manipulated me—I seized control of the prince he loves, and I made sure he watched his prince destroy in my name.

And Violetta, darling, *dearest* sister who turned her back when I needed her the most. I cast her out. I finally said everything to her that I wanted to say.

I have hurt back.

You've won, Adelina, the whispers say.

I reach the throne. It's beautiful, an ornate structure of

gold and silver and stone. Lying in the center of its cushion is Giulietta's former crown, heavy with gems. I reach down and pick it up, admiring the jewels as they wink in the light, running my fingers along their hard surfaces. I walk once around the throne, gripping the crown. *This is mine.* I lift the crown to my head, then put it on. It is heavy. Finally, I sit in the chair, then lean back and rest my arms on its sides.

How long ago it was, when I used to crouch along the stair railings in my old home and fantasize about this, of wearing such a crown and looking down from my own throne. I lift my head high and stare out at the chamber. It is empty.

This is what I have fought so hard for, what I sacrificed and bled so much for. This is everything I ever wanted—revenge against my enemies for what they've done to me. And I've achieved it. My revenge is complete.

I force a smile onto my face. In the silence, I sit alone on my throne and wait eagerly for all the satisfaction and triumph to hit me. I wait, and wait, and wait.

But it doesn't come.

Acknowledgments

The Rose Society is the darkest book I've ever written. Taking Adelina down to a place where she not only lets her pain consume herself but consume others was a necessary task—but it was also an emotionally difficult one. Being in the headspace of a villain-in-training for months at a time meant seeking out the best hearts I know in order to balance out all that negativity. So:

Thank you to my editor Jen Besser, who *gets* Adelina's story down to the core, who always knows exactly what to say, and who believes in me even when I don't believe in myself. I don't know what I'd do without your friendship and advice.

Thank you to my agent, friend, and champion Kristin Nelson—you are somehow both extremely badass and incredibly kind. No matter what, you always sail us in the right direction.

Team Putnam and the Penguins: that sounds sort of like the coolest indie band ever. You guys rock the house every time! Thank you for having my back, for believing in these books, and for being downright awesome people.

Thank you to my wonderful film agent Kassie Evashevski, for taking *The Young Elites* under your wing and finding it a great home. You are amazing, in every sense of the word.

I am so grateful that *The Young Elites* is with none other than you guys, Isaac and Wyck. Your thoughts, encouragement, and friendship mean the world to me.

Amie, seriously, what would I do without our Fat Emails and your incredible, smart self? You helped pull me through this book, even if you had to half drag me part of the way. JJ, thank you for always being there to lend an ear and talk about anything. Leigh, you have the wits of a thousand wits. Thank you for calming me down, building me up, and always making sure there is cake involved. Jess, Andrea, and Beth, I can't wait until the next time we are all reunited, because it will be so epic. Jess and Morgan, afternoon tea forever!!! Tahereh and Ransom, you guys are totally maxed out on the Best People Meter. Margie, Kami, Mel, and Veronica, the world needs so many more of you. Thank you for being an inspiration.

Thank you to my family and closest friends, for long conversations day or night, for endless fun, and for your love and joy. Most of all, thank you to Primo, my best friend and my rock. I am thankful every day for you.

MARIE LU is the author of the *New York Times* bestselling Legend series and *The Young Elites*. She graduated from the University of Southern California and jumped into the video game industry, working for Disney Interactive Studios as a Flash artist. Now a full-time writer, she spends her spare time reading, drawing, playing *Assassin's Creed*, and getting stuck in traffic. She lives in Los Angeles, California (see above: traffic), with one husband, one Chihuahua mix, and two Pembroke Welsh corgis.

Visit Marie at **www.marielu.org**
www.theyoungelites.com

AUTHOR PHOTO: PAUL GREGORY